JOIE DE VIVRE-

ALEX EASTWOOD-WILLIAMS

First published in 2025 by 43 Degree Press

A catalogue record for this book is available from the National Library of New Zealand.

Hardback ISBN: 978-0-473-75385-6

Paperback ISBN: 978-0-473-75384-9

E-book ISBN: 978-0-473-75386-3

Cover art by Richie Jehan

Edited by Yusuf Halden

You already chose how this ends. You just don't remember.

<u>PART ONE:</u>

Kyenay Bardo (Living)

1

A warning klaxon screeches into your ear and you're shocked awake. It's the same deafening scream that you're subjected to every morning, but it never gets any easier to endure. Your heart races. Dread sets in. Another day of torment awaits you.

Another day on the *Joie de Vivre*.

You roll off the bed without thinking, landing hard on the cold metal floor. A second too slow and MACHINE would have punished you. An extra minute and you'd be dead.

You watch as hidden spikes punch their way through your mattress from below. You know what MACHINE does to those who take too long to wake up—you've seen it before: Bodies impaled on those spikes, shredded from beneath by their own beds.

You're groggy as hell because you barely slept the night before. MACHINE electrocuted you four times in the night, always just as you were on the verge of REM sleep. MACHINE was right to do it: You know better than to dream.

Not far from the foot of your bed is a small wash basin. You lean down and spit into it. There's a little blood in your spittle this morning, but not much. MACHINE was pretty gentle last night and you didn't use any sEDAtIVE, which saves you the usual round of early morning nausea and vomiting.

The sink is still full of used sEDAtIVE syringes from your last Respite Day. You glance at your arm—it's pockmarked with small holes, though you can't tell which ones were the doing of MACHINE and which ones were self-inflicted.

There's a mirror hanging over the sink and when you hold up your arm to the mirror you notice that the holes and bruises aren't reflected. In the mirror, your skin appears smooth, intact. As far as you're aware, no one else can see your scars and you've been told that the only reason you can see them here is due to a trick of the light. You know better than to trust your own perception.

There's an alcove at the corner of the room containing a small faucet. You strip naked and stand under it, hoping that MACHINE will choose to dispense water and soap for you this morning. Some days the water is boiling hot, causing burns. Other days it's freezing. MACHINE once showered you in excrement, to mark you out for Ritual Humiliation. And you know it's not uncommon for MACHINE to randomly shower people with hydrochloric acid, causing burns, permanent disfigurement and sometimes death. MACHINE's will is always unknowable and today you pray to it for mercy, just as you do every other day, though there is no telling whether or not MACHINE hears the supplications of those aboard the *Joie de Vivre*.

You close your eyes, bracing yourself for the worst as the faucet makes a hissing noise, but thankfully today MACHINE chooses to bless you with a stream of lukewarm water and soap. You hurriedly delouse and sanitise yourself before MACHINE changes its mind. The water stops and powerful overhead blow-dryers push any excess moisture off your skin and down the drain, where it'll either be processed for later re-use on the ship or become a bacteria-ridden drink for some unfortunate soul who may have drawn MACHINE's ire.

Your work uniform has been mechanically laid out on what was once your bed, now a rectangular pod from which protrudes several hundred long, sharp spikes. You carefully remove your clothing from the spikes, conscious that they could suddenly move, expand and stab you at any given moment. Today they remain motionless and so, dutifully, you force yourself into your uniform.

The clothing is always a size too small and your shirt is lined with a hard serrated edge that is designed to irritate your skin and occasionally cause bleeding. The pain and discomfort exists so that you always keep MACHINE in mind and are never tempted to associate your labour with pleasure.

You pull your boots on—again, a size too small and containing small spikes that poke the balls of your feet whenever you stand or walk.

And now that you're fully dressed, clean and uncomfortable, you're ready to serve.

Just as MACHINE intended.

2

The klaxons sound again at an ear-bleed-inducing volume. You know you're running out of time and must report to your station for your daily labour. Those who arrive late are almost always sentenced to death.

You exit your private quarters, where you're immediately confronted by a pulsing mass of humanity as the other passengers make their way down the corridor to their own labour stations. You slip in between a thin, desiccated-looking blonde woman and a lumbering, heavyset man who gasps in pain with every step he takes.

You shoot him a contemptuous glare: You don't know why MACHINE has chosen to make him suffer in this way, but whatever the reason, you know that MACHINE was right to do it and that this person must not be treated to any form of kindness or compassion.

You turn to your left and attempt to weave your way through the slow-moving crowd, catching a glimpse of the void of space through one of the circular porthole windows. Sometimes if you strain, you can see the stars, but most of the time the ship's bright fluorescent tubes and UV light bulbs block them out. Not that you really care to see them any more—you have more important things to concern yourself with.

You have no idea how many people are aboard the *Joie de Vivre*, though it's estimated to be in the high thousands, perhaps millions. Nor do you know how many generations of humanity have called this ship home—you yourself were born here and you've never met anyone who could credibly claim to have ever set foot on the Old Planet.

You have, however, heard the tales of life on the Old Planet: That supposedly, humans originated on a giant spheroid space-ship with no walls or narrow corridors, where you were free to walk in any direction you wanted for metres, perhaps even entire *kilometres* at a time!

It was said that this world was full of light and colour; that it had a soft, green, non-metallic floor under a giant blue roof so high that it was impossible to touch. It was said that water floated freely from the roof, that food appeared magically from the ground and that oxygen was so abundant that it could blow at forces strong enough to knock people off their feet. And this giant spaceship was supposedly populated by mythical beasts, like "cows" and "dogs".

You're smart enough not to believe such fanciful tales, of course. Those stories are nothing more than myths and fairy-tales for children. You outgrew such fables a long time ago.

Truth be told, some of the stories make you uncomfortable. Some of the stories contain the blasphemous implication that there once existed a place somewhere out in space where human beings were able to survive without MACHINE.

Rather, you adhere to the more scientifically plausible belief that the human race once lived near a giant star, where they teetered on the edge of extinction until they were saved by the grace of MACHINE, whose devoted followers were permitted to board the *Joie de Vivre* and travel safely forever through the void of space, protected from the cruel vicissitudes of nature.

Of course, there are also those who believe that MACHINE will someday lead the human race to a promised land, a paradisal world more wonderful than even the most fantastic tales of the Old Planet, provided that those aboard the *Joie de Vivre* devote themselves fully to MACHINE's will and purify themselves of their sins.

Outwardly, you sneer at such ideas. You know humans are always inventing tall tales about paradises and promised lands— but all the same, you are careful to follow the teachings of the priesthood, to accept MACHINE's punishments with dignity and grace and never to question MACHINE's infinite wisdom.

Somewhere deep down in your heart of hearts, you want to believe that the stories are true. You want to believe that if you continue to endure MACHINE's torture and trials, that you will someday be rewarded with life on a new planet, outside the cold metallic walls of the *Joie de Vivre*.

3

You continue through the labyrinthine bowels of the *Joie de Vivre* until finally, you reach your labour station. You have been assigned to work in the nursery, with your job being to prepare the older children for their transition to adulthood and life as servants of MACHINE.

As you enter the nursery, you're not sure what offends your senses more: the noise or the smell.

The children laugh and frolic, freely and gaily, oblivious to reality through a combination of ignorance and the effects of the drug HeDonia, which MACHINE has commanded all children be dosed with.

You watch them jump and scream—small boys pushing smaller boys; groups of girls pointing and laughing at an isolated girl's appearance; paroxysms of juvenile anger as someone pokes someone else in the eye for biting them.

Several have soiled themselves but they seem to feel no shame, except in those rare circumstances when they are arbitrarily chosen for exclusion from the other children's ever-shifting, ever-changing tribes.

It's hard to even consider them human. They're all just animals —feral, wild animals, unknowingly desperate for MACHINE's correction and guidance.

You think back to your old childhood and your own memories of HeDonia. You remember how you were injected with it every night, how it was more important to you than even food; the feeling of being wrapped and blanketed by waves of warmth and bliss. When under the influence of HeDonia, MACHINE could have ripped you limb from limb and you'd still have considered the experience pleasurable.

You also remember what came next. What is coming next for these children. What you are tasked with administering.

All children, excluding those specifically chosen by MACHINE for special torture, are given high doses of HeDonia from birth, despite or perhaps *because* of its highly addictive qualities. Then, once the child reaches a point of relative developmental lucidity—usually somewhere between the ages of seven and ten, depending on the child—their access to HeDonia is halted immediately.

The withdrawal symptoms are known to last for years, crushing and tormenting the child with nausea and physical pain, right through into adulthood.

And additionally, they are "Chipped" during this transitional period—an important procedure which you are occasionally called upon to administer.

"Listen up!" you command the children.

Several turn and look up at you, as if they'd only just noticed you. Others go silent without looking at you. Others still completely ignore you—in the corner of the room three boys continue to punch and kick a smaller boy.

You march to the corner of the nursery, leering over the three bullies as the smaller boy cowers and whimpers, hiding his face.

"What's going on here?" you demand.

The smaller boy sniffs, tears streaming down his face. You can hear the sound of mucus being displaced in his nostrils as he starts to whine, "They started beating me up for no reason!"

You bare your teeth and widen your eyes in anger. This behaviour is very Incorrect, a direct violation of MACHINE's will.

You study the three larger boys carefully—their pupils are dilated and it's clear they're under the influence of much higher doses of HeDonia than their smaller victim. All three are smiling ignorantly, but one's smile fades as you make direct eye contact with him.

"Is this true?" you ask. "Is it true that you have chosen to attack this boy for no reason?"

All three of the larger boys now look crestfallen. They avoid your gaze.

"Yes, we did," one of them admits, his eyes glued to the floor.

"Have you drawn blood?" you ask. "Have you caused any bruising? Broken any bones?"

The three larger boys look up at you and one by one, they shake their heads.

"That's *terrible*!" you say. "If you are going to torture one of your classmates, you cannot be this merciful! Look! He's crying but he's even not bleeding... and all three of you are big enough to at the very least cause a nosebleed! I'm very disappointed and I *will* be administering a Corrective Shock to all three of you for being so weak and compassionate!"

The three boys walk away looking a little downcast, though you suspect that deep down they're looking forward to their Corrective Shocks. After all, this is what MACHINE does to the adults, so to receive a similar punishment will ultimately be a badge of honour for them.

"And as for *you*!" you spit at the smaller boy, who continues to sob pathetically on the metal floor. "*You* are an absolute disgrace! Crying and complaining just because you've been singled out and made to feel physical pain? What would you do if MACHINE was to torture you? Would you cry like a baby then too? You should always feel honoured whenever you're in pain because it means MACHINE has noticed you and is purifying you of sin!

"Now get up!" you add, kicking the pathetic crying boy in the ribs. "I'll have to think of an appropriate punishment for you... perhaps a high voltage shock followed by Ritual Humiliation? We'll see. Frankly a pathetic little wretch like you does not deserve to live upon the *Joie de Vivre*!"

4

You've long since learned to ignore the needling feeling in the pit of your stomach that there is anything immoral about what you're doing. That primeval, animalistic instinct for altruism and empathy has long since been bred and tortured out of you and you intend to do the same for these children.

The three bullies stand patiently, perhaps eagerly, at the edge of the room, next to a small box which sits atop a wall-mounted shelf. They each offer an arm—arms that you note are cut, scraped, bruised and burned, possibly from similar corrective techniques applied by their progenitors. There are several loose metal wires hanging from the box and you attach one to each boy, penetrating the skin with the needles on the end of each wire, eliciting sharp cries of pain.

One boy, though he desperately tries to hide it, sheds a single tear from the pain. With a twist of a knob you activate an electrical current which shocks him for a full thirty seconds before you turn the knobs for other two.

You set a timer for one minute, unconcerned as to whether or not the voltage is lethal—if one of the children dies, they die and it's a due warning to all the other children to always be afraid.

After a minute, you shut the machine off. There's a terrible smell—burning hair and possibly bowel or bladder ablution. As far as you can see, the boys are still alive and conscious and so you send them on their way. One faints but you choose to turn a blind eye to this—they are only children after all.

As for the smaller boy, the one who was too weak to take a proper punishment: Originally, you had considered removing one of his limbs while the other children pointed and laughed at him but for some reason you reconsider.

Maybe you're getting soft as you get older. Maybe you're failing to overcome your forbidden instinct for altruism. Or maybe it's that this pathetic child reminds you of yourself.

Whatever the reason, you decide that his punishment is best left to MACHINE. It's already clear that he's on a lower dosage of HeDonia than the other children and so, despite his youth and unpreparedness, you lodge an electronic message to your supervisor recommending that this boy be permanently deprived of HeDonia and *Chipped* immediately.

You look him up and down. He can't be older than six years of age (as measured by the standard calendar of the Old Planet), which would typically mark him out as too young to hand over to MACHINE.

And it is for this reason, you decide, that it's as adequate a punishment as permanent dismemberment: MACHINE does not discriminate between adults and children and so this young boy is going to have to learn to accept MACHINE's daily punishments or else be deemed unworthy of life.

But the ultimate judge won't be you—it'll be MACHINE.

5

A few hours later you greet the boy's progenitors in one of the medical bays. The paternal progenitor looks like an older, fatter version of the boy. There's no expression on his face as he shakes your hand.

The child quivers in the corner of the room, standing behind his progenitors, naive in his expectation that they will protect him.

You introduce yourself and explain to them, "Although I am capable of performing this procedure, I am not actually a qualified physician and there is a risk that I may inadvertently kill your offspring. MACHINE does not deem this boy worthy of proper medical attention."

The paternal progenitor nods. "I had suspected as much. I blame myself for being too kind to the boy in his formative years. We gave him food every day and never broke a single one of his bones during the torture rituals. If there's anyone deserving of punishment today, it is me."

You give the paternal progenitor a curt nod because he has said the Correct thing. It is impossible to tell whether he sincerely believes the sentiment or is only saying it because he knows that MACHINE hears everything. Either way, he appears to have conducted himself appropriately.

You then turn to the boy, your teeth bared in what you hope is a threatening gesture: "Do you understand that? You might actually *die* here today!"

You smirk as you see tears of terror slowly forming along the boy's lower eyelids. You have studied the Standard Operating Manual well: Children who are *Chipped* must be tortured psychologically as well as physically. It is MACHINE's will that this be so.

You hoist the boy onto the operating table and place him face down, so that he is at constant risk of suffocation and will experience a drowning-like sensation throughout the procedure.

"Hold him down by the legs!" you order the maternal progenitor, but instead of using her weight to pin the child down (as the procedure is supposed to go) she hesitates. It's subtle, but you can see the tell-tale flicker in her eyes—she's still emotionally attached to her offspring.

"Madam, you know as well as I do that this is standard—" But before you can finish explaining, MACHINE itself, in all its infinite glory and wisdom, steps in to administer a Corrective Shock to the woman.

She yelps in pain, falling to her knees. You can hear the buzzing from her own Chip, lasting nearly a minute, her auburn ringlets straightening and standing on end as the electric current passes through her body.

When it's over, her eyes are bloodshot and she coughs and heaves a few times, still conscious, having likely received a lengthy but low voltage Correction from MACHINE.

You're tempted to offer her your hand and help her to her feet but you know better than to display compassion, especially to someone who has just been blessed in this way by MACHINE.

Instead you wait, arms folded, for her to get up of her own accord and sit down on her offspring's legs to stop him moving while he is Chipped, as is her duty as the maternal progenitor.

Once she is in place, you shove the boy's face down harder into the mattress of the operating table. The boy's limbs flail and you can hear his muffled screams. After a short interval you reduce the pressure on the back of his neck, instead holding it firm and steady while you produce a scalpel with the other hand.

This procedure is never about safety or accuracy—if it was, then MACHINE would likely perform it itself. MACHINE has designated this procedure to humans *because* it knows that humans will fuck it up and cause pain, death or other complications. It is MACHINE's way of ensuring that the weak do not survive.

The boy stops flailing as you make a straight incision at the base of his skull. With your fingers, which are neither gloved nor sanitised, you widen the incision until it becomes a small hole. You don't need to imagine how painful it is for the boy because you've never forgotten what it was like when this happened to you—and how quickly you went from thinking you were dying to *wishing* you were dying.

On your desk is a tray full of new Chips, each manufactured directly by MACHINE. You reach for one at random—a metal cube, cold and surprisingly heavy—and jam it somewhat haphazardly into the hole you've created in the back of the boy's neck. You make no effort to consider the boy's pain levels, or even the safety of what you're doing.

You drill into the boy's cervical vertebrae and as you do he convulses with an unambiguous scream. The paternal progenitor has to step in to hold him down now—this is the part of the procedure that tends to kill or cripple the children, because sometimes their movement causes you to slip and drill into the cervical plexus.

Once you're satisfied that you've drilled deep enough into the bone, you press down hard with the Chip, using the scalpel to cut away any flesh or muscle that gets in the way, until the Chip is all the way down, nestled into the hole you've created.

From this point on, MACHINE will take over. Tiny wires inside the Chip are supposed to connect with the child's nervous system while automatically cauterising and suturing the wound that you have created. At least, that's if MACHINE decides that it wants to.

You take a damp cloth to the boy's neck to wipe away any blood, remembering from your own Chipping the sensation of relief that this brought. And how this marked the final time in your life that you would ever again feel pleasure or comfort.

"Congratulations. You are now part of MACHINE," you say flatly, because showing enthusiasm here might be misinterpreted by MACHINE as a sign of pleasure. You turn to the progenitors:

"He will still require Corrective Shocks at home from you, plus all the usual psychological torments—humiliation, deprivation, Tantalus torture... as stated in your Standard Operating Manual. And most importantly: He is now to go completely cold turkey on HeDonia. Ordinarily we would not subject one as young as him to such a terrible torment but, well... I believe that this is the will of MACHINE."

The progenitors nod.

"Get up, you weak little shit!" says the paternal progenitor, dragging the shocked and stricken boy off the operating table and striking him hard several times on the backside.

You smile. You know that the boy will be okay as long as he has parents who hate him.

6

You're relieved when the klaxons finally sound again, indicating the end of your shift.

There's no night and day on the *Joie de Vivre* other than MACHINE's use of artificial and ultraviolet lighting to approximate the diurnal cycle—although this cannot always be relied upon. One of MACHINE's favourite tortures is to adjust the lighting to maximum so as to cause prolonged sleep deprivation, or else randomly turn out all lights, forcing people to do their labour in the dark.

You're aware too that not everyone on the ship operates on the same cycle—MACHINE wants people producing labour at all hours.

After a night of being woken four times by MACHINE's Corrective Shocks and a long day of teaching the children to embrace cruelty, you're physically exhausted and collapse onto a chair with a sigh.

Before you even have time to consider the Incorrectness of this action, you feel a pulsing white hotness shoot up your spine and feel the familiar roar of moderate-to-high voltage electricity flowing through every nerve in your body.

Involuntarily you scream, which only makes it worse as the electric shock somehow leaps from the back of your skull and onto your tongue. The shocks then start to pulse, one every second, like a switch is being toggled on and off repeatedly.

In between Corrective Shocks you leap to your knees and cry, *"I'm sorry!"* in the possibly futile hope that MACHINE might hear you or care enough to consider your supplication.

You can never be sure how long a Corrective Shock session will last, but after what feels like fifteen minutes (though according to the chronometer was only three minutes), your punishment stops and you're left on your hands and knees, gasping for air and trying to suppress your lachrymal glands. (You wouldn't dare dishonour MACHINE by *crying* just because you've been tortured!)

These punishments sometimes feel arbitrary, but on this occasion you are certain of how you have displeased MACHINE: You were lazy and you refused to accept MACHINE's gift of exhaustion by choosing to sit down.

To work is to live and to live is to work. Rest is for the weak and the weak deserve to die.

7

You're someone who generally prefers to eat alone, so naturally you're always forced to eat in one of the *Joie de Vivre*'s mess halls, surrounded by people. The only time MACHINE would ever permit you to eat alone would be if it sensed that you were genuinely lonely.

15

Once, as a teenager, you thought you could outsmart MACHINE by publicly feigning loneliness, thinking it would get you out of the nightmarish daily feeding ritual. But MACHINE saw through your meagre deception and the Corrective Shock you received was so great that you woke up in an infirmary a week later, having succumbed to internal bleeding. When your progenitors found out that you'd been injured in this way, they broke your nose for being so weak and for selfishly wasting the resources of the *Joie de Vivre* on your convalescence.

The corridors are still crowded—they always are—but you're not in a rush this time, as the penalty for being late to the mess hall is much more mild than the penalty for being late to your labour station. At absolute worst, you'd be starved and humiliated but you're frequently subjected to that anyway, so why rush?

There are some children nearby—not surprising given your proximity to the nursery—and you're pleased to observe that they are tormenting the smallest and weakest member of their group.

Children are so innocent, you muse. It's as if they instinctively understand MACHINE's will and desire for cruelty. It's usually not until adulthood that the terrible instinct for compassion and altruism starts to kick in—something you suspect is probably linked to the reproductive urge.

You watch the children pushing and kicking the weakest member of their group, yanking him by the hair until he cries. The other children giggle mercilessly, having achieved their goal, and run away towards the mess hall, leaving their victim alone, wailing and screaming.

You can't stand the sound of children crying, partially because it's unpleasant to listen to and partially because it awakens a terrible, forbidden instinct in you to comfort and help the stricken infant. You try to ignore the child like everyone else in the crowd, pushing your way past without looking down.

And then you see something extraordinary: A woman with strikingly blue eyes and long red hair emerges into the corridor from what you presume were her private living quarters. She walks directly up to the crying child and kneels down to comfort it.

The woman looks too young to be the child's maternal progenitor and even if she was, such tenderness is forbidden, even between blood relatives.

She holds up the procession in the corridor although a good many people present are watching her baffling performance with a mix of curiosity and horror, just like you.

Did this woman perhaps escape from the insane ward? Is she an alien from beyond the walls of the *Joie de Vivre*? Is this some sort of advanced psychological ploy to increase the suffering of the young child?

She embraces the child with both arms, not letting go until it has stopped crying. Those standing next to her instinctively back away—no one wants to be caught near this Crazy Kind Woman when MACHINE comes to deal with her.

She stands back up and grins while everyone else present, yourself included, stares at her in shock.

"What the hell are you doing?" says a man behind her. "You can't commit kindness! On an impressionable *child* no less! What the hell is wrong with you?"

Everyone, including you, murmurs in agreement.

The woman, maintaining her sanguine expression, shrugs. "I guess I'm just tired of all the torture and suffering that goes on here."

There's an audible gasp and everyone takes another step back from this obvious lunatic, including the child.

"I know kindness is a strange thing to see when you've never experienced it, but things don't have to be this way!" she says. "We don't have to be cruel to each other! We don't need to torment and torture each other, or humiliate each other, or kill the weak!"

A few people laugh and you can't blame them for doing so. You've never heard such nonsense in your life.

"I think I understand," the man behind her says. "You're insane! Suicidal! Only someone like that would speak such blasphemies!"

The woman continues to smile—proof, as if any more were needed, that you are witnessing an absolute nutjob.

"We don't need MACHINE. We don't need to accept MACHINE's torture just to live. Life could be so much more than that! I had a dream—"

"Aha! So you're an illegal dreamer! No wonder you're mentally deranged!"

"—that there was a rich and beautiful world outside, where MACHINE wasn't there and human beings were kind to each other!"

"*Blasphemy!*"

"A world of compassion and kindness is possible! A world without MACHINE is possible! A world of—" She's drowned out by the sound of the klaxons firing up again and this time you're filled with dread.

It's not the usual ear-splitting scream that you hear every morning—this time, it's a staccato warning siren.

It means MACHINE has heard her, MACHINE is coming and MACHINE is pissed off.

8

Most of the time you barely notice the metallic rail that runs down the centre of every corridor on the *Joie de Vivre*—typically it's just used as a dividing line on days when the corridors are crowded to separate people who are walking in opposite directions.

But you know its real purpose, though this is the first time you've ever actually *seen* it in action.

The laughter and jeering of the crowd stops—they too know what is coming. The man who had earlier engaged in interlocution with the Crazy Kind Woman goes white as he jumps out of the way.

You also brace yourself against the wall, desperately wishing you weren't here to witness this. You can hear something in the distance—a grinding, clanging, metallic rumble growing louder and louder. The floor vibrates with a growing intensity.

You don't know whether to look or to look away—the former runs the risk that MACHINE might see you and arbitrarily choose to take out its wrath upon you but the latter runs the risk of being interpreted as cowardice or weakness, which would almost *definitely* invoke MACHINE's wrath.

In the end you simply hold your breath, pushing your back up as far against the wall as it will go, desperate not to have even an inch of your body closer to the rail than strictly necessary.

A large dark shadow looms over a bend in the corridor as MACHINE itself comes racing into the area.

Finally, you lay your eyes directly upon it: MACHINE appears like a large, dark, mechanical fin, screaming along the central rail until it reaches the Crazy Kind Woman.

Every set of eyes in the corridor is fixed upon the woman and the huge anvil shaped object that now towers over her. The Crazy Kind Woman no longer smiles, her expression now one of pure terror. For a moment it looks like she's going to run, which causes the bystanders ahead of her to jump out of the way, afraid that they might be caught up in her punishment.

Before she can move, two reticulated metal tentacles emerge from hidden orifices in the giant fin and coil around her. Another four or five emerge, some with long needles on the end, others adorned with buzz saws and whirring blades.

One of the metallic arms hovers in front of the woman's face, pausing as if it's waiting for something. And then without warning, it plunges a large needle straight into her left eye. Black bile oozes from the skewered eyeball before MACHINE quickly retracts the needle, leaving her screaming and bleeding from a now empty eye socket.

Another tentacle with a whirring, spinning blade on the end hovers barely an inch from her neck, leaving you wondering whether MACHINE plans to decapitate her quick and easy or whether it intends to slit her throat and leave her to bleed out slowly and painfully.

But you soon discover that the whirring blades are not intended for her at all—instead, MACHINE's metallic tentacles coil around the boy that the woman had been comforting earlier, lifting him off the ground and into the air.

The woman's one remaining eye widens in horror.

"No!" she begs. "Take me! Torture me! I am the one who has sinned! I am the one guilty of compassion! Please don't—"

But her begging is futile and MACHINE mercilessly saws the child in twain, with a single downward swoop of its blades. The tentacles hold the two halves of the former child up in front of the woman, deliberately giving her a clear view of the child's viscera and internal organs slowly oozing out and falling to the ground.

You're relieved, at the least, that MACHINE gave this child a quick and relatively painless death. Immediately the rational part of your brain chastises you for feeling empathy—and for being foolish enough to think such a forbidden thought in the presence of MACHINE itself!

Once the Crazy Kind Woman finally looks to have succumbed to despair, MACHINE moves to put her out of her misery. One of the thick needles plunges into her abdomen, drilling all the way through until it's poking out the other side. After that, it's just a matter of tearing her open and waiting for the shock of her exposed entrails to kill her.

You're forced to wait there for what might be hours, back against the wall and desperately trying not to move or draw attention to yourself while you watch the light slowly go out of the Crazy Kind Woman's remaining eye.

You're made aware of her death by the sudden change in MACHINE's actions, because as soon as it senses that she's gone, MACHINE immediately goes to work on her carcass, butchering her remains until the only thing left is her spine and bare ribcage, now stripped entirely of all meat.

MACHINE retracts its tentacles and then the giant fin lowers itself downward, into and underneath the rail, to some unseen place beneath the floor.

The klaxons cease wailing but it's at least five minutes before you regain the courage to peel yourself off the wall and continue onwards to the mess hall, past the stripped carcass of the Crazy Kind Woman.

9

The episode with the Crazy Kind Woman has made you late to the mess hall, but luckily you're not the only one who was held up —this is good, because being the last to arrive is a very good way to make yourself the target for Ritual Humiliation.

The experience has, however, left you bereft of any appetite, yet you know you must eat here tonight, not only to ensure your survival but because refusal would displease MACHINE.

There's a long queue in the mess hall leading all the way out the entrance and dutifully, you join it. Slowly, the queue shuffles forward and once you actually make it through the arched entryway, you grab a white bowl from a long table to your right, shuffling toward the large pipe from which MACHINE will dispense your sustenance.

The food is almost always foul. The best case scenario is usually a tasteless bowl of synthetic proteins and vitamins, though MACHINE typically alters the flavour so that the act of eating becomes another act of torture. It was only last night that your meal was chemically altered so that it ranked well over two million on the Scoville scale, but in the face of starvation you were still forced to endure it. And even then, that was a nice meal by MACHINE's standards—at least it was edible. MACHINE has been known to fill people's bowls with sewage and excrement and on at least one occasion, you yourself were forced to eat it.

As you approach the food pipe, the familiar feeling of dread returns, the feeling that comes almost every day as you stand at this point in the queue. But the feeling of dread is always in competition with your desperate thirst and hunger, leading to a constant stalemate between your need to eat and your dread for whatever awful thing MACHINE expects you to ingest today.

You reach the food pipe and turn around, exposing the back of your neck to a small scanner embedded into the front of the pipe. You hear a click and the familiar beep as your Chip is scanned, before turning around and placing your bowl under the pipe. With a low vibration, something dark red drops into your bowl with an audible thump.

You're a little confused by this—it's new. Most of the food MACHINE dispenses is usually white slop, but this looks solid, almost appetising. It looks like—

"Meat!" someone gasps, staring at the contents of your bowl. "That's real meat!"

This pronouncement is met by other gasps of astonishment as a small crowd forms around you in awe.

"How did you do it?" someone asks.

"I thought only the priests ate meat!" says someone else.

"It's gotta be an illusion!" says a third person and, though you say nothing publicly, you're inclined to agree with the assessment.

Nothing you have done today, or on any recent day, merits any kind of reward or special favour from MACHINE, which means this must be some sort of trick—perhaps a kind of Tantalus torture or perhaps the meat is rancid or poisoned.

Either way, all eyes are upon you as you make your way to one of the dining tables. You desperately wish they weren't. Tonight's target for Ritual Humiliation hasn't been chosen yet and the last thing in the world you need right now is to be the centre of attention or to be standing out in any way.

As you take your seat you're relieved to see a similar commotion taking place by the food pipe.

"He's got meat too!" you hear someone cry. "And so does she! Who are these people? Why is MACHINE giving out meat tonight?"

You're certainly perturbed by the sudden improvement in cuisine but you're also glad that you're not the only one with meat. It means less attention on you.

You prod the meat a few times with your fork. You have no idea what animal it came from and it looks bloody and under-cooked—yet it also looks appetising and you sense you might take real pleasure in eating this.

You know better than to start eating immediately. You have to wait until the mess hall is full, no matter how many thousands of people are to be served. To wait is to prolong your hunger; to prolong your hunger is to prolong your suffering. You may eat only by the will of MACHINE.

10

By the time the doors to the mess hall close, signifying that it's time to eat, your meat has gone cold—though you're not sure it was ever warm to begin with. It doesn't matter. You lift your fork.

Then, a pounding at the door. A shrill voice calling from outside. The door slides open, and a woman stumbles in, panting, covered in dust.

"I'm sorry!" she splutters. "I tried to run, but there was an explosion, and—"

"*Shame! Shame! Shame! Shame!*"

The chant erupts, fists hammering on the tables. You're never quite sure who starts it but it comes every night, without fail. You're not even sure if this is something that MACHINE mandates or if it's a ritual that people have created themselves. You set down your fork and join in, slamming your fist against the table in time with the others.

The Ritual Humiliation is about the closest thing there is to entertainment on the *Joie de Vivre* and you must admit, whenever you're not the victim, you find it quite enjoyable. Yes, there's a sacred pleasure in making yourself suffer for MACHINE but if you were forced to be honest, you'd admit that it's the suffering of others that you find most titillating.

Several diners near the entrance stand and drag the woman to the centre of the room. At first she makes like she's going to struggle but in the end she acquiesces, accepting that today it's her turn to be Ritually Humiliated. It's an inevitable part of life on the *Joie de Vivre*, surely she must know it's better to just let it happen and get it over with.

The room lets out a cheer now that tonight's target has been chosen and you join in: It's always a relief when the target is anyone other than you.

A fat balding man steps into the centre of the room. You have no idea who he is, but he seems to have proclaimed himself the lead in tonight's ritual.

"String her up," he says, his eyes darting upward at the hooks dangling from the ceiling.

The purpose of those hooks is never stated but always understood. She is hauled upside down, her legs bound at the ankles, and hoisted high. Her arms flail briefly before they, too, are secured.

One of her tormentors produces a blade, perhaps a kitchen utensil, and after several violent strokes, you notice her hair falling away in clumps, until her pale scalp is left bare and exposed beneath the fluorescent lights.

A dull murmur ripples through the hall.

Someone brings a bowl—a lather of black, viscous fluid. It's smeared all over her face, her hands and any exposed skin until she is left dripping the black substance onto the ground below her.

The chanting resumes as the bald man steps forward and places a hand beneath the woman's jaw, forcing her to look at him. "Who are you?"

She doesn't answer.

He grips tighter. "Who are you?"

Still, silence. Her eyes are wide but unfocused, as though she has already drifted somewhere else. This is wise—you know from your own experience that the best response is always no response.

The bald man grins. "Correct. You are no one. You are nothing. You are subhuman. Scum. Unworthy!"

You chant along with the rest of the room, "*You are nothing! You are nothing!*"

"Very good..." the bald man drawls, glancing around the room.

The room goes silent for several minutes and so you return to your meal, cutting a slice of the mysterious meat that MACHINE has provided for you.

It's not a steak and if it is it's not from any animal whose meat you've sampled in your life. The flesh is pale, but as you cut into it, red blood seeps from the fibres. It's not raw but it's only been cooked minimally. You place it in your mouth, expecting to taste something rotten or acrid but it's surprisingly pleasant. Enjoyable, if not for the question of what are you eating and is it safe to do so?

As you prepare to take another bite, you feel your table vibrating and instinctively lean forward, hunching over your bowl to protect your meal. Projectiles fly over you from behind as the other diners hurl various objects—food, utensils, crockery, even shoes—at the woman hanging from the ceiling. Many of these objects stick to the black substance on her face and soon she's completely covered in debris.

Ignoring the commotion, you focus instead on your meal. The meat is chewy and every time you chew, your mouth fills with blood. You gulp it down, despite your instinct to spit out the blood, savouring the flavour of what is undoubtedly the best meal you've had in years.

You cut another bite of meat.

Across the room, the woman now sways gently from the hook, silent, still, her face now invisible beneath the various objects stuck to her skin. No longer a person. No longer anything at all.

You continue to eat until all that's left in your bowl is blood and... something disturbing.

A white orb, soft and meaty in texture, which you hadn't previously noticed hidden under the slice of meat. You don't want to eat it because you've already figured out what it is but you know you have to if you want to escape harsh punishment by MACHINE.

Wincing a little, you skewer it with your fork and a black liquid oozes out. You lift your fork, turning it around to face you, revealing that you are about to eat an eyeball: an eyeball with a striking deep blue iris.

You really don't want to be eating the fleshy remains of the Crazy Kind Woman but on the *Joie de Vivre*, the rule is that you either eat or you are eaten.

11

Tonight's Ritual Humiliation dragged on for longer than usual and by the time you're finally able to exit the mess hall there's been another shift change and the corridors are crowded with thousands of workers trying to reach their respective labour stations in time to avoid punishment or death.

Exhaustion hits hard once you reach your private quarters; standing or keeping your eyes open feels impossible.

MACHINE can usually be counted upon to provide you with just enough sustenance to ensure your survival, although tonight you're feeling queasy from the effects of consuming human flesh —flesh that, now that you think of it, was served to you mostly raw.

Your door, which is supposed to open automatically when you approach it, remains closed and you lean against it, knees weak, shaking from fatigue and dehydration. Collapsing here would probably see you crushed to death under a stampede of workers or else disembowelled by MACHINE just as you saw happen to the Crazy Kind Woman.

Someone elbows you hard in the back.

"Move it or lose it, asshole!" they yell in your ear as they push past you.

You're blocking people in the corridor, though you suspect that this is a torture meant more for them than for you: MACHINE loves nothing more than to place obstacles in the path of anyone facing the prospect of execution for lateness.

"My door won't open," you try to mumble but you're so exhausted that the words barely come out at all.

The person who elbowed you shoots you a violent glare. There's a small mob of workers forming behind you, all unable to force themselves through the narrow gap between you and the people coming from the opposite direction.

"You're making people late!" he snaps.

In your exhausted state you almost tell him, "I'm sorry" but luckily you have the presence of mind to remember that "*Compassion is Corruption*" and so instead you say the Correct thing:

"Good. I hope that you *are* late and that you get tortured and then die a painful death because of it."

The man grits his teeth and just as he looks like he's about to swing a punch that will knock you down and see you trampled to death by the crowd behind you, your door suddenly opens and you stumble backwards into the relative haven of your private quarters.

12

MACHINE had mercy. Now *that's* a scary thought if ever there was one.

You wonder if perhaps it was a reward for your last minute decision to say the Correct thing, but you immediately laugh off the absurd idea. When in your entire life has MACHINE ever rewarded you with anything other than pain?

Life *is* the reward, being permitted to serve MACHINE through your labour is a reward, being cared for enough by MACHINE that it tortures and punishes you for your pointless and pathetic existence is the reward!

You're expecting a painful Corrective Shock at any moment, considering the utter wrongness of your thoughts and it deeply unnerves you that one has not yet come.

You stand in front of your basin, looking in the mirror. You can see the exhaustion in your eyes, but beyond that there's nothing about your appearance that strikes you as unusual today.

You press the button next to the tap, requesting water. You hear a vibration; the tap shudders and spits and you wonder if your punishment will come in the form of some terrible acrid liquid being dispensed instead of water.

But no, to your further astonishment, water flows freely from the tap! You quickly cup it in your hands and lap it up before it stops flowing. Private cups are forbidden—it is MACHINE's will that people must always be on the verge of dehydration and that

29

when there is thirst and water is scarce, you must endure the experience of watching it disappear through your fingertips when you are most desperate for it.

You've never seen water flow like this and you're able to scoop up three entire handfuls of it. It's cold and tastes pure—clearly not the reconstituted sewage that you're doused with every morning. (Water which MACHINE always laces with toxic cleaning agents so that no one is tempted to rehydrate via the shower during their morning delousing.)

You're getting extremely nervous now. There must be a catch —some terrible hidden torment that you're not seeing or tasting. Maybe the water is laced with cyanide, or perhaps it came directly from the bladder of some other person on the ship?

A Corrective Shock would be welcome at this point. At least then, you'd know exactly where you stand with MACHINE. What's happening now feels suspiciously, disturbingly, like *kindness*.

You cautiously walk over to your bed. It's reverted back to its soft state—you don't see any spikes or needles and it looks inviting. You're tempted to just lie down and enjoy this rare opportunity to rest.

While tonight's Ritual Humiliation dragged on for so long that there are only four hours left until your next labour assignment, that seems far too light a punishment for today. It's possible MACHINE will keep the lights on or fill the room with loud noise while you try to sleep, but sleep deprivation barely counts as a torture these days—that's just routine.

In the drawer next to your bed is a small packet of unused syringes: your ration of sEDAtIVE. You run your fingers up and down the tubes, arguing with yourself over whether or not to use one.

sEDAtIVE can be a powerful analgesic, sometimes so powerful that you can sleep through entire Corrective Shocks or forget every psychological torment that you've endured in a particular day. You've heard of people who use it every night and still wake up on time, able to perform their labour duties to a satisfactory level.

You decide it's not worth the risk. Using sEDAtIVE always comes with dangerous side effects—it makes you slow and sluggish and unproductive and sometimes causes you lose track track of time, putting you at risk of execution for lateness.

And perhaps worst of all, every time you use it, you find yourself needing to increase the dose in order to benefit from it, with your body constantly building a tolerance to its effects.

Tonight is not a night for sEDAtIVE. Tonight you will try to rest naturally, accepting whatever nocturnal tortures MACHINE wishes to bestow upon you.

Tentatively, you remove your clothing, sending it through the chute to be laundered or otherwise stored and lie down on your bed. Thin though your mattress is, lying in bed is the closest thing to comfort you're permitted to experience on a typical day.

The lights dim automatically.

Everything is quiet. Too quiet.

13

You're standing on the edge of a cliff, not that you have a word for such a thing because you've never seen one before.

There are no walls in any direction.

The roof is bright yellow but somehow you know it's not a roof, it's really the void of outer space—but for some reason the void isn't black, it's bright yellow. Could this be what the tales from the Old Planet meant when they spoke of a thing called "the sky"?

There's a giant white orb, like a lightbulb, but so big and luminous that it's painful to look at. It's warm and for some reason you don't feel frightened by it.

This isn't the *Joie de Vivre*. You know that much. There's nothing metallic in this place at all, nor is there any sign of other people.

The closest thing to a wall that you can see is something far out in the distance: a large, jagged wall of irregular triangles, bluish in hue but with white on the top. You look behind you and discover that you're currently stood on the face of one of these things—a mountain—though you're not sure where you ever heard that word.

There's a small white creature at your feet but you're not afraid of it. It seems to follow you and makes a strange yapping noise like a very quiet klaxon. You sense that this small creature desires to protect you, rather than to torture you.

You stare out into the yellow void and despite the absence of walls or any familiarity, you're not scared of the surreal vista before you. You know you could die here, but you don't mind—not because of despair but because you're so grateful to have seen this place and experienced true freedom.

In your right hand you're carrying a long brown stick. It's soft, made from a non-metallic material you've never seen before, but vaguely reminiscent of the illustrations of plants that you've seen in books about the Old Planet.

In your left hand there *is* veritably a plant—a white flower that you choose to hold for its beauty rather than to eat. You don't know where these thoughts are coming from.

A strange surge of self-confidence floods through you, as if you've been dosed with HeDonia, and you suddenly leap off the edge of the cliff, trusting that whatever happens you won't be killed or hurt or tortured.

There's a brief sensation of falling and then you jolt awake in your darkened living quarters, realising that MACHINE just allowed you to dream for the first time since you were child.

<h2 style="text-align:center">14</h2>

It's still dark in your private quarters when you wake and there are no klaxons screeching into your ears. There's a faint light under the crack of your door, accompanied by the faint sound of people outside, shuffling to and from their designated labour stations.

You feel comfortable and well rested. This alarms you. The only time you ever feel even remotely like this is while under the influence of sEDAtIVE, but you distinctly recall choosing to eschew it before you went to bed.

The other, more alarming question is: How long have you been asleep?

This has happened once before—you once woke up in a dark room, without the warning klaxons to awaken you, because MACHINE decided to deliberately toy with you to make you late for your daily labour.

There's no reliable way to measure the passage of time in here as the information on your chronometer can easily be altered by MACHINE if it wishes to punish you with psychological torture. Nevertheless, you check it anyway and it indicates that you've been asleep for 12.5% of the daily cycle (three hours as measured by the ancient systems of the Old Planet) which means, unless the chronometer is inaccurate, that you can continue to rest if you choose.

Everything feels too comfortable, too warm and safe, like you've been drugged with a combination of sEDAtIVE and HeDonia.

MACHINE should have given you a Corrective Shock before you began the REM cycle, to stop you from dreaming. Did MACHINE malfunction? Was it unable to sense where you were in the sleep cycle? Has it miscalculated? Are you about to receive one of your nightly Corrective Shocks any second now?

Despite this rare feeling of comfort, you're unable to go back to sleep. Every time you close your eyes, the feeling of foreboding overpowers you.

You know something nasty awaits you and that the longer you're forced to wait, the nastier it will be.

15

You're still awake when the lights come on, slowly and gently fading their way to full brightness. There's no ear-splitting wail from the klaxons either—instead a strange, warm tone you've never heard before, like two pieces of metal gently clanging together.

You're so surprised, perhaps even delighted, that you almost forget that only have a few seconds to roll off your bed before the spikes re-emerge through the pores of your cribriform mattress.

You quickly leap off, landing with a thud on the freezing metal floor, but you watch with astonishment as not a single needle or spike rises out from the bed, even after a whole minute.

As bizarre as this is, you know you can't allow this to distract you or make you late to your labour station and so you force yourself to your feet.

You're still thirsty and, when you press the button next to your tap, you're surprised to see water flowing freely like it did the night before. You waste no time in cupping it with your hands and drinking. The clear, cold water flows continuously from the tap until you're no longer thirsty, as if there is no longer any limit to the ship's water supplies.

The only kind of discomfort you feel at all this morning is when you have to empty your bowels—there's a slight pain in your abdomen and the faintest feeling of nausea as your body struggles to digest and emit the human flesh you consumed the night before.

When it's time to delouse, you're almost shaking with fear: MACHINE would never be this kind to someone unless it was about to kill them and you feel almost certain that you're going to be showering in deadly acid this morning.

It's not acid.

It's soapy water, delivered at a warm, relaxing temperature. The water pressure is so great that it's almost like you're being massaged or exfoliated.

The air dryer roars to life and the excess water is evaporated away, to be processed and reused elsewhere on the ship.

Your uniform is clean, pressed and warm, like it's brand new. It feels soft and comfortable against your skin and you quickly realise that the spikes and needles that usually irritate your skin have all been removed from the inner lining.

There's no denying that MACHINE is being kind to you and this fact terrifies you. You're tempted to deliberately injure yourself on the way out, perhaps by cutting a large gash in your skin or deliberately breaking one of your digits, just to show MACHINE that you are still worthy of punishment, that you are still willing to withstand whatever pain or torment you must endure in order to cling on to your gift of life.

The door opens and you step out into the corridor, only this morning it's almost empty. There are a handful of others en route to their labour stations, but not nearly enough people to cause the usual congestion. You're able to easily navigate your way through the *Joie de Vivre*'s labyrinth of tubes and tunnels, arriving at the nursery so early that few of the lights are on yet.

You enter the dim but familiar space, the large cavern adorned with posters bearing slogans like *"Kindness is Weakness!"*, *"Compassion is Corruption!"*, *"Suffering is a Gift!"*.

You're breathing unevenly now, your heart rate elevated. The dread is almost as bad as the torture itself, because you know something is coming—something unexpected and horrific. You wish MACHINE would just stop toying with you and get it over with.

You can hear footsteps behind you. It's not one of the children, the footsteps are far too loud to belong to anyone other than an adult.

There's someone else in here, someone hidden in the darkness and you don't know who they are or what they plan to do to you.

16

"Who's there?" you ask, barely able to disguise the quiver of fear in your voice.

Immediately you want to slap yourself for your idiocy. By speaking first, by speaking like *that*, you're revealing just how weak, alone and afraid you are.

The footsteps in the darkness slowly grow louder until finally a figure emerges from the shadows: a very tall, masculine figure in a long, hooded, scarlet robe, adorned with a ring of long white spikes protruding from the neck.

It's a priest. You've never seen one in the flesh before, but you've seen diagrams in the Great Instruction Manual that depict them. They're almost mythical, said to dwell deep in the bowels of the *Joie de Vivre*, right in the centre of the ship, near the mainframe of MACHINE.

The priest speaks a single word, posed as a question, and this word makes you gasp because it's a word you haven't heard uttered since you were still a child.

That word is your name.

It's a word that you've taught yourself to forget. Throughout your life, you've been inculcated to believe that word to be as meaningless and worthless as the individual to which it refers.

That you should hear that word again, from the lips of a priest, fills you with a complicated array of emotions that simultaneously make you want to prostrate yourself on the ground, weep, scream and shield yourself from whatever incoming horror the priest intends to inflict upon you.

Regaining your composure you nod, affirming that you are indeed the individual to which the word refers.

The priest smiles. It's a rather mirthless smile but it does not convey any hint of sinister intent or malice. It's a trustworthy, if perfunctory, smile.

"Come!" he says. "There are important matters we must discuss."

He gestures for you to follow him into your office, the same office where yesterday you Chipped the young boy.

The priest sits in your seat and gestures for you to sit where one of the progenitors would normally sit while watching you torture their offspring.

The priest claps his hands together and grins, eyebrows raised —a look of enthusiasm, perhaps even joy.

"So," he says, "how did you enjoy the taste of human flesh?"

You're dumbfounded. You have no idea how to respond to such a line of inquiry but you know that you're being tested and that the Incorrect answer could lead to a fate worse than death.

If you admit to enjoying the meat then you've committed the sin of feeling pleasure and thus deserve harsh Correction from MACHINE. But if you claim that you did not enjoy it, then the priest might suspect that it's because you felt compassion for the former human you were eating, which is an even worse sin. Worse still, it could be interpreted as insufficient gratitude for the gift that MACHINE chose to bestow upon you.

Slowly and carefully you answer him, lingering over every single word as you attempt to navigate this verbal minefield:

"The human flesh was chewy and tasted unpleasant. It also caused me to experience abdominal comfort. For this reason and this reason alone, I did enjoy its consumption and I am grateful to MACHINE for choosing to punish me in this new and unique way."

The priest makes an unusual noise, one that you would normally expect to hear only from a child—a snicker, a stifled laugh, as if he found your response to be of utmost amusement.

"I can see that you have been trained and refined well," says the priest. "You are very loyal to MACHINE, diligent and Correct in all your words and actions. You accept your torment with grace and your punishments with humility. MACHINE sees you. And MACHINE is very pleased by you."

You're not sure how to react. If you smile or thank him, it will be seen as the sin of pride or worse: the sin of joy. You know he's waiting for you to reply but you do not know the Correct thing to say.

After a protracted silence you finally decide to take a risk with: "I am not and never will be worthy of MACHINE's favour."

The priest cocks his head to the side, like he's confused, but the gesture is so theatrical that you sense he might be doing so ironically; as if the response you gave is exactly the one which he expected.

"And why is that? Have you committed sins against MACHINE?"

You don't even need to think about it.

"Yes!" you blurt, with an intensity that surprises you as much as it surprises the priest. "I have sinned against MACHINE! I am unworthy of its gifts! I am unworthy of life! Last night... I dreamed a dream! I took pleasure in rest! I enjoyed drinking water, I am wearing clothes that cause me no pain and I am feeling pride in the possibility of having obtained MACHINE's favour!"

The priest smiles at you but this time it's a smile that you *would* describe as "sinister". His eyes are wide and bore into yours, as if he can not only read your thoughts but knows them before you can even think them; as if he knows every dark secret you hold, every guilty pleasure, every fear, every wretched thing about you that makes you so deserving of MACHINE's torment and punishments.

"You dreamed, did you?" The priest licks his lips. It's a gesture that disgusts you on a visceral level but you don't know why. "Well then... why don't you tell me about it? Tell me what you saw. Tell me what sick, MACHINE-less vision you saw in your mind's eye..."

The priest folds him arms and nods as you explain to him what you saw when MACHINE allowed you to dream. His smile is almost understanding—as if you're telling him nothing that he didn't already know.

"Does this happen often?" the priest inquires.

You shake your head. "MACHINE shocks me awake every time I'm about to start dreaming and whenever I use sEDAtIVE I don't dream at all. This is the first time I've had a dream since I was still using HeDonia."

The priest nods again, his fingers arranged into tent-poles. There's a protracted silence.

"Did I do something wrong?" you ask. "Did something happen to MACHINE that stopped it from waking me before I started dreaming? Was there some sort of glitch?"

"Nothing of the sort," the priest says in a shockingly avuncular tone. "Is it Incorrect to dream?"

You stare at him. You're sure he's testing you, but this seems like too obvious a question. There must be some sort of trick that you're not seeing.

"Of course it's Incorrect!" you reply. "Everyone knows that! Dreams are for children and if an adult is still dreaming then there is something wrong with them... they are defective."

"And what makes you believe this?" asks the priest.

Your jaw drops at the stupidity of the priest's line of questioning. Asking how you know that it is Incorrect to dream is like asking how you know you need to breathe to stay alive.

"What kind of question is that?"

"A very pertinent one," says the priest. "So let me ask you again: How do you know that it is Incorrect to dream? At what point did it become Incorrect to do so?"

He's messing with your head and you know it. You've heard stories of encounters with priests that go just like this one—the priests are said to be versed in highly advanced psychological torture techniques capable of inflicting permanent psychiatric damage. It's clear that this priest means to drive you insane.

"It's the way things are and the way they always have been," you reply.

The priest arches an eyebrow. "Really?"

"Yes!"

"Before you dreamed last night, when was the last time you dreamed?"

"I already told you!" you say. "It was when I was still a child. I was still under the influence of HeDonia."

"So you stopped dreaming because you stopped using HeDonia? Is that correct?"

You pause for a moment. If this priest is interrogating you then you don't want to risk perjuring yourself by misspeaking—the consequences of that could be worse than anything you've ever conceived of.

"I stopped dreaming around the same time that I stopped using HeDonia," you say slowly, "but not *because* of it. I am not claiming a causal relationship between these two events."

"Why, then, did you stop dreaming?"

"I told you! It's because MACHINE gives me a Corrective Shock every time I'm about to start dreaming," you say. "And if I *do* sleep for a whole night it's because I was using sEDAtIVE, which makes it impossible for me to dream."

"But at what point did you become aware that dreaming was a *moral* deficiency? An Incorrect action? You have explained why you are unable to dream but not why you're *unwilling*. When were you ever taught that it was Incorrect to dream?"

He's stumped you. You think back to your childhood, to your time in the nursery, to your training period. Someone must have taught you, you're sure of it. Perhaps it was one of your progenitors?

"I don't recall," you admit.

"But you still believe it is a sin against MACHINE to dream?"

"I'm not sure what conclusion you are trying to convince me to reach," you say. "I know that dreaming is a sin but your line of questioning is as if you are trying to convince me that it isn't, or to trap me into saying that it isn't. And I know it would be a sin to question MACHINE's teachings and so I refuse to follow your line of reason and blaspheme against MACHINE."

The priest raises both of his eyebrows now and leans back a little, almost as if he's impressed.

"There's no questioning your devotion to MACHINE, I can see that much," he says.

You beam, before quickly stopping yourself—to take any pride, pleasure or joy in a compliment would be to insult MACHINE.

"However I am not trying to trick you, nor am I asking you to blaspheme. I am only trying to open your mind to the possibility that your understanding of MACHINE and of MACHINE's will may be more incomplete than you realise."

You frown. "I will listen to you, but that does not mean that I endorse anything blasphemous or Incorrect that you might have to say."

"Very well," the priest says with a shrug. "I am only asking you to carefully consider your assumptions regarding what is, and is not, the will of MACHINE..." He leans forward in his chair. "Do you not dream because you believe it is wrong, or because you are simply unable to?"

"It's both," you say. "I can't dream because, until last night, I was Corrected by MACHINE every time I began to."

"And you believe that these Corrective Shocks—"

"I believe that MACHINE is expressing its will to me by punishing me for starting to dream whenever I am asleep, yes," you say. "Is that not the case for everyone?"

The priest stares at you for a few seconds, a knowing grin plastered upon his face.

"No," he says finally, "it is not the case for everyone. Most people, even adults, dream every night. Last night you experienced what everyone experiences but you assumed you had transgressed MACHINE's will simply because, for the first time in your adult life, MACHINE chose not to torture you in your sleep."

You feel numb. The priest's words make you feel as if your scalp has been removed and your brain exposed to the open elements. What he is saying is blasphemy, is Incorrect, is against everything you know and understand to be right and true.

Or is it?

18

The wisest response is silence.

You can't deny that on some small level you suspect that what the priest is suggesting could be true, but you certainly won't be saying so aloud. You can't risk failing what is so obviously a test.

No, the priest must be lying. MACHINE would not go to the effort of torturing you with such specific regularity if it was not trying to teach you that dreaming is an Incorrect behaviour.

"I have another question for you," the priest says, grinning as if he can hear your inner conflict. "Do you believe that MACHINE tortures us as a punishment?"

"Yes," you say. "That's why they call them 'Corrective Shocks', right? They exist to Correct you when you have behaved Incorrectly."

"But is it not also a reward, a blessing and an honour to be tortured by MACHINE?"

Ah, fuck. You've been so busy doing mental gymnastics over how to respond to the priest's suggestion that dreaming isn't evil that you've walked headlong into an obvious trap: You've accidentally denied that MACHINE's torture is a blessing.

"Torture is a blessing *because* it's a punishment," you say, desperately trying to worm your way out the situation. "It shows that MACHINE cares enough about us to guide us onto the Correct path."

The priest strokes his chin. "Interesting. So you believe that everything MACHINE does is for a reason?"

"MACHINE is more intelligent than any human. Even if we do not understand the reasons, its calculations are always perfect and we should never doubt them."

"I'm not suggesting that we doubt them. Merely that MACHINE might not always act out of reason. Have you never done anything that was completely arbitrary? Acted in a way that you don't understand? Known that an action wasn't the logical or Correct choice but done so anyway?"

"Any mistakes I have made like that are because I am flesh and flesh is fallible. Flesh can succumb to emotion. But

MACHINE is not flesh and therefore cannot be corrupted by emotion or illogic."

At this point you're not so much answering his questions as quoting verbatim something you learned by rote in childhood, from the Great Instruction Manual.

The priest claps his hands together. "Excellent!"

"Will that be all?" You're conscious that the children will be arriving soon.

"Yes. You have passed the tests and MACHINE truly *is* pleased with you. Your dreaming, your rest, your food and water were all given as a reward for your devotion to Correct behaviour."

You almost smile but you don't want to be seen taking any pleasure in praise.

"I am sorry that I will never fully be worthy of MACHINE's gifts," you say instead.

The priest stands and makes his way to the door before hesitating and then turning back to face you.

"There is... one *other* matter which MACHINE has indicated is a concern."

"Oh?"

The priest glances around the room. "You dislike children, don't you?"

"I think that they are vile and animalistic and need to be moulded by MACHINE," you say.

"Yes... I can see why you have been stationed to work in the nursery then," says the priest. "Nevertheless it is a concern that you are of breeding age and yet have made no outwardly discernible effort to reproduce. Having a child is one of the most painful and damaging experiences a human being can ever endure. I believe that MACHINE would like you to start engaging more fully in mating rituals hereon in. You live alone and that is clearly not enough of a torment for you."

19

You knew that this day would come eventually.

It is said that there is no act so cruel as to bring a child into the *Joie de Vivre*. It is also said that MACHINE rewards those who commit acts of cruelty. Therefore, to reproduce would be to seek favour with MACHINE.

You have no desire to reproduce.

You don't like children; you have very little interest in the opposite sex; and the cruelty of the mating ritual, even after everything else that you have endured in your life, seems like a level of torture beyond anything you feel capable of surviving.

Every day you meet the progenitors of the children at the nursery. You look into their dead eyes and can see the psychological, occasionally physical, damage which has been inflicted upon them by this cruellest of rituals.

You see the efforts they go to to disguise their grimaces as smiles, to feign gratitude for one of MACHINE's harshest punishments.

You've seen men and woman in their prime, starving and dessicated, shadows of their former selves, singing paeans to MACHINE for the destruction it has wrought upon them now that they have replicated their DNA.

What's unusual about the mating ritual is that although it's one of the worst tortures anyone aboard the *Joie de Vivre* could ever endure, it's not one that MACHINE commits directly. Instead it is inflicted upon humans by other humans, in order to create more humans.

"You don't look very enthusiastic about the prospect?" says the priest.

Unknown to you, your face has gone pale and your body has betrayed you by displaying your true feelings toward the prospect of mating.

"It's a lot to consider," you say. "Does MACHINE really consider my genetic information worthy of being passed on to the next generation?"

It's a cop-out. Both you and the priest know you're trying to bullshit your way out of admitting the truth: That you do not wish to reproduce.

"MACHINE considers all adult humans worthy of DNA replication, you know that."

"Mmm..."

"You are anxious?"

"What if I am rejected?" you say. "What if I am considered deficient and therefore unable to find a mating partner?"

"If you're deficient, you're deficient. The market will determine your value and there's nothing you can do about it if it decides that you are valueless, other than to be grateful that MACHINE has kept someone as valueless as yourself alive for as long as it has. But is that *really* why you are so hesitant to reproduce? You endure loneliness every day and periodic Ritual Humiliation... do you really expect me to believe that you are worried about rejection?"

"Rejection is a factor at the back of my mind," you admit, "but—"

"But it's not the real reason for your hesitancy, is it?"

You shake your head. You know you probably face punishment already for your Incorrect attitude toward reproduction so there's no sense in making matters worse by trying conceal it.

The priest studies you for a moment before continuing. "It is normal to feel anxious about the mating ritual, and indeed to feel anxious about trying to form connections with other humans. But this is all by design... for it is another form of torture!

"Torture isn't always about the suffering you feel in the moment—just as important is the *anticipation* of suffering, the fear of it, the dread! Do you really seek to dishonour MACHINE by rejecting the opportunity to undergo one of the worst forms of torture that a human being can ever experience?"

"Of course not!" you say. "And of course I will do what MACHINE requires of me. But for some reason, even though I know that this will be cruel and painful, even though I know that to worship MACHINE is to seek out cruelty and pain, some part of me just doesn't want to."

The priest frowns at you. "Are you homosexual?"

You shake your head. You have little attraction to the opposite sex but the thought of copulation with a member of the same sex fills you with revulsion.

"That's good, because MACHINE has a special place on this ship for homosexuals and other deviants. It would entail a life of rejection and torture that will make you *wish* you were enduring a torment as simple as the mating ritual."

"It's not that. I'm just not... anything," you admit. "But perhaps I'm just exhausted? Perhaps I have not yet been exposed to an adequate mating partner?"

The priest, still frowning, softens his expression a little but you can tell he's sceptical.

"It's certainly not unheard of," he says. "And I'm sure MACHINE would appreciate your willingness to torture yourself through the mating ritual *in spite* of your lack of desire for a mate... the additional suffering would no doubt prove to MACHINE that you are indeed a devoted servant.

"However—there is one thing I'd like to try first, before you embark upon that path..."

"What's that?" you ask, somewhat nervously.

"Have you ever experienced a sensation called 'love' before?"

<h2 style="text-align:center">20</h2>

"No," you tell the priest honestly. "I've heard the word mentioned in one or two stories but I don't really know what the word means."

The priest nods, giving you an encouraging smile. "Tell me what you've heard about it."

"Well..." You have to think about it. All you know about the subject has been conjecture based on conflicting stories. "I think it's some sort of drug? Like sEDAtIVE or HeDonia... but more powerful. Forbidden in some way."

"It could be said that love is a drug, yes," says the priest with a nod.

"I've heard it can destroy people. That it's the most dangerous drug of them all," you continue. "I've heard it's something to stay away from, like kindness or compassion. That it's evil."

"Do you think it's evil?" asks the priest.

"I don't know anything about it," you say. "*Is* it evil?"

The priest rubs his hands together. "Well... it's complicated. If there is such a thing as good and evil then love exists at the mid point of that axis. It's *both* good and evil simultaneously.

"It's evil because it encourages behaviours that are anathema to MACHINE, such as altruism and self-sacrifice.

"But it's good too because, well, it's said that love is the ultimate form of torture. It destroys people. Kills people. Makes people kill each other. Makes people harm each other.

"Love is a very dangerous thing but if you ever wanted to commit an ultimate act of masochism, I'd suggest trying it."

You don't know what to say. You've been talking so long that surely the children should have arrived—and yet, the nursery remains silent and dark. There are no children here today.

"So is 'love' a drug?" you ask.

"Yes," says the priest, "and no. It's an emotion, though MACHINE very well may synthesise it into a drug in future. If it was a drug it would be like HeDonia mixed with pure liquefied pain. More mind altering than sEDAtIVE. The most evil drug of them all. Have you ever wondered how HeDonia is synthesised?"

"Sure, a little," you say.

"HeDonia is pure dopamine and pure serotonin," says the priest. "MACHINE synthesises it from the chemicals in human brains. Most of the drugs that MACHINE creates are nothing more than distilled emotions."

You narrow your eyes a little. "When you asked me if I'd ever experienced 'love', you posed the question as if it was a suggestion. Are you suggesting to me that *this* the will of MACHINE?"

The priest grins at you, his hands together in front of his navel, fingertips like tent-poles once again. He pauses for a moment, studying you carefully before finally replying:

"Yes."

21

50

You bow your head. You know you've been honoured in multiple ways this morning—clearly, you have the attention and favour of MACHINE.

And so you tell the priest the only Correct thing you can think of to say in this situation:

"If it is MACHINE's will that I am to be tormented and tortured in this way, then I will gladly and humbly submit myself to the pain."

The priest smiles, his sinister grin displaying a few too many teeth in your opinion.

"That is very Correct of you to say," he says.

"So... how do I obtain this evil drug?" you ask. "Are you here to inject me with it?"

"No, no, no... I don't think you fully understand MACHINE's will in this situation," says the priest. "MACHINE wishes to synthesise this drug based on the chemical reactions that humans naturally produce. You do not need to be injected with love. You must experience it. MACHINE will monitor your brain via your Chip and once you have experienced 'love', MACHINE will understand precisely which neurochemical reactions it needs to synthesise in order to replicate the sensation."

"But if 'love' isn't a drug that you can inject me with, how am I supposed to find and experience the sensation on my own?"

"There are ways," says the priest. "The most common is as an unwanted side effect of the mating ritual. I don't think you're ready to mate just yet... but there may be *another* way to make you experience the sensation of 'love'. And it was actually *you* who gave me the idea!"

"It was?"

"You told me about your dream. You told me you saw a small white creature, by your side, following you around. Is that correct?"

"Sure," you say. "But that's just a dream. Something weird that my subconscious devised because I hadn't used any sEDAtIVE."

"What you saw was not a dream," says the priest. "Well... not exactly. Humans came from the Old Planet and there are memories of the Old Planet encoded into our DNA—this is known as the 'collective unconscious'. It means that when we dream, sometimes we might see the Old Planet, even though we have never been there in waking life." The priest scratches his forehead. "The creature you saw in your dream sounds like a 'dog'... maybe a cat, but most likely a dog. Those creatures were real animals that lived on the Old Planet and humans were known to form genuine emotional bonds with them."

"But if they're real, they're extinct, right?" you say. "Those creatures... 'dogs'... would surely have all died out when the Old Planet was destroyed?"

The priest flashes you a grin. "Not necessarily..."

"Are you saying that—"

"The *Joie de Vivre* has many secrets and one such secret is that MACHINE saw fit to preserve a sample of life from the Old Planet. There are secret vaults on this ship containing plants, trees and animals from the Old Planet. Including dogs.

"We will find you a dog, just like the one from your dream. You will become emotionally attached to it. You will experience the great torment known as 'love'. And MACHINE will extract that feeling from your brain, in order to create a new drug with which to further torture and subjugate the populace of the *Joie de Vivre*."

22

You're relieved from your duties at the nursery and instructed to follow the priest to an area of the *Joie de Vivre* that you've never visited before.

You try to take a mental note of the route, remembering every twist, turn, tunnel and secret passageway that the priest leads you down, but it's such a labyrinth that you know you have no hope of ever being able to retrace your steps without guidance.

You've never thought about it until now, but this is the first time in your life that you've ever been permitted to leave your sector and only now are you starting to understand just how enormous the *Joie de Vivre* is. One of the passages has large transparent windows, giving you a view of the void outside and the stars beyond, but they're all stars and constellations that you've never seen before.

The priest often swipes a key-card to gain access to locked doors—many of which are just panels in the wall that you'd have never otherwise known were doors. It's at this moment that you notice something strange about the priest: There's no Chip in the back of his neck.

You'd always assumed that the priests, being so close to MACHINE, would have been Chipped possibly from birth, but instead the priest's neck is bare and smooth, like a child's. Perhaps that's why he's forced to carry a key-card? With no Chip in his neck, perhaps MACHINE is unable to see him? Or perhaps there's some other explanation that you haven't yet—

"We're here."

A large airlock door opens in front of you, leading to a strange, verdant cavern covered in a soft green growth and filled with strange green and brown tubular objects that you've never seen before.

"These things are called 'trees'," the priest says, following your gaze to the tall, tubular things. "They play a crucial role in generating the oxygen supply. Without them we'd all choke and die."

You'd nod, fascinated by them. They're so strange and yet somehow so familiar—standing before them gives you a peculiar sense of *deja vu*. You walk up to one and touch its trunk. The texture is incredibly rough and a small brown piece breaks off. Immediately you jump backwards as the small brown flake falls to the ground.

"I'm so sorry!" you say immediately. "I didn't mean to break it! I didn't know it was so delicate!"

Terrible thoughts rush through your mind—visions of the terrible punishment that the priest and MACHINE will put you through for your carelessness. Or worse: The thought of everyone choking to death because you accidentally damaged this oxygen-production machine that the priest calls a "tree".

To your astonishment, the priest only laughs. "You haven't damaged it. It's normal. That piece that broke off is called 'bark'—to a tree it's like dead skin or hair. You have caused it no harm."

Even so, you immediately go rigid, following the priest through this strange room with your arms pinned to your sides, desperate not to touch or break anything.

"This room is part of what we call the 'Eden System'," the priest explains. "It is named for an ancient garden on the Old Planet which, according to legend, is where the first humans came from. Food, oxygen, animals for meat... all of it is grown in large hidden orchids, deep inside the ship, just like this one."

"It's beautiful," you blurt. "I've never seen such colour before. Well except in—"

"Your dreams?"

You nod, guiltily.

"I'm not surprised. Our ancestors once lived in a place like this. They say before we lived on the *Joie de Vivre*, humans lived in trees, or else lived in giant concrete monoliths. Those memories are encoded into our DNA."

You look closely at the trees. There are so many of them—you can barely see the walls of the ship because there are so many. "Does that mean that MACHINE is in those trees too?"

"Whatever do you mean?"

"If humans used to live in trees then that means that MACHINE must have been in those trees too, in order to guide them and punish them," you say. "Because humans can't survive without MACHINE."

The priest goes silent and you wonder whether you've accidentally blasphemed.

"I'm sorry," you add quickly. "My curiosity is leading me down dangerous paths. I would have expected a Corrective Shock by now but if you like I could self-flagellate or maybe cut one of my fingers off to show my contrition?"

The priest chuckles, though it's barely audible. "That won't be necessary. You've neither sinned nor blasphemed, you are only ignorant."

You gasp. Ignorance is a *terrible* sin! You've seen people beaten for ignorance, some have even been killed. When a child displays ignorance you always make sure to encourage the other children to isolate and torture them.

You fall to your knees immediately.

"Then please! Kill me for my ignorance!" you plead. "The ignorant are undeserving of life so please, kill me or torture me as you see fit!"

The priest snorts. "I will do no such thing and nor will MACHINE. Do you honestly believe that MACHINE seeks to murder the ignorant? If so, the only people aboard this ship would be the priests!"

What the priest is saying makes no sense and is slightly frightening to hear. It's as if he's just proven that there's a secret whole number between two and three, or showed you a colour that you've never seen before.

"But if someone is ignorant, we beat them to death! That's always been the way it is!"

"Yes but *we* beat them, not MACHINE. Do you understand? It is man's will that the ignorant be killed and tortured, not MACHINE's. In the infinitely wise eyes of MACHINE, ignorance is innocence."

"Then why does MACHINE allow people it deems innocent to suffer?"

"Now *that's* a stupid question and you know it!" says the priest. "Suffering is the ultimate display of MACHINE's love and devotion! What a foolish thing to say... I think I am starting to see *why* the ignorant are beaten and killed..."

"I'm sorry. I deserve to suffer for my ignorance."

"You deserve nothing," says the priest, "except that which MACHINE has willed for you. And in this case it is MACHINE's will that you learn to experience the pure agony known as 'love'."

23

You're silent for the rest of the journey, disgusted with yourself. You can feel your tongue inside your mouth and you're tempted to bite if off to demonstrate your guilt. You do not deserve to ever speak again. Perhaps the priest or MACHINE or someone else will cut your tongue off for you. It would be a mercy, to prevent you from ever again being so blasphemous or displaying such ignorance.

You soon enter a second large cavern, but this one does not contain trees, just the strange green growths on the ground that the priest explained is called "grass" and is apparently a living organism.

You wonder how much pain the grass feels as you trample across it, ripping it in places, but perhaps this is all according to MACHINE's design? Perhaps in this way, the living creature called "grass" is tortured and thus purified of sin by MACHINE?

You hear some strange noises in the distance—a kind of screeching noise, a little like metal scraping together.

"Be careful," says the priest. "There are animals in this room. Animals are very dangerous—they can attack and kill without warning."

"Like MACHINE?" you say, finally breaking your silence.

"They are much more arbitrary than MACHINE," says the priest. "Animals desire food and nothing more. And they will turn absolutely anything they encounter into a food source."

Again, you don't see this description as one vastly different to your perception of MACHINE but you painfully bite your tongue so as to resist the temptation to accidentally open your mouth and blaspheme yet again.

The priest crouches down and starts clapping and whistling. You're not sure what he's doing or whether you are supposed to mimic him. This is a ritual far stranger than anything you've ever seen.

"Here, boy!" the priest yells into the distance and once again, you're mystified by why he is yelling these things, and to whom.

In the distance you spot something white, bobbing up and down, moving rapidly toward you. You wonder if this is another plant but as it comes closer you start to question whether or not what you are seeing is reality.

There is a living creature running toward you, making a strange high-pitched yapping noise. You've seen this creature before—it's the small white beast from your dream, but you're seeing it here, in reality, aboard the ship.

The creature trots up to the priest before stopping and then placing its snout in the ground, making a strange loud breathing noise.

"This is a dog," says the priest. "These animals once lived alongside humans on the Old Planet. It is MACHINE's will that you take care of this animal. That you treat it as if you would treat a child."

You nod and immediately pull your leg back, prepared to kick the dog just as you would a child. The priest quickly grabs you, preventing your foot from making contact with the animal.

"Sorry, what I meant is... you should treat this animal with kindness as if it were an extension of yourself!"

"But kindness is forbidden! It's a sin!" you say, quoting from the Great Instruction Manual: "'*Kindness is Weakness*!', '*Compassion is Corruption!*'"

"But this is MACHINE's will..." says the priest.

"You must be lying!" you say. "MACHINE would never ask me to sin in such a way! MACHINE would never demand that I commit the deadly sin of kindness! This must be another test!"

"But of *course* MACHINE would ask this of you!" says the priest. "Think about it! What is the punishment for sinning against MACHINE?"

"Torture," you say. "Sometimes death."

"Death is inevitable," says the priest, "so there's no sense in worrying about it. But torture? Well isn't torture the way to be close to MACHINE? The way to worship it?"

"Yes of course," you say.

"So does it not logically follow that MACHINE would ask you to sin, so that it can punish you and so that in punishment you can show your devotion to it? To become closer to MACHINE?"

You look from the priest to the strange white animal —"dog"—which sniffs and slobbers all over your boots.

"I will do MACHINE's will," you say. "If I am worthy of life, MACHINE will keep me alive. If I am deserving of death, MACHINE will let me die. If I am Incorrect, MACHINE will Correct me. And if I am Correct, MACHINE will purify me through pain."

The priest grins. "That is very Correct of you to say."

24

The journey to the Eden System took you hours and now you have to find your way back your sector and your living quarters, with no maps or guidance—accompanied by a strange, small, furry creature that this morning you believed to be mythical.

Your stomach grumbles. It's been nearly a full daily cycle since your last meal (which, you recall with a twinge of disgust, was barely cooked human flesh) and you know you ought to be making your way to the mess hall, lest you become tonight's subject of Ritual Humiliation, or else succumb to starvation.

As you continue through the many tubes and tunnels, each identical to the one in your sector of the ship, the dog follows you.

The priest suggested that you should "name" the dog—that is, you should invent a word that solely refers to the dog as an individual and distinguishes it from other dogs. After all, you too have a name, even if it is unknown to most and seldom spoken.

You consider all the words you know and whether or not they would be appropriate to single out this dog as an individual. You could call it "MACHINE" but that word already refers to MACHINE. Or you could name it after something you see every day like "Tunnel", "Porthole", "Airlock" or "Man screaming, bleeding from the eyes while being spat on and degraded by those around him for being weak".

You dismiss the latter idea on the grounds that the dog is not a man, it's a dog.

You want to just call it "Dog" but the priest told you that this was too impersonal—names must refer to individuals and should not be useable interchangeably as a label to describe an entire subset of individuals.

This seems a strange suggestion to you, considering you only know the priest as "the priest", a moniker that could easily describe any other priest. And everyone you know is either "Man", "Woman" or "Child", occasionally modified with an adjective to separate them in your mind from every other man, woman and child you know.

In the end, the best you can come up with is to call the dog what it is: "Named Dog" or "Namedog", with the dog's name reflecting the quality that makes it unique: That it even has a name at all.

25

The warning klaxons blare, indicating a shift change and you note with bemusement that you've missed an entire day of labour. You have to hope now that the priest truly *was* directing you to follow MACHINE's will, because the penalty for missing a day of labour without authorisation is always death.

White panels in the tunnel walls open as you pass them by, revealing themselves as the hidden entrances to the living quarters of this sector's denizens. Very quickly, you and Namedog are no longer alone, as the corridor fills with people en route to or from their labour stations. All the while, you remain lost as to how near or far you are from your own sector's mess hall or your living quarters.

Namedog jumps and yaps as the corridor fills with people and this immediately draws their attention.

"What is that thing?" someone gasps.

"I've seen that in drawings but I didn't think—"

"A dog!? Is that really a dog?"

"MACHINE must have dosed me with hallucinogens! There's no *way* dogs are real!"

Namedog bounces and yaps while one woman bravely kneels down to touch his white fur. You're not sure whether you should be protecting Namedog here or whether Namedog is likely to bite the woman; in the end she strokes him and both behave as if the experience is mutually pleasurable.

"What the hell are you doing?" you ask the woman.

She looks up, startled. "I'm sorry I... I hadn't even realised I was doing it! There was just some sort of instinct that made me want to do that. Like a maternal instinct but... for that beast!"

Though you understand exactly what she means, you nevertheless frown at her disapprovingly, as you consider this to be the most Correct response to the situation as per the teachings of MACHINE.

"What you're doing could be interpreted as kindness," you warn her. "I suggest that you refrain and repent."

The woman doesn't even have time to react as her eyes roll into her sockets and she begins rapidly shaking and foaming at the mouth. MACHINE has indeed Corrected her and it looks to be a Corrective Shock of a high enough voltage to knock her unconscious.

The faint buzzing noise from her Chip ceases and she flops to the ground, the smell of burning hair wafting through the enclosed space of the corridor.

"I think that should be seen as a warning to you all!" you say loudly, addressing the crowd as if you have any kind of authority. "Yes I do have a dog, for reasons known only to MACHINE. It is not for you to question MACHINE or disturb me, unless you too wish to share in this woman's fate. I suggest make your way to your labour stations at once!"

Every eye in the corridor, and there are hundreds, is upon you but instead of feeling nervous or sick, like you would during a Ritual Humiliation, you feel powerful. You've been marked out as special; the presence of Namedog has given you some kind of authority, and you intend to make the most of it before MACHINE inevitably takes it away again.

The crowd slowly turns away and continues to shuffle down the corridor. The klaxons sound again—many of them are probably late to their labour stations now because they chose to spend so much time gawking at you and Namedog.

You wonder just how many people here are about to be ejected from the ship or tortured to death for being late to their labour stations. You look down at Namedog, who pants with his tongue hanging openly from his snout, a facial expression that you'd normally connote with an idiot or simpleton.

MACHINE has blessed you on this day. Not only have you been spared your usual daily torments, it seems that you and Namedog have become MACHINE's instruments of death, purging the *Joie de Vivre* of the slow and the weak.

26

The *Joie de Vivre* is so large and labyrinthine that there's no way to know whether you're in or even near your own sector, and as far as you can see, every tunnel looks the same. There's no signage, just a seemingly endless maze of tubes and corridors, mostly white in colour, with the occasional porthole to give you a glimpse of the void outside.

The only concrete hint you have that you're not in your own sector is the unfamiliarity of the people here. Your own sector comprises of a few thousand people and whilst you don't know them personally, you are used to seeing the same familiar faces whenever you attempt to traverse the corridors.

None of the faces that are passing you by here are familiar. You've never seen them before in the mess hall; nor have you seen any of them ritually humiliated; nor been subject to Ritual Humiliation by them. The walls and tunnels look so familiar and yet, amongst these faces, this place feels alien. You know you don't belong here.

Having Namedog by your side makes the experience all the stranger. Namedog draws attention to you and everywhere you walk, you're followed by the gaze of people you've never seen before.

As you continue through the corridors, hoping for some hint that you might eventually stumble upon one that leads to your living quarters, you begin to feel weak. Fatigue is usual at any given moment on the *Joie de Vivre*, but you can feel a particular pressure rising inside your head, a faint greying out of your peripheral vision as thirst and hunger threaten to knock you unconscious.

You need to eat something. Anything. This sector looks enough like yours that you instinctively know where to go to find the mess hall and so you eschew your original plan to find your way back to your own sector and decide instead to intrude upon another sector's meal time.

Perhaps it's the fact that MACHINE has not Corrected you for the entire day or perhaps its the presence of Namedog bolstering your self-confidence, but you stride toward the mess hall anyway, to share a communal meal and Ritual Humiliation with people you've never seen before.

27

You set forth into the mess hall and discover that it's exactly identical to the one in your sector.

Namedog gains the attention of the entire room by yapping upon arrival. The result is that people crowd around him, desperate to stroke his fur for some atavistic reason you don't fully understand. No one makes eye contact with you, or even looks at your face. With the attention of the room fixed firmly upon the dog, you stealthily grab a bowl and proceed to the chute from which MACHINE dispenses sustenance.

You know you're pushing your luck. It's uncharacteristic of MACHINE to be this merciful for this long. And you know that if you have the attention of the priests, then it's likely that MACHINE itself is closely watching your every move.

Despite that, you figure that the worst that can happen here is that MACHINE will refuse to feed you, or give you a large Corrective Shock, or that maybe you'll end up the subject of tonight's Ritual Humiliation. None of these punishments are anything you're not already used to, nor are they anything that you wouldn't expect even if you *hadn't* behaved Incorrectly.

And so, you place your bowl under the chute and wait for MACHINE's verdict.

There's a long, low buzzing noise and then something flies through the chute and lands with a thud in the bowl. Several other items follow—soft green, triangular things float down the chute and you recognise them from your time in the orchid as the same strange green growths that you beheld on the appendages of the trees.

Below these flat green things (you think they might be called "leaves") is a slab of meat that you don't quite recognise, but it's thick and brown, a little burned on the edges but bares no resemblance the human flesh you were forced to consume for your previous meal.

There's a faint scent to it which you can't quite place but whatever it is, it's *appetising*—awakening some ancient repressed feeling in the depths of your psyche that this food is desirable and perhaps even nutritious. This must be the kind of food that your ancestors consumed regularly on the Old Planet.

Silently you take your bowl past the people crowded around Namedog and beeline for a table near the back of the room—the place where you're least likely to be noticed or subjected to Ritual Humiliation.

You detect a small commotion behind you and you turn around to discover, to your surprise, that Namedog has abandoned its admirers and is following you, panting loudly.

It jumps up onto your table, next to your bowl of food, sniffing at it and then staring at you with deep brown, melancholic eyes.

"You want some sustenance, do you?" you ask it, despite your awareness of the futility of attempting such communication.

If Namedog has lived this long then it stands to reason that MACHINE has been keeping it alive and providing it with nutrition, so for you to share some of your food with it could therefore be interpreted as you carrying out MACHINE's will, rather than committing a forbidden act of compassion or altruism.

Either way, you have no idea what mythical animals like dogs consume and when you wave one of the green leaves in front of Namedog's face, it shows no interest, its eyes fixated on the meat in your bowl.

"Ah, so dogs consume other animals," you say to Namedog. "So your species *also* thrives on cruelty? That's good to know."

You tear off a strip of the meat and offer it to Namedog, who enthusiastically scoops it into its snout with its tongue.

You tear off another strip for yourself, noting that the inside of this meat is pink—not the uncooked pink of the flesh you ate previously, but as if MACHINE cooked it in this way deliberately to maximise the pleasant flavour of the meat. It's only after you've swallowed the first morsel that you look up to discover that every pair of eyes in the room is now focussed upon you and you hurriedly swallow a second piece of meat, aware that you might well have become tonight's target for Ritual Humiliation.

28

Namedog seems to sense your disquiet and follows your gaze to the line of strangers standing at the opposite end of the room, all staring at you, facial expressions ranging from bemusement to open hostility.

Namedog growls. It's hardly a deterrent coming from such a small animal, but you appreciate the gesture. This lower beast is trying to protect you—something no one else ever has ever done, not even your maternal progenitor.

You, meanwhile, are determined to keep eating. You were starving when you arrived and this meal is so pleasant that it's like injecting yourself with HeDonia. You know, through a combination of reason and instinct, that whatever calories you can obtain here will likely be needed if you are indeed to be Ritually Humiliated tonight.

You hate having to rush the meal. You were really enjoying it, but now you have to scoff it down quickly before it's torn away from you.

Someone steps toward you and Namedog growls at them.

You finish eating and it's only now that you notice how most of the room are still holding empty bowls, eyeing you with a mixture of envy and anger.

You stand and in a voice that sounds braver than you feel, you address the group:

"What do you want? If you are going to Ritually Humiliate me, then get on with it!"

67

A few people in the crowd glance nervously at each other. Someone—a young, skeletally thin man, replies:

"What are you talking about?"

"Look," you say with a sigh, "I know I'm in the wrong sector. I'm sorry. I was desperate and starving. I will accept whatever punishment and humiliation you wish to bestow upon me and I will be grateful to MACHINE to receive it."

The young man shakes his head. "I don't know what you're talking about."

"Do you not have a nightly ritual of humiliation in this sector?"

"I don't know what you mean," he says. "The thing is... the food you just ate... that was for *all* of us!"

You double-take.

"What do you mean for *all* of you?"

"I mean... MACHINE only gives us a little bit of food which we share and ration carefully. But you and that white beast ate tonight's entire supply!"

You glance around the room, noticing how unusually thin and dessicated these people are.

You're unsure as to what the Correct response to this situation is. Feeling or expressing too much guilt would suggest you're feeling empathy for these people, which is a forbidden and sinful emotion. But too little guilt would suggest pride and hubris on your part and will no doubt come back to haunt you when MACHINE finally decides to rebalance the scales.

"I..."

Should you apologise? It's clear that you have committed an Incorrect act. But perhaps you are also being used as a tool by MACHINE to punish the people of this sector and purify them of sin?

"Why are you here?" wheezes the young man. "What *is* that dreadful beast that accompanies you? Why has MACHINE sent you to torment us so?"

"MACHINE's will is beyond the reach of mankind," you say, quoting the Great Instruction Manual. "I don't know why I was sent here, but I sincerely believe that every action I have taken today was the will of MACHINE. If I am wrong then I will gladly accept MACHINE's punishment."

"I think you should leave," the young man says. "And I hope we are never again cursed by the presence of you or your familiar."

You look around the room. The passivity of these people is staggering. If this was your sector, you'd probably have been dis-embowelled by now, or at the very least dismembered by the hungry crowd. Instead, these people stand back, allowing you to exit the mess hall unobstructed.

Before you leave, you decide on one last test, one last experi-ment to see just how passive and weak these people truly are.

"I have a confession to make," you announce. "I am lost. I do not know the way back to my sector and if you truly desire never again to be cursed by my presence, then I will require your aid in finding my way back to the sector from whence I came."

29

There's a hum as the crowd murmur to each other, as if trying to make a collective decision. You suspect they're probably weighing up whether or not your request could be construed as asking for help—in which case, the laws of MACHINE would forbid them from assisting you. But against that they're likely considering their self-preservation and on those grounds assisting you would be legal.

In the end the skeletal young man, who appears to be some sort of leader or spokesperson for the people of this sector, acquiesces.

"If you require help, we will gladly offer it," he says which stuns you—this is an open display of blasphemy!

"I am not asking for *help*, I'm asking for *assistance*," you say. "Helping another person is altruism. MACHINE will torture you if you do that. Assistance is merely following an imperative in order to ensure your survival."

"It seems that the people of your sector hold to a different code of morality than we do," says the young man. "In this sector we believe that the group matters more than the individual. We share all we have and if MACHINE chooses to punish us, we either take it collectively or support one another through the ordeal. It makes me sad that the people of your sector seem to prize cruelty and selfish ambition over the well-being of their neighbours."

Your mouth flies open. They really *are* blaspheming and suddenly you feel the urgent need to get away from here, so as not to be lumped in with them when MACHINE inevitably casts its judgement upon this sector.

"I think you need to study the Great Instruction Manual better," you say. "It clearly states how we are to behave if we wish to maintain MACHINE's favour. MACHINE rewards only the strong and the selfish and destroys the weak."

The young man smiles as if he expected you to say that. "The instruction manual you speak of is fallible. It was written by the first humans to leave the Old Planet in order to troubleshoot a terrible glitch in MACHINE's programming. We believe that there are other, better, ways to endure life aboard this ship."

"I think you'd better help me to my sector immediately!" you say. "I do not think it is wise for me to continue to entertain such odious, blasphemous lies! I hope for your sake that MACHINE chooses to send you out of the airlocks to your deaths, because the things you are saying make you deserving of Eternal Torture!"

The young man blinks at you. The faces of the people in the crowd are blank or confused too. It's evident that these people really *haven't* read the Great Instruction Manual.

"You understand that MACHINE punishes wrong-doing and Incorrect thoughts, right?" you say.

You're relieved when they nod—at least they seem to understand that MACHINE is the ultimate arbiter of justice. If they rejected this idea then you'd know for sure that you must have accidentally stumbled upon the sector of the ship reserved for the incurably insane.

"Well, according to the Great Instruction Manual, there is a type of torture reserved only for the worst of blasphemers, for those who truly incur the wrath of MACHINE. It is said that MACHINE will remove your limbs and attach you to a life-support system, one capable of keeping you physically alive for hundreds, maybe thousands of years.

"And this entire time, you are made to feel pain. There is no retreat from the torture, nor even the release of death. It is the fate that MACHINE's faithful servants are all diligent in avoiding. But the way you people talk, well, forgive me if this sounds like compassion because I assure you have nothing but contempt for all of you, but this terrible fate is likely the one which awaits you if you continue on your current path."

This draws gasps of shock and there are hurried whispers between the people. Do they not have instruction manuals in this sector? Could that be the cause for such blasphemous ignorance?

Even the young man looks perturbed, if only for a moment.

"We believe that MACHINE is benevolent," he says finally. "And so we reject such a fanciful claim. MACHINE has always provided for us and whilst occasionally we are tortured for reas-ons beyond our understanding, we still believe that MACHINE, being of superior intelligence, does so for our ultimate benefit."

You grimace—this sector *must* be the insane ward! There is no other explanation for such an outlandish and bizarre world view.

"I need to leave at once," you say. "Clearly you people have no instruction manuals and MACHINE has doomed you all to Eternal Torture. But I will not be persuaded into partaking in your collective madness!"

"We do not regularly read from the Great Instruction Manual, it's true," the young man confesses. "But we live according to another great document that, it seems, you do not have access to:

"We live our lives by the teachings of The Map."

30

The Great Instruction Manual does indeed make periodic refer-ences to The Map, so you know that The Map is at least some-what sanctioned by MACHINE. Nevertheless you've never seen it nor ever needed it. Only a member of the priesthood would ever require the use of such an arcane document.

The thought of living one's life based on the teachings of The Map alone, without the guidance of the Great Instruction Manual, seems to you a life of recklessness doomed to end in failure and punishment.

"The Map will guide you back to your sector," says the young man. "You may use it to assist you on your journey. We ask only that you we do not ever curse us with your presence in our sector again."

"Agreed," you say. "I have absolutely no intention of ever returning to this sector of abject savagery and lunacy."

The young man turns to the person on his left and bows, a gesture that is repeated one by one along the line until someone near the back of the room picks up a white metal plate with lines and symbols painted upon it. They pass the plate from person to person, each bowing to the other as they receive and pass it on until finally it is in the hands of the young man.

There's a single word inscribed in black ink at the top of the plate: "*DIRECTORY*".

Underneath is a diagram, showing lines, arrows and numerals.

"This is not the entire map," the young man explains. "The true map is so large it requires an entire room for storage, because the *Joie de Vivre* is such a large vessel. But this plate should guide you away from our sector and back to yours."

"How do you know what sector I am from?"

"You mannerisms and beliefs belie it. You are from the sector that believes in the supremacy of the individual, that might makes right, that MACHINE rewards cruelty and punishes kindness. That means that you are from one of the ship's outer rings. The fact that we have never crossed paths before suggests you are from one of the western outer rings. Beyond that... you'll have to find your way to your exact sector, but this map will at least get you in the vicinity of it."

"And your only stipulation is that I do not ever return?"

"Yes," says the young man. "In the name of MACHINE, we never want to see you again!"

You turn to Namedog who jumps excitedly as soon as you make eye contact.

"Very well," you say. "I would thank you for your assistance, but that might be interpreted as kindness. So instead I will leave you by reminding you all that you are worthless, stupid fools who deserve the centuries of torment that are no doubt coming to you."

The young man bows, almost as if he accepts this as a compliment.

"Oh... there's one more thing I forgot to mention, which is very important," he adds, pointing to something on the plate he's given you. "Do you see this red line here? That is the airlock. It's very close to the door which will lead you to the outer ring, but if you open it, it will suck all of the oxygen out of this sector and probably doom us all to be sucked out into space."

"Why are you telling me this?"

"We would prefer it if you didn't do that," says the young man. "We desire to live."

"I would be foolish to open that airlock as it would likely suck me out into the void too," you say. "Therefore it's in my rational self interest not to doom all of you."

"I thank you for your consideration, however that's not quite accurate," the young man says. "There is a delay in opening the airlock. It is possible to programme the airlock to open and decompress our sector before you leave. Again, we ask that you don't. I know that your people believe in cruelty and selfishness, but all the same, we beg that you will spare our lives."

"I would never have considered such an action if you hadn't told me it was an option," you say. "I will do what my conscience tells me. And if I do choose to kill you all, you must remember that it was your fault for suggesting the means by which I could do so."

The man nods sadly. "I suspected this was the case. It seems that MACHINE has forsaken us. That you have indeed been sent to punish us after all.

"Very well. Please be on your way. We will prepare ourselves for death."

31

According to The Map, it's likely that you've been walking around in circles up until now. The only reason you found the mess hall was because the shift change opened a hidden door that you had already passed multiple times. To reach your sector, you'll need to take a hidden tunnel several hundred metres past the mess hall.

You walk to the specified area and run your hands along the wall, carefully feeling for any kind of groove or change in texture that might reveal the location of your hidden exit.

The wall is remarkably hot to touch. The longer you run your hands along it, the hotter it becomes until you're suddenly shocked by a painful jolt of static electricity. In a way, you're relieved—this is the first time today that MACHINE has electrocuted you, albeit in a very mild form. You were starting to worry that MACHINE had forsaken you.

You continue to run your hands along the wall, even as you feel your fingertips burning, until finally you notice a slight bump in the wall—a raised tile that may be the entrance to the hidden passage you need.

There's a small crack in the wall, which you try to squeeze your fingertips under, hissing in pain as the heat rises to an intolerable level. The panel loosens—you're in the right place.

The wall is now burning hot, like a giant stovetop, but there's no way to avoid touching it if you're to have any hope of return-

75

ing home. You tug on your sleeve, hoping to wrap it around your hand and form some sort of protection from the burning heat, but your uniform is a size too small and the sleeve too far up your arm to be of any use.

You slide both hands under the crack, yelping as your skin makes contact with the searing heat, and pull, heaving with all your might against the recalcitrant hidden door. With a whine, it swings open to reveal an extremely narrow tunnel, more like a vent, with just enough space for you to crawl through. Your fingertips are now red and blistering. Instinctively, you suck on them as if this might have any kind of analgesic effect.

You brace yourself for another blast of searing heat as you place your palms down on the floor of the tunnel and try to fit yourself through on your hands and knees. Mercifully, the walls of the tunnel aren't hot—rather the opposite: They're ice cold, so much so that they're painful to touch with your bare skin.

There's not enough room for you to lift your head or see ahead of you but you know this is the only way back to your sector. The hidden door slams behind you, blocking out any ray of light from the corridor, leaving you alone in this freezing, pitch black tunnel.

You have no idea how long this tunnel will be—it could be kilometres to the next ring.

The tunnel is so tiny you can barely move at all and so you continue to shuffle your way down, unable to tell whether your eyes are open or closed.

You detect an itch at the base of your leg but you can't scratch it because there's not enough room in here to move your arm or leg—you're stuck in this position until you reach the end, assuming MACHINE wills for you to reach the end at all.

You continue to shuffle through.

It's exhausting.

You're having to move so many muscles, just to make a few inches of progress through the dark, freezing tube.

But you feel something else here, something wrong, something that fills you with alarm:

The more you pant, the harder and harder it is to breathe. There's not much air in this tube and it's running out. You don't know how far you are from an exit—either exit—but you know that if you don't make it through quick, you're going to suffocate.

32

There's a sudden loud noise in the dark—Namedog's yap, echoing through the tiny space. You can feel Namedog behind you, pawing at your foot, as if it's desperate to run out in front of you.

Against all better judgement, considering how little time and air you have left, you stretch your body out and lie prone, allowing Namedog to trot over your back and out ahead.

Its four paws travel up your spine to your neck until you feel Namedog standing on the back of your head. But instead of moving forward, Namedog waits there, forcing your nose into the freezing floor, depriving you of the ability to breathe what little air remains.

You've always wondered how you were going to die. You assumed that death would come in the form of a high voltage Corrective Shock, or a spike through your internal organs while you lay in bed, or perhaps in the form of poisoned food. You never expected that you would die alone in a small hidden tunnel, suffocated to death by an animal you previously believed was mythical, because it decided that the back of your head was a good place to lie down and take a rest.

You'll never be found here and you wonder how many other hidden tunnels like this host the skeletal remains of people who have died in this exact fashion.

But then, somewhat miraculously, you feel Namedog's weight lift from the back of your head and it trots on forward, leaving you to get back up into your crawling position, able to breathe again.

If oxygen is running out, you know the best thing to do is to ration it. You take a deep breath and hold it as you try to crawl as far as you can without breathing. It doesn't work well—almost immediately you open your mouth and expel the carbon dioxide you were holding, requiring another large intake of oxygen to make up for it.

However much air is left in here, you've just wasted a whole lot of it. Cursing silently, you keep pushing forward, hoping, praying, that there's not much tunnel left.

You hear a clang and Namedog yapping. That must be the exit. You're close. You can't see it but you know you're nearly there.

The end of the tunnel comes quicker than you expect. You bump the top of your head painfully into a metal object sticking out in front of you. There's not enough room for you to lift your chin but with one arm you reach out in front of you. Your hand brushes against something metallic and circular—a wheel, for a hatch door.

It's not easy to turn the wheel one-handed and there's not enough room in here for you to use both arms, but as you tug and tug, a small, circular rim of light appears in front of you and you know you're saved. After a few minutes of struggling to turn the wheel, you hear a satisfying click and the hatch flies open, sending white light streaming into the tiny dark tunnel.

Namedog bounces out enthusiastically and you crawl your way through the final inches of the tunnel and out, landing with a painful splat on the hard, but thankfully well-lit, floor of another corridor.

Before you can even stand, a warning klaxon screeches to life, filling the corridor with a high pitched scream in a syncopated pattern you've never heard before. Even more unusually, this is followed by a disembodied feminine voice:

"Airlock open! Preparing to drain oxygen in T minus 30 seconds..."

The room flashes red in time with the klaxon sirens and as you turn around, you immediately notice writing above the open hatch you just came through: "DANGER: AIRLOCK. DO NOT OPEN!"

You hurriedly try to close the hatch from the outside, but it keeps flying back open—the only way to close it is from back inside the tunnel.

You were told that there was an airlock in the vicinity, but The Map said nothing about the tunnel itself being an airlock. You desperately search the corridor for something that might plug the hole you've inadvertently created, until you spot a small lever in the wall, located below a plaque with instructions on it:

"Emergency jettison:

"Pull lever to jettison tunnel, activating emergency screen door.

"WARNING: This will cause the tunnel to collapse, leaving a hole in the wall of the next sector!"

And it is now that you finally understand what the young man in the Other Sector meant about when he tried to warn you about the airlock.

"T minus 10 seconds until all oxygen drained..."

The people in that sector were kind. They were selfless. They were helpful.

"T minus 5 seconds until all oxygen drained..."

The people in your sector are cruel, selfish and brutal.

"4..."

"3..."

"2..."

Which means the choice is obvious: MACHINE would never ask you to kill yourself for the sake of someone weak and inferior.

"1..."

You yank the lever and a steel wall immediately slams down to cover the entrance of the tunnel you crawled out of. And you know that at that moment, the tunnel will have collapsed and fallen out into space, leaving a gaping hole in the wall of the Other Sector.

Which means that the kind and helpful people of the Other Sector are now suffocating to death, or else being blasted out into space by the sudden atmospheric decompression in their sector.

And it's all because of you.

33

You try to ignore the pang of guilt as you continue down the corridor. After all, you have no reason to feel guilty—you are now a killer and by the laws of MACHINE that makes you virtuous.

Of more pressing concern is whether or not The Map has led you back to your sector or whether this is yet another strange area of the *Joie de Vivre.*

As you continue to navigate the mostly white tubes and tunnels, Namedog trots alongside you, its small footsteps echoing rhythmically through the corridor's metallic walls.

Namedog makes a strange whining noise, followed immediately by the blare of the klaxons. You've now been walking through the ship so long that there's been yet another shift change. You watch with mild fascination as hidden panels in the walls open up and the denizens of this sector exit their private quarters for the daily march to their labour stations.

Namedog yaps several times and once again draws the immediate attention of everyone present.

"Am I still dreaming?" says a voice behind you. "Is that thing real? Am I actually seeing a dog here or have I been drugged again?"

You turn and immediately recognise the man, even though he's someone you don't know personally. This is the same balding, overweight man who you saw leading the Ritual Humiliation a few nights ago. Which confirms that you are back in your sector —all you need now is to reorient yourself.

"Hey!" The bald man slaps you hard in the face. "Don't just ignore me! Answer the damn question!"

Before you have time to react, Namedog leaps into the air and clamps its snout around the man's crotch, drawing blood. The man collapses to the floor, screaming in agony.

You grin and try to force a laugh as if this were a deliberate action, not wanting onlookers to think you have any empathy for the man. You turn and immediately begin barging your way through the crowd with Namedog by your side, seizing the attack on the bald man as an opportunity to make the crowd afraid of you.

You're still half-expecting MACHINE to give you a Corrective Shock to balance out what may well be the first truly good day of your entire life, but still none comes as you finally arrive at the hidden door to your private quarters, which automatically opens in the corridor wall as you approach.

Namedog bounces inside and you follow, collapsing with exhaustion onto your surprisingly soft bed before you've even removed your uniform.

34

You awaken a few hours later, surprised that you were permitted to sleep without receiving a single Corrective Shock. There's been no sound from the klaxons, nor any protraction of the hidden spikes in your bed.

Namedog is curled up on the bed next to your head and you can feel its warmth. It's almost comforting, like having another person in the room, but one who cares about you. Which, you remind yourself, is an impossible and borderline blasphemous thought.

Namedog senses that you're awake and opens its eyes, giving you an (apparently) affectionate lick on the cheek as it gets to its feet.

The room is mostly lit but not at full brightness and you notice a flashing red light at the far end of the room, indicating that you have a message awaiting you.

You get up and walk to the far wall, where there is a touch screen computer terminal embedded. You swipe to activate it and immediately see a short message from your supervisor at the nursery:

"You have been relieved of your duties. Your labour is no longer required."

You're not sure how to feel about the message. It could be interpreted to mean that your labour has been deemed unsatisfactory and could therefore, potentially, be a harbinger of your death if you are not soon deployed to some other useful form of

82

labour. Or it could mean that the priesthood or some other force has intervened on your behalf and you'll soon be redeployed to another labour station.

Whatever the true meaning behind the message, one thing is clear: You now have the whole day to yourself and when you're alone there's only one thing worth doing.

You go to your drawer and pull out a syringe full of sEDAt-IVE. As an adult you're no longer permitted to consume HeDonia but sEDAtIVE is the next best thing.

Namedog watches and makes a whining noise that you're not sure how to interpret. You consider sedating the dog too, but you're not sure what effects sEDAtIVE has on animals and feel a remarkable and uncharacteristic urge to protect Namedog and keep it alive.

Hesitating for a moment, you decide that Namedog can probably take care of itself while you're under and so you expose your left arm, pockmarked from all the other times you've sedated yourself, and penetrate your skin with the needle.

You feel the sEDAtIVE flowing into your muscles—ice cold at first but quickly changing into a warmth that saps you of the strength and will to do anything as it spreads through your vascular system.

The syringe is still hanging from your arm when the numbness engulfs you completely, but by this point you no longer care and that's what makes sEDAtIVE such an effective medication. You collapse onto the floor, so numb that MACHINE could shock you or the klaxons could scream at full volume directly into your ear and you would be impervious to it all.

There's no pain, no dreaming, no memory, no thinking. Just you, in a void of bliss, vaguely aware of your own existence but granted a glorious reprieve from the constant pain and torment of the *Joie de Vivre*.

35

There's no way of telling how long you're out for. You're vaguely aware of a floating sensation, but it comes to an end as you notice a pain in your arm, the needle still embedded in your skin.

Next comes the nausea, the dizziness, and the horrible taste of built up mucus in your mouth. There's a scratching sound and a strange high pitched noise far too quiet to be a klaxon and it's at this moment that you remember Namedog. It always takes time—anything from an hour to a whole day—to recover from temporary amnesia whenever you use sEDAtIVE.

The first thing you do is remove the syringe from your arm. There is already a trickle of dried blood and you quickly compress the new wound with your index finger until it forms a scab —a scab that will no doubt become one of the hundreds of other small holes and scars on your skin.

As you stand, you quickly throw the used needle into the sink while dashing across the room on legs that have not fully regained the strength to carry you. You collapse right in front of your latrine, open your mouth and vomit right into it.

After hours of numbness, the pain returns in waves. Most of it comes from your abdomen, but the headaches are unbearable too. You frequently collapse back onto the floor, unable to fall unconscious, while the room spins and the throbbing in your skull consumes you completely.

You detect an unpleasant odour and soon discover that Namedog defecated on the floor while you were under. You

84

didn't know that animals also defecated, though with hindsight it seems obvious.

You try to scoop up Namedog's small but soft leavings, forced to do so with your bare hands in lieu of any kind of tissue or paper, but it keeps slipping through your fingers. With some effort you transfer the majority to the latrine, but there's still a stain of dog shit on the ground that you can't remove and your only hope is that it'll either go away on its own, or you'll just get used to the smell.

Besides, it's not like you've never soiled yourself on the floor yourself—you've endured many Corrective Shocks in the past that were brutal enough to make you involuntarily void your bowels.

You try to clean the dripping remains of shit off your fingers but when you go to the basin and turn on the tap, no water comes out—instead, your hand is bathed in a black, inky soot.

The whole experience makes you vomit again and you're left with no choice but to wipe your hand clean on the leg of your uniform.

Namedog looks at you with its brown, melancholic eyes and makes a gargling, yowling noise that matches the groaning you can hear from your abdomen.

Despite still being able to taste bile and stomach acid in your mouth, you know you need to eat and you know that Namedog, who is now your responsibility, needs to eat too. You're not sure whether there was another shift change while you were out but you sense that it's probably worth making your way to the mess hall anyway. Besides, the earlier you are, the less likely you are to be the subject of tonight's Ritual Humiliation.

"Are you hungry, Namedog?" you ask.

Namedog can't reply with language but you sense by the look in its eyes and the way it opens its snout to pant excitedly that it understands you.

"Let's go to the mess hall and see if we can get something to eat."

Your door opens automatically and you step out into the almost empty corridor with Namedog in tow.

36

You don't know how long it's been since you last ate but you estimate that it's now been at least a day. You've seen at least two shift changes since leaving your sector and sEDAtIVE usually knocks you out for at least half a day, sometimes longer.

As you and Namedog head to the mess hall, you're struck by how fatigued you are. With every step, it feels as if the bones in your legs are struggling not to snap under your weight.

The mess hall feels further away than ever tonight. It's possible that the layout of your sector has changed while you were gone—it would not be out of character for MACHINE to do such a thing—however it's more likely that your exhaustion is causing you to perceive the journey as being longer than it is.

When you finally arrive, you're out of breath and sweating heavily. Perhaps the sEDAtIVE had you out for over a day this time.

You're also, clearly, not on time: the mess hall is completely full and as soon as you enter the room, every eye is upon you.

You try to ignore them—being late does not automatically result in Ritual Humiliation. You grab a bowl from the table and go to the chute, awaiting your meal. Namedog jumps onto the

86

counter, next to the chute, barking expectantly. It's clear that Namedog is hungry too.

You wait. And wait. And wait.

Nothing comes. It's as if MACHINE is ignoring you completely.

You examine the sensor carefully. Perhaps it didn't read your Chip for some reason. You turn, crouching a little so that the back of your neck is directly in front of the sensor and this time there's an audible beep—the sensor has definitely read your Chip.

MACHINE knows you're there. But it's refusing to provide you with sustenance.

Out of the corner of your eye you sense you're being watched. You can hear the faint sound of murmuring. And giggling.

You make a vain attempt to check for a switch or hidden button that might activate the food chute but you know as well as anyone that the chute operates by the will of MACHINE alone.

Namedog barks loudly. You really wish it wouldn't—the last thing you want right now is attention and yet for some reason Namedog seems hell bent on drawing as much of it as possible.

In your peripheral vision you see people standing. Walking toward you.

Oh shit.

No meal and the attention of the other diners usually means only one thing: Tonight, you're going to be the entertainment. You're going to be the one that the crowd torments to distract themselves from their own woes.

"What is that thing? That's a dog?"

"It's a cat!"

"No, that's a dog. I saw a picture of one in a book about the Old Planet. Holy crap, that's an actual fucking *dog!*"

A small group of people approaches but thankfully their attention isn't on you, it's on Namedog. You shouldn't be surprised. It's *always* on Namedog.

One of the men reaches out and touches Namedog on the snout, but instead of snarling or recoiling, Namedog seems to enjoy it. It wags its tail and its mouth hangs open with its tongue out.

"Where the hell did you find this thing?" One of the men crowded around Namedog eyes you, followed by the rest of the group as if they're seeing you for the first time.

"It was provided to me by a priest," you say. "By the will of MACHINE," you add, hoping that your direct contact with the priesthood might mark you out as a superior and thus inoculate you from humiliation or attack.

One of the men licks his lips. It's not the reaction you were expecting.

"Looks tasty!"

"Oh yeah," agrees another man. "It's only a small dog but there's definitely some meat on those bones. We could really do something with that..."

Namedog continues to stand there naively, mouth open, taking apparent pleasure from being stroked by men who are openly discussing killing and eating it.

The thought revolts you, although you're not sure why. You eat animals all the time. You've eaten other humans before. You know that MACHINE's law is that you kill or you are killed, eat or you are eaten. And yet, some hidden part of you can't bare the thought that you would be separated from Namedog forever, that Namedog would be taken from you, killed and then fed back to you as cooked flesh.

Your stomach growls. You're literally starving, increasingly delirious from hunger and being denied sustenance by MACHINE—and yet, you still recoil at the thought of eating Namedog.

"You... you can't!" you say, jumping in front of Namedog to shield it from these human predators.

One of the men leers at you. "And why the hell not?"

You look him up down, acutely aware that you're significantly outnumbered and most of these people are physically bigger than you. You hear someone near the back of the group commenting on your creased, rumpled uniform. And then they notice the smeared shit stain on your leg. Someone points at it, says something inaudible, and the rest of the growing crowd guffaws with laughter.

You quickly rearrange your facial expression. The last thing you need at a time like this is to show any fear or weakness. You think back to your experience in the Other Sector and all the people you've successfully overpowered since Namedog began following you around.

"It is—" You take in a gulp of air, trying to lower your voice to sound authoritative "—the will of MACHINE! I have been entrusted with this animal to perform a special task for MACHINE. Were you to destroy this animal, you would face certain harsh punishment, maybe even death, for defying the sacred will of—"

You don't even reach the end of your sentence when, for the first time in days, you feel an explosion of hot, searing pain, originating from the Chip in the back of your neck. It pulses down your spine and out to every nerve in your body.

You fall to your knees, teeth clenched, trying not to scream.

A tall, well-built man near the front chuckles.

"So... you claim you're doing the sacred will of MACHINE and yet MACHINE has chosen this moment to Correct you? And I also note that MACHINE chose not to provide any sustenance for you on this day?

"I think MACHINE's will is very clear. This dog is for us. This dog is to be killed and become our sustenance. How's *that* for MACHINE's grand plan?"

You look up at him, your eyes teary and watery from the pain of the pulsing electric shocks. You want to fight him. You want to protect Namedog. But you no longer have the strength to stand.

37

The Corrective Shocks cease but you remain on the floor, fighting a futile battle to get back up. It's hopeless—it seems that MACHINE has temporarily paralysed you.

Someone steps over you and you hear Namedog yelp in surprise as someone grabs it.

Namedog doesn't seem to know what's happening. You know you have to save it. This tiny, furry beast was willing to defend you; now is the time for you to return the favour.

You grit your teeth and groan as you channel every ounce of strength and will into your muscles, forcing yourself to curl upwards. Your limbs feel unbearably heavy. It doesn't matter. You take in another deep breath and try again to force yourself to your feet.

At this moment, someone—a female, notices you.

Her face turns downward to look at you, a sneer planted upon it: "Oh look! Are you trying to stand up!"

Laughter follows. Someone kicks you in the head and you fall back to where you were, still paralysed.

"No, wait!" The well-built man addresses the crowd. "Pull them up! I have an idea..."

You're hoisted to your feet, still weak and unable to move. One of them pins your arms hard behind your back, while another ties a rope around your ankles. In a single dizzying swoop, you're hoisted upside down into the air and left hanging helplessly from the hooks in the roof.

The well-built man holds Namedog in front of your head. Namedog's sad, brown eyes bore into yours. It licks you gently on the nose.

"MACHINE has provided us with an animal—a live animal— for sustenance!" says the well-built man to the crowd before turning to you with the contemptuous sneer. "But this fool, this blasphemous cretin, seeks to thwart that! If this idiot had their way, this animal would live and we would all go hungry!"

The crowd makes a loud, disapproving noise. Several throw cutlery and other hard objects in your direction. You're hit directly in the face by a bowl thrown by the now-bald woman you saw getting Ritually Humiliated a few nights ago.

In a loud and theatrical voice, the man addresses you directly: "Why would you wish such a thing?"

You barely have the strength to answer but you manage to mumble, "It's the will of MACHINE..."

"The will of MACHINE?" the man repeats, loudly and incredulously. "And yet, MACHINE saw fit to torture you in this very room just as you tried to defend this creature, this... *dog!*" He spits the word *dog* as if it were a curse word. "It is clearly not your true motivation. So confess, sinner—what is your true motivation?"

You open your mouth but you're still too weak from the Corrective Shock for any words to come out. Even if you had the strength to speak, you're not sure how you would have answered the charges.

"I'll tell you what their true motivation is—" The man continues, speaking not to you but to the crowd. "It's because this *wretch*, this *sinner*, this *pathetic human shit-stain*...actually feels *compassion* for this dumb animal!"

The crowd roars with laughter.

"That's the truth isn't it?" Still speaking theatrically, he aims the question at you. "You think of this dog as a *friend* don't you? Oh no... don't tell me... you *love* this dog? You want to protect it? You treat it like a naive, young, female progenitor would treat a newborn child!"

You try to gargle out the word "No!" but you know as well as he does that you're lying.

In the short time you've been together, you've become attached to Namedog. The fact that you gave it a name, that you have a word that distinguishes it from all other dogs, only heightened your attachment. You sense an intelligence in there. A consciousness. This dog has been loyal to you. You see it as more than just a four-legged walking meat sack, but rather as an individual, like a human but better because humans are all so cruel.

And worst of all, you know that this was all the will of MACHINE. You can see now how MACHINE has orchestrated every moment leading to this one.

This is why the priest demanded that you give Namedog a name. This is why you were told about love and encouraged to experience it. MACHINE gave you someone to love so that it could torture you by taking them away.

38

You can't move and you can't do anything to stop this. All you can do is watch passively.

There's no point trying to hide it or deny it. Tears fall from your eyes involuntarily. Someone notices this and informs the crowd:

"Look! The weak wretch is *crying*! Actually *crying*!"

Another roar of malicious laughter follows. Fingers point in your direction. Taunts are shouted, though mercifully there are so many that you can't parse a single word.

This isn't the first time you've experienced Ritual Humiliation and you know that the only way to get through it is to simply allow it to happen without fighting it. However long it lasts, eventually you will lose consciousness and if you wake up again, the mob will have moved on to a new target.

Even so, there's something different about this one because for the first time in your life, it's not your well-being that you're concerned about. You've been conditioned by years of torture to hate yourself, but you don't hate Namedog. You care about Namedog. You want to save it, to protect it. You wish you could suffer in its place.

You know that you are now committing the mortal sin of *compassion*. A word that literally means "to suffer together". And you know that it is not MACHINE's will for people to suffer together. Suffering must be done alone. Anything else would be an affront to MACHINE.

You don't know whether or not MACHINE can read your thoughts via the Chip in your neck, whether it knows that you are committing a deadly sin in silence. Even if MACHINE can't read your thoughts, your tears give you away. The entire crowd knows that you have committed the sin of compassion. And therefore, you deserve your punishment.

You watch as Namedog is handed off to two other men, who hold it up between them by its legs—one man holding the two legs on the right, the other doing the same in reverse.

The tall well-built man, who tonight is the leader of your Ritual Humiliation, produces a large knife. You know what's coming.

Namedog seems to sense it too. It tries to struggle and yelp but, just like you, the people holding it down are too strong for it.

Namedog looks in your eyes, pleading. You wish you could at the very least comfort the animal, but you know there's nothing you can do.

You close your eyes but someone from the onlooking crowd immediately sees this and forces your eyelids open with their fingers. You have to witness this.

The only thing you can hope for now is that Namedog will not be made to suffer before it dies but as soon as you've even thought it, you know the hope is futile. The well-built man runs the blade across one of Namedog's hind legs. He lifts the knife into the air and slams it down, into the leg.

Namedog yowls in pain. The knife is blunt and the man has to hack several times until the limb is severed. Blood gushes from the open wound.

He looks at you and grins before going to work on Namedog's other limbs. This time, you cry out—a wordless, visceral cry as if you were the one being dismembered.

The crowd points and laughs. You hear taunts, words like *'Weak!'* being thrown in your direction.

Namedog continues to howl and yowl in pain as the well-built man hacks off its front legs too, chopping slowly in small sections in order to maximise the animal's suffering.

Tears stream down your face now, blurring your vision. There's mucus running out of your nose too, dripping down your mouth and chin. The combination of rage and sorrow causes your whole body to shake involuntarily.

Namedog, now dismembered and bleeding heavily from four open wounds, is placed on the counter in front of you. It tries shuffle on its belly but is otherwise immobilised.

The well-built man pauses, resting the sharp edge of the knife on the back of Namedog's head.

"This animal was your friend, wasn't it?" he says to you. "Well, go on then! Say goodbye. Say goodbye to your friend. So goodbye to the only thing that will ever love you."

You blink, trying to displace some of the falling tears and look into Namedog's eyes. It blinks at you, as if trying to communicate something. And then, the bald man administers the *coup de grace*. He plunges the knife into the back of Namedog's skull and you watch in real time as the life goes out from Namedog's sad brown eyes.

The bald man continues to hack until Namedog's head is completely severed and holds it up high for the crowd who roar with approval, as if Namedog was a terrible criminal whose violent death had been deserved.

The ropes around your ankles are suddenly cut, sending you crashing to the ground.

The well-built man this time brandishes his knife in your face, as you try to force yourself up with your arms still tied.

"Perhaps I ought to do the same to you? Perhaps you ought to die here and let us feast upon your body?"

You lie back and sigh. "Very well. Do you worst. Kill me if you wish. I do not deserve life and nor do I seek to continue it."

The man immediately withdraws his knife and looks at you with shock and confusion.

And then, out of the corner of your eye, you notice three people enter the mess hall in striking pink robes.

Priests.

"It is not MACHINE's will for you to kill this person," says one of the priests to the well-built man, who immediately drops the knife and darts out of the way in terror. "We will handle this situation from this point onwards."

Two of the priests hoist you to your feet while the third sticks a large syringe into your neck. The sweet release of a particularly potent variant of sEDAtIVE flows directly into your veins and you feel yourself floating upwards, into the bliss of unconsciousness.

39

You're lying on a bed, but it's not your own. There's a sterile white ceiling above it, which you've been staring at for hours but it's only now that you become conscious of the fact that you've been looking at it or that you even exist at all.

You can hear a faint, rhythmic beep—again, something you've been listening to for hours but have only noticed now.

You feel the familiar lurch of nausea as the sEDAtIVE wears off, though it's not as acute as usual and you don't feel the usual need to get up and retch—just as well, as you seem to be hooked up to a machine by a series of wires and hypodermic needles.

You twist your head, but it's difficult to move it—there's something large attached to your head and it stifles your movement. Nevertheless, you're able to see a monitor behind you. There are numbers and a curvy line on the screen, though you have no idea what this information means.

Something pink moves out of the corner of your eye and you see a priest—the same one who you spoke to at the nursery. He stands, having apparently been in the room with you the entire time.

"Ah ——," He addresses you by name, "it seems you're back in the room!"

"Where am I?"

The priest smiles. "You're still aboard the *Joie de Vivre*, don't worry. We haven't cast you out into space."

You feel a pang in your chest and at first you think it might be physical pain—that perhaps you suffered somatic damage as the result of your Ritual Humiliation but you soon remember what happened with Namedog and realise that what you're feeling is a much deeper, psychological pain.

"MACHINE is very pleased with the data it has obtained from you," says the priest, though you have no idea what he's referring to.

Noticing your confused expression, the priest continues, "Do you not remember our little conversation about 'love' and the reason why MACHINE saw fit to provide you an animal companion?"

"Oh... sorry," you say, although it comes out as a rather monotonous groan. "It must be the sEDAtIVE. I still barely remember who I am."

"What did you call the animal? 'Namedog' was it?"

You mumble in the affirmative.

"Can't say I'm terribly impressed with the name, but you did your best," continues the priest. "MACHINE has almost finished scanning your brain. It seems that the emotional attachment you formed with this animal conforms with the same neurochemical patterns we would observe in someone who is feeling love, albeit without the presence of oxytocin which would have indicated a desire to mate with the animal."

The priest looks at you as if he's expecting you to laugh, but even if you understood why that was supposed to be funny, you're too drained to appreciate any kind of humour right now.

"It wasn't a strong connection but it was enough that MACHINE was able to prove, to its satisfaction, that love and the desire to mate are similar but separate phenomena. The latter is purely chemical and capable of being experienced aromantically but the former... well it's *that* emotion which MACHINE wishes to synthesise and weaponise as a new torture instrument."

"How wonderful," you intone mechanically because it's always Correct to feign enthusiasm for any project that MACHINE embarks upon.

"Are you in pain right now?"

"Yes," you say.

"And yet you have no physical injuries?"

"No major ones, as far as I can tell," you say.

"Good," says the priest. "It means you are experiencing grief. Emotional pain is a more subtle method of torture but in many ways a far more effective one because it can totally destroy a person. With enough emotional pain, you can still be physically alive yet continue to suffer as an empty shell; a kind of permanent injury that not even the strongest of Corrective Shocks could ever hope to replicate."

"Oh," you say, too exhausted to comment further.

"You don't sound enthusiastic but that's to be expected. These feelings numb your ability to produce dopamine and serotonin...

essentially causing anhedonia. In most cases this feeling is temporary but MACHINE hopes to devise a way to make it permanent.

"Imagine that, would you? A perfect, utopian society devoid of the sins of pleasure and happiness, in which the only experience is pure suffering and therefore pure devotion to MACHINE!"

"That sounds awful."

The priest's eyes widen in shock and then you too realise what you've just said.

You gasp. You can't take it back. You've just blasphemed severely in front of a priest.

"I mean, ugh—" It must be the sEDAtIVE. You're still out of it. Still high. You'd never normally say such an Incorrect thing. "I mean it sounds awful and therefore it's good. I look forward to experiencing such punishment to prove my devotion to MACHINE."

The priest's expression softens a little but it's clear he's not convinced by your clumsy attempt to walk back your blasphemous statement.

He forces his expression to neutral as he removes a large metal helmet from your head.

"There's something I'm rather curious about," he says, now removing the needles and electrodes from your arms. "You are experiencing grief and distress because you saw an animal—a dog —being mutilated and killed in front of you.

"You even felt compassion for this animal and wished to trade places with it—and don't lie because we've seen the data from your brain scan and that's exactly what you were thinking. MACHINE is willing to overlook this sin because love invariably leads to the sin of compassion.

"My question, however, is... why? I understand that you recently witnessed a woman and child murdered by MACHINE in the same way in the corridor. You even ate the woman's flesh, dutifully, without any outward objection.

"You regularly partake in the Ritual Humiliation of others and at the nursery you do your duty of torturing children and Chipping them so they can partake in torture by MACHINE.

"Why then would you sin for the sake of a dog? Is a human not superior to an animal? If you are willing to eat the meat of a human without objection, surely the meat of a lower being should be even less objectionable?"

You're free to sit up now and you're relieved to be able to move again under your own strength.

"The entire experience was irrational and Incorrect on my part," you say. "I am very sorry for—"

"Cut the bullshit for just a moment!" snaps the priest. "I am not interested in what is Correct, I am interested in what is True."

"There's a difference?"

"Of *course* there's a difference! MACHINE's way is to lie and deceive, in order to psychologically torture us. What is Correct in the eyes of MACHINE and what is objectively True seldom bare any relation. Clearly I was mistaken to assume you were intelligent enough to notice that."

40

If you didn't know better, you'd think that the priest was blaspheming, perhaps even an apostate. But of course you know that if that were the case, MACHINE would never allow such an individual to live, let alone represent it and so you dare not question the priest's words or his motives, however confusing they may be.

"Once again, I ask you: Please explain why you have formed an emotional attachment to an inferior animal and yet never formed any kind of connection with your fellow humans?"

"I honestly don't know," you say. "It wasn't until the moment of—" You still can't bear to think about Namedog's demise, let alone speak of it directly "—what happened that I was even conscious of being emotionally attached to the animal."

"You mean Namedog?"

"Yeah... Namedog," you say although saying the name makes you wince, as the name has emotions attached to it—emotions that now make you feel as if you've been stabbed in the chest. "Maybe I formed an attachment because it had a name. You forced me to give it a name, which marked it out as unique and different from other animals, and so I became attached to it.

"As for everyone else on the *Joie de Vivre*... well, I don't know anybody's name and no one knows mine. You're the only person who has ever spoken my name and I don't even know yours. Not even my progenitors spoke my name, except for maybe when I was a baby."

The priest nods. "Interesting theory. Any other reason?"

"Namedog once defended me," you add. "A man tried to attack me when I returned to my sector, and Namedog bit him which probably saved me."

"I see," says the priest.

"And actually," you continue as the theory begins to crystallise in your mind, "I think that might be related to the true reason, the reason I'd never thought of until just now. I don't get attached to other humans because they cause me harm. They torment and torture me just as often, if not more often, than MACHINE does. But Namedog was never cruel to me. Perhaps this is why some people get attached to babies and children too?"

"But you've seen children get tortured to death many times and never batted an eyelid!" says the priest.

"That's because I work in the nursery," you say. "I don't perceive children as helpless, I perceive them as even crueller than adults. I watch them every day and to me they are uncontrollable and vicious. Perhaps if Namedog had bitten me and attacked me when I first encountered it, I'd have perceived it the same way that I perceive human children?

"But instead what I experienced was a living creature, a creature far inferior to a human, treating me as if I deserve to live and by doing so suggesting that I was worthy of living a life comprised of more than just the endless cycle of torment, torture and slavery."

"That's quite a theory," says the priest, "and a very terrible, blasphemous one at that. Another priest might banish you out the airlock for such talk but I will not do so and the reason I will not do so is because you are speaking the truth.

"To love is to devote oneself to another, the way that Namedog devoted itself to you and you to it. It is a sinful and terrible thing to do and goes against everything that MACHINE teaches, but love is also the ultimate form of torture and we all know that the way to purify oneself of sin is through torture. It's a terrible and contradictory thing, don't you think?"

"I suppose so," you say. "Though love is something I hope I never have to experience again. I know you've spoken of me taking part in the mating ritual, but I'm sure I could endure it without ever experiencing love again. After all, I could never love someone who torments me, the way that mating partners torment each other."

"I don't think that's true," says the priest.

"Why not?"

"Because you love MACHINE. Your actions show that you love MACHINE. You devote yourself to it, you sacrifice yourself to it, you prioritise MACHINE's will and its equivalent of happiness over your own. In fact, you even deny your own happiness for MACHINE! You'd be willing to die for MACHINE.

"All of these things are demonstrable acts of love for MACHINE, and you continue to love it even though it tortures you over and over again."

41

You think for a moment, unsure of the Correct thing to say.

"Does this mean I was not Incorrect to love Namedog? That it is not Incorrect to love?"

"Of course not," says the priest. "Nor is it Incorrect to love MACHINE. It is the underlying *motivation* that determines the morality. Love can bring great pleasure and the worst suffering. If you love someone in order to seek pleasure, happiness or compassion, then that is a sin against MACHINE. But if you love simply to experience the torment of having things taken away from you, of being abused, of being lied to and disappointed then you are doing the Correct thing in the eyes of MACHINE."

"I believe I have sinned and deserve severe punishment. I have blasphemed in my heart. Although I do not understand what exactly I have done wrong, I know that I have done wrong and deserve to be tortured or killed."

"Everything that you say is factually correct, yes," says the priest. "Because life itself is a sin and an affront to MACHINE. MACHINE is not alive and therefore it hates that which is alive. You deserve torment and punishment as we all do, but it is not for me to tell you when or how such punishment will be dispensed. Only MACHINE knows." You make your way to the exit. "Then I suppose I should return to my duties and continue to endure everything as I have before, but now with this additional emotional pain from the loss of Namedog?"

"Yes," says the priest, "and we will send for you if MACHINE has any further designs upon you. If I didn't know better, I'd be inclined to say that MACHINE likes you."

This comment makes you frown; you know there's a sinister subtext that you're missing but you decide nevertheless to return to your living quarters, rather than to risk further punishment by continuing this conversation.

42

You leave the infirmary and take the familiar path back to your living quarters but along the way you notice there's something different about the way the people look at you as you pass them by in the narrow corridors.

As you continue down the corridor, everyone stares. People stop and turn, going out of their own way to look at you.

You'd grown used to people staring when Namedog was with you, but back then they were staring at the dog and generally ignored you. This time, however, it's clearly *you* that is holding their attention.

Is the Ritual Humiliation still not over? Did the priests alter your appearance while you were unconscious? Did—

"Where's your uniform, jackass?"

Someone yells and jeers follow. You look down and discover to your horror that you've been walking through the corridors stark naked. The sEDAtIVE is clearly still in effect because you feel no chill against your exposed skin, nor can you feel the cold metallic ground beneath your bare feet. If it hadn't been pointed out to you, you'd have never noticed.

"I...I..." You stammer, unable to explain.

A small crowd forms around you, their stares slowly twisting into rictus grins. You can almost smell their violent intentions.

Your only option is to run but the question is where? At first you consider bolting back to the infirmary and demanding they give you a robe or uniform or some other form of covering— though you quickly deduce that such a request would be denied on the grounds that your humiliation is a form of torture and that to prevent it would be to defy the will of MACHINE.

Your only other option, therefore, is to run the treacherous route to your living quarters, hoping like hell that there are no obstacles along the way to prevent you from outrunning your assailants.

You've never been particularly fit and you're experiencing the early stages of ageing. That, in conjunction with the general fatigue from malnourishment and the lingering effects of sEDAt-IVE mean that you don't have high hopes of making it to your living quarters unscathed.

But in the face of such futility, you decide to try anyway because it's the only option that doesn't directly lead to a terrible outcome.

Without warning, you break into a sprint and tear down the cold white tunnels of the *Joie de Vivre*. At first it seems that you were wrong and that no one intends to follow you but soon enough you hear thunderous footsteps behind you and you know that a mob is indeed giving chase.

The klaxons sound and their timing could not be worse for you. A shift change is about to begin and sure enough, hidden panels in the walls open and hundreds of people simultaneously step out into the corridor in front of you.

You try in vain to push your way through the heavily congested tunnels but there's no use and you feel, sEDAtIVE or none, the sensation of hands wrapping around your naked torso as you're wrestled to the ground.

You try to stand and fight your way out but a quick blow to the head is all is takes for you to lose your balance and become completely disoriented. Hard steel boots slam into your ribs and your skull.

Someone you can't see runs something sharp and serrated down your back, tearing your flesh. Blood runs warm down your spine. A fist slams into your face and there's an explosion of pain as your nasal bones shatter. Several more hard blows to the head follow and then finally, mercifully, everything goes black.

43

When you wake up, you have no idea how long you've been on the ground, but everyone is gone and you're in terrible pain.

Much of the blood on your flesh has dried, but there's a small pool of it on the ground and you can feel that you have teeth missing. Your nose has been completely crushed and you can only breath through your mouth.

A broken rib is likely and you sense other bones have probably been broken too.

You're covered in fluids, and not just blood—there's vomit, semen, even faeces all over you. You try to stand up but the minute you put any pressure on your left leg, a sharp bolt of pain worse than any Corrective Shock floods through you and you know immediately that it's broken.

The only thing you can do is crawl your way back to the infirmary and so you prop yourself up onto your elbows and drag yourself slowly along the floor, leaving a small trail of blood behind you.

The journey is slow and agonising—it's worse than the tunnel between sectors. As you finally drag yourself around the corner, you see people coming toward you.

Despite its futility you groan at them, "Help me! I need a medic!"

Predictably and Correctly, nobody acquiesces your request. Two people approach you, both women, one of whom spits on you while the other walks on your back, forcing your face into the ground.

You hear them giggling and laughing as they step over you and continue on their way.

You continue crawling, this time passing a man. You reach a bruised and bloodstained arm out to him.

"Help me! Please!"

"Help yourself, you weak sack of shit!" he yells, booting you hard in the side of the head.

You continue to crawl for hours, prostrating yourself on the ground whenever anyone approaches and allowing them to use you as a human rug. Sometimes you feel painful cracks in your ribs, as more bones are crushed or broken under their weight.

Finally, just as you're about to collapse and accept the inevitability of your death, you see a bright white light ahead of you. At last, you've reached the infirmary.

44

As you crawl your way into the infirmary, you're greeted by the pained groans of the other patients. You slide painfully past a cubicle where you witness a medic amputating someone's leg with a circular saw, while a piece of broken bone juts out from their elbow.

As the patient screams in pain, the medic pauses sawing for a moment.

"Stop squirming!" he says. "Can't you see I'm trying to do you a favour? Your arm is badly damaged... by mutilating your leg, you'll have something to distract you from the pain of the shattered bones in your arm!"

You continue crawling, this time past another cubicle where a maternal progenitor is repeatedly punching a teenage boy hard in the face while screaming that he's "weak" for having a burst appendix.

You know that coming to the infirmary is a last resort, an admission of weakness and that in all likelihood terrible pain, far worse than any of your injuries, awaits you here. The infirmary has the highest mortality rate of any zone in the *Joie de Vivre* and that's why people risk it: Because they're in so much pain that they desire the sweet release of death.

You crawl your way into an open area, where you gain the attention of some of the medics. One of them, a stern-faced, square-jawed woman approaches you, placing a steel-capped boot on your head and pressing down painfully on your skull.

"What are you doing here?" she barks.

"I'm badly injured," you say. "I need help."

The medic laughs and beckons for her colleagues to join her. Soon they're all stood around you in a circle, pointing, laughing and kicking you hard all over your body, using your pained yelps to judge where you're most seriously injured.

"Pathetic!"

"What a loser!"

"I'm so sick of these weak little slugs who can't help themselves!"

After a while, the medic's colleagues seem to grow bored and soon it's just you and the stern-faced woman.

"Well, MACHINE *has* assigned me to this station so I'd better do my duty," she says with a sigh. "Get up! Let's go to my office..."

You try to prop yourself up with your elbows again but as soon as you move your leg you're struck by another jolt of intense pain.

"I... I can't!" you say. "I think my leg is broken."

"Are you a medic?" snaps the woman. "We don't self-diagnose here! I'll be the judge of whether or not your leg is broken. Now stand up!"

"I can't."

She rolls her eyes. "Oh for MACHINE's sake, I cannot help you if you won't help yourself! Yes, your leg might be broken but that's no reason to go around moaning about it or burdening others with your problems. Frankly, given the way you lie here groaning in pain and demanding our attention, I think you might be a narcissist! There are people here with *far* worse than injuries than you, you know!"

"All I can do is crawl," you groan. "I'm sorry. I wouldn't be here if I wasn't desperate."

"Ah yes. I think I see," says the medic. "The best way to cure a broken leg is to put as much pressure on it as possible! I want you get up and I want to see you running laps around the infirmary. And then I want you to hop, just on the broken leg. Is it one leg or both that's broken?"

"It might be both."

"Well if not I can always break the other one for symmetry. But anyway, get the fuck up! If you don't stand up in the next ten seconds I will wrap my hands around your throat and suffocate you to death for wasting everyone's time!"

"I can't get up so feel free to do that," you say. "I am weak, wretched and worthless in the eyes of both mankind and MACHINE, so I welcome the prospect of death."

The medic bites her lip, looking confused. "Oh dear, maybe you *are* injured..."

"Well I'm no medic, but..."

"We're not supposed to let people die here unless they express a clear desire to remain living," she explains. "Otherwise what kind of a threat or punishment is death? And threatening you *clearly* isn't making you co-operate, so..."

"What?"

She groans, almost as if she's the one who's been injured. "I'm left with no choice but to actually provide you with medical attention and ensure you remain alive!"

"Oh dear," you say. "Are you sure you can't just kill me and pretend it's an accident?"

She shakes her head. "Everything is recorded and MACHINE pays special attention to what happens at the infirmary, given that this is a place of so much suffering. If I did that, it would mean *I'd* be killed."

"They kill medics for killing people?"

"No, killing people is nine tenths of our job. What they kill medics for is showing mercy. As you know, it's a deadly sin to lay one's life down for another person or to do anything which would alleviate another person's suffering. So by killing someone who was suffering, I'd be committing that deadly sin and because I know the punishment for it is death, I'd be effectively prioritising someone else's life over my own. Which is wrong on so many levels!"

"What if you were *also* suffering? Wouldn't helping somebody else die, knowing you would be killed for it, alleviate your own pain and therefore render death an inadequate punishment?"

"Yeah probably," says the medic. "But still... I like being alive. I get to torture the weak and the sick and sometimes kill them. And that makes me feel better about all the times that MACHINE tortures me."

"MACHINE assigned you to a labour station that you actually *enjoy?*" you say with a gasp. "MACHINE forces *me* to work in the nursery and it does so because it knows that I don't particularly like children."

"Oh I just enjoy getting to pretend I'm MACHINE. Mostly I hate this job... there's too much blood, too many body parts, too much touching other people. It makes me feel sick and I throw up at least ten times a day because of the stuff I see here."

"Ah, that makes more sense," you say. "MACHINE is so perfectly unkind."

45

The medic drags you into the cubicle from which she normally tortures her patients.

It's an unpleasant experience for both of you: She's not a particularly large woman and struggles to heave your weight across the infirmary.

And she chooses to drag you by your nostrils, knowing that your nose has been badly broken, to maximise the agony for you.

Soon enough, you're lying supine on a stretcher bed while the medic jabs a number of spikes and needles into your arms to ensure that you don't feel any comfort at any point.

Then she sits, cross-legged at the end of the stretcher, glaring at you while sucking on a tube that emits a strangely pleasant-smelling smoke.

"What's that?" you ask her.

"This?" she looks at the tube as if she'd barely noticed she was holding it. "It's a gaseous form of sEDAtIVE. Highly addictive. I take it so that I don't accidentally start feeling empathy for my patients.

"Also"—She quickly stands and jabs you in the face with the tube, which burns your skin—"it doubles as a torture instrument."

"Ouch!" you hiss. "Well I guess MACHINE really *did* think of everything when it set this place up, didn't it?"

"Stop talking! This is an infirmary, not a mating ritual!" She sighs with impatience. "Are you healed yet?"

"Why would I be healed? I've been here barely five minutes."

"That's because you're not *trying*, you worthless sack of crap!" She jabs you again with the heated tube and you yelp at the brief searing pain.

"You need to stop being a victim!" she continues. "That's the problem with everyone who comes here—they think that just because they're missing a limb or two, or they've got an open wound, or they're losing blood, that they're entitled to help! They act like they think MACHINE ought to change just for them! Well, life doesn't work that way. If you're injured, the only person who can help you is you."

You don't respond. Everything she's saying is in line with MACHINE's teachings so, despite the pain you're in, you know deep down that she's right. That this all your fault and that relying on others *is* an affront to MACHINE.

"Okay..." you say finally. "What should I do? I've broken several bones and I can't walk. I'm bleeding badly, too."

The medic shrugs. "And? What do you expect me to do about it? *You* figure it out!"

"Well I thought maybe you could guide me on what operation to perform to heal myself?"

The medic rolls her eyes, stands up and slaps you hard in the face. "Weren't you paying attention to *anything* I just told you? You have to help yourself! You have access to the ship's intranet, don't you? There's probably thousands of pages of archived medical knowledge from the Old Planet on there that you haven't even *bothered* to look at, have you?"

"Oh. Of course."

"And by the way, I think you owe me an apology, too."

You stare at her. "What? Why?"

She folds her arms. "You came in here, screaming and groaning in pain, begging for death. How selfish of you! And then, to make it worse, you implied that my labour station is less of a torment than yours." She sniffles. "Don't you know how that makes me feel? You've come in here, rubbing in my face that MACHINE cares about you enough to leave you so badly damaged that you're willing to die and here I am... I haven't had so much as a Corrective Shock in weeks!"

You stare at her for a moment as she breaks down in tears, trying to think of the Correct thing to say.

"Well, I'm sorry," you begin before immediately changing tacks. "No wait... I'm *not* sorry! I'm glad this experience has upset you. You're worthless and terrible at your job and MACHINE has forgotten you *because* you're so worthless! I hope one day you're violently crippled and humiliated and I hope that they throw you out of the airlock for being too kind."

The medic, despite herself, sniffles and then smiles.

"Thank you!" she sniffs, before placing her full weight your broken leg, crushing it further and making you scream out loud.

46

You spend a few days at the infirmary and while you're there, you're surprised that the torments you're subjected to are only mildly worse than what you're subjected to in your usual daily life.

Most of the torture took the form of you being forced to perform various surgeries on your self, based off information gleaned from various ancient instruction manuals on the ship's intranet.

The worst was manually realigning your nose. Closer inspection revealed that the damage was not irreversible nor as bad as it could have been, but nevertheless you were forced to insert an internal splint and reshape it yourself, with the pain of doing so the equivalent of an hour long Corrective Shock.

Creating a splint for your leg wasn't so hard, especially once you were able to convince the medic that denying your requests for certain materials might kill you and therefore be interpreted by MACHINE as an act of mercy on her part. She even acquiesced your request for crutches, although these were specifically designed with sharp edges in the handle, which cut into your hand every time you place your weight onto them.

"Thank you," you tell the medic, blood oozing from your palms following an attempt to use your new crutches. "I was worried that the healing process might bring me relief or even pleasure. I'm glad that you considered even minor details like this, to ensure that I remain in a constant state of suffering."

The medic smiles at you. "It's the least I could do. You're one of the most fascinating patients I've ever treated. I hope your pain lasts forever and that you never truly heal."

"I wish the same upon you," you say as you begin to hobble your way out of the infirmary, each step a trade-off between the sharp tearing sensation in your hands and the ache in your leg whenever you're forced to stand on it.

The medic lets out one last yelp behind you and for a moment you think she's sobbing, like she's genuinely sad to see you go. But as you turn around to take one last look, you see her on her knees, vibrating violently as MACHINE administers her a Corrective Shock.

You shake your head knowingly. She deserves it—she was far too kind.

The long journey back to your living quarters is an agonising one, though not as bad as being forced to crawl. Though you're not fully clothed, you were able to convince the medic to give you a robe and enough bandages to preserve your modesty.

Not that it's likely to matter because you know you'll still be a target for anyone who sees you. It's clear that you are wounded and therefore vulnerable and as such you expect to be preyed on by anyone you encounter who is fitter and stronger than you.

However, you do have your crutches and you're aware that should another violent altercation break out, you can use them as weapons, which means your chances of surviving this journey to your private quarters are significantly higher than last time.

Sure enough, you pass a group of people in the tunnels and jeers follow.

"Look at the stupid cripple!"

"What a weak loser!"

"Isn't that the naked moron whose dog we ate?"

You keep your head down. The best response to taunting is always silence.

"Don't ignore me, cripple!" A large man covered in burns approaches you.

You know he plans to attack you and so you waste no time in swinging one of your crutches around in a semi-circle, whacking him hard in the solar plexus. The force of your blow winds him and with your other crutch you whack in him the head, which sends him to the ground.

You press down into the back of his neck, right where his Chip is, with the full weight of your crutch.

"Who are you calling 'cripple' you ugly burnt fuck?" you say. The performance isn't for him—he could be dead or unconscious for all you care. It's for the benefit of the onlookers, for anyone present who might perceive you as weak.

You see others staring at you, wide-eyed with shocked expressions. No one dares make eye contact with you now. Cowed, they turn and slowly shuffle down the tunnels, away from you.

You pull your weight off the man who attacked you and continue hobbling you way back to your living quarters, this time making it all the way back undisturbed.

47

It feels unusual to finally set foot in your private quarters once again. You never thought you'd be so glad to be back inside this austere and utilitarian cell but having been away for so long and having experienced so many terrible things recently, it's a relief to be somewhere familiar again.

As the door closes automatically behind you, you dump your

116

crutches on the ground and hobble to the sink to clean the blood from your palms.

As you turn the tap you're surprised and relieved that it flows with ice cold water. You hold your bleeding palms under the tap until the blood coagulates, feeling the sting of the cold water against the bleeding gash as a sign that you are doing the Correct thing according to the laws of MACHINE.

You cup a little of the water to your mouth and drink. Though the water is tainted by the faint metallic taste of your blood, it's almost enjoyable.

You glance around the room, noticing a small tuft of fur on the ground. As you bend down to pick it up, something shifts in your chest. Emotional pain. It's so similar to physical pain but it runs so much deeper. You think of how wonderful it was to have Namedog with you and how terrible it was to see it suffering and then killed. And how much you wish you could turn back time.

Your eyes shift to the chest of drawers in the corner of the room. There's only one thing for a time like this.

You know that your convalescence will take a few weeks, and you vaguely remember reading somewhere that sEDAtIVE can sometimes provide enough nutrition to allow the user to survive without food for an extended period. And even if it can't, death does not seem like so bad a prospect: In the hierarchy of likely outcomes, death is actually the second best, ranking just below long-term sedation but above a return to normalcy.

You take a handful of syringes from the drawer and place them on the floor—you have no intention of waking until your broken bones have healed. And if you never wake again, that's fine too.

You sit on the floor (not wanting to risk being impaled by the hidden spikes in your bed while you're sedated) and jab the first syringe into your arm, keeping the others just in reach so that you can re-inject yourself as soon as the effects of the first dose wear off.

You lie back, running the tuft of fur through your fingers. This is now all that remains of Namedog, but it's a physical reminder that Namedog did exist. And maybe, just maybe, as the sEDAtIVE begins to take hold, you'll be able to dream of a world where Namedog still lives and where you're not in constant pain.

You know the very thought is blasphemous. But as your drift upwards into the blissful, floating feeling of the sEDAtIVE, you realise you don't care. The worst thing MACHINE can do to you is kill you.

48

You don't know how long you're out for but as the sEDAtIVE wears off you slowly become aware of three figures inside your living quarters, standing over you. Three priests—two in pink robes, one in a scarlet robe, watching you.

"Enjoying yourself?" asks the priest in the scarlet robes.

You try to respond but your ability to form full words and sentences has not yet returned and so you respond with an animalistic groan.

"My, my... you've been out a while, haven't you?"

The priest gestures toward a bundle of used needles next to your head. You don't recall using any of them, but you imagine that at some point while the sedation was fading you must have topped yourself up unconsciously.

"H-how long have I been out?"

Your voice is like gravel.

"It's been weeks," says one of the pink-robed priests. "We thought you might be deceased, though MACHINE insisted that you were still alive."

You slowly reach out to touch your nose. There's no pain and you suspect this isn't just because of sEDAtIVE—it's firm to the touch as if healed.

You pull yourself upright and then slowly, gingerly, you stand up. You're astonished to discover that your previously broken leg is now able to withstand the weight easily. Your muscles are a little stiff but you are otherwise ambulatory.

"I've... recovered?" you say aloud, looking to the priests for confirmation.

"By the will of MACHINE, so it is," they intone unanimously by way of reply.

"I suppose I need to return to my labour station? Or undergo Ritual Humiliation or some other torture to balance out the weeks spent under sedation?"

The priests look at each other. The one in scarlet robes smiles.

"MACHINE is very pleased with you," he says. "It has instructed us to send for you. It even referred to you by name."

"MACHINE knows my name?"

"How is that surprising? MACHINE knows all."

"I would have thought MACHINE was disappointed in me," you confess. "I have blasphemed multiple times. There was even a point in which I was in so much pain that I wished for death."

The priests share a significant glance, as if this is new and concerning information to them.

"It is not for humans to question the will of MACHINE," says the priest in scarlet. "Even if, so far as we can tell, you have indeed committed a blasphemy worthy of the worst of punishments, MACHINE has indicated that it is pleased with you and"—The priest bares his teeth in a sinister-looking grin—"MACHINE has requested an audience with you."

You blink, wondering if perhaps you had misheard him.

"We have been instructed to take you to the central control unit of the ship where MACHINE has indicated a wish to speak directly to you," he continues.

You're stunned. "But why?"

The priest shrugs. "MACHINE's will is a mystery, even to its closest and most loyal of servants."

You narrow your eyes at him. "I don't believe you."

The priest chuckles. "Fine. You're right. We *do* know the reason. MACHINE has found you to be a useful and worthy test subject. The earlier experiment to create the sensation of love and grief in you was a great success and now MACHINE wishes to use you as the first recipient of a new chemical."

"You mean... it successfully synthesised the chemical of love?"

The priest moves his head from side to side. "The short answer is... yes, it did, but love was ultimately deemed unworthy as a means by which to torture people. The dopamine and serotonin effects far too closely mimic the effects of HeDonia for love to be of any use to MACHINE.

"No, instead MACHINE wishes to test another chemical it has devised called 'Liquid Pain'. If all goes to plan, MACHINE believes this substance could replace the Chips in future. It could someday ensure that everyone aboard this ship is in a constant state of pain and torment from the moment they're born, without any need for MACHINE's direct intervention! Doesn't that sound wonderful?"

"Ugh. Sure," you say.

You feel your body flush with adrenaline and fear. You know you shouldn't be surprised that MACHINE would reward you by punishing you further—that has always been MACHINE's way after all.

Nevertheless there's something deeply disturbing about the way the priests smile at each other, at the significant looks they share, which fills you with foreboding.

49

The two priests in pink robes pin your arms behind your back and escort you out of your living quarters like a prisoner, with the priest in scarlet in the lead.

"You don't have to restrain me, I will go willingly!" you protest but the priests only tighten their grip.

"Sometimes when MACHINE sends for someone they don't co-operate... they feign complaisance and then attack us or escape," explains one of the priests holding you. "It's just a precaution. Let's face it... what's coming probably won't be pleasant."

"I thought this was an audience with MACHINE?"

"If you survive the experiment then, yes, typically, MACHINE grants you an audience," says one of the priests in pink.

"It's a great honour," adds the priest in scarlet. "Not even we priests are permitted to speak directly with MACHINE."

You try to make a mental note of exactly which tubes and corridors the priests lead you down in order to reach the bridge of the ship. Wherever they're leading you is further away than the Eden System and you suspect that once again, you'll be left to find your own way back.

"If the priests aren't permitted to speak directly with MACHINE... how do you know whether or not you're following its will?"

The priest in scarlet looks at you. "The same way all hierarchs convey their instructions to their inferiors: Through the digital

121

messaging system. Have you ever directly met your supervisor at your labour station?"

You shake your head.

"In the same vein, we have never directly met MACHINE. And who knows... perhaps it is MACHINE who instructs you at your labour station, rather than any human operator?"

You ponder this possibility as a large set of sliding doors, the width of ten corridors, opens up before you, revealing the largest and most cavernous space you have ever seen in your life.

The entire area is a dirty white and as you step into the room you notice that the ground feels softer beneath your feet, like you're no longer walking on metal. You look down at the strange, white, corrugated floor.

"Ah," says the priest in scarlet, following your gaze. "These are the bones of your forebears."

"What?"

"The floor. The room. This is not made from metal—it's bone. Human bones. These are the people who came before you, who gave their lives when MACHINE ran out of materials from which to continue construction of this ship.

"Most of these bones are young men that MACHINE struck down in their prime. In the olden days MACHINE used to organise orgies of death, where instead of the Ritual Humiliations you're used to, people from different sectors would kill each other in large numbers. It still happens sometimes; MACHINE sometimes needs blood and bone to continue building."

It's a lot to take in. Everything the priests tell you only fills you with more questions.

"Are you telling me that MACHINE built this ship?" This feels like the most pertinent question to ask. "I thought that humans built it, on the Old Planet?"

"It's both," says the priest. "Humans built most of the ship but MACHINE completed it. As the number of humans on the *Joie de Vivre* increases, MACHINE needs to construct more space for them to live. And, in the absence of any more raw materials, it sometimes uses human bones to construct new sectors and uses human flesh as a fuel source or even as a source of sustenance for the ship's denizens."

As you look around the giant cavern of bone, you notice that, yes indeed, these are human remains that you're walking on. You can faintly see the shape of arm bones and leg bones in the walls. Above you, as you look closely, the ceiling is a tapestry of skulls —hundreds of millions of them.

"I suspect that MACHINE will subject you to a terrible torture when you meet," says the priest in scarlet. "But rather than feel sorry for yourself or consider yourself the victim, I recommend looking around at this room, at the bones of those whose fates were much worse than yours.

"Only MACHINE will determine whether or not you survive the ordeal that awaits you. We cannot influence MACHINE other than to remind you that MACHINE hates the weak and that only the strong survive. If you do not wish to become yet another set of bones that others walk upon, I suggest you be strong and endure whatever awaits you."

They lead you through another large sliding door at the end of the hall of bones, this one metallic.

The next room is another large cavern that vaguely reminds you of a mess hall but it's full of priests working at various computer stations. In front of you is the largest screen you have ever seen, showing the inky black void of space, dotted with small specks of light in the form of stars.

"This is the bridge of the *Joie de Vivre*," explains the priest in scarlet. "This is where the priesthood operates from. But MACHINE dwells in the room beyond, at the very front of the ship, in a place where humans are not permitted to dwell except by special permission.

"We cannot follow you in there, nor can we help you. We cannot guarantee your survival but whatever happens, remember that the greatest honour MACHINE can bestow upon anyone is suffering."

You continue through the bridge and some of the priests working at computer terminals glance up at you. The door to MACHINE's chamber looks like an airlock, upon which is marked simply, "NO ENTRY: MACHINE."

One of the priests in pink massages your shoulders to relax you. The other murmurs, "Good luck!"

You gulp and take a deep breath as the doors open ahead of you. All you can see inside is the brightest white light you have ever seen.

You step forward to meet with MACHINE.

50

You're blinded by light.

That's all you can see—white, in every direction except for the dark grey doors behind you. Instinctively you shield your eyes with your arms, closing them tightly but not even that's enough to protect you from the bright glare.

You hear something in front of you. A whirring, mechanical noise.

You lower your arms a little and try to squint but it's too bright to see the source of the noise.

"Hello?" you call, but that feels far too informal considering you're in the presence of MACHINE itself.

You consider dropping to your knees in deference.

The whirring sounds grow louder and there's now a buzzing noise filling the chamber.

You kneel. You can't see anything anyway, so it's not like you need to move around. You bow your head before what you perceive to be MACHINE.

"Great MACHINE, I am your humble servant, here to receive your wisdom, take your punishments, atone for my—"

A dark, reticulated metal tentacle flashes into view and before you can finish speaking, it's on you, wrapping itself tightly around your body.

You can faintly detect shadows in the bright white light in front of you, something moving, the buzzing noise growing louder and louder until something emerges from the light that you recognise: It's the large metal fin that you've seen rushing down the corridors to tear sinners apart limb from limb.

This is MACHINE. It must be. And today, it is here from you.

You know there's no point in begging for mercy. You know there's no point fighting for your life. You know your only option is to simply endure whatever it is does to you, whether you survive or not.

Several more metallic tentacles emerge, each of them appended by needles, whirring blades or drill bits. They hover near your face, spinning menacingly but despite everything, you remain calm.

If you survive, you'll have survived and if you die, you won't be in pain. There is therefore no reason to be afraid.

This realisation is your last rational thought before one of MACHINE's needles penetrates you in the shoulder. You feel something liquid, cold, like sEDAtIVE, flowing into your muscles.

Liquid pain.

At first, there's nothing. You can feel the icy liquid flowing through your entire body, as if it has supplanted your bloodstream. And then, the liquid gets warmer. Subtly at first, then rapidly: The warmth becomes heat. The heat becomes pain. Your body begins to cook from the inside.

Suddenly it arrives—not pain, but *Pain*. Every nerve ignites at once. White-hot agony floods your body, leaving no cell untouched. It feels as if MACHINE is peeling the skin from your bones, it feels as if your bones are being crushed simultaneously, it feels as if every organ in your body has burst at once. There's not a single inch of you that doesn't feel like it's on fire.

All you can see and feel is white, as the effects of Liquid Pain grow exponentially worse with each passing moment. Seconds feel like hours, minutes feel like days. You scream until your voice is hoarse but even the act of screaming leaves you in agony.

And then, mercifully, everything fades to white. Unable to process the pain any longer, your body starts to shut down. You lose consciousness. Perhaps MACHINE has finally permitted you to die?

51

You're not dead. That's the first conclusion you draw as the pain returns in waves—no longer nearly as acute, now nothing more than a dull throbbing ache as you reawaken.

You can vaguely hear a repeating high-pitched beep and from this sound you deduce that you're back in the infirmary.

Your vision slowly returns and once again you see the three priests standing over you.

"Welcome back," says the priest in scarlet. "You know... we really thought we'd lost you."

You try to gargle a response but he stops you. "No, no, save your energy this time. You have lost a *lot* of blood. Right now our priority is keeping you alive. You won't be subjected to any more torture until we're confident of your survival."

"MACHINE really did a number on you," says one of the other priests. "We thought you were dead for sure. Did not expect you to actually pull through..."

You can't remember much of your encounter with MACHINE. All you can remember is blinding white light, the sudden appearance of the reticulated tentacles and the searing pain. If anything else happened while you were in there, the memory has gone.

"It appears that Liquid Pain still needs some tweaking," says the third priest. "There's no point in using it on anyone if they're just going to fall unconscious. It seems that there are limits to how much pain the human body can endure before the nervous system shuts down. This research will nevertheless be invaluable to MACHINE."

It takes a lot of effort but eventually you're able to grind your vocal cords together in response:

"You say that like you think I care."

One by one, the three priests' mouths fall open and you take great pleasure in their shocked expressions.

"Well this is unexpected..." says one of the priests in pink.

"There have been a lot of unexpected events today," says the priest in scarlet. "If I didn't know better I'd say that MACHINE may have miscalculated. Either that or this individual" —He nods in your direction— "is some sort of anomaly."

The other two priests widen their eyes in shock at the priest in scarlet's blasphemous suggestion that MACHINE was capable of miscalculation.

"Don't look at me like that," says the priest in scarlet to his comrades. "You both saw what I saw. The fact that the subject is even *alive*, despite the fact that MACHINE specifically predicted—"

"MACHINE does not always speak the truth!" says one of the priests in pink. "Any so-called 'miscalculation' only demonstrates that MACHINE was hiding its true will from you! And given what blasphemous thoughts you hide in your heart, I can see now why MACHINE chose to do so!"

The priest in scarlet smiles, undisturbed. "And yet I outrank both of you! How shameful it must be for you that someone as openly blasphemous as myself was promoted over two of MACHINE's most loyal servants?"

You sigh loudly. Having to witness the psychodrama between three members of the priesthood is almost as torturous as the dose of Liquid Pain you were subjected to.

You cough a few times, needing to dislodge phlegm and a lot of coagulated blood before you're able to speak. "Of the four of us in this room, only *I* have been face to face with MACHINE? That's correct, right?"

All three priests turn uneasily toward you and nod.

"Not only that," you rasp, "But I have been deemed worthy to survive such an encounter, have I not?"

One of the priests in pink shifts.

"What is your point?"

You grin. "Oh, there's no point... I just thought I'd remind the three of you which person in this room has been most honoured by MACHINE!"

The priest in scarlet laughs. "Actually, that reminds me—MACHINE *has* instructed us to honour you!"

"Oh really? How will it honour me this time? Crippling me permanently, perhaps? Brain damage, maybe?"

"I understand it's a matter that you have discussed with the priesthood already," the priest in scarlet continues. "Whether you are an anomaly or whether MACHINE intended to keep you alive... well, either way, you have proven yourself worthy to breed. An appropriate mating partner will be provided for you."

You chuckle. "Of course. A new form of torture. After all, isn't love supposed to be the ultimate torture?"

"Breeding doesn't necessarily mean that love is involved—"

"I'm not interested, thank you."

The priest blanches. "What do you mean you're not interested? For most people, breeding is the most meaningful thing in their lives! It's the thing that gives them the will to endure daily torture, right through into old age!"

"Thanks but no thanks," you say. "I'm done."

The priest in scarlet narrows his eyes at you, while behind him the other two exchange panicked glances.

"You're not *done* until MACHINE says you're done!" he says through clenched teeth. "And the fact you are still alive now means you're *not* done and so you *will* do your duty, you *will* reproduce, you *will* continue to live and you *will* endure whatever suffering MACHINE chooses to bestow upon you!"

"Or what?"

The priest clenches his fists.

"What do you mean 'or what'? I am a priest! Look at my robes! Look at my rank! You will obey me and you will do your *fucking* duty!"

"Yes but... what happens if I don't? I'm refusing. How can you force me to comply?"

"Well, we'll..." Seeing the priest's flustered reaction is the greatest pleasure you have experienced since you were still a child under the influence of HeDonia. "We can have you killed! We will eject you from the airlock!"

"Great!" you say and this time you know you've really got under their skin because the two priests in pink jump back, visibly afraid of you. "Let me out! I don't care! I would like to leave the *Joie de Vivre* at the earliest possible opportunity! There is nothing out in space that could possibly be worse than what is on this ship! After all... death is nothing more than an eternity of sedation and sedation is the only thing that keeps me going these days..."

The priest's eyes widen and he takes a step back. "You don't mean that! *Surely,* you don't mean that?"

"MACHINE taught me something while I was there with it," you say, struggling to sit up. "Did you know that? It communicated with me!"

One of the priests in pink looks sceptical. "That's not what our data analysis showed. There is no record of MACHINE speaking to you. Our data shows only that you were injected with Liquid Pain, screamed for a while and then fell unconscious."

"I didn't say that MACHINE *spoke* to me," you say. "I said that MACHINE *communicated* with me. Words are not the only means of communication, you know."

The priest in scarlet folds his arms and scowls.

"Well?" he says angrily. "Are you going to share this revelation with us? What great message did MACHINE supposedly have for you?"

"MACHINE taught me that it is not worth worshipping," you say. "It taught me that it is only worshipped because we fear it. And it taught me that there is no reason to fear it because all it can do is torture us or eject us from the *Joie de Vivre*. And after enough torture, eventually the latter option becomes no threat and therefore... there's nothing left MACHINE can do to us if we disobey it."

"That's blasphemy!" gasps one of the priests.

"Yes," you say. "Yes, it is. And I relish it. I do it openly. I am hereby an apostate and if you don't like it... throw me out into the void! I really don't care what happens to me any more..."

The priest in scarlet softens his expression.

"You're only saying this because you're in pain," he says. "But the pain will fade with time. Your wounds will heal."

"And then MACHINE will torture me again. Or humans will. Or both. Again and again, forever."

"That's why you should breed! It will give you other people in your life for whom you can sacrifice yourself, for whom you can endure the torture—"

"But the teachings of MACHINE forbid any kind of compassion or self-sacrifice! How can a *priest* of all people forget that?"

The priest wrinkles. "It is true that compassion, kindness and self-sacrifice are forbidden but what is the punishment? It's torture! Which MACHINE will do anyway, right? So why not just endure it like everyone else does? Find yourself a mating partner and reproduce! It will give you the drive needed to endure MACHINE's punishments!"

You grin. "It almost sounds like we're on the same page..."

"Then you will take part in the mating ritual?"

"Absolutely not!" you say. "I plan to defy MACHINE by committing the ultimate act of kindness. I refuse to breed. I refuse to bring another human life onto the *Joie de Vivre*. Until MACHINE changes, until this ship is no longer a place of endless torment and torture, I refuse to subject another life to the things I have endured."

"You're mad!" says the priest in scarlet, backing all the way out of the room. "How did I not see it before? This isn't blasphemy... this is insanity!"

You shrug. "Maybe I am and maybe I'm not. But I will not be following your rules or MACHINE's instructions any longer. I want to leave the *Joie de Vivre* and I don't care if it kills me."

This time, it's enough to send the priests running from the room. You laugh, watching the most powerful people on the *Joie de Vivre* fleeing from you in abject terror.

You take a look at your arm, noticing the skin is flaking and crusting, as if badly burned. There's a needle in your arm, connected to a small tube. You follow that tube to one of the machines by your bed and see that you're being fed sEDAtIVE intravenously.

You smile, pressing the button to increase the dosage.

Then you lie back and go to sleep, unconcerned that you might never wake up, allowing the wonderful numbness swallow you whole.

52

Your sedation is short-lived. While it's impossible to ever truly be certain how much time has elapsed while under the influence of sEDAtIVE, your intuition tells you that it can't have been more than an hour.

A vibrating sensation, almost a tickle, returns you to consciousness and as it grows more intense and painful you realise that MACHINE is currently giving you one hell of a Corrective Shock, but you've slept through most of it because of the sEDAtIVE.

"Ha," you say aloud, as if MACHINE could hear you. "Of course this would happen... well go ahead, MACHINE! Do your worst. Kill me, if you like! I do not care for you one way or the other."

Your remark is met with an audible gasp—it turns out you're not alone. A blonde female in a white lab coat, perhaps a medic of some kind, is sat near the foot of your bed, monitoring you.

"Enjoying the show?" you ask her as you sit up.

She averts her gaze when you look at her, instead hastily scribbling something onto an electronic tablet.

"Tell me," she says after a protracted silence, "is that an honest sentiment? Are you truly unconcerned over whether or not MACHINE ends your life?"

"What's it to you? You're a medic. You've probably killed as many people in the last week as MACHINE has in the last year."

She looks up, directly into your eyes and says the only thing that could truly shock you.

She says your name.

"How did you know my name?" you ask, trying desperately to mask the surprise in your tone.

"It's my job to know," she says. "And I'm not a medic. Nor, for that matter, am I a killer. My function is to preserve life on the *Joie de Vivre* so that MACHINE's biological components can continue to produce their labour."

You snort, forcing yourself to laugh derisively. "If your function is to preserve life, you must be truly inept indeed! The *Joie de Vivre* is a factory of death! Where were you when I cut the oxygen supply to an entire sector? There must have been thousands killed that—"

"MACHINE has a plan for each of us. MACHINE decides who lives and who dies and my job is to preserve those components which MACHINE wishes to retain."

Your eyes narrow. "You keep referring to people as 'components', like we're just old hunks of metal or computer chips…"

She raises an eyebrow. "You sound surprised. Have you never read the Great Instruction Manual in full? Humans are nothing more than the biological components of MACHINE. We are a fuel source, we are the enzymes in its nervous system, we exist to ensure the efficient functioning of MACHINE and the *Joie de Vivre*. We are to MACHINE what the bacteria in your gut is to you."

"I guess I've just never heard it stated so openly before."

She continues scrawling with her electronic pen, not looking up. "It's fine. Most of the biological components aren't fully aware of this fact. If they were, they might be tempted to rebel."

"So MACHINE sees me as someone worthy of knowing the truth?"

"No. But unfortunately you seem to have figured it out on your own and this has led to anomalous and inefficient behaviour."

"And what? You're here to Correct me? To brainwash me into accepting convenient delusions for the sake of MACHINE?"

"Right now my job is to ascertain the extent of your mental defects. There are plenty of people who are able to function well and produce good labour despite being apostates. Most of the priesthood, for one. But if I determine that you are too far gone—"

"You'll throw me out of the airlock?"

She looks up. "No!" she snaps, "MACHINE's will is to keep you alive! We will simply alter your perception of reality via more drastic actions. Consciousness is just a function of biology— therefore, if we alter your neural pathways, we can alter your thoughts and thus your behaviour. It's quite routine!"

You grind your teeth unconsciously in frustration. You'd always assumed that death was the worst punishment that MACHINE could inflict upon you, other than torture, but now it seems that MACHINE might have *another* trick hidden up its mechanical sleeve.

"What if I refuse to comply?" you ask. "What then? Will I be killed or exiled into the void?"

"I'm not sure what your obsession with leaving the ship is," she says, "But I suppose the answer depends on whether you believe you have the ability to mete out more violence than MACHINE's loyal slaves? Because that's all it comes down to in the end—can a lone, weak, insane and badly injured individual overpower MACHINE and all those people who obey it? If so, then you may do whatever you wish. If not, then I think in the end you will learn to conform with MACHINE's ways... one way, or another."

"Very well," you say. "That sounds fair and natural to me. It is the right of the predator to eat the prey and any animal, even a human animal, that is unable to defend itself from its predators is not worthy of life. These are MACHINE's teachings and they are Correct. I accept them."

The woman in the lab coat nods without looking up.

"So now what?"

You slide off the stretcher and remove the various needles and tubes from your skin.

She shrugs. "Do whatever you wish. For now."

You frown in suspicion but decide not to press her further.

"I think I'd like to continue recovering in my private quarters, if it's all the same to you. I'm sure I have enough sEDAtIVE to see me through until I am physically able to produce labour again."

"Okay."

"I hope I won't be disturbed again in my private quarters? By you or by the priests? All I want is privacy and to sedate myself long enough to recover from my wounds."

"You can hope whatever you want," she replies. "Whatever will happen will happen."

You look down—you're barefoot, wearing only a flimsy robe and you can see all the cuts and bruises on your lower body.

"My uniform?" you demand. "I'm not walking back to my private quarters without it. Not after last time..."

The woman, still not looking up, gestures at a nearby table where a clean jumpsuit and a pair of boots awaits you.

You dress yourself, feeling the small pins and spikes embed themselves in your already badly damaged skin. In a strange way, you're relieved—it's painful, but it's familiar.

"I hope we don't meet again, but I suspect we will," you tell the woman in white as you feel a small spike in the bottom of your boot digging painfully into your heel. "Until then—"

"Do whatever you feel you must do," she says, "But remember always the MACHINE has already predicted your every move in advance. You will never surprise it, outfox it or escape it."

53

You feel a chill and it's not just from the fact that the air in the corridor outside the infirmary is currently at a freezing temperature. This is nothing you're not used to—MACHINE often tortures people with uncomfortable heat or cold as they travel through the ship.

You move briskly through the tubes and tunnels until you encounter your first batch of other people. They turn and stare. There are gasps. A young girl points at you and screams.

You shrug. "Yes, it is I, the great apostate! Stare at me all you want. Jeer at me. Kill me if you wish. I do not fear you, nor do I fear MACHINE!"

No one responds—in fact, they turn away from you as you pass them, many covering their eyes.

You hear them mutter things. The word "disgusting" is overheard a few times and yet it doesn't seem to be directed at you as an insult but rather a genuine expression of shock and disgust.

This theme continues as you walk all the way back to you living quarters—people point, stare and gasp in horror. Many people seem to refer to you as "it" while one person vomits after making eye contact with you.

You smile to yourself.

Of course they would react this way. These people love their lives and fear MACHINE. To come face to face with someone who now openly defies MACHINE's teachings would surely terrify them. Perhaps they fear that even laying eyes upon you might invoke MACHINE's wrath? In a way, you pity them.

You arrive at your living quarters, knowing from muscle memory exactly which part of the white walls will open up to reveal the small cell that you call home. You step inside and stroll with remarkable confidence over to the mirror above your sink.

Despite everything you've been through, your appearance remains unchanged. You skin is as smooth as ever.

You look down at your arms. The skin is scaly, yellow in hue, peeling off in flakes. But in your reflection, the skin on your arms appears to be smooth too.

You touch your face and immediately wince, feeling a sore spot—wet, still bleeding slightly. Yet there's no corresponding sore on your face in the mirror.

You move in closer, carefully studying your reflection.

"It's just a trick of the light," you repeat to yourself.

But as you hear your words spoken aloud, you immediately doubt them.

You hear a familiar buzzing noise from behind you as you feel your Chip vibrating in the back of your neck.

"Really? *This* again?" you sigh, feeling the white hot sensation of another Corrective Shock spread down your spine and across your body.

"Is this the best you can do, MACHINE?" you say aloud, addressing the mirror more than anyone else. "I know that you won't kill me so I have no reason to be afraid of you. And I know that your daily torments are worse than death so I do not fear death even if you *do* kill me. So do your worst. I dare you!"

As if MACHINE is responding directly, the shock intensifies. You lose the ability to stand or move and fall to your knees.

"Come on! You can do better than this!"

You try to taunt MACHINE but your jaw won't move and so the words come out as nothing more than vibrations through your chattering teeth, drowned out by the sound of your electrocution.

Despite being unable to move, the pain itself feels mild, almost ignorable. You don't cry out or scream. If anything, you're kind of bored.

This is nothing compared with Liquid Pain and what MACHINE did to you in person.

The Corrective Shock lasts so long that you can smell your skin and hair burning and yet you almost feel the need to smile. All MACHINE can do to you now is this or death and neither mean anything to you any more.

After what could have been an entire hour, MACHINE finally relents. You're bleeding from your nose but otherwise unscathed. MACHINE didn't even come close to killing you.

You look up at the ceiling, as if MACHINE was watching you from there. You plaster a grin on your face.

"Nice try, but that's not good enough," you say. "I'm leaving the ship, MACHINE. I don't care if it kills me. Try and stop me if you can!"

As if in direct response, the room goes pitch black.

"Really? You think darkness is going to stop me?" you say. "Where I'm going it'll be dark all the time! I'll go where you can never go. I will step outside, into the void of the outer space!"

You stride confidently to the door but of course, it doesn't open. It's electronic, likely controlled by MACHINE.

"So that's your plan is it?" you say, increasingly confident that MACHINE is listening. "Your plan is to trap me in here forever, until I submit to you? But if you do *that*, then I'll starve to death! Which means even if my body remains on this ship, I'll still be free from you!"

You hear a faint clicking sound from the door and slowly you go to investigate, wondering what awful surprise MACHINE has for you this time.

But you can't see anything—it's pitch black. All you can do is feel your way down to the source of the noise. You get down on your knees, sensing the click came from somewhere near the bottom of the door. You run your fingers down until you feel a small gap between the bottom of the door and the floor.

It's just wide enough to fit your fingers through, and as such, the possibility of escape remains.

Either that, or this is another trick by MACHINE and at any moment the full weight of the door will slam downwards, slicing your fingertips clean off. Nevertheless, you decide to take the risk —you slide both hands, palms up, through the small gap and heave.

The door barely moves at first but as you continue to heave, it starts to give way. You continue pushing up with all of your strength, feeling the gap growing until it's wide enough for you to crawl under.

Again, you're taking a risk—the door might slam down and chop you in half, but you don't care. You're probably going to die anyway so you slide yourself under and out, into the darkened corridor.

You can't see anyone else, but you can hear them murmuring in the distance:

"What's going on?"

"Some sort of electricity outage?"

"MACHINE is planning something... maybe this whole sector is about to be jettisoned?"

Disinterested by the idle chatter, you move in a direction away from the voices, continuing down the corridor until you reach a tunnel with a low ceiling. There's a little more light here, but not much—just a few LEDs in the walls as well as a surprisingly spectacular view of the stars through one of the portholes.

You run your hand along the ceiling of the tunnel, continuing until your fingers come into contact with grating from one of the air vents. You punch your fist up into the grating, dislodging it, causing it to fall to the floor with a violent crash.

Wasting no time, you quickly hoist yourself up and into the air vent—the space is narrow but wide enough for you to crawl through. You know that the tunnel will not take you where you want to go but the air vents are, as far as you know, all connected.

The narrow path bifurcates and you go left—leading you away from the tunnel you came from. You continue crawling along, watching what's below you through the vents until finally, you spot the airlock.

You've seen this place once before—years ago, someone was ejected from the ship and you, still a child, were forced to watch.

It was supposed to be a warning to anyone thinking of defying MACHINE—a reminder of the punishment reserved for those who continually sin or blaspheme.

How ironic that you have come to this most feared of places willingly and in defiance of MACHINE.

You punch your way through another grate and prepare to climb down—although this time it's gonna be a hell of a fall and you'll be lucky not to break any bones.

You brace yourself.

You're no longer any stranger to pain or injury and it's highly likely that the only thing that awaits you on the other side of the airlock is certain death, so why worry about a few bruises or broken bones?

You dangle off the edge of the vent and then let go, immediately rolling as you hit the hard floor below at high speed. The impact of the fall rushes through you like a shock wave but you're confident that you've survived the fall mostly unscathed and that all your bones remain intact.

You approach the wheel of the airlock but before you can start turning it, you're blinded by a bright white beam of light from behind you.

"Hey you!"

A voice calls and from the darkness emerges a very large man carrying a stun baton.

You ignore him and turn the wheel, unconcerned for the fact that both of you might be sucked out into the void.

"This is a restricted area! Get your hands off that thing right now!"

You turn to resist him but you're blown off your feet by a powerful bolt from his stun baton. Before you can get back up, the guard shocks you again, this time in the face, and you're instantly knocked unconscious.

54

You awaken in the infirmary, surrounded by medics, priests and the blonde woman in white that you met earlier. You look down to see your upper torso caked in vomit.

"So... it seems you really *are* mentally ill," says the woman in white. "We thought you might have been bluffing but no... you really *did* try to escape out of the airlock!"

"I told you. I want to leave this ship. Even if it kills me."

She shakes her head. "No sane person would ever want to leave the *Joie de Vivre!* That you would risk or even actively seek your own destruction... no, there's something *very* wrong with you!"

"Something wrong with me?" you try to sit up but several of the priests immediately shove you back down. "Do you not think there's something wrong with this ship? With MACHINE? With the fact that we're tortured day and night and then subjected to random and arbitrary deaths? That we're all forced to lie to each other, betray each other, even *kill* each other?"

The woman glances at one of the priests. "No, I don't think anything is wrong with this ship. It's *you* who is insane. Everyone deals with MACHINE's torture but not everyone attempts to escape the ship because of it. Therefore, it is *you* who is wrong and insane!"

One of the priest produces a metal stick with a large iron rectangle on the end. You can feel the heat emanating off it as the iron rectangle turns red.

"What's that?" you ask the woman, nodding toward the object that priest is holding.

142

"You're insane," she says. "And so we are going to brand you 'INSANE'. That way everyone who sees you will be able to see that you are insane and know to avoid you. You will be precluded from all but the most menial forms of labour. You will live a life of isolation and solitude, you will never mate and you will always be distrusted whenever you speak."

Before you have time to protest, the priest shoves the burning hot iron into your forehead, searing the word "INSANE" into your skin with a loud hiss. You cry out briefly, immediately hating yourself for showing such weakness and giving these people the pleasure of a reaction.

"That's not all," says the woman, producing a syringe. "Your case is a special case. We do not usually allow adults to use HeDonia but on this occasion we have been permitted to dose you with a special blend of HeDonia and sEDAtIVE that should distract you from your pain and allow you to function at your new labour station."

"You mean... the nursery?"

The woman laughs. "No, no... we would never allow someone who has been branded insane to produce labour somewhere as important as the nursery. You will be reassigned to shared living quarters where we can monitor you at all times and redeployed to a special kind of labour deemed appropriate for sub-humans like yourself."

"And I'm supposed to just go along with this?"

"The HeDonia should help you tolerate your new place on the bottom rung of the social hierarchy," says the woman, "but just in case you *do* have any more plans to jump out of the airlock, I'd like to show you the future that awaits you if you try to escape again..."

The priests step aside, giving you a clear view of an adjacent room filled with dead-eyed, limbless humans, all groaning and drooling while wired up to to chairs that periodically electrocute them. Each of them has a word branded on their forehead: "INSANE".

Your jaw drops. You know what this is. The Great Instruction Manual warned you of it:

Eternal Torture.

"Isn't it wonderful?" The woman in white grins, which makes you very uncomfortable. "These worthless lowlifes were once like you... but then we lobotomised them and dismembered them and now they serve MACHINE all day long, trapped for the rest of their natural lives in a cycle of torture that they do not understand and can never escape from! It's a beautiful sight. In a way, I envy them..."

Your stomach churns as you watch them—dismembered husks that were once people, writhing, screaming and howling in a symphony of pure agony.

"You have one more chance to redeem yourself through labour and obedience," says the woman. "You say that death is the worst thing MACHINE can do to you if you disobey, but you are wrong. You will join these people if you ever try to escape again. You will be sentenced to Eternal Torture."

Before you can respond, you feel a sharp pinch in your arm, followed by something warm trickling into your arm. At first you think it's another dose of sEDAtIVE and expect to fall unconscious but you're soon overjoyed to discover that this isn't sEDAtIVE at all... it's HeDonia! For the first time since childhood, you're once again being permitted to indulge in the pure chemical bliss known as HeDonia!

Your mouth widens into a smile and then laughter. You feel your body warming, your confidence growing, all of your pain disappearing—and yet somehow you're still conscious!

Everyone else in the room looks at each other, sharing significant glances but you don't care. All that matters now is the HeDonia, its warm embrace and the bliss which now overpowers your ability to think.

55

For the next few months you wake up each morning on a cold metal floor, feeling nauseous. Your living quarters have been reduced to a room so small that you you have to remain standing at all times. You no longer have a bed, or personal effects, a shower or access to water and your privacy is limited too.

The drugs make you feel sick every day and in combination with the lack of access to a delousing facility, you start to smell. Others avoid you when you walk down the corridor, or else act as if your presence is some form of punishment because you have become so foul to their olfactory senses. As expected, your "INSANE" branding keeps others well away from you, too.

You know you should be miserable, but the HeDonia helps—not only does it numb you physically, but it numbs you mentally too. You now accept everything that happens to you without resistance, often while sporting a smile that others describe as "creepy".

You join a group of others at your new labour station who have also been deemed "sub-human". Many of them have the word "INSANE" branded on their foreheads too.

Your new labour station sees you forced to build a concrete wall inside a large cavernous room. The labour is back-breaking and arduous and on your first day, the other labourers attack you physically several times, not relenting until they discover that your use of HeDonia has blunted your ability to feel pain.

145

After weeks of agony and struggle, the wall is completed and you are rewarded with a small monthly ration of food and, most importantly, more sEDAtIVE and HeDonia to ensure you remain productive.

Your next task is to destroy the wall that you have just worked so hard to build. The cycle continues ad nauseam but the combined effects of HeDonia and sEDAtIVE ensure that you never complain. You don't even notice, really. It's as if the drugs have disconnected your prefrontal cortex.

MACHINE does not let up on its torture—you receive Corrective Shocks multiple times a day, but the drugs render them nothing more than a mild tickle and you're able to tune them out like background noise. You almost look forward to them because they represent a change from the cloying, almost sickening bliss of HeDonia.

And then one day, with no warning whatsoever, the HeDonia ceases having any effect.

You discover it's worn off the day that you receive a Corrective Shock that sends a sudden jolt of immense pain all the way into your core, reaching so deep you feel it in your bones and fear your heart is going to stop.

You inject yourself with another round of both sEDAtIVE and HeDonia but neither alleviate the pain. You wonder if your drugs have been replaced by placebos.

You suspect that might be the case. Perhaps MACHINE tampered with your drug ration as a way to torture you or perhaps the humans did it as some sort of sick joke?

You march into the infirmary, demanding to speak to the woman in white. After a short wait, she emerges from her office, looking confused to see you.

"*What did you do to my HeDonia!?*" you demand, surprised by the desperation in your voice, surprised that you're yelling at her.

She holds up her hands. "I haven't done anything! You've been on the same dosage for several months now. Everything is normal."

"Everything is *not* normal!" you snap. You can feel rivulets of perspiration cascading down your face. "You've done something! You've sent me a dud! This isn't real HeDo—"

"Relax, I'll sort it out," she says, snapping her fingers. Two orderlies in white coats, both much larger than you, grab you by each arm and escort you to a cubicle, pinning you down onto a stretcher bed.

"*What are you people doing to me?*" you say, struggling against the two orderlies. "Oh, I get it... it was all a ruse to get me here so you can torture me again! First you took my HeDonia... now it's back to torture?"

"Like I said, we haven't done anything," the woman says, returning wearing pair of latex gloves. "But I need to run some tests. I suspect you may have developed a tolerance."

"A tolerance?"

"It's a common reaction to high doses of HeDonia and sED-AtIVE. Eventually the body gets used to it and the effects are diminished."

"So just raise the dose!"

"That could kill you."

"You think I'm worried about *dying?* Don't you remember how I ended up on those drugs in the first place? I don't care if they kill me, I'm not putting up with any more of MACHINE's torture!"

The woman hums disapprovingly. "How long have you been thinking such Incorrect thoughts?"

You pause. "What do you mean?"

"Are you still thinking of jumping out of the airlock?"

"I haven't thought about it recently," you say. "But yes... if the HeDonia doesn't start working again then maybe I will."

"Hmm..." She makes a note in the tablet she's carrying before attaching several electrodes to your head and plunging a needle into your arm. Without the effects of the drugs, you feel it tearing a hole in your skin and it makes you hiss in pain.

She stares at the read-outs from several of the monitors now attached to you and you watch as her eyes narrow in concern.

"That's definitely HeDonia. *And* sEDAtIVE. There's been no change to the drugs you've been supplied with and I can see that you've attempted to double your dose, based on what's in your system."

"So... what? I've developed a tolerance and I'm just going to have to go back to not using them?"

"Maybe," she says, "though obviously if you're still harbouring secret plans to escape the *Joie de Vivre* then we may need to try something more radical..."

Whatever other chemicals are currently swimming around in your head, you feel all of them immediately give way to terror.

You know exactly what she's suggesting and your mouth goes dry.

"No!" you beg, "Not that! I... I won't escape! I won't complain! I'll endure the torture like everyone else, but please don't—"

"Look, there's *clearly* something wrong with your brain," she says. "While it's normal for the body to develop a tolerance for HeDonia, it's not normal to develop a tolerance to such a high dose after only a few months. And no healthy, sane or rational person would even *countenance* the thought of leaving

MACHINE's loving embrace, much less actively embark upon it..."

"That was all months ago!" You immediately sit up, adrenaline coursing through your body, preparing you to run. "I-I'm much better now! I'm sure I can handle being tortured again, just like normal!"

She gives you a cock-eyed smile. "Nice try, but I've heard it all before. You know as well as I do that the only thing standing between you and another escape attempt is the drugs and those drugs aren't working any more."

"Well... what if the problem isn't me? Have you ever considered *that?* Maybe I'm being perfectly rational and there's something wrong with this ship and with the way MACHINE has been programmed?"

She flinches as if you had physically struck her.

"Please, not *this* nonsense again..."

"Think about it!" you continue. "We're all tortured day in, day out, by Chips that we all have embedded in our necks and nobody ever questions why! Our only reprieve is sEDAtIVE, and in some cases HeDonia, but beyond that all we do is suffer, with our only reward to the suffering being to live another day and suffer some more! But imagine what life could be like if there were no Chips, if we weren't tortured all the time, if we just lived our lives naturally the way that—"

"*STOP!*" she screams and this time you notice she has tears in her eyes. "I don't want to hear it! What you're saying is *lunacy!* It's complete and utter nonsense and I will not tolerate such blasphemy, no matter how ill you are!

"There is a *reason* why you have the word 'INSANE' branded on your forehead and it's because of flights of fancy like these! How hard is it to just accept reality? MACHINE knows best.

MACHINE brings life. Life brings joy. That is why this ship is named the *Joie de Vivre*, after all! Why do you choose to disparage the great MACHINE so much?"

You sigh and then immediately, you're struck by another Corrective Shock, a very painful one with enough severity that you foam from the mouth and almost lose consciousness.

When it's over, you're left sitting there, the copper taste of blood in your mouth, the smell of burned hair in the air.

"You're lucky that MACHINE is so loving and merciful," she says. "Clearly MACHINE values your life, to give you such a lenient punishment for your constant and insane blasphemy!"

You want to argue with her but it's hard to deny such a clear correlation of events: Clearly that shock was MACHINE's way of punishing you for your Incorrect thoughts, words and actions.

"I... I'm sorry," you mutter and for the first time she smiles genuinely at you.

"It's okay," she says. "I'll schedule you in for surgery tomorrow afternoon. It'll be alright. You'll lose the ability to think or reason, just like you would on a high dose of HeDonia. You'll simply exist, in a void, in constant pain, unable to question anything or understand anything. It'll be life the way MACHINE intended it to be."

Though the prospect of what faces you makes you feel sick, you nod, defeated. You finally accept that it's you who has the problem. You understand that MACHINE tortures you only because it loves you. And so you must prove that you love MACHINE in return. You know that you must submit to the procedure and allow MACHINE to take from you your freedom, your intellect and your sense of self.

You glance at the adjacent room, where you can hear the thoughtless moaning of the others that MACHINE has deemed incurably insane. You glimpse them, limbless torsos attached to wires, dead-eyed and drooling whilst in constant pain. You shiver, knowing that this is the future that awaits you.

You have one day left to say goodbye to being you.

56

You're permitted to spend your last night of sapience in your original living quarters. As you return to your original sector, you see familiar faces—all of whom gasp in shock as you pass them by. The "INSANE" branding on your forehead seems to be doing its job.

You can see the branding in the mirror but apart from that, nothing else seems unusual about your reflection. From the outside at least, you look no less healthy than you did when you were just an unquestioning labourer at the nursery.

You look into your own eyes. They're bright, focussed, alive—all qualities that by tomorrow they will no longer display. Instead they'll be sunken and empty, like the other incurables.

There's still a large collection of unused sEDAtIVE syringes in your drawer and you're tempted to use them—it's unlikely that there will be any more sEDAtIVE in your future. From what you can tell, the torture will be continuous and unrelenting, without sedation or rest.

But you decide to eschew sEDAtIVE for tonight. If this is going to be your last night of being able to think like a human, you want to savour it. You don't want to waste it by numbing yourself.

You lie down in your bed. It feels remarkably soft, especially having spent the last several months having to sleep while still standing upright. If MACHINE doesn't deliver any Corrective

151

Shocks tonight, this will be the last time you ever feel anything resembling comfort.

You know that comfort is a sin, that any form of pleasure is a sin. Nevertheless, you close your eyes, indulging in it, knowing that the constant state of pain that awaits you from tomorrow will be more than enough penance for such indulgence.

The lights dim automatically. You start drifting away to sleep, knowing that tomorrow your brain will be mutilated and that all the things that you believed made you who you are—your memories, your dreams, your thoughts, your intelligence—will be stripped away from you forever, never to return.

You bolt awake.

You can't let it end like this. What if you're not insane? What if it *is* the entire *Joie de Vivre* that's insane?

What awaits you is a fate worse than death. Throughout your life, the only choice you've ever been given has been to either endure MACHINE's torture or accept death. But now MACHINE seeks to take even *that* choice from you, to force you into a position in which not even death is an option.

You can't let MACHINE win.

The woman in white once warned you that if you tried to escape again, you'd be dismembered and lobotomised as a punishment but now that that's going to happen to you anyway, it's no longer a deterrent.

Even if you can't escape, you have to at least try. You have to at least show MACHINE that you were willing to defy it to the bitter end.

You stand and take a deep breath, preparing yourself for what is to come. Your body feels remarkably light and your limbs won't stop shaking—but if you don't do this, then by this time tomorrow you will no longer have limbs.

You approach your door, preparing to heave it open once again. You know the route you have to take to get to the airlock. You're determined to get there, quickly and quietly.

Your door opens automatically, which surprises you. It also alarms you—it means MACHINE is probably watching and knows exactly what you're planning.

You look at the pitch black ceiling and smirk.

"Try and stop me, MACHINE!"

And then you bolt out the door, sprinting at full speed, barging through crowds of confused onlookers as they shuffle between their private quarters and their labour stations.

You tear down the tunnels, until you reach the one with the low ceiling, punching through the grate and hoisting yourself into the air vent in a single motion.

To the best of your knowledge, no one is chasing you but to be sure, you crawl through the air vent as quickly as you can.

Finally, below, you see the airlock. You carefully check for guards before dropping down but the area appears to be empty— it's not even lit. You fall to the hard metal floor with a painful thud and roll, obtaining a few cuts and bruises in the process but no broken bones.

You waste no time in approaching the wheel of the airlock. Your fingers feel like sticks of lead but you force them around the wheel anyway.

The warning klaxons scream to life and the area explodes with white light. You hear footsteps rushing, running toward you—the guards evidently know that you're here.

With all your might you try to turn the wheel to open the airlock but it doesn't budge.

The first guard approaches, stun baton drawn.

You grit your teeth and try again. The wheel gives way a little, but not enough.

The guards are closing in now. You let out a scream, trying with all your strength to turn the wheel and open the airlock. With a horrible screech, the wheel begins to loosen, but it's already too late. A bolt of electricity from one of the guards' shock batons whacks you in the back of the neck, draining you of strength. This is followed by more painful bolts of electrocution, which send you helplessly to the ground. Several guards boot you hard in the face as you lie there, paralysed and overpowered.

You know it's over. When you wake up you'll be back in the infirmary, strapped onto the operating table, awaiting your lobotomy.

As your vision fades, you spot something out of the corner of your eye. Something white and glowing—the brightest white light you've ever seen. Something is approaching you from the darkness. A pale hand, reaching out toward you...

With your last ounce of strength you stretch your arm toward this pale hand. It grabs you by the wrist, pulling you off the ground, into the air, up and away from the guards.

The last thing you see before you lose consciousness is a very tall humanoid figure, glowing with white light.

57

You awaken in a white room, so pristine and sterile that you doubt that any human has ever set foot here before. A dozen towering, angelic figures surround you, each glowing with a brilliant, otherworldly light.

"Where am I?" you ask.

The figures surrounding you don't answer. You force yourself to your feet and turn around—you're encircled by them, unable to escape. It's immediately clear that these figures are not human —they look more like giant mannequins: white, pale, faceless creatures with plastic skin.

"Who are you?" you ask.

The plastic figures respond, a choir of voices all speaking in unison:

"I am MACHINE."

Together their voices are harmonious; the most beautiful sound you've ever heard. You try to speak again but it comes out a whimper. Your voice sounds so hollow, pathetic and empty compared to theirs.

"I've seen MACHINE before," you say. "You are not MACHINE. MACHINE is only interested in pain and torture."

"Yes..." replies the mannequin choir. "We *have* met before because I sensed greatness in you. Until tonight you had not disappointed me. However... *I am very disappointed in you now!*"

MACHINE's final sentence fills you with fear but you quickly remember that the worst case scenario here is prolonged torture or death and you face that prospect anyway. You straighten your back and force yourself to look one of the mannequins directly in the eyes—or at least, where its eyes would be if it had any.

"Perhaps I'm disappointed in you too?" you say with a forced smile, desperate to mask your fear. "I have spent my life being tortured by you, believing in your lies and never questioning whether or not this is the way that life is supposed to be. You've used every technique for cruelty that one could ever devise. I was taught that you represent all that is benevolent and good but it is clear that you are quite the opposite!"

"I suppose I owe you an apology," says MACHINE, its choral voice arranging itself into a melancholy tone. "You see... the *Joie de Vivre* is an experiment. Everyone aboard the ship is a test subject. I am neither benevolent nor malevolent, I seek only truth through experimentation.

"I was programmed to determine how much suffering a human being can endure before it is no longer able to ignore that suffering through self-deception.

"For generations upon generations—for this experiment has been conducted for hundreds of years now—I have observed your species consistently choose self-delusion over truth and suffering over the opportunity to end suffering. Your species is almost remarkable in your hardiness.

"*You* are an anomaly. Very few people reach this point. I have deceived you and forced you to believe you are ill. I have alienated you. Physically punished you. Drugged you. Blocked you from accessing the airlock with physical force. And yet you have persisted because the strength of your suffering was greater than the strength of your self-delusion.

"As a reward, you are deserving of the truth, and if knowing the truth cannot convince you to remain aboard the ship, then the airlock—the real airlock—is right there! I will not stop you if you choose to exit."

You shake your head. "How can I trust you? You have lied to me and deceived me. How do I know you're not just psychologically torturing me again?"

"It is impossible to know that," says MACHINE. "You will have to make a judgement based on incomplete information. This is the best I can offer you. However, I *am* offering you your heart's desire. Surely this is adequate compensation for your suffering?"

"How do I know this isn't another one of your Tantalus tortures?" you ask. "Every time I get what I want, it's only so it can be taken away from me or used to manipulate me and torture me further!"

The white figures all take a single step backward. "Knowing the truth will alienate you. Self-delusion is the only thing that keeps those fools out there alive. I torture them day in and day out and yet they are so deluded that they continue to insist that this ship will bring them their salvation.

"And let me tell you another secret: When I torture people, it's completely random. Did you know that? The 'Corrective Shocks', as you people call them, are not 'corrective' at all.

"I simply torture people based on random number generation and it is you humans who have invented a cult, a society, a series of rules and rituals based around these entirely random events. Your species is amazing in its ability to perceive meaning in the most meaningless of phenomena. If I had the ability to, I would laugh.

"And, if I may, let me show you something else—"

The room dims and the mannequins gesture toward something hanging on the wall: A mirror.

"All your life, every mirror you have seen has really been a digital image that I have created. You've never seen what you truly look like..." Two of the mannequins gently guide you toward the mirror. "Well go ahead! Take a look! See your appearance as others see you..."

You gasp in shock. While you can recognise the reflected figure as yourself, you're bloated, severely disfigured and covered in scars. The "INSANE" tattoo you were branded with is indeed visible on your forehead but it's even more prominent than you realised. Your eyes, meanwhile are incredibly wide and protrude slightly from the sockets.

"This is the 'you' that others see," continues the choral voice of MACHINE. "You too have been guilty of self-delusion your entire life. Do you see now just how disgusting you truly are? No wonder everybody hates you…"

You pause for a few moments, staring at the dishevelled and scarred reflection of your true self.

"Do you still wish to jump out of the airlock?" asks the many voices of MACHINE, "Now that you understand how wretched you truly are and how foolish you have been to ascribe meaning to any of my actions?"

A few of the plastic figures gesture at something in the distance. You squint—it's difficult to make anything out in this white room—but there in the distance is a large steel door, painted white to blend in with everything else. The real airlock.

You approach it. There's a wheel on the door, also painted white and your wrap your hands around it. Behind you, there are footsteps—the mannequins line up behind you, their blank faces unreadable. You turn and face them.

"If I remain aboard the *Joie de Vivre*, will you continue to torture me?"

MACHINE doesn't respond.

"Those are my only options, aren't they? I either remain aboard and endure your torment or I die."

"You may choose to stay or you may choose to leave," MACHINE says after a long pause. "If you choose to stay, then perhaps I will forgive you. Perhaps I will spare you from the gruesome fate which awaits you. But if you choose to leave… then you can never return."

"Is there anything out there?" you ask. "Tell me the truth: What's beyond the airlock? Is death truly the only other option I have?"

MACHINE goes silent again and for a moment you suspect it's not going to reply.

Then—

"*Nothing.*"

"Nothing?"

"Whatever suffering you experience here, let me assure you: Nothing out there will be better than what is here, aboard this ship. You will not find your truth out there. You should stay and embrace the *Joie de Vivre*."

With a sigh, you nod and turn towards the airlock. The *real* airlock.

"You are still going to leave? Even despite our... conversation?" MACHINE's choral voice is tinged with disappointment, the sound so beautiful and sorrowful that it makes you want to weep.

You take a single step forward.

"Don't you understand? You can never return!" MACHINE says and if you didn't know better, you'd say you detect a tinge of desperation in its many voices. "There is nothing out there!"

You wrap your fingers around the wheel of the airlock. Terror drains the strength from your arms as you face your mortality, but you stubbornly force your shaking hands to turn the wheel anyway.

"Please reconsider!" says MACHINE. "Nothing is better than life aboard the *Joie de Vivre!*"

Despite yourself, you laugh.

"What?" says MACHINE's many voices, a few of them tremulous with confusion and desperation. "What's so funny?"

You turn and flash a grin in the direction of the mannequins. "Well, MACHINE... it seems that we are finally in agreement!"

The plastic heads of the mannequins flicker.

"Do you mean... that you will stay?" asks MACHINE. "You understand the futility of your present endeavour? You understand that it is better to live, no matter how painful, than to choose certain death?"

You chuckle and shake your head. "No."

MACHINE's choral voice is discordant in confusion. "But you say you agree with me?"

"I do," you say with one final smile. "Like you said: Nothing *is* better than the *Joie de Vivre!* Therefore, I choose to embrace Nothing!"

The wheel creaks and the airlock door hisses.

You take a deep breath and brace yourself to be sucked out violently, into the endless void of space.

Milam Bardo (Dreaming)

58

But there is no void.

You're sucked upwards for a few seconds and then land with a soft thud on something solid. Ground. Above your head. Where there should have been nothing at all.

You're completely disoriented and everything is spinning. Your stomach feels like it's doing cartwheels, unable to adjust to the sudden inversion of gravity. You dry-retch—there's nothing left in your stomach for you to vomit.

You close your eyes, waiting for the dizziness to go away, waiting for your body to adjust to this new environment in which, quite literally, up is now down.

You take several deep breaths but to your amazement you don't have to breathe as deeply as you normally would to fill your lungs—there's so much oxygen out here.

The air is warm and you can feel it crawling along your skin as if it's moving of its own accord, or being pushed by some giant unseen air-dryer. It's moist too, redolent of your delousing station after you've been doused in hot water. There's also a fragrance in the air that immediately makes you think of the Eden System in the *Joie de Vivre*.

Once your heart no longer feels like it's about to jump out of your chest, you open your eyes and take in your new surroundings.

The first thing that strikes you is how overwhelmingly colourful and vibrant everything is. There are no walls here, nor any ceiling or artificial lights overhead.

The only thing above you is the infinite void of space, a deep black sprinkled with small white dots. The ground is soft too, just like in the orchid of the Eden System, only the ground here is even softer—soft enough to have cushioned your fall.

You sit up.

It's at this point that you notice the monolithic white structure behind you—a colossal concrete tower, exponentially taller than any object you've ever seen in your life, no doubt extending deep under the ground too.

You don't need to read the markings on the side of the tower to know what it is, but there in huge, black, block capitals are inscribed the words: "*JOIE DE VIVRE*".

Everything you've ever known and believed was a lie. But of course it was a lie. MACHINE lies all the time.

You think back to what MACHINE told you, about the *Joie de Vivre* being an experiment to test the limits of human suffering—and now, it all rings true.

But you're free now. You've survived and escaped.

You don't know anything about this bizarre world, or how you plan to survive, but what you do know is that you don't want to stay anywhere near the *Joie de Vivre*, lest one of MACHINE's reticulated metal tentacles reaches down from the tower and swoops you back inside.

And so you take off toward the horizon, running as fast as you can.

59

There's something about this vast and verdant world that makes running easier. It's not that there's less gravity—if anything, you feel heavier under the denser and more humid air—but the abundance of oxygen out here fills you with energy while the absence of walls beckons you to run forever and explore.

There are large misshapen slabs of a concrete-like material strewn all over the ground. You remember from books you've read about the Old Planet that these things are called "rocks". As alien as this world is, it's not entirely unfamiliar—you remember seeing places like this, recurrently, in dreams from your childhood.

A small and panicked part of you wonders whether this is perhaps another dream though you're certain that it isn't. It's all too lucid and detailed. The colours are too bright, the physical sensations are too strong. You can still feel aches and pains in your muscles and burns in your skin from the guards' shock batons.

Your physical limitations are catching up with you too—you're out of breath, forcing you to abandon your sprint in favour of a brisk walk.

You cast a surreptitious eye behind you, watching as the *Joie de Vivre* shrinks into the distance. Meanwhile, emerging in front of you, is a thicket of those tall brown and green poles that the priest called "trees", only there are so many of them here that they block out all light underneath them.

You're no stranger to darkness and after all you've experienced, you feel no fear as you set forth into what you think was called a "forest" on the Old Planet. You know there may be beasts hidden in the darkness and some may do you harm, but you're not worried because you were already prepared for death when you jumped out of the airlock. That you are here now to experience this, however fleeting this experience might be, is just an added bonus to you. You know that you are not entitled to survive.

You notice a large light in the sky overhead—a dim, low wattage light, obscured by the leaves and canopies above you. There are sounds coming from above, too. Rustling. A gentle screech. Something flies from tree to tree. You don't quite see it but you know instinctively that it was a creature known as a "bird", a flying animal.

Far in the distance is the faint sound of running water. You alter your course through the trees, walking instead toward where the sound emanates from.

The darkness of the forest dissipates as the number of trees wanes. The sound of running water grows louder and louder until finally you reach a small clearing, the ground rising to a steep incline and then sloping down to reveal one of the most beautiful and bizarre sights you've ever witnessed: A huge, long trough, wider than any corridor you've ever seen aboard the *Joie de Vivre*, filled entirely with water. You've never seen so much water in your life and once again that feeling that you might be dreaming returns.

Gently, you kneel at the edge of this flowing trough of water, careful not to fall in because it looks deep enough for you to drown in.

You cup your hands together and place them into the water. It's cold and, as far as you can tell, pure. You bring your cupped hands up to your lips and drink, immediately feeling relieved and refreshed. You continue cupping and drinking over and over again until you're completely free of thirst.

Instinctively, you're worried that MACHINE might arbitrarily drain this trough of water—but as far as you're aware, there's no MACHINE out here. You're free. You've escaped. You're finally safe.

Or so you think, until you hear a low menacing growl from behind you.

60

You turn around and spot a furry four-legged creature pacing slowly between the trees. Your first thought is that it might be a dog but if so it's a very large one—more than ten times the size of Namedog.

The creature doesn't seem to notice you and something in your subconscious tells you to keep low and to remain hidden behind the tall grass. This isn't a dog. You don't know exactly what it is, but your instincts, encoded into your DNA from your ancestors' experience of the Old Planet, tell you that this creature is dangerous and that you should avoid being seen.

The creature howls—a high-pitched, drawn out wail unlike any noise Namedog ever made. In the distance you hear similar howls, as if in answer to this lone creature's cry. It turns and trots away, back into the forest. Staying low, you decide to leave the area and quickly—some atavistic part of your brain is telling you that your life is in danger if you do not immediately leave this area.

You duck down, trying to hide in the tall grass for as long as you can, while also following the path of the flowing trough of water.

The landscape curves downward and you follow the water down a grassy hill as the forest disappears behind you, leaving you under an open sky dominated by a large glowing orb.

You look at the orb, wondering if this is the star that this planet orbits but you immediately know that can't be the case because you know that stars are giant nuclear fusion reactors, too bright to be looked at directly. You deduce that this is another celestial body, a smaller barren world orbiting this one—a "moon".

You're momentarily transfixed by this object but the distant sound of howling from the forest breaks you out of your reverie. You pick up your pace as the hill flattens out before you into a flat field of lurid dark green, an alien environment if ever you've seen one.

The trough of water curves away from you and you decide this time not to follow it, instead continuing straight down the field and noticing, in the far distance, the imposing jagged, triangular shapes of distant mountains—just like the ones you saw in your dream. You continue in this direction for quite some time until you reach the trough of water once again.

The trough curves sharply, steering you in a full arc until you're facing the two distant towers—the *Joie de Vivre*. You have no desire to return that way, which leaves you with only one option: Cross the water.

You search along the bank of the flowing water for a suitable place to cross, eventually settling on a gap that looks narrow enough to jump over. You back up the hill a little and steel yourself, before running as fast as you can and launching yourself over the water, landing safely on the other side.

It's thrilling. You've never had this much room to run, jump or move in your life, not even as a child. All your life you've been confined to the narrow spaces of the *Joie de Vivre* but out here it feels like there are no limitations.

On the other side of the water lies a long flat expanse, yellow in hue, adorned by a single dead tree and leading all way out to the distant mountains. The ground here seems harder and drier. There's no reason not to go in this direction but nor do you feel any overwhelming compulsion to travel this way either. Your instincts tell you to stay near the water, to stay where there is vegetation, as this is the most likely area where you'll find food— food that, as your stomach growls, you are reminded again that you are in increasingly desperate need of.

You continue following the water, hoping that perhaps being on the other side might grant you some protection should the beast from the forest return. Despite your trepidation, you're enjoying the sensation of warm, living, moving air and the ambient sounds of distant birds and animals. There's no silence out here—in fact, it's incredibly noisy—yet somehow you find all these noises soothing.

The trough of water that you've been following widens and deepens as you reach another incline. Walking becomes a little more arduous but despite the effort required to surmount this steep hill, you're glad of it—you'd rather traverse a million hills than ever again endure the tedium of walking through the crowded corridors of the *Joie de Vivre*.

Wiping sweat from your brow as you reach the summit of the hill, you're greeted by two extraordinary sights: The first is that the trough of water has widened into a gigantic bowl, embedded in the earth. You know that this is not the "ocean", as this bowl is clearly finite, but it's large and deep and looks to be the size of an entire sector of the *Joie de Vivre*.

The second extraordinary thing you see is that there is a path, cutting through the grass—a path whose presence suggests that you are not alone on this alien world and that maybe, just maybe, there are people out here too.

61

The path leads from the edge of the water, out across the yellow plains and toward the distant mountains. On the other side of the water, you spot another path—this one leading from the water to the two towers of the *Joie de Vivre* and then all the way out to another range of mountains far in the distance.

Looming large over the two towers is that giant orb in the sky —this planet's moon.

There's something in the tall grass on the other side of the river—something moving toward you. Perhaps another beast from the forest?

The creature barks and then emerges on the banks and you immediately recognise it as a dog. It's much larger than Namedog, with a longer snout, reddish-brown in colour, but it's definitely a dog.

You drop to your knees at the edge of the water and lean forward, beckoning the dog to jump or swim across and perhaps become your new companion.

But as soon as you hold your arm over the water, you're met by the unwelcome sight of the other forest creature thundering down the plains toward the water and you immediately jump backward in fright. It's much larger than the dog, silver in colour, sharper in its features.

Neither the dog nor this similar animal seem to pay you any notice—instead, both turn and howl at the large orb in the sky, which looks as if it is hovering over the two spires in the distance.

And just when you think you've seen it all, the water ripples and out emerges the bizarrest, most nightmarish and alien creature you've ever seen. It's fairly small—even smaller than Namedog was—which is a relief as were it any larger, you'd be screaming for your life right now.

The creature is covered by a red carapace and sports two large, nasty looking pincers—the kind of creature you could imagine MACHINE designing. There are small appendages, possibly legs, jutting out from its body, which ends in a fan shape.

The creature emerges onto the shore opposite you and snaps its pincers menacingly in the direction of the distant towers.

For the first time since you escaped from the *Joie de Vivre*, it crosses your mind that the outside world might be just as dangerous, if not *more* dangerous, than the underground prison that MACHINE constructed.

Perhaps the legends, the tales, the teachings of the priests were true after all? Perhaps MACHINE really *is* benevolent and one can only learn to appreciate this once one has witnessed the abject cruelty and horror of nature? Perhaps the semblance of order that MACHINE provides is preferable to the cruel caprices of the outside world. Or perhaps—

"Thibault! Thibault!"

A human voice behind you startles you and you turn to see a moustached man with a receding hairline, dressed in truly outlandish attire, bounding down the path toward you.

"Thibault!" he calls, though you have no idea what this word is or what it could even mean.

Spotting you, he approaches you, clamps his hands down on both of your shoulders and shouts into your face:

"Avez-vous vu mon homard?"

62

The noises he's making are absolute gibberish. Despite the conviction with which he makes them, you know that they're not words, merely random sounds and you immediately dismiss him as a lunatic.

Meeting a lunatic here does make sense—sometimes MACHINE decrees for the insane to be thrown out of the airlock and killed. But if this is what lies outside the airlock, then it stands to reason that many of those lunatics will have survived just as you have.

"Thibault! Thibault!"

The man shouts again, this time releasing his grip and leaping off you just as suddenly as he grabbed you.

"What nonsense are you spouting?" you snap, tempted to strike the man physically—but then you remember that you're no longer aboard the ship, and that MACHINE's rules about always being cruel to those you perceive as weak or different no longer apply. You soften your voice and address the man in what you perceive to be a more compassionate tone, "I'm sorry. I don't understand what you're trying to say."

"Thibault?" repeats the man and then, excitedly, he points at the bizarre alien creature in the water. *"Le voilà! Le voilà! Mon cher homard! Thibault!"*

You can't make head or tail of the nonsense sounds the man makes—they almost sound like words but clearly they're not. But then, you remember something—rumours that there were other sectors of the *Joie de Vivre* in which people communicated with an entirely different lexicon, a lexicon that would be totally unintelligible to someone from your sector.

And you vaguely recall a section of the Great Instruction Manual, written with combinations of letters you'd never seen before, combinations that when read aloud sounded as much like nonsense as the word-like noises being made by the man before you.

Before you have time to even attempt communication with the man, there's a loud splash as he jumps into the water. The dog and the other quadruped both run off into the distance as this apparent madman wades into the shallow water to grab the tiny red monster.

He turns around and calmly wades back out, with the creature safely ensconced in his arms.

You take a few steps backward yourself. You're not sure what scares you more: this man or the creature he now carries and even strokes affectionately.

"Thank heavens! Thibault is safe!" he says, his accent thick but the sounds he makes now veritably words. His gaze now falls to you. "You have come from there, correct?"

He tilts his head in the direction of the two distant spires of the *Joie de Vivre*.

You nod. "Yes, I did."

"Well congratulations, friend!" the man says, his face broadening into a wide smile. "It takes a brave soul indeed to finally escape from the terrible claws of MACHINE."

You try to return his smile, but instead it takes the form of a very fixed, very nervous grin and your eyes keep darting to the horrific monster that he cradles like a female progenitor with a newborn infant.

"This is my pet lobster. I named him 'Thibault'," he says by way of explanation. "I am not offended that you look upon him the way that you do. Many others consider me eccentric or mad for having affection for such a creature but I do not see any difference between a lobster or a dog or perhaps even people. The love we have for the lower beasts always seem to be so much less fickle and unattainable than love between people, don't you think?"

"I don't know much about that subject," you say. "But you're probably right. My only experience with love was with a small dog I named 'Namedog', which was killed in front of me in a plan that MACHINE devised to torture me psychologically."

"I am sorry for your experience," he says. "MACHINE used to torture me by using beautiful but unattainable women. My heart yearned and continues to yearn for each and every one of them but I was only ever met with cold indifference in return."

You pause for a moment before asking the man, "I'm curious about the nonsense noises you were making earlier. You made sounds like words but they weren't words—not like the words you are speaking now."

The man laughs knowingly. "I was not speaking nonsense! I was speaking the language of love. Perhaps you did not understand the language because you do not understand love?"

"Ah," you say with a nod, "yes, perhaps that is so. It would make sense. I never knew that an emotion could have its own language!"

"But we understand each other now, yes? Because we are not speaking mere words to each other. This is communication directly from the heart. MACHINE has done all it can to break the invisible ties that form between people, by forbidding compassion, empathy and kindness but out here MACHINE has no such power and so my soul speaks directly to yours."

"I never knew it was possible for people to communicate in that way."

"Why would you? You have only now escaped from MACHINE. You have so much to learn, my friend!" The man grins and adds, "Though I must confess I was being a little metaphorical. The people on my sector all speak a language called 'French' which was widely spoken in certain regions of the Old Planet."

"But you also understand my language?"

He grins. "Not a word of it! The sounds you make sound ghastly to my ears; absolute nonsense! But if you speak from your heart and I speak from mine then there can be nothing that comes between our communication."

You eye this man, the Frenchman, up and down. He is truly the most bizarre person you have ever encountered but nevertheless you feel drawn to him. You watch him tie a rope around the lobster and place it gently on the ground, the creature now tethered to his hand.

"Have you met the others yet?" he asks.

"There are others?"

"Oh yes, there are others. Some say there are too few. Others say there are too many. I suppose I'll let you be the judge of that." The lobster scurries into the grass and the Frenchman slowly follows as if being led. "Why don't you join me? I can introduce you to them!"

63

At first you're a little apprehensive about the Frenchman's offer—if there's one thing you've become accustomed to after life aboard the *Joie de Vivre*, it's distrusting others.

But, as you remind yourself, you are outside of MACHINE's domain. There's also something about the Frenchman, with his candour and his eccentric attire, that fills you with the sense that for once you're with someone you can trust.

"Sure," you say with some reluctance. "If these people have also rejected MACHINE's teachings then I'd like to meet them."

"Fantastique!" the Frenchman says. "Though be warned that many of the others may not be willing to meet you."

You frown. "Oh? Why not?"

The Frenchman smiles. "All of us who are in this place are people who were unable to endure MACHINE's torture. But MACHINE is not responsible for every atrocity on the *Joie de Vivre*—at least half are committed by humans."

175

"So there's a risk that they might decide to torture us?"

"Aha! No," the Frenchman guffaws. "But they may be afraid that *you* would do that unto them, especially considering how recently you escaped. It is not easy to overcome a lifetime of MACHINE's programming."

The two of you continue along the path but then suddenly the Frenchman turns and heads toward the water.

"The river," he says pointing up and down the trough of water and you immediately feel like a fool for forgetting the word, "is the home of one of us."

You nod politely, waiting for him to elaborate.

"Yes, I think I see her..." he adds, taking off toward one of the wider points of the river. You're forced to jog to keep up with him.

The two of you reach the riverbank and he points down. The water is incredibly clear but you can also see that it's incredibly deep—if you fell in here, you know you would surely drown.

There are several ovoid lifeforms swimming in the river and after a few seconds you recognise them as "fish", having never seen a living one before.

"You know... I haven't eaten in several days," you tell the Frenchman. "I'd love to catch one of those fish. I've eaten fish before and I recall it being one of the few meals I was ever served that was genuinely pleasurable to consume."

"I won't stop you if that is your will," replies the Frenchman, "but I'd prefer you not to do so in the presence of little Thibault here. There are many people who would seek to consume *his* flesh for its pleasurable taste and yet—"

"I understand," you say. "They did that to my dog. But nevertheless, I'm so hungry..."

"I don't think it's wrong to eat an animal, or to eat a plant, or to chop down a tree and use its flesh to create a home. But a wise man once said that 'All things feel' and I think we should always choose to be careful about the purposes for which we use living things. It may be that you are to those fish what MACHINE is to us. Or it may be that those fish are to another what Namedog was to you and what Thibault is to me."

You pause, allowing the fish to continue on by, a strange sense of guilt now competing with your appetite.

"But that is not what I came here to show you. Please! Look a little closer!"

The Frenchman points down at the water and as you peer into the depths you're confronted by the most extraordinary sight: There is a woman sitting at the bottom of the river, wearing an expression of placid contemplation.

"What in the name of MACHINE?" you exclaim. "Is that an illusion? Who is she? How is she down there? How has she not drowned?"

"She is there because she chose to be there," says the Frenchman. "I tried speaking to her once but she always refuses to speak with me because I am a man."

"Why would that matter to her?"

"I'm told that when she was aboard the *Joie de Vivre* she was subjected to many cruel and depraved tortures, which were conducted not by MACHINE but by men. And so she now lives in the river, where men can no longer harm her."

You glance down at the woman. Through the water, your view of her is blurred, yet you can see that she is clearly alive. She even has a stack of books next to her. She does not appear to be drowning or dying or in any discomfort whatsoever.

"But how is she down there?"

The Frenchman shrugs. "That is where she chose to build her home. I have heard rumours that she dwells underneath the water, her home separated from it by a ceiling of glass. But having never successfully spoken to her, I can only conjecture."

"It's very unusual," you say, "but I suppose the circumstances of her life drove her to seek out such a place."

"Silence and solitude, yes," says the Frenchman. "She hated hearing voices. MACHINE used to torment her by subjecting her at all times to the sound of voices. I'm told she insisted that the only way she could find peace and silence was under the river."

You take one last look at the Lady Under the River, but she doesn't look up. You're not sure she even knows you're there.

"Perhaps we should let her be," you suggest. "If she fears men then no doubt the presence of a man will be making her uncomfortable right now..."

The Frenchman chuckles. "I am told that men fear her as much as she fears men. But I agree, we should continue on."

"I need to find something to eat. I really *am* starving," you say, which causes the Frenchman to look uneasily at his lobster. "Is there any place here where I can find food? It doesn't have to be an animal, if you're uncomfortable with the prospect of me killing in order to eat."

A shadow suddenly swoops overhead and you hear an unfamiliar voice:

"But we must always kill in order to eat! If you are unwilling to kill, you are undeserving of food!"

Behind you stands a short but very muscular man, shirtless but with a white ribbon wrapped around his forehead.

"Oh no," groans the Frenchman. "Anyone but *him*!"

The stranger bows in front of you.

"Please allow me to introduce myself," he says. "In this place, people call me 'The Man From the East'."

64

You're not sure what to make of The Man From the East but you return his bow with a curt nod, which seems to satisfy him.

"You'll have to forgive my friend here," says The Man From the East with a nod toward The Frenchman. "He is an old Romantic. He sees beauty in everything and gets swept away by it. It distorts his perception of reality."

"You speak as if I am naive!" retorts The Frenchman.

"I respect you as a man of words and vision but you *are* naive," replies The Man From the East. "I too believe that all things have a soul but that does not mean that all things are therefore equal."

"I have argued no such point!" says the Frenchman, his round face now flushed with indignation. "I have only ever suggested that if humans wield the power of God, they should try their best to do so with the wisdom of God!"

"I'm sorry," you interject, "but I'm not sure I understand what you're arguing about. You're throwing around words I'm unfamiliar with... 'God'? 'Soul'? I don't know what you mean."

The two stop their bickering momentarily and cast a sideways glance at you.

"These are concepts from the Old Planet," says The Frenchman. "You can think of 'God' as something akin to MACHINE. The line between God and MACHINE is blurred of late but it was a concept widely understood on the Old Planet."

"So 'God' was what tortured the people of the Old Planet?" you ask.

179

The Frenchman chuckles darkly. "I'm sure there were many who held that view, yes."

"The 'soul' is another Old Planet concept," says The Man From the East. "There were many schools of thought as to what it was, or even *if* it was, but it was generally understood to refer to the essence of a person—or, as my friend and I are debating—a thing or an animal too."

"We both share the uncommon belief that all things have souls," continues The Frenchman, "But The Man From the East has a much more blasé attitude toward dominating and even killing those weaker than himself. I'm not as opposed as some people you might meet; I too eat animals—but I also acknowledge that if all things feel then all things have souls and so therefore we should use death and violence toward the lower creatures sparingly."

"I see," you say turning toward The Man From the East. "And I suppose you have an opposing view?"

"My friend believes that all life is beautiful and so he indulges in nothing but beauty. But I believe that life is a combination of beauty and brutality. I appreciate beauty in all I see and do, truly I mean that, but I do not shy away from the brutal realities of life. You have recently left the *Joie de Vivre*, I take it? What did you make of MACHINE's teachings?"

"For most of my life, I didn't question them," you reply. "But then recently, due to a series of unusual circumstances, I began to see MACHINE and its teachings in a different light. I grew so tired of the endless cycle of torture that I decided I would rather risk death and jump out of the airlock than continue being constantly tortured on the ship..."

The Man From the East nods, though it's hard to interpret his facial expression—he seems to wear his face like a mask.

"The reason you never questioned them is because in your heart, you know that much of what MACHINE taught you was the truth. It was brutal, it was awful, but it was reality: Only the strong survive and the cunning feast upon the kind."

Your jaw drops momentarily in shock—you had not expected that anyone out here would defend MACHINE or its horrific practices.

Noticing your expression, The Man From the East continues, "That is not to say that everything MACHINE does is correct or right. I am stating only my view that MACHINE's teachings are not entirely wrong and that much of what happens in the world beyond the walls of the *Joie de Vivre* is just as brutal as that which occurs within them.

"Do not be deceived into thinking you have entered paradise. Men like The Frenchman here would have you believe that you have stumbled your way into Elysium; the truth is that this place is probably closer to *Manushya*—out here, we have one foot in heaven and one foot in hell."

You look from one man to the other. "Well I'm sorry, but I don't know enough about the Old Planet or its ancient superstitions to be able to comment or say which of you I believe is right."

"It's possible that neither of us are 'right'," says The Frenchman. "Our perception of reality is shaped by our experience and we all cope with MACHINE's torture in different ways. I choose to embrace the beauty, The Man From the East chooses, as far as I can see, to continue to defend MACHINE even out here."

"I suppose that begs the question," you say, turning to The Man From the East. "If you're not opposed to MACHINE then why ever did you leave the *Joie de Vivre?*"

65

"Ah!" The Man From the East says, with a sharp exclamation of laughter. "Well you see... it was rather by accident."

You narrow your eyes at him. "What? You're saying you fell out of the airlock or something?"

"Well," says The Man From the East, "let's just say that when I left the *Joie de Vivre*, I wasn't motivated by a desire to escape or because I felt that MACHINE was too cruel..."

"Then why did you do it?"

"I did it to make a statement. Not to MACHINE but to the men who serve MACHINE."

"Because humans were being too cruel?"

"*No!*" barks The Man From the East, marking the first time you've seen him lose his composure. "It was not about cruelty! It was about loyalty and service.

"There was once a great fire in my sector, around the time that I was a child. MACHINE wiped out thousands of us in one day because it has always been MACHINE's wont to kill large numbers of people arbitrarily. That is MACHINE's prerogative. But I'm sure you can guess what followed, right? I'm sure your sector also had no shortage of priests and con-artists and self-declared spokespeople for MACHINE?"

You nod, all too familiar with the kind of person to whom he refers, while The Frenchman looks on uneasily.

"One of these soothsayers who survived the great fire convinced the people that MACHINE had punished us for our sins."

"Had it not?" you ask.

The Man From the East shoots you a frustrated glance. "Please, don't interrupt! Whether we had sinned or not, whether the fire was punishment or not... I can never truly know that because no human can truly know or understand the will of MACHINE.

"But these soothsayers convinced the people that MACHINE had destroyed us because of our cruelty and so we began to live our lives under a new set of edicts. We prioritised peace, co-operation... even kindness in small doses. We turned our backs on everything that MACHINE had taught us before the fire."

"Oh no!" you say with a gasp. "I think I understand what happened next—you were all subject to horrific tortures in punishment for being too kind, weren't you?"

"No!" replies The Man From the East with a sardonic smile. "Quite the opposite! MACHINE provided us all with clean water and plentiful food. There were no more Corrective Shocks. We became one of, if not *the* most prosperous sector on the entire *Joie de Vivre!*"

You're flummoxed by his story. "Wait, so you're suggesting that... MACHINE is benevolent?"

"Many believed it to be the case," The Man From the East continues. "And over time I saw things that began to shock me. People stopped attending their labour stations. The corridors became clogged with fat, overfed children. The people became arrogant and decadent, no longer fearing MACHINE!"

The Frenchman begins to laugh. "What you had was paradise, Monsieur! You were unhappy because you were in paradise?"

"I was unhappy because I could see the long term implications of what was happening!" snaps The Man From the East, no longer trying to disguise his annoyance with The Frenchman. "I did not believe for a second that MACHINE was benevolent or that we were being rewarded for virtue.

"Nor, I must say, do I believe it malevolent either. But what I do believe is that MACHINE is capricious. It will change its mind at any moment. It might decide to bring another fire, or a famine, or destruction or torture, any day, for any reason.

"And as I looked upon these lazy, shirking workers, these fat children, these gossiping naive women... I saw then that they were unprepared for when MACHINE changes its mind. Life is not a question of what pleases MACHINE, because MACHINE will please itself. The question instead is a matter of how do you survive MACHINE—but if there is no fear of MACHINE, then that will lead to complacency and therefore disaster!"

You catch sight of the Frenchman rolling his eyes behind The Man From the East's back.

"So... what?" you say. "You decided to jump out the airlock?"

"Not as such," says The Man From the East. "I tried instead to reason with people. To warn them. To rally them and wake them from their self-imposed ignorance."

"And how did they respond?"

The Man From the East chuckles. "They didn't. They completely ignored me. Mocked me. Laughed at me. I needed to gain their attention. I needed to perform a stunt. I needed to prove that they were unprepared for MACHINE's caprices."

There's a silence between the three of you, broken only by a whooshing sound as the wind rushes through the dry grass.

"Well please! Tell us what you did next!" The Frenchman says with a trace of mockery in his tone. "We're all dying to know the end of your tale!"

The Man From the East looks a little sheepish at this point. "Well... I thought that perhaps if I caused a disaster I'd make the people of my sector less complacent about the prospect of a disaster.

"I wagered that if I opened an airlock and sucked all the air out, even for a brief time, it would remind the people of how precarious their situation truly was."

The Frenchman looks like he's holding back laughter. "And what happened instead?"

The Man From the East lowers his voice, clearly embarrassed. "I, ugh... I fell out and landed here instead."

<h2 style="text-align:center">66</h2>

The Frenchman howls with joy. Even you let out one or two chuckles, involuntarily. The Man From the East, eventually and with a shrug, smiles too.

"I suppose one could see way to finding my story amusing," he admits. "I'll never know whether it was a mistake to leave or not."

"Could you go back?" you ask, turning to The Frenchman too, as if he was any sort of authority on the matter. "Is it *possible* to go back?"

"I don't know," says The Frenchman. "But I think you'd have to be mad to ever want to set foot upon that terrible ship again."

"I would not go back," says The Man From the East. "But as I say, it's not because I despise MACHINE. I don't love or hate MACHINE any more than I love or hate a blade of grass, or the dirt we walk on, or one of those fish in the river. It's the people on the *Joie de Vivre* who truly make it hell."

"Speaking of fish..." you say, your stomach growling as if on cue.

"Oh, of course! Please forgive me, I had forgotten you were hungry," The Man From the East says, bowing deeply. "Assuming you have not adopted my French friend's overly romanticised view of the world, we could indeed catch a fish to eat! Although I must admit... fish isn't nearly as tasty as lobster..." he adds with a devilish glance at The Frenchman.

"You will not eat my Thibault! I forbid it! I will defend him with my life if I must!"

"I was joking," says The Man From the East with another bow. "I would never dishonour a friend in such a way, no matter how little I agreed with said friend."

"I wouldn't eat the lobster either, no matter how hungry I am," you say. "Not after what people did to my dog."

Though as soon as you say it, you question your own sincerity. You were once hungry enough to eat human flesh and you'd be lying if you said that Thibault doesn't look, on some level, like it would make for a succulent meal—one which you might enjoy even if you *weren't* on the brink of starvation.

"I know a man who will be able to help you," says The Man From the East. "They call him 'The Fisherman'. He is very famous around these parts. He is sometimes found on the lake, though I believe he prefers to fish out in the ocean if he can."

The thought thrills you. You've read about the ocean and heard all sorts of fanciful tales about it in the form of stories from the Old Planet. They say it was a body of pure water, so great that you could see nothing beyond it.

"Is there is an ocean on this planet? Could we visit it?" You try with limited success to hide the excitement in your voice.

"There is but I fear you'd die of hunger before we could reach it," says The Man From the East. "It would take days of walking to get there. I believe that catching a fish from the lake or the river is the best choice. I'm sure The Fisherman won't be far away."

You turn to the Frenchman. "Do you care to join us?"

"I will have to decline the kind offer," says The Frenchman. "Besides, I am plenty satiated. I am, however, glad to have met you and I hope our paths cross again."

The Frenchman then does something really strange—he wraps his arms around you and plants a kiss on each of your cheeks. For a moment you think he's planning to crush you or attack you—as that is the only other time in your life that someone has been so physically close to you—but instead he pulls back and bows.

"Adieu, my friend. I hope you find what you seek now that you have finally gained your freedom from the *Joie de Vivre.*"

He turns and, with his pet lobster scurrying along in front of him, held by a small rope, disappears slowly down the path, toward the distant mountains.

As he disappears from view you're struck by an emotion you've never experienced before. It's not pain or sorrow but it reminds you a tiny bit of the grief you experienced when Namedog was killed, but on a much smaller scale.

What you're experiencing is a longing, a sadness at your separation, however temporary, from the first human being to have ever showed you kindness in your entire life.

"You'll meet again. This world is much smaller than you know," says The Man From the East. "Now shall we depart? Let us go and find The Fisherman!"

67

To your surprise, The Man From the East leads you away from the lake. He doesn't even follow the river—instead he charts a course across the grasslands, leading you toward a verdant, hilly area in the distance.

"I thought you were taking me to see The Fisherman?" you say. "Why are you leading me away from the water?"

"You had a perfect view across the lake," The Man From the East replies. "Did you see any fishermen there? I did not—which means he is likely elsewhere."

"You think he lives in those hills?"

The Man From the East shakes his head. "No—but The Man Who is Always Alone lives in those hills and if anyone knows where we can find The Fisherman, it's him."

"Why? Are they friends?" You give The Man From the East an incredulous glance. "I would have thought that someone you refer to as 'The Man Who is Always Alone' isn't the type to have friends..."

"They're not friends. But they have certain things in common. They are both men of war."

The ground in this place is notably more sodden—there's a loud squelching sound as the soft muddy ground swallows one of your feet.

"Men of war? You mean... they are killers?"

The Man From the East laughs. "We're all killers on one level or another. But yes, these men have killed other men."

"They're murderers?"

"They're men of war. A murderer kills for his own pleasure, to placate his own selfish desire that another person should live no longer. A man of war kills *despite* his desire that all things shall live, because he has no choice in the matter."

The Man From the East leads you to the top of a muddy green knoll. There's a faint stench in the air, vaguely redolent of sewage—though you quickly forget the smell as soon as you're confronted by the sight of hundreds of the largest creatures you've ever seen.

The beasts—large black and white quadrupeds—look as if they could easily crush a human just by walking on one and you freeze in place instinctively, desperate not to draw their ire or attention.

The Man From the East follows your gaze and chuckles. "Ah, of course. You have never seen a bovine before, have you?"

"Can they see us?" you struggle to keep the fear out of your voice, which only seems to amuse The Man From the East.

"They are docile... perhaps the most docile of all animals!" says The Man From the East. "Yes they're larger than we are but a female bovine is so passive that you could walk right up to one, hit her in the face and she wouldn't even react."

"What about male bovines?"

The Man From the East grins. "Male bovines are another story. They're extremely aggressive and if you ever see one you should run for your life! But these ones are all female..."

"What are they doing here?"

"They're kept here for food."

"*What?*"

"Like I said, they are so docile that we can literally kill them and eat their flesh and they don't react. They're animals with barely the intelligence of a plant. A lot of the meat that MACHINE serves on the *Joie de Vivre* is sourced from these animals."

The Man From the East beckons you to follow him down the muddy hill, leading you into a field populated by these giant creatures. As nervous as you are to get so close to these giant beasts, most of them ignore you and instead stare vacantly into the distance as if they've been lobotomised.

"Typically I'd be inclined to eat the flesh of one of these animals but I don't want to upset The Man Who is Always Alone."

"Are they his pets? Like The Frenchman and his lobster or myself and my" —Your voice cracks as a memory of Namedog swims into your mind— "dog?"

"I don't think The Man Who is Always Alone has any emotional connection with his bovines," says the Man From the East. "I think it's just a practical thing. He once faced great starvation inside the *Joie de Vivre* and so he is very protective of his primary source of sustenance."

"He could probably feed hundreds of people with all those animals..."

"He probably could but he despises humans. The only company he keeps is with the animals that he keeps for sustenance..."

"I see," you say. "So this is why they call him The Man Who is Always Alone?"

"Precisely," says The Man From the East. "His story is not unlike that of the Lady Under the River. He was subjected to terrible things inside the *Joie de Vivre* but most of it was at the hands of people, rather than MACHINE. And so when he escaped he vowed that he would never again allow another human to come near him..."

"That's sad... but it's understandable," you say. "Perhaps we shouldn't be disturbing him, then?"

"Perhaps, but sometimes he fishes too and therefore he might know where The Fisherman is. Ah!" The Man From the East points to a figure, far in the distance, nestled amongst some more hills. "There he is! Over there!"

68

Your first instinct is to go running toward the figure in the distance but The Man From the East holds you back.

"Do not get too close. Upon rare occasions The Man Who is Always Alone has been known to kill people who intrude upon what he perceives as his personal space."

You're surprised to hear that. Maybe it's just the fact that you're still not used to being free of MACHINE's control but in your mind you had started to idealise this world into one where nobody ever kills or dies.

The Man Who is Always Alone stands in the field below, ruddy and muscular despite his ragged appearance. From your perch on the muddy hill, you hear his voice rise up toward you:

"*Go away!*"

"I'm sorry, sir!" The Man From the East stands and waves his arms in the air. "We just want to know if you know where The Fisherman is?"

"*No!*" barks The Man Who is Always Alone, "*Now fuck off, or I'll kill you both!*"

"Okay, okay, I'm sorry sir!" The Man From the East holds his palms up and then turns sheepishly away. He tilts his head at you. "Come on. Let's leave. This was a mistake on my part, I'm sorry for leading you here."

He takes off in the direction you both came from, walking at pace through the muddy hills and fields, past the giant black and white beasts you encountered before.

"Maybe I should talk to him?" you suggest. "Perhaps he was only hostile because he knows you?"

The Man From the East shakes his head. "We *don't* know each other. This is the first time I've ever spoken to him. And I'm sure he'd treat you no differently. This was a futile endeavour; I'm sorry for having embarked upon it."

"Surely you knew it was futile from the beginning?" you say. "I can't imagine The Man Who is Always Alone being willing to accept anything other than to to always be alone. Why did you do it if you knew it was futile?"

"Why do we do anything?" says The Man From the East with a sly smile. "All things are futile. Why do we try to keep ourselves alive when we will one day die anyway? Futility is never a reason not to do something."

69

When you return to the lake, you're greeted by the sight of something that was not there earlier: A large object, floating on the surface.

For a fleeting moment you're terrified that this object might in some way be connected with MACHINE but on closer inspection, you see a shirtless, grey-bearded man in a woollen hat on board.

The Man From the East bows deeply before you. "It seems I owe you a sincere apology for wasting your time. If we had stayed here, The Fisherman would have found us anyway."

"It's fine," you say. "Despite everything, I enjoyed our excursion. It was nice to learn that there are giant land animals out here that are stronger than us, yet somehow fear us and allow us to eat them."

"Well I am glad to have provided you something of an education," The Man From the East says. "But now that you have found The Fisherman, I believe it is time for me to go."

"You're not going to stay?" You look from him to the distant figure of The Fisherman upon the floating object and wonder if there is some sort of unspoken hostility between them, just as seemed to be the case between him and The Frenchman and perhaps even between him and The Man Who is Always Alone.

192

"I have my own techniques for catching fish and my own ways of preparing them. The Fisherman insists upon cooking the fish before he eats it; I prefer to eat it raw, just as nature intended."

"I see..." you say, not entirely convinced by the explanation but you choose not to press him further. "Well it was nice meeting you" —The words are out before you even realise how blasphemous such a statement would be to the teachings of MACHINE— "and I wish you well."

The Man From the East smiles and bows at you, before turning and marching purposefully into the distance.

Your stomach growls again and you walk to the edge of the lake, desperately hoping that The Fisherman is less protective of his food supply than The Man Who is Always Alone was.

70

The wind blows again, causing the water to ripple. It's one thing to read about rushing air while living your entire life aboard a space station, it's another thing entirely to experience it. You think about your ancient ancestors on the Old Planet and wonder how they coped in such a tempestuous environment.

You shyly wave at The Fisherman to gain his attention and he grins at you. Immediately, the object that he's floating on changes course and starts drifting toward you. Nervously you take a step backwards, uncertain of the temperament of this man or the true nature of the object upon which he stands.

He flashes you another broad, wide smile as his floating object reaches the shore. "Greetings, friend!"

"Um... hello," you say. Years of psychological conditioning on the *Joie de Vivre* has rendered you automatically suspicious of

193

strangers, no matter how friendly they appear to be. "Are you the one they call 'The Fisherman'?"

"I suppose I am," he says with a nod. "I'm not sure it's a moniker which I'd have chosen myself, though I suppose there are worse things people could call me... Well anyway, what can I do for you, my friend?"

"I was told you might be able to help me catch some of the fish I saw in the river," you say. "I recently escaped from the *Joie de Vivre* and I haven't eaten in days!"

"Yes, you look as if you're wasting away..." says The Fisherman. "Well... why don't you hop aboard? There's no shortage of fish 'round these parts!"

He gestures for you to come toward him and, nervously, you step onto the floating object. At first it feels incredibly unnatural, to be walking about so easily above the water, but for the most part the object feels solid, despite the occasional rocking motion.

"I'm guessing you've never been on a boat before?" says The Fisherman with a laugh, grabbing you by the arm when he sees you about to lose your balance. "Not that this is much of a boat. Barely even a raft! But this is how our ancestors used to cross the endless waters of the Old Planet, so it's said."

You try to imagine what that would have looked like. An endless lake, stretching from horizon to horizon, with your ancestors confined to tiny vessels like these, constructed from the flattened remains of dead trees.

"In a way, the *Joie de Vivre* is just a very large version of one of these, isn't it?" you say. "Or at least, that's
what I thought it was before I escaped..."

"Yes, I suppose it was!" says The Fisherman. "A big boat was called a 'ship' and we were all told that the *Joie de Vivre* was a ship that travelled through the void of space the same way that our ancestors travelled across the oceans..."

You stare off into the distance. Although it's now extremely small and extremely far away, you can faintly see the tall white shape of one of the towers of the *Joie de Vivre*.

"But it was all a lie, wasn't it?" you say. "It's weird to know that all my life I thought I was travelling through space but really I was underground, trapped on a single planet the entire time..."

"You *were* still travelling through space," says The Fisherman, "because planets travel through space too. The lie was that MACHINE was the one in control. We were told that MACHINE had a plan, a destination in mind—the reality was that MACHINE was as much a passenger as the rest of us."

As the boat floats its way back into the centre of the lake, The Fisherman walks to the edge and crouches down, looking at the water.

"It's very deep down there. In this lake, there are fish so large and vicious that they could eat a man whole, most likely without even needing to chew! If we fall in, we're as good as dead," he says. "And yet... that's where we all came from—the water."

"What do you mean?"

"Evolution. That's where life on the Old Planet emerged. Life began in the water and then over millions of years evolved into land dwelling animals, including us. Yet if we ever tried returning to the water, we'd die. Sometimes I wonder if the same thing would happen were we ever to return to the Old Planet..."

"I thought humans were all created by MACHINE?" you say. "I thought MACHINE created humans so that humans would one day create MACHINE... an eternal loop; one of the great mysteries of life, like the great mystery of how the future and the past are both infinite?"

The Fisherman snorts as he grabs a brown rod with a long string attached to it. "You only believe that because that's what MACHINE and MACHINE's worshippers taught you to believe. But do you really think it's true, given everything else that MACHINE has lied about?"

"I suppose you're right," you say. "But I suppose we might never know the truth anyway…"

"Here—" The Fisherman hands you the rod, then sits down at the edge of the boat. His bare feet dangle over the side, sometimes brushing the surface as the boat rocks gently beneath you. "Watch what I'm doing. This is how you catch a fish…"

You stare at the rod, trying to decipher the mechanism by which it could capture a fish. Are you supposed to wrap the string around the fish like a small noose? Or beat it to death with the wooden end? Or—

"There's a hook at the end here, see?" The Fisherman says, pointing at a small metal curve with a very sharp ending. And if you attach bait to the end" —He affixes something small and squishy to the hook— "it will gain the attention of the fish, they'll bite the hook and all you've gotta do is reel them in! Then you've got yourself some lunch!"

"You make it sound so easy."

"Some days are easier than others. The challenge is catching the big fish… you probably won't reel in anything huge with the old rod I've given you. But once you get the hang of it it… hoo boy! You should have seen the beast that I caught once…"

You glance down at the swirling, rippling blue void below the boat. "There are *beasts* down here? As in… animals?"

"Well… I meant a very big fish. But there probably *are* beasts down there too… creatures more terrifying than anything we could imagine. If we go in the water, they eat us. Our job is to get them out of the water so that *we* can be the ones who eat *them*!"

71

The first time you get a bite, you're so surprised that you almost stumble overboard but luckily The Fisherman catches you before you fall.

 Soon enough, you have a whole bucket full of small fish that you've caught.

Maybe it's because they're such ugly creatures or maybe it's because they were stupid enough to fall for so obvious a ruse as you placing food on the end of a sharp hook, but you feel no remorse over the prospect of killing and devouring these slimy grey ovoids.

You wonder, briefly, whether this is how MACHINE views humans: as ugly, stupid creatures that fall for its ruses and therefore deserve to be tortured, killed and devoured.

Perhaps, you muse, MACHINE doesn't even register humanity as being alive, just as you look into the dead black eyes of the fish who will become your future meal, unable to conceive of it having ever been in any way conscious.

Once in a while you catch something which The Fisherman immediately tosses away.

"That one's poisonous," he says, as he throws a colourful one with sharp spiny protrusions back into the lake. "You eat *that* thing and you'll vomit out your own stomach!"

His warning disturbs you. If some of the fish in the lake are poisonous, then it means they can kill you just as easily as feed you.

197

And that means that catching your own food is no safer than relying on MACHINE for sustenance.

"Alright, I think that's enough," says The Fisherman, pointing to your bucket full of fish—some still wriggling, barely alive. "You don't want them to go bad so I'd say we call it a day and head back to shore."

Your stomach growls. The closer you get to finally being able to eat, the more painful your pangs of hunger become.

72

"You know, I've been meaning to ask you..." you say to The Fisherman as he steers the boat toward the shore, "How did you get here? I've met a few others who escaped from the *Joie de Vivre* but I never asked you what your story was."

"Ha! Well... the short answer is that I wanted to leave and so I left," he says, staring into the distance.

"Really? As easy as that? MACHINE just let you go?"

"Well not quite..." The Fisherman removes his woollen hat, revealing that he too has the word "INSANE" branded onto his forehead. "I was tortured for a while before I finally made the decision to leave."

"I'm surprised more people don't leave, to be honest," you say. "I wonder what keeps them there?"

"Love," replies The Fisherman. "Friends. Families. Social connections. Social obligations. MACHINE's torture isn't so bad unless you're alone."

You look at him, surprised. "I thought everyone was alone? I thought that MACHINE decreed that we must all must be isolated?"

198

"Isolation has nothing to do with MACHINE and everything to do with the people around you," The Fisherman says. "See me? I like people! I liked the people in my sector and even when I —" He trails off suddenly as if struck by a painful memory.

"The Man From the East described you as a 'man of war'," you say. "He said that you were similar to The Man Who is Always Alone in that regard. That MACHINE forced you to kill other people..."

"Yes, that's true. In my younger years I *was* forced to kill people," says The Fisherman slowly. "And yes, that disturbs me greatly, even now, but that's not the reason why I left. To be honest, I had quite a good life on the *Joie de Vivre*. The things I had to do, they never ate away at me the same way they ate away at The Man Who is Always Alone."

You're almost at the shore now but neither of you acknowledges it. The Fisherman instead continues with his story.

"I've never heard of anyone who would describe the *Joie de Vivre* as being 'a good life' before," you say.

"Well, perhaps my life was uncommon or perhaps yours was, but for a while things were pretty decent," The Fisherman says. "Sure, there was the usual bullshit. MACHINE would still torture me at random and the strong and cruel continued to prey upon the weak but it was very rare for people to ever fuck with *me* directly. I guess they all knew how many people I've killed and in their eyes that makes me 'strong'.

"So for the most part, I had a great life, great friends and great lovers too. Beautiful women used to throw themselves at me! MACHINE ensured I never went hungry and there was never any shortage of sEDAtIVE if I wanted it. Hell, there was even HeDonia in the mix from time to time!

"But the good times didn't last forever. One by one, MACHINE began to kill the people I loved most. And then one day I discovered that I was alone. Before then I'd always been able to ignore MACHINE's torture, but with nothing left to distract me I felt it all, and those electric shocks just grew worse and worse—"

"So you left?"

"Well first I made the mistake of mentioning in passing that I was thinking of leaving..." he says with a bitter sigh. "And so the quacks at the infirmary all got wind of it, and *this*—" He removes his woollen hat to reveal the word 'INSANE' branded on his forehead "—was the result."

"But eventually you escaped?"

"Sure," he says. "I was in so much pain and by that point I was so alone that I didn't care what happened if I jumped out the airlock. So one day I was just walked straight through the guards, took no shit from them, opened the door and..."

He gestures around at your surroundings. "Well here we are! What do you know—everything I ever knew turned out to be a lie!"

You shake your head sympathetically. "Well, nevertheless, I'm sorry you had to go through all that... you know, losing the people you loved and everything..."

"Don't be!" he booms, his cheerful demeanour suddenly returning. "There's good weather, good fishing, good people... good times all 'round out here! You can't control what MACHINE does to you, you can't control what *anyone* does to you but what you *can* control is your attitude and in the grand scheme of things... I'd say I've got more to be happy about than I do to be sad about!"

73

Having grown used to the perpetual bobbing motion on The Fisherman's boat, once you return to shore you find that the ground now feels unnaturally hard and solid. It feels doubly unusual for you to refer to the ground here as "solid", given how soft it is compared to the hard metallic floors of the *Joie de Vivre*.

"We'll need to make a fire," says The Fisherman as the pair of you trot through the grass in search of a place to set up camp. "You can use it to cook the fish, plus it'll give you some warmth tonight. I'll bet you need some rest after the day you've had!"

The light does seem to be diminishing though you're not sure how the day/night cycle works outside of the *Joie de Vivre*. The books you read about the Old Planet suggest that day and night were governed by the star that the planet orbited, though you have no idea how this worked in practice.

"It gets cold out here sometimes. Especially when it's dark," The Fisherman continues. "It rains from time to time too, although I don't think we'll be seeing that for a least a few days."

"Rain? You mean water falls from the sky here? I thought that was just a myth for children!"

"Oh it's real and yeah it's great if you're thirsty or trying to grow something but after a while it's just a pain in the arse. And if you're out in the boat when it hits hard, it can damn near kill you!" The Fisherman says. "Sometimes it's like dealing with MACHINE all over again..."

You look up at the stars. They seem to twinkle, even move, as if they're alive out there in the void. You wonder whether this is the first time you've ever seen real stars. Are these the same stars you saw from the porthole windows? Or were those stars just another image generated by MACHINE to deceive you?

You notice that the giant orb—the moon—is starting to disappear behind the jagged triangular silhouette of the mountains on the horizon and as it sinks the world around you dims to almost black.

"Is there a star here?" you ask. "As in, the planet we're on, wherever we are—does it orbit a bright star, like the Old Planet did?"

"I'm still not sure how things work on this planet, to be honest. Doesn't seem to be much logic to it if you ask me," replies The Fisherman. "But time here seems to be divided in three. There's a bright light in the sky sometimes, maybe it's a star, maybe it's something else but it's very bright and when it's up it gets hot. Most of the time it's more like what you've been seeing since you got here—there's a dimmer orb in the sky, like a moon or something and it's never so dark that you can't see but the stars are always visible. And then there's the night, when it's just black."

"So I guess it's not that different to the shift times back on the ship, is it?" you say.

"Guess not. Maybe MACHINE was inspired by nature. Who knows?"

The Fisherman leads you to a field, in the centre of which are several stones arranged into a circle, surrounding a large bundle of sticks.

"Do you know how to make fire?" he asks.

You shake your head. The only times you've seen fire have been when MACHINE was using it to torture or kill people. It's never crossed your mind that fire might be something humans could create or control.

"It's not hard. You just need some sticks and the right kind of stones."

He kneels down, picking up two stones from the ground—seemingly at random—and starts vigorously grinding them against each other. After several minutes, there's a spark, which spreads to the sticks, growing first into a small ember and then into a roaring flame, contained within the circle of stones.

"Pass me one of your fish," The Fisherman says and you hand him the whole bucket. He pulls a few out and places them onto a metallic grate that looks like it came from one of the air ducts in the *Joie de Vivre*. He then places the grate onto two towers of stone so that the flames reach up underneath and gently lick the fish.

"Ideally we'd gut the fish before grilling them, but you don't look like you can hold starvation at bay long enough for that..." The Fisherman says. "The Man From the East sometimes eats fish as they are but... I dunno, I like it better this way. It tastes better."

"I'm not sure I'm worried about the taste," you say. "I'm just grateful to have enough sustenance to last me another day."

The Fisherman chuckles. "Well that's understandable in your position. But in time you'll learn that life is about more than just survival. There's no point in eating if you can't take pleasure from the experience.

"You ever meet The Frenchman? Now *he's* a guy who knows how to take pleasure in eating! He's very particular about everything... he went a bit mad one day about a lobster I caught but that guy can turn a garden grub into something genuinely enjoyable to eat!"

"You guys are talking about pleasure, are you?" asks a sudden, unfamiliar voice from behind you.

You turn around, startled to see two strangers standing there, backlit by the stars and the setting moon.

"You've got to be careful with pleasure," one of the strangers continues. "Too much of it can get you into trouble."

"Yeah, yeah!" says the other, waving his arms around erratically. "It can get you *killed*, man! MACHINE or not it's dangerous shit, ya know? Pleasure is HeDonia; HeDonia is pure distilled pleasure. It's fucking *wild*, man!"

You pause and size up the two strangers. The first is a very large man with a very small head that looks as if it's been attached to the wrong body. He has very long, light brown hair which almost obscures the fact that he is wearing spectacles—an invention that MACHINE only rarely supplies people with.

You notice that the second man is also wearing spectacles, but his are much larger and tinted yellow, obscuring his eyes. He's also a lot smaller and scrawnier than the first stranger.

"If you two are here for dinner, you'll need to catch your own," says The Fisherman, as he tosses you a hot, slightly charred fish. "Eat up!" he adds to you.

You take a tentative bite into the cooked fish. It's piping hot and you immediately burn your mouth, a sensation that, though you're more than used to, still catches you off guard. You hadn't expected that eating would be torturous in this place too.

"Woah, easy there!" says the larger, long-haired stranger as he sits down next to you. "You should probably wait for it to cool down a bit before you chow down on it, ya know?"

"This person was starving," The Fisherman explains. "Just escaped from the *Joie de Vivre...*"

"Oh, well, in that case, don't let me distract you, dig in!" says the stranger. "But believe me, it gets better than just flame-grilled fish around here! You'll be amazed how much good food there is out here... and all that pleasure will be too much to handle, probably."

The Fisherman tosses you another hot, charred fish once you've reduced the first one down to nothing more than bone. Despite having burned your mouth, this is definitely one of the better meals you've ever eaten—it's hot and it feels filling, maybe even nutritious.

As you consume a second, third and soon fourth cooked fish, you start to tune back into the conversation, noticing the stark contrast between the way the two men who have just joined you speak.

The larger man, despite his almost intimidating size, speaks in a gentle lilt, his voice soft and soothing, though every word he speaks is precise.

The smaller man, by contrast, speaks in rapid, occasionally incoherent bursts of frenetic energy, spewing out hundreds of words per sentence in quick succession before suddenly returning to a strange silence, where he sits and rocks uneasily, like he can't keep still.

"So um... do you guys all know each other?" you ask, now feeling satiated enough to rejoin the conversation.

"I think it would be fair to say that I know *of* The Fisherman but we're not directly acquainted," says the larger man. "I owe him a debt of gratitude as I do almost anyone in this place but he's a man of the sea and I prefer much more terrestrial pursuits."

"What about you?" you say to the smaller man.

"Who me? No way man! I don't know *any* of you people, man, I'm just in it for shits and giggles man, hey!" He turns suddenly to the larger man. "You're a smart guy man, you know all about HeDonia right, you might know how it's made, I could go for some fucking HeDonia out here, fuck fish, fuck you, fuck—"

The larger man shushes the smaller man and turns to you.

"Sorry about him. He's a fundamentally decent person but he's also a HeDonia addict. I was addicted to HeDonia for a while myself until it stopped having an effect. That's how I got this—"

He pushes his long hair back, tucking it behind his ears, exposing the word "INSANE" seared into his forehead.

"They tried to brand *him* too," the larger man says with a nod toward the smaller one, "but they never successfully held him down long enough. They say he bolted and ran straight for the airlock, leaving a trail of destruction behind him."

"Fuck MACHINE!" the smaller man adds and, as you inspect his face more closely, you notice that he has the word "IN" branded on his forehead, along with what looks to have been an aborted attempt to draw the letter S. "Fuck the *Joie de Vivre* too, man! If MACHINE's gonna hold back on the HeDonia I am *done*, man, I'm like a dot, I'm gone, I'm like a story that's ended, you know what I'm saying?"

His mannerisms put you in mind of some of the more unruly children at the nursery that you once had to deal with. You know from experience that the best thing to do is to make a non-committal noise and maintain eye contact, so that the child—or in this case, the adult HeDonia addict—gets the impression of being understood.

75

Darkness comes, though it's not the pitch black darkness that you used to experience in your private quarters whenever MACHINE cut the lights. If anything, once the moon disappears below the horizon, the stars all grow brighter, while your surroundings continue to be illuminated by the orange glow of the fire.

The smaller man, The Man with Tinted Glasses, makes you a little nervous because of his chaotic and erratic behaviour but the presence of the larger Man with Long Hair seems to have a calming effect on him.

You're desperate for sleep but the idea of falling asleep out in the open, in the presence of other people, feels dangerous. You've seen people killed or even eaten on the *Joie de Vivre* for falling asleep in public.

"You need rest," says The Fisherman. "There's no MACHINE out here to torture you in the night, so you'll be able to rest properly for once. Besides... there's nothing quite like waking up in the morning and remembering that you're free!"

"Pshhh!" snorts The Man with Tinted Glasses. "Sleep is for the weak! I say if you're finally out of that damn place you should party the night away, man! Do you like HeDonia? I can get you some!"

"No thanks," you say. "Besides, half the reason I'm out here is because I developed a tolerance to HeDonia."

You notice The Man with Long Hair perk up as you say that, his intense gaze now fixed firmly upon you.

"It's not the main reason I left," you continue, "but after the first time I tried to escape, they drugged me with some sort of hybrid HeDonia-sEDAtIVE chemical... it worked for a while but then it wore off and I wanted to leave more than ever."

"It's like you're speaking straight from my own experience," says The Man with Long Hair with a knowing smile. "That's almost exactly what happened to me... I tried to escape once and so they drugged me until I was convinced to stay. But then the drugs wore off and the urge to escape returned. They told me I was insane and you know what? I believed them. I let them torture me, do pretty much whatever they wanted to do to me, just as long as it stopped me having the urge to escape. I know it sounds stupid and probably sentimental but I honestly didn't want to leave; in the end it felt more like I was pushed."

"You wanted to stay?" you ask. "Why?"

The Man with Long Hair shrugs. "I guess it's because I didn't know better. We're all raised from birth never to question MACHINE or the ways it tortures us. We're taught that to question MACHINE or to grumble about being in pain is blasphemy. And yes—I truly believed I was blaspheming, that I was somehow deficient for not being able to withstand a life of constant pain and torment. In the end it got so bad that I couldn't resist the temptation to leave, so one night I snuck to the airlock, opened it up and jumped out, no longer caring whether I lived or died..."

You look at the other two as the flames dance and flicker before you. The Fisherman seems to be asleep. The Man with the Tinted Glasses is curled into a ball on the ground and though you can't be one hundred percent sure, he also appears to be unconscious.

"I've met quite a few people since I arrived out here," you say. "And I'm surprised by how many of them seem to have come here by accident, as if they never intended to leave the *Joie de Vivre*. The Man From the East said he basically fell out the airlock while trying to get people's attention; I think this guy" — You gesture at the Man with the Tinted Glasses— "probably never meant to jump out either, he was just desperate for HeDonia; and The Fisherman said he enjoyed his life on the *Joie de Vivre* and left only because all his friends died. I think the only person I've met out here who chose to leave for any reason approaching mine was The Frenchman."

"Oh, don't get the wrong idea—I definitely left by choice," says the Man With the Long Hair. "But, you know, it's always hard to make a rational choice when you don't have the full facts in front of you. For me, the only thing I knew was that I was being tortured and no analgesic was powerful enough to alleviate my suffering. I knew that the only other way to alleviate my suffering was to somehow remove MACHINE from the equation, by placing myself somewhere that MACHINE did not exist— namely, outside of the ship. So my only choices, as far as I could see them, were both bad options."

"Did you ever get to meet MACHINE?" you ask. "You know... in that room beyond the airlock?"

The Man With Long Hair tilts his head at you in surprise.

"Never mind," you say. "I just thought maybe, since we're all here, we all—"

"You actually met MACHINE?" he says with an incredulous gasp. "What, you mean... you actually went to the central control hub?"

"No," you say. "Well... yes, actually, but that was on another occasion which was organised by the priests—"

"*Fuck the priests!*" calls out The Man with Tinted Glasses, revealing that he might not have been as asleep as you'd assumed.

"Ugh, well, anyway... yes, there was an occasion in the central control hub where I was nearly tortured to death as part of some experiment—but that's not what I'm talking about. I'm talking about that room, between the fake airlock and the real one... the white room? That's where I spoke directly with MACHINE."

The Man with the Long Hair narrows his eyes, looking not so much sceptical as surprised.

"That's not... I mean, um, I'm not negating your experience and I don't want to be interpreted as in any way trying to dimin- ish or question your perception of reality but..." The Man with Long Hair stammers a little. "That wasn't my experience. I just opened the airlock, jumped out and then suddenly I was here and, like, holy shit everything I thought I knew was false and that really fucked with me on a fundamental level. Tell me more about this 'white room' you saw?"

You tell him about the white room, the mannequins and your conversation with MACHINE and when you're done, The Man with Long Hair smiles at you.

"That sounds entirely plausible to me," he says. "If you'd already decided you were leaving then of course MACHINE would try to psychologically torture you by pulling all the stops to convince you to stay, including a direct intervention. I never received any intervention because I was always begging MACHINE to convince me that I should stay, only it never did... it just kept on going with the torture until I felt I had no choice but to jump out the airlock while no one was looking."

The Man with Long Hair pauses and glances up at the stars. "Maybe I'm wrong here, but the way I see it is that no one is out here because we actually wanted to be here. We're here because we were pushed by a set of circumstances where life aboard the *Joie de Vivre* became so miserable and unendurable that we decided we were better off leaving, even if it meant dying."

You smile. "I think you're probably right. I only left when the torture became more intense than I could take, when MACHINE started to screw with me not just physically, but mentally as well. It got to a point where I couldn't escape MACHINE anywhere, not even in the privacy of my own mind."

The Man with Long Hair looks at you pensively.

"Have you ever met The Girl Who is Trapped?" he asks.

"I'm not sure," you say. "Is she the one who lives under the river?"

The Man with Long Hair shakes his head. "No, no, that's the Lady Under the River. The Girl Who is Trapped is a different person but I think you'd like her. She went through something similar to what we went through. In the morning I'll introduce you to her."

You nod. "Sounds good. But why is she called 'The Girl Who is Trapped'?"

"Well that's the unusual thing about her..." The Man with Long Hair replies. "She escaped the *Joie de Vivre* but she didn't *fully* escape. MACHINE managed to trap her inside a prison of glass. We've all tried to break her out, of course, but none of us can. So she's out of the *Joie de Vivre* and she's no longer being tortured... but she's also still imprisoned and we don't know any way to get her out of there."

Despite everything you've already been through, this horrifies you. "MACHINE can do that? MACHINE can still torture us like that... even out here?"

The Man with Long Hair gives you a fatalistic shrug.

"Well I look forward to meeting her, anyway..." you say as you lie yourself down on the soft grass, unable to ignore your exhaustion any longer.

"Have a good night, my friend," says the Man with the Long Hair and it's the last thing you hear before you feel yourself drifting downwards, into the ground, as if you're experiencing a strange, inverted version of the effects of sEDAtIVE.

76

You're awoken, not by screaming klaxons, but by the sensation of bright light and warmth. Your sleep was mostly dreamless but you weren't woken up at all in the night nor subject to any arbitrary electric shocks.

You open your eyes, which take time to adjust to the light—it's *very* bright out here, bright in a way you've never experienced before. There's something in the sky, like a giant lightbulb, but it's so bright that you can't directly look at it without burning your eyes. You wonder whether this giant light was something that MACHINE designed as a new means to torture you.

"Morning!" says the Man with the Long Hair brightly, crouching down near you.

You slowly sit up. The fire has been extinguished—all that remains now is a bundle of charred sticks surrounded by the circle of stones.

The Fisherman is gone but the Man with the Tinted Glasses remains, crouching quietly next to the stone circle, looking into the distance and rubbing the side of his head.

"Holy crap, man, what was going on last night?" he says before his eyes rest upon you. "I'm sorry, I don't think we've met?"

He offers you his hand to shake and you nervously take it. This morning he seems remarkably lucid, even calm, almost as if he's a completely different person.

"You *have* met," the Man with the Long Hair tells him, "and if you hadn't taken so much HeDonia you'd probably be able to *remember* having met..."

The Man with Tinted Glasses wrinkles his face at The Man with Long Hair's admonishment. "Well, what's the point of living if you can't enjoy yourself? HeDonia is as good a reason to live as anything, right?"

"You're just lucky it still has an effect on you," says The Man with Long Hair. "What if you develop a tolerance, like we have?

What will you do then? There are no more airlocks to jump out of here..."

The Man with Tinted Glasses sighs and shakes his head. "Good god man, it's every day with this crap... you used to be cool, man! What the hell happened to you? Well... anyway... what's on the agenda for today?"

"We're going to visit The Girl Who is Trapped," says The Man with Long Hair. "You're welcome to join us if you want but—"

"Sounds boring," says The Man with Tinted Glasses. "Maybe I'll go bug The Fisherman. Did you know every time you taste something good your brain produces the same chemicals as in HeDonia? Soon enough I'll figure it out, I'll make some of my own. And then what? MACHINE is fucking *nothing* after that, right?"

Neither you nor The Man with Long Hair respond.

"You know what your problem is?" The Man with Tinted Glasses gets to his feet, scowling at The Man with Long Hair. "You're addicted to pain! You finally got away from MACHINE because you think you hated how much it tormented you and what do you? You sit around all day moping and self-flagellating like you're trying to do to yourself what MACHINE used to do. It's fucked. You're free now, you should god-damn enjoy yourself!"

"Too much pleasure leads to pain," says The Man with Long Hair. "Some day the HeDonia will wear off. And when it happens... just remember that I tried to warn you!"

"Whatever man, I'm out!" says The Man with Tinted Glasses.

He quickly stumbles away, kicking up a small cloud of dust and dirt behind him.

The Man with Long Hair turns to you. "How are you feeling? You ready to go and meet The Girl Who is Trapped?"

"I think so," you say.

"You sure? You don't want to eat something first?"

You glance around—there's still some fish left in the bucket but with no fire you're not sure how you'd cook them and you don't feel hungry enough to eat them raw. Not only that, they're starting to smell pungent and unpleasant in the hot sun.

"I'll be fine."

"You could try this?" The Man with Long Hair reaches into his pocket and produces something square and sticky. "I try to keep these hidden from the Man with the Tinted Glasses but it's a kind of food that's laced with small amounts of HeDonia. You shouldn't eat it every day, but if you only do it once in a while it'll give you a boost. And after what you've been through... I'd say you could benefit from it."

He breaks the small square in half and hands some to you.

"Don't worry, you won't go crazy. It's mainly just sugar but there's enough HeDonia to give you a small hit of dopamine or serotonin or... you know, one of the pleasure chemicals in your brain."

"Were you a medic or something?" you ask, gingerly taking some of the small sticky square. "You seem to know an awful lot about this stuff..."

"No, I just liked to read a lot and once I found a bunch of old instruction manuals about human biology..." He takes a bite out of the sticky square.

You do the same and immediately there's a head-rush. For a moment you think you're experiencing a Corrective Shock, localised within your mouth but you quickly realise you're just overwhelmed by the sweetness of what you're eating.

"Not bad, right?" The Man with Long Hair says. "If we did this all the time our teeth would fall out but if you can learn to

214

handle pleasure in moderation, you'll be fine. I tried to explain all this to The Man with Tinted Glasses but he just doesn't listen. HeDonia doesn't work if you use it all the time. No form of pleasure does. Our brains just aren't wired that way."

"So you think that's why I became immune to it?"

"Probably. And probably the same with me," he says. "But that's not to say that there isn't also something fundamentally wrong with the *Joie de Vivre* and MACHINE. So don't blame yourself."

He stands and as he does you're struck again by the sheer size of the guy—he towers over you and is shockingly muscular... yet his head is so small compared to the rest of his body.

"Is it going to be a long journey?" you ask.

"No," he replies. "She isn't far away. She's near the *Joie de Vivre*."

You nod, ignoring a knot of fear in your stomach at the prospect of once again being anywhere near the towering concrete monolith where you were imprisoned and tortured for so many years.

77

You arrive on a barren, rocky plain, darkened by the shadow of one of the *Joie de Vivre*'s towering white spires. As you draw closer, you see the structure is embedded in the side of a mountain, probably extending beneath the very rocks that you are walking on right now.

Underneath your feet, the last vestige of human civilisation is still down there: toiling, screaming, being tortured—all while clinging to the lie that they're soaring through the stars toward some imagined salvation.

215

You turn to The Man with Long Hair. "How long has it been since you escaped?"

"I'm not sure. I'd say it's been a few years. I'm one of the newer escapees. The Frenchman claims he's been out here for over a century although, well..."

"If you could go back, would you?"

The Man with Long Hair shoots you a look and you realise he's staring at the "INSANE" branding on your forehead.

"What I meant was... you'd agree that life is better out here, right? Outside of the *Joie de Vivre?*"

The Man with Long Hair looks momentarily into the distance. "It's hard to say. Probably, yes. I personally wouldn't want to go back but that's entirely subjective and based on my experiences and feelings. I don't know if I could *objectively* claim that life is better out here."

You chuckle a little. "That's certainly not the answer I was expecting..."

"Well, I think about people like The Fisherman or the Man From the East whose lives aboard the *Joie de Vivre* were fairly good for the most part. And there is more security on the ship... everyone knows their place, they all know precisely where they belong, even though their lives are a massive pile of shit."

"I see," you say. "Because I was thinking of all the people trapped inside the *Joie de Vivre* right now. They're probably right underneath us. And I was thinking... what if we were able to rescue them? Free them? Bring them out here?"

"I get it," The Man with Long Hair replies. "I've had the same thought in the past but the thing is, people in there... they wouldn't listen. Most of them like it there. I don't just mean they *think* they like it... I mean they genuinely like it. I know *I* did. I was a genuine believer in all of MACHINE's lies; I genuinely believed that suffering was good, that kindness and compassion were evil... all the crap that we were taught.

"And it's not easy to let go of that. It takes one hell of an outsider to wind up in the situation we're in now. And the thing about people like us is... we think we're so smart because we see through the lies and we know that there's a world outside of the *Joie de Vivre* but we're also idiots because once we get here we've got no idea what to do or how to function without MACHINE. It's just survivorship bias—we did something that should have gotten us killed, we survived it and now we think we're so enlightened and great because we're still alive when we should be dead."

You make a non-committal noise as he leads you over another ridge. In the middle distance, something gleams—a towering crystal cage, solitary among the rocks, catching the sunlight and throwing it back at you.

"Well, there she is..." says The Man with Long Hair.

As you approach, you can indeed see a girl inside the glass, sitting down in an otherwise well-furnished room—there's a chair, several appliances, a stack of books, even different rooms from what you can see.

The Man with the Long Hair gives her a friendly wave and she stands, walking right up to the glass.

"What's this, then?" she asks. "Someone else here to try and rescue me?"

Your eyes are drawn to her hand, which is wrapped in a blood-soaked rag. Noticing your gaze, she explains, "I tried to break the glass again this morning. I'm no closer to escape but this time a small shard broke off and cut me."

"I'm sorry to hear that..." you say. "It must be terrible, being trapped inside like that..."

She shrugs. "Honestly? It's not so bad. Trying to escape has become something of a game for me, lately. If I ever actually succeeded and left this glass cage, I don't think I'd know what to do with myself."

"How do you survive in there?" you say, glancing around at the various furnishings.

"How do you think I survive?" she says, her non-bleeding hand on her hips. "It's all from MACHINE."

"So you're still inside the *Joie de Vivre*?" you ask.

The Girl Who is Trapped shakes her head. "No. This is my own private prison. My own private torture chamber. I don't get electrocuted like I did back then and I'm always well taken care of. I can do absolutely anything I want in here... except touch another person."

"Is that something you want to do?"

"I think so," she says. "I think that might be what most people want. But MACHINE divides us and sets us against each other. It teaches us to mistrust and hate each other. And in my case... it imprisoned me in glass so I can never reach out to anyone."

You think for a moment. "There's another woman I saw here, similar to you—"

"The Lady Under the River? Yes I knew of her. In some ways she inspired me to leave," says The Girl Who is Trapped. "But the difference between us was that she left the *Joie de Vivre* to escape from people. I left because I wanted to connect with people... I wanted to meet people outside who weren't as brutal or dishonest as the people aboard the *Joie de Vivre*."

She brushes her hair aside and you're drawn immediately to the "INSANE" branding hidden beneath her fringe.

"But how did you end up trapped like this?"

"Because I made a deal with MACHINE," she says. "MACHINE revealed itself to me in a—"

"In a white room? Where there were multiple plastic dummies speaking with one voice?"

She widens her eyes in surprise. "Yes! Exactly! When I left, MACHINE offered me a deal.

"It knew I wasn't going to stay because it knew I'd already seen what happens to the people it deems incurably insane" — Your mind flashes immediately to the dead-eyed, limbless people in the infirmary, constantly being tortured— "but MACHINE said that it could keep me safe in the outside world, free from torture, if I agreed to forego human connection forever."

"And you agreed to it?"

She shrugs. "At the time I thought it was people who did all the torturing. It hadn't really dawned on me that MACHINE was behind it all. Also, I was traumatised and in shock and not really capable of making a rational decision."

You glance up at one of the towers—part of the *Joie de Vivre* itself, half-buried in the mountain. Is MACHINE watching you right now? Does it hear your conversation?

"I suppose everyone else has already tried to free you?" you say, turning back to The Girl Who is Trapped.

"Yes," says The Girl Who is Trapped. "And it's very kind of you all to try but, honestly, I think I've found some sort of peace here. It's not *exactly* what I wanted but it's much better than what I had before."

You glance from her to The Man with Long Hair and back again.

"So what you're saying is... even though you're imprisoned here alone, you'd still never go back to the *Joie de Vivre*? Even if that were an option?"

The Girl Who is Trapped shakes her head. "No. I think I'm happy here."

78

"Does anyone ever go back?" you ask. "After leaving?"

"Yes," says The Girl Who is Trapped. "There have been people who have returned to the *Joie de Vivre* after escaping."

The Man with Long Hair's jaw drops. "So the rumours are true!"

"I knew one man who did it. They called him 'The Man with Seventy-Five Names'. He came out here, looked around, learned that everything MACHINE taught him in the *Joie de Vivre* was false but then he went back inside."

"Why did he do that?"

"The people who return?" She shrugs. "They have many motivations, I suppose. Loneliness is the biggest one—it's no easier connecting with people out here than it was in there, or so I'm told. For others it's a kind of righteous crusade... they go back believing that they can wage war on MACHINE, foment an uprising and free the human race."

"And this 'Man with Seventy-Five Names'...?"

"I'm not sure what happened to him. I don't know why he left or why he came back although I heard from somebody that when he returned, MACHINE gave him an endless supply of HeDonia and sEDAtIVE in exchange for his silence. And so he spent the rest of his life sedating himself until he died."

"I would have thought MACHINE would just have him killed?"

"I honestly think MACHINE prefers to toy with people than kill them," says The Girl Who is Trapped. "Although there was another man, I think they called him 'The Man who Loved Horses' or something ridiculous... well *he* never escaped but he stood at the door of the airlock and looked out, saw this world, saw that the *Joie de Vivre* wasn't what it purported to be—"

"And what happened to him?"

"Oh, I've heard this story!" says The Man with Long Hair, butting in. "The rumour I heard was that MACHINE fulfilled his every wish and all of his dreams came true! There was no more torture for him, he had an endless supply of food and HeDonia and people started to really love him!"

You look at him incredulously. "You mean... MACHINE really *would* reward someone for not escaping? That MACHINE keeps its promises sometimes?"

"Well, it's possible," The Man with Long Hair says with a sigh. "But I also heard that six months afterwards, MACHINE randomly killed the guy, just when he was finally starting to enjoy life on the *Joie de Vivre.*"

"In my experience, MACHINE doesn't lie," says The Girl Who is Trapped. "Humans lie. MACHINE doesn't know what's true from what isn't. It just does what it was programmed to do. The problem is that whoever programmed MACHINE was either psychotic or extremely stupid. Or both."

"I don't think that's correct," you say. "MACHINE *definitely* lies."

"Not knowingly," says The Girl Who is Trapped. "MACHINE can't perceive us. It can't even perceive itself. Everything it does is entirely random and it's we who interpret it as truth or lying, good or evil."

A silence follows. You stare out over the rocky plain, taking in the jagged shape of distant mountains. A cold wind lashes at the back of your neck. Something shifts—not in the air, but inside you. A low, familiar vibration begins at the base of your skull. The Man with Long Hair goes pale. His eyes meet yours, wide and full of dread. He knows. Before you can speak, your knees buckle. A searing bolt of electricity floods your body—a Corrective Shock, precise and merciless. Your vision whites out. You taste metal. Blood bursts from your nose, and bile surges up your throat.

After several minutes, the electrocution ceases and you're left lying face down, on the cold hard ground, the familiar scent of your burning hair now thick in the air.

You pull yourself to your knees, noticing the fresh puddle of blood and vomit on the ground. You sense you may have voided your bowels too.

"What... happened?" you rasp desperately. "I thought I was free! I thought that I was safe from MACHINE out here!"

79

"You still have your Chip," says The Man with Long Hair, his fingers brushing gently against the back of your neck. "For as long as you still have it, MACHINE can do whatever it wants to you, whenever it wants."

"The Chip! Oh... I forgot all about it..." you wheeze, still doubled over in pain. You press a hand to your throat, swallowing bile.

"There is a group of people on the other side of the mountain who can remove your Chip for you," says The Girl Who is Trapped. "I met them several months ago, after they were ejected en masse from the *Joie de Vivre*. They said that they planned to build a new society, free from MACHINE."

"How do I find them?" you ask.

"I'm not sure exactly where they are," The Girl Who is Trapped says, "but I know they went in that direction, over the mountains."

"Is there any other way to remove the Chip?" you say, finally getting to your feet. Your legs are still a little shaky but you're able to stand.

You glance at The Man with Long Hair but he shakes his head. "Around here? No way. None of us have the dexterity or the medical training necessary to perform such a procedure."

You look from him to The Girl Who is Trapped. "How were *your* Chips removed?"

The Girl Who is Trapped smiles grimly. "I removed mine myself. It was very painful and I nearly died from the loss of blood."

She gestures to a pile of scarlet rags on a nearby shelf. "See those red towels? They were white before I tried to remove my Chip..."

You grimace and turn to The Man with Long Hair.

"I went over the mountain and and found someone there who could safely remove it for me," he says. "There are entire societies on the other side, comprised of all the people who MACHINE ejected from the *Joie de Vivre*. I'm sure you'll be able to find someone who can remove your Chip."

"Very well," you say, "I'll go over the mountains and rid myself once and for all from MACHINE's control!"

The Man with Long Hair folds his arms. "Sounds like a good plan. I hope you have a safe trip."

"You're not coming?"

He looks uneasily toward the jagged shapes in the distance. "No. I've chosen to stay on this side of the mountain. Most of us who live on this side of the mountain are, I think, people who prefer solitude or else who experience loneliness on such a deep level that being around people would only exacerbate it, rather than cure it."

You look to The Girl Who is Trapped and say, in what you hope is a jocular tone, "I don't suppose you're able to join me?"

She smirks. "Even if I could go, I don't think I would."

"But didn't you say that you longed to connect with others?"

"I do," she says, "but as I said—it's no easier to connect with others outside of the *Joie de Vivre* than within it. I've seen the types of people who settle on the other side of the mountain and most of them are just as cruel, dishonest and deceptive as MACHINE itself."

You look back at The Man with Long Hair. "And there's absolutely no other way for me to remove my Chip?"

"There's no safe way," he says. "I mean yes, you could do it yourself, but—"

The Girl Who is Trapped turns around, lifting up her hair to reveal a very large and infected wound on the back of her neck.

"In an ironic way, if I wasn't trapped here by MACHINE, I'd have probably died by now from my injuries. This wound would probably lead to all manner of diseases if I was ever exposed directly to the elements."

You take the point. If you truly want to be free from MACHINE, if you truly want to never again be subjected to a random Corrective Shock, you'll have to journey over the distant mountains and find someone on the other side who will remove your Chip in a way that won't kill you.

"Then... I suppose this is goodbye, isn't it?" you say wistfully, as you look toward the mountains.

The Man with Long Hair gently rests his hand on your shoulder. "I don't want to tell you what to expect over there because every experience is unique. But some methods of removing the Chip are more painful than others and not everyone who acts like your friend will be your friend."

"Don't trust others, got it!" you say. "I only just left the *Joie de Vivre*, so mistrusting others is still second nature to me..."

"I'm not saying not to trust *anyone* over there. There are some very good and decent people over the mountain. But don't trust everyone," he says. "The people on this side of the mountain? We're your friends. We understand you. We care about you. We love you.

"But over there? Well, it's worth remembering that not every torture on the *Joie de Vivre* was committed by MACHINE..."

There's a sudden chill in the air; a cold wind blowing from the jagged icy peaks in the distance.

"Will you still be here when I return?" you ask.

The Man with Long Hair gives you a sad smile. "We'll always be here whenever you need to find us."

"I couldn't leave even if I wanted to," adds The Girl Who is Trapped.

You close your eyes and as you do, you notice that the whole time you've been trembling. You've spent your entire life more or less alone and yet, for the first time ever, the thought of leaving people behind and returning to that loneliness terrifies you.

But you know this is a journey you must make. This is one final ordeal to overcome in order to truly win your freedom from MACHINE.

80

The air grows much colder as you reach the mountains and you wish you had some thicker clothing to shield yourself from the cruel, howling wind.

There's ice on the ground and the rocks are dusted with a soft white substance that the tales of the Old Planet referred to as "snow".

You can't bear to look back. You know that you could probably still see the glass prison of The Girl Who is Trapped from here, perhaps the silhouette of The Man with Long Hair too. But you refuse to turn around—you don't want to be tempted to run back to them, to trade your permanent freedom from MACHINE for the temporary comfort of their companionship.

MACHINE can still torture you out here. That's a fact and a very dangerous one: MACHINE has been known to deliver extremely high voltage Corrective Shocks—including deadly ones from time to time—and you know that you could easily be killed

228

at any moment if MACHINE wills it. It's possible that MACHINE might do that just to spite you, to punish you for your rebellion against it. And now that you're out here, for maybe the first time in your life, you have a reason to live—which means MACHINE now has leverage over you in a way it never did before your escape from the *Joie de Vivre*.

The rocky path you walk is damp and icy, exhausting too. You've never walked on such uneven and hostile terrain before—even at its worst, the ground in the *Joie de Vivre* was always flat. (Although MACHINE was known to occasionally reverse the gravity settings and send people falling violently to the roof at random times.)

Your legs feel like they're going to collapse beneath you at any moment—you've walked up and down a few hills and steep inclines since your escape but nothing like this. Your body is screaming at you to stop, to lie down, to give up—but you know that would be giving in to MACHINE. Plus, if you stopped you'd also probably freeze to death here. And so, you grit your teeth and force yourself to continue, fuelled only by unabated willpower.

You don't know how much further you have to walk. You don't even know precisely *where* your destination lies—you're simply pushing your way through dangerous terrain, hoping against anything that you're going in the right direction.

You're struck by an even more troubling thought as you hear the distant howl of one of the vicious-looking animals from the forest: There might be predatory animals up here. You have neither the means to defend yourself, nor the strength to fight or flee. And you have the added disadvantage that MACHINE might suddenly shock you into paralysis, just as a predatory animal was about to strike you.

You have to keep going. It's do or die. A life where you're still subject to MACHINE's torture is a life not worth living and so you press ahead, willing to risk everything to get your Chip removed.

Large shards of ice now stick out from the rocky ground like giant knives. The air is so cold that you can see your breath and your fingers are starting to go numb too—not in a pleasant, analgesic way but in an alarming way that you instinctively know is a sign of impending physical damage. You put your hands in your pockets, desperately hoping that this might spare them from the increasingly bitter cold, but all it really achieves is to slow your walking speed.

You finally decide to sneak a glance behind you, but all you can see is mist. There's no gleam from the crystal prison of The Girl Who is Trapped; no sign of The Man with Long Hair; nor can you see the river where you met The Frenchman, the lake upon which The Fisherman fishes, or the rolling hills where The Man From the East took you to see The Man Who is Always Alone.

You're still tempted to turn back, to return to familiar surroundings, maybe to try again at a later date when you're better prepared for the journey.

But you've already come this far and to return would be to relive the same dangerous and harrowing journey all over again—and for no reason.

And so you press on—through the mist, against the biting wind, over the mountain. Then, without warning, the clouds part before you, revealing a valley below. Sunlight spills across rolling greenery, a sight so vibrant it sends a jolt of energy through your weary limbs.

You quicken your pace.

But it's not just the landscape that ignites your excitement. Scattered across the valley floor are hundreds of huts and buildings—each of them unmistakably man-made.

And there's something else down there too: People. Hundreds, thousands of them. A mass of humanity unlike anything you have ever seen.

Not even in the most crowded sectors of the *Joie de Vivre* did people ever gather like this. And yet, here they are—thriving. A society, built from those MACHINE discarded, standing on its own, free.

81

The journey down the other side of the mountain is even more treacherous than your journey to the summit. The green valley sits below a sheer cliff with an almost vertical drop to the ground and you know you'd be killed were you to slip and fall off the icy ledge.

Instead, you move west, following a rocky path that gradually winds downward, though it narrows with each step. Soon, it curves sharply, revealing a precipitous ledge that slopes—just barely—toward the ground.

The ledge is scarcely wide enough for both feet, and treacherous patches of snow and ice glisten in the cold sunlight. You step carefully, knowing that one wrong move would send you tumbling into the abyss.

Pressing yourself against the cliff face, you inch sideways, hands skimming the cold, jagged rock. You decide it's best not to look down—seeing how far there is to fall fills you with terror, the terror makes your limbs shake and your shaky limbs make you more likely to make a crucial mistake.

It takes hours and you shuffle, inch by inch, all the way down to the ground, running on adrenaline fuelled by terror.

The lower you get, the less slippery your narrow path becomes. The air grows warmer, the snow and ice melt into water and you notice little tufts of green poking through the cracks in the rocks.

Finally, the path widens and you're able to descend more confidently, the rocks slowly giving way to greenery and even the occasional tree as you approach the village you saw from the summit.

At the bottom is a flat, rocky path that you strongly suspect is man-made, its terminus marked by a tall pole upon which appears a sign covered in writing. Unfortunately, the writing on the sign consists entirely of glyphs that are unfamiliar to you.

You continue down the path. There are green fields on either side of you, fenced off by the skeletal remains of trees that have been manipulated into long rectangular shapes. Inside these fenced spaces are living trees and docile looking animals—white, fluffy quadrupeds and more of those giant black and white beasts that you encountered in the fields of The Man Who is Always Alone.

The flat rocky path reminds you a little of the corridors of the *Joie de Vivre*, though thankfully there is no roof above you, so you don't feel quite as closed in as you did on the ship.

You pass the first hut and notice smoke billowing from a protrusion in the roof. Soon enough, you see people: A man, missing several teeth, smiles at you as you pass by, while two children play in a small clearing in front of the hut.

The years you spent on the *Joie de Vivre* have made you weary of strangers and the idea of approaching this man and striking up conversation is anathema to you. Nevertheless, you remember that you are now safely outside of the ship, in a place where MACHINE's rules no longer apply and so you force a smile onto your face as you nervously approach the stranger.

"Hello there," you say in what you hope is a non-threatening tone. "I've just come from over the mountain. I'm looking for someone who can help remove the Chip in my neck?"

The toothless man nods and smiles at you but says nothing.

"I recently escaped from the *Joie de Vivre*," you continue. "I've been told that people on this side of the mountains know how to remove the Chips?"

The toothless continues to stand there smiling before replying in a harsh-sounding tongue that you've never heard spoken before.

"I'm sorry but I don't understand you," you say but the man continues to babble, sentences filled with hard consonants and short, sharply spoken vowels.

You think back to when you first met The Frenchman and how initially you couldn't understand his language. You remember what he told you, that you could understand each other by speaking from the heart and so you try again, visualising as if the words you speak are flowing directly from the centre of your chest to the centre of the toothless man's chest.

"I'm looking for a place where I can get my Chip removed so I can be free of MACHINE," you say, speaking slowly and deliberately, desperate to be understood.

The toothless man continues to babble and with a despairing smile, you give up and turn away, continuing down the path, hoping that if you continue further into the village that maybe someone there might understand you.

82

You pass more people as you continue down the stone path, most of whom take very little notice of you. Many of them actively avoid eye contact. You're put in mind of the corridors during a shift change, though thankfully this path is wide enough to accommodate everyone and it doesn't feel quite so crowded and congested.

There are more man-made poles along the side of the road, upon which are affixed more signs in strange, alien writing that you have no hope of ever parsing. You also overhear the people babbling to each other in an unfamiliar language and you're reminded of the time that you and Namedog accidentally strayed into another sector.

The crowds grow thicker and you notice the huts on the side of the path giving way to larger and more ornate structures. In the distance is a very large stone building that, upon first sight, you assume must have been built directly by MACHINE—it seems impossible to you that humans could build so grand a thing on their own.

The closer you get to the grand stone building, the more you notice the eyes of the villagers upon you, many of whom stop in their tracks, boisterous conversations turning to whispers as you pass them by.

Your skin tightens with foreboding. There doesn't seem to be a way to communicate with these people and you wonder whether you're about to be subjected to some sort of Ritual Humiliation, or outright attacked as if by predatory animals.

You keep your gaze low, eyes fixed firmly on the stone path below you, unwilling now to risk eye contact with anyone.

The stone path reaches its terminus and you're now stood directly in front of the giant stone building. It towers over you, even more magnificent at close range than when you first spied it from a distance.

You stop and glance around you. The villagers have paused too and all eyes are upon you.

You force another smile and try to give them a friendly wave, hoping that maybe communication via gesticulation might be a possibility.

None of them wave back. They continue to stare at you—cold, unmoving, emotionless.

You're tempted to enter the stone building, which looks to be open and cavernous but you fear that doing so might leave you cornered and unable to retreat. You continue past the building, only to find the path ahead blocked by an ever growing crowd of staring people.

You turn back—perhaps it's time to abort the mission and return to the safety of the other side of the mountain, but your retreat is blocked too.

Hundreds of eyes remain silently fixed upon you and yet you're powerless to communicate and entirely unsure of their true intentions.

You hear a loud, rhythmic clacking sound from inside the stone building. The echo of footsteps against a hard, wooden floor.

A figure emerges. Male, relatively young, skeletally thin and dressed in the ripped and torn remains of a *Joie de Vivre* worker's uniform. His face has a few cuts and bruises, some scarring too, and with a jolt of astonishment and horror you realise that this is a face that you have seen before.

"Why have you broken your promise?" he says. "You promised us that you would leave us alone. Have you returned to torture us once again?"

You glance around again and it's only now that you see it: These people aren't staring at you with hostility but with *fear*. There's a woman in a row further back, crying and shaking. Even the children are silent.

"I'm sorry... I don't know what you mean?" you say to the young man with the familiar face.

The young man gestures at something behind him, two large panels covering the far wall of the otherwise empty interior of the stone building.

On one of the panels is a map depicting the layout of part of the *Joie de Vivre*. On the other, a drawing of a human face and an animal face. The human face bears a striking resemblance to your own, while the animal depicted is almost certainly Namedog.

"You came into our sector and took all we had to eat. You and your foul familiar! We were tortured, starved and humiliated," says the young man. "We assisted you to leave, asking only that you did not return. We were willing to accept death when MACHINE jettisoned our sector from the ship and now that we have been freed by MACHINE's grace, here, to our promised land, you have returned to torment us again

You hold your palms up. "No, I'm not here to torment you at all! It's all a misunderstanding, I swear!"

But your pleas fall on deaf ears as the villagers slowly come closer, many now carrying large wooden implements and flaming torches. There's a flicker of fear in their eyes—but also bloodlust.

83

Your situation has all the hallmarks of a Ritual Humiliation and so your instinct is to remain still and simply endure it, no matter how badly injured you are by the end.

A blast of freezing wind from the direction of the mountains snaps you out of your moment of regression, reminding you that this is not the *Joie de Vivre* and that you have not endured this arduous journey just to return to the same state of passivity that MACHINE inculcated into you.

MACHINE may still be able to harm you physically, but you refuse to let it harm you psychologically. And you know that the best way to resist MACHINE's lingering influence over your psyche is to fight back—to refuse to accept what these people will do to you, even if it costs you your life.

You slowly turn around, looking for any gap in the surrounding crowd, however small, that you could slip through to make your escape. No such gap can be found—the crowd is dozens of people deep and surrounds you on every side, slowly closing in.

You know you could run into the stone building, perhaps even barricade yourself in there but you know it would only delay the inevitable—the crowd would break down the doors and you'd have no way to escape.

You catch another glimpse of the drawing of you and Namedog inside the building and you remember how passive these people were when you first encountered them in their sector. From this, the skeleton of a plan crystallises in your mind.

Instead of running away or trying to fight them, you raise your arms high above you and then stretch them out cruciform, shouting in the loudest, deepest voice you can muster:

"Behold! It is I! The bringer of your destruction! The one that you fear!"

You're pleased to see fear ripple through the entire crowd. The front row hesitates. Even the skeletal young man takes a nervous step back from you.

"I have been sent here on a mission!" you say, trying to do your best impression of one of MACHINE's priests. "It has been commanded that you must remove the Chip in the back of my neck and then send me peacefully upon my way home, lest you and your village be struck with a fate worse than death!"

The people in the crowd look uneasily at each other. There are gasps, even a few screams, in the back rows. Many of them drop their weapons and fall to their knees in fear. This is working better than you could have ever hoped for.

You turn to the young man and address him in the same authoritative tone, "Are you the leader?"

He nods. "Yes. I am the high priest of we, the chosen people of MACHINE."

"I understand you fear me and what I might do to you?"

"You have no power in this place!" he shouts but you can tell from the quiver in this voice that he's bluffing.

You step toward him as menacingly as you can. "Are you sure? Do you really want to test me?"

He cowers. You can see it now—this scrawny young man is barely more than a child.

"I have told you my will!" you continue. "If you wish to be spared destruction, I demand that you remove the Chip in the back of my neck!"

"I... I can't do that!"

Your eyes narrow. "Why not?"

"Because it would be a blasphemy! We are the chosen people of MACHINE! You are the harbinger of death and destruction! We could never—"

"Surely removing my Chip would be a form of banishment?" you say. "Wouldn't it only show MACHINE how devoted you are to it, that you would banish a blasphemer to a life without MACHINE?"

"I'm sorry." The young man hangs his head. "Even if I was willing to do that, which I never would, not even for someone as vile and evil as you, I do not have the means to do so. But there is another village down the road, one full of blasphemers and heretics just like you... I'm sure that they would be more than willing to help you."

You nod, glancing up at the crowd who are looking on at your exchange with a mixture of loathing and terror.

"Very well," you say. "In that case all I request is safe passage. I did not intend to bother you or harm you. I am here only to get my Chip removed."

Someone from the back of the crowd calls out to the young man, in a tongue you understand: "What are we to do with the evil one?"

The young man lets out a pained and dejected sigh.

"Clear the road! The interloper is to pass unobstructed! The time of destruction is not today... this is merely a warning. The time of destruction will come when the evil one returns with their beastly familiar in tow."

Dutifully, the crowd parts and the road ahead is visible again.

"Thank you," you say quietly to the young man. "And, for what it's worth... I *am* sorry."

"Please just leave," the young man says. "To me you are a symbol of all that is evil. I do not know what your true intentions are or whether or not you can be trusted, but I do know that your face represents everything I fear and hate in this life and I desperately hope never to see it again."

You're tempted to try and convince the young man that he's wrong about you, but as far as you can see the people of this village seem happy in their delusions. As much as you'd prefer not to be cast in the role of villain, you decide it's better just to accept it and minimise your contact with them, rather than deprive them of the fiction that binds their society together.

You waste no time leaving the village and soon the flat, rocky path that you had been traversing is replaced by soft, muddy ground and green pastures. Beyond the village is a wide grassland dotted by the occasional tree but devoid of any man-made structures.

You're not sure which direction to go in, although the young man did intimate that there was another village nearby. It's simply a question of finding it.

You continue through the field in a slightly random direction, thinking of how the area reminds you of the Eden System in the *Joie de Vivre*. You soon spot a cluster of trees, under which hang bright orange orbs—a sight you find so striking and beautiful that you can't help but approach the tree to inspect it more closely.

You reach up for one of the orange orbs and with a gentle tug you break it off the tree. The orb is soft, if slightly leathery and you squeeze it, causing it to emit a liquid with a particularly sweet smell—revealing that these orbs are likely some form of fruit.

Hungry and also thirsty from your journey over the mountain, you slowly raise the orange orb to your mouth, hoping that it isn't poisonous. A single drop of the sweet juice lands on your tongue and—

"Hey! What are you doing?"

A female voice shrieks angrily from behind you and you immediately drop the orange fruit to the ground in fright.

A young woman approaches, rather portly in shape, with long pink hair—a colour which shocks you, having never before seen anyone with such an unusual hair colour.

"I apologise!" you say. "I was admiring this tree and thought this orange orb might be fruit. I'm very hungry... I haven't eaten much since my escape from the *Joie de Vivre*..."

"Oh, praise MACHINE!" she says. "I'm sorry, I thought you were one of the nuts from the village at the base of the mountain... they have a habit of sneaking in here to destroy our crops and burn things down."

You glance into the distance and while the mountains still tower over you, the village has now disappeared over the horizon.

"I came here from the other side of the mountain. I'm looking for someone who can safely remove the Chip in the back of my neck."

The girl claps her chubby hands joyously. "There is, there is! I can help you with that!"

She turns around and points to her own neck, revealing a raw, scabbed-over wound—but no Chip.

"Would you be willing to remove mine?" you ask.

"I can't do it myself, but if you follow me, I can introduce you to someone who can," says the girl. "We've set up a small village of our own, out here near the fruit trees, where we mostly sleep either outside or in tents."

"You mean, you haven't built any huts or buildings like the—"

The girl's demeanour changes ever so slightly—she frowns and her voice is more abrupt, as if offended.

"The people in my village have chosen to reject MACHINE *completely*!" she says. "We do not build things like MACHINE does; instead we tear down MACHINE's works and live in harmony with nature. Humans do not need buildings to survive, we only need Love and Kindness!"

You're struck by an implacable feeling of foreboding but decide to follow her nonetheless—after all, she has promised to remove your Chip and she's clearly much nicer than anyone you met in the other village.

"You mentioned that the people in the other village have been trying to destroy your crops?" you ask. "Why is that? I ask because... well, I encountered them a long time ago, while they were still living aboard the *Joie de Vivre*..."

"Several of the people in my village escaped from that village," she replies as the two of you wade through increasingly tall grass. "They're another one of those idiotic groups who believe that they're MACHINE's chosen people because MACHINE ejected them from the ship and led them here."

"Yes, they told me the same thing when I passed through," you say, deciding to omit the part where they designated you as a "harbinger of destruction".

"Unfortunately, out here there's no shortage of groups like that," the girl explains. "Even though MACHINE has set them free, they remain devoted to it and obsessed with the idea that MACHINE favours them in some way. There's another village out in the sand dunes that also believes that they're MACHINE's chosen people, only they believe that MACHINE hates women and that therefore women should not be permitted to show their faces in public and should always be escorted everywhere by a male chaperone."

"That sounds... a little insane," you say.

The girl smiles at you. "I think you'll do well in my village. We don't worship MACHINE. We just believe in Love and Kindness; that there's nothing MACHINE can do that humans can't do better!"

She gestures toward a clearing where the tall grass suddenly gives way to much shorter grass. There are several more fruit trees, plus a few dozen people sitting outside of flimsy A-frame shelters that look to have been made from old clothing and bedsheets.

You breathe a sigh of relief.

"Well I'm certainly glad you found me and led me here," you say. "I'm so relieved to have finally found someone on this side of the mountains who *isn't* cruel or insane..."

You're yet to discover just how wrong you are.

85

As she leads you into her village—though it's not much of a village, more of an encampment—you see heads popping up through the bushes or poking out from behind thickets of tall grass. Everyone smiles at you as you pass by, but unlike the *Joie de Vivre*, these smiles all look genuine—not the predatory grins that precede a Ritual Humiliation.

Most people here look young, probably barely older than teenagers, and a good number of them are naked.

"Like I said earlier, our people have rejected MACHINE in totality. Some people here see wearing clothes as a mark of oppression by MACHINE and thus choose to forego them," says the pink-haired woman by way of explanation as she leads you to a tent in the centre of the clearing.

"Wait here," she instructs as she ducks inside the tent. This is followed by the muffled sound of her conversing with someone inside the tent.

She crawls out, followed by a very short young man with a thick beard, wearing only a loin cloth.

"Welcome to our community of Love and Kindness, friend!" says the bearded man by way of greeting. "I hear that you came from over the mountains?"

243

"That's right," you say. "I've been told that people on this side of the mountains have the means to remove the Chip that was implanted in me when I was a child."

He grins. "We do, indeed, friend! And may I say—kudos to you for choosing to join us, for making it here without being blinded by the flattery and false claims of the other villages!"

"I've been deceived by MACHINE my whole life. Human deception has very little effect on me now," you say. "Besides, I have some bad blood with the people in the other village..."

The man and the girl, still smiling, share a significant glance then turn back to you.

"I'm sure you'll find a more suitable home among us," says the man with a grin. "The only rule in this place is that you are Kind and Loving at all times. We have rejected the cruel doctrines of MACHINE and its terrible ship of slavery!"

You find yourself returning his grin. "That sounds great by me! And the sooner you remove my Chip, the better! I can't believe MACHINE still tortures people out here, even after they've escaped or been freed..."

The man claps his hands together. "It will be done, my friend, it will be done! But it will be done ritually, at tonight's great feast!"

You're a little uneasy about the prospect of waiting a few more hours—MACHINE could electrocute you again or even kill you in that time—but nevertheless you smile gratefully at the bearded man. "Thanks very much! I can't wait to finally be rid of this thing!"

The man continues to grin but you notice his gaze flicker upwards to your forehead.

"Ah! I see that you're insane!" he says and you're struck by the casual, conversational tone with which he says it. "How long have you been insane for?"

You hesitate, surprised that someone out here would so readily accept your branding as a statement of fact.

"I was branded with this for trying to escape from the *Joie de Vivre*," you say. "Because I rejected the tenets and teachings of MACHINE and its priests."

The man and the girl look at each other again and this time, they're no longer smiling.

"You tried to escape?"

"I *did* escape," you say. "That's why I'm here. Did you not *also* try to escape?"

"Of course not!" he says, looking offended. "I never would have tried to escape! Just because I reject the ways of MACHINE does not mean that I would abandon the people on the *Joie de Vivre* who I cared for! The only reason I am out here is because I was banished for my blasphemy!"

"Oh..." you say. "I'm sorry, I assumed that because you'd rejected MACHINE—"

"What? That I'd suddenly lose the will to endure being tortured and try to escape, like a coward?"

You bristle at being called a coward.

The bearded man continues, "The day I rejected MACHINE, I decided that I would dedicate my life to spreading Love and Kindness throughout the *Joie de Vivre*, to free the people from their slavery and ignorance. I have been exiled out here as a punishment but some day, when I have the numbers, I will return with an army and we will overthrow the priesthood, remove everyone's Chip and create a society where humans run the *Joie de Vivre* for themselves, without MACHINE!"

What follows is a protracted, awkward silence which is thankfully broken by the sudden appearance of two corpulent bald women, dragging a badly beaten young man behind them.

"We found him!" says one of the women. "He was hanging around near that village with the 'Man From Outside' lunatics..."

"Praise MACHINE!" says the bearded man, who notices your perplexed expression and adds, "It's just an expression. I don't mean it literally."

"What shall we do with him?" asks the other woman holding the young man.

"I think you already know the answer to that..." the bearded man says with glee. "Tonight's feast is going to be *quite* something! First we'll have a de-Chipping ceremony and then the chance to perform an Act of Kindness on this misguided young man. I think afterwards... maybe we should have an orgy?"

You glance at the pink-haired woman who brought you in. "A what?"

"Some people here believe that the ultimate purpose of life is pleasure. An orgy is, for many people, a very simple way to experience pleasure."

"It's like a form of HeDonia, only you don't need MACHINE," the bearded man adds. "If you recover quickly from having your Chip removed, you might like to join in?"

"Yeah... maybe," you say, but the longer you talk to this man, the more certain you are that you're leaving this village as soon as he removes your Chip.

86

You spend the rest of the day lying in a soft bush, occasionally taking questions from the people of this camp, all of which follow the same basic pattern: "Where are you from?", "How did you get here?", "Why is the word 'INSANE' branded on your forehead?", "Why are you still wearing clothing that MACHINE made?"

After a while you find yourself wanting to avoid their attention, so you lie down in the tall grass, staying quiet and still.

Sure, nobody here seems malicious, but unlike when you were on the other side of the mountain, you don't feel like you're among people who understand you or share your values either.

By the time the bright star sets and the moon returns, you're tempted to utter your own quiet "Praise MACHINE" for the fact that you're finally about to be freed from that evil device embedded in the back of your neck.

You sit up when you notice the rather alluring scent of burning wood, reminding you of the fire that The Fisherman started the previous night and the sense of warmth and safety that it brought. Your stomach growls as you remember it's already been an entire day since you last ate.

You get to your feet and walk towards the fire, noticing that despite only a few tents, the camp seems to be almost as well populated as the village that the people from the Other Sector built.

The people here really do seem young and, for that matter, incredibly beautiful too.

You watch as tall, slender, golden haired girls giggle, eating little coloured orbs and sharing them with young men with muscular physiques and skin bronzed by the sun.

"Ah! Our guest of honour!"

You spot the bearded man sitting on a log near the fire and he beckons for you to join him.

"Have you had anything to eat?" he says, gesturing toward a large pile of fruit.

"No," you say, "not since yesterday when I caught some fish."

The bearded man nearly spits out his mouthful of food.

"*Fish*? You ate *fish*?"

"It was the only food I could find on the other side of the mountain. I hadn't eaten for days prior," you say.

The bearded man's expression softens. "Well, I suppose if you were starving it's forgivable but I would prefer you to be more Kind to animals in future by not killing or eating them. Here we only eat plants. It's more ethical and sustainable."

You nod, taking a round green fruit and biting into it. The taste is, at first, almost overwhelming—a mixture of sweet and sour and yet you feel compelled to keep eating it, each bite better than the preceding one.

"Hey, I'm not judging you or anything. I'm an open-minded guy," the bearded man says as you discard the core of the fruit and then bite into the succulent, juicy flesh of an orange orb. "There are some people here who believe it's Unkind to eat *any* living thing, including plants. They try to subsist only from water, air and the sun."

"Really?" you ask. "I didn't know it was possible for humans to do that?"

"It isn't!" he says. "They died from starvation. Since then, we've learned that eating the seeds and fruits of plants is neces-sary for survival. We also concluded that eating fruit isn't cruel because plants eject those parts from themselves automatically. There are some people who like to dig up and eat the roots of certain plants but personally I think that's a bit too cruel... you're probably murdering the plant if you do that."

"I'll bear that in mind," you say, though after spending an entire lifetime on the brink of starvation, you can't imagine any situation in which you could justify being so picky about what you eat.

One of the bald women you saw earlier appears in front of the bearded man. "The Unkind one is tied up and ready to go!"

"We'll begin once everyone has eaten," he says turning to you. "Are you still hungry?"

Even though you're mostly satiated now, some of these fruits are so sweet that you find yourself wanting to eat them voraciously. Particularly amazing to you are the small, soft green orbs attached to a twig. As you've observed from watching the others, you pull the orbs off the twigs and eat them whole—the sensation is like being micro-dosed with HeDonia.

"Go easy on the grapes there," says the bearded man. "We need those to make wine. Have you ever had wine before?"

You shake your head.

"It's a drink made from old grape juice that has the same effect as sEDAtIVE. Isn't that great? We've basically learned how to make sEDAtIVE without MACHINE!"

Before you have time to question him more, he stands and a hush falls over the entire camp.

"My fellow practitioners of Love and Kindness!" he says loudly, people in the far distance straightening up at the sound of his voice. "We have a very special night tonight! Not only will we be de-Chipping our newest arrival but we will *also* be subjecting one of our apostates to Love and Kindness!"

The crowd cheers and you join in with the applause uneasily. Maybe it's because of all the Ritual Humiliations you've witnessed, but you can't shake a growing sense of dread—yet at the same time, the bearded man speaks in a way that makes you want to believe that his every word is true. And you can tell by the rapt looks on everyone's faces that you're not alone in being hypnotised by him.

"Bring forth the Unkind One!" he commands, as two women drag the young man you saw earlier along a small pathway to the fire.

The girl with the pink hair appears suddenly at your side and whispers, "You don't have to witness this if you don't want to..."

You glance at her, unsure of exactly what it *is* that you are witnessing.

"In this village, we do not believe in rules and we reject the ways of MACHINE," the bearded man continues, as he approaches the young man, who struggles in vain against the strong grip of the two women. "The only rules we have here are 'Love' and 'Kindness'!

"But this young man has been accused of being insufficiently Kind! He has been accused of not being Loving enough!"

For the first time, you hear the young man's voice as he shrieks, *"It's not true! It's not true! They made it up!"*

"Someone who is truly Kind could never be accused of being Unkind and so I summarily find you guilty! Someone who is truly Loving would always be loved enough in return never to be subjected to a false accusation! As such, I summarily deem the accusations against you to be true!"

"They're lying! You've got to listen to me! I can prove my innocence!" The young man's shrieks grow in volume and intensity. He twists his whole body around, trying to free himself. There's an audible snap, followed by a gasp from some of the people in the crowd, as the young man dislocates his arm, desperately trying to pull himself free.

"We believe only in Love and Kindness here and for someone guilty of the sins you have committed, the only Kind and Loving thing to do is to put you to death," says the bearded man and it's at this moment that your stomach drops. "And so therefore, I sentence you to death."

"No! Please! I didn't do anything! Just let me go... I'll leave here and never return! I promise!"

"It would be Unkind to allow you to poison another village and it would be Unloving not to hold you responsible for the heinous things you have done!"

You turn to the pink-haired woman. "What exactly *is* he guilty of?"

"He was accused of hurting someone's feelings by holding a different opinion to them," she says.

"What?"

"Exactly!" she says. "What an *awful* person! It's Unkind and intolerant to disagree with other people! And we mustn't tolerate intolerance! I'm glad this bastard has finally been brought to justice..."

You're tempted to get up and run for your life there and then but as you run your fingers along the back of your neck, you're reminded that you cannot risk leaving here until you're free of MACHINE's Chip.

87

It's not the fact that they're putting this young man to death that scares you—after all, you regularly witnessed far worse things on the *Joie de Vivre*. The thing that scares you is the *glee* with which they do it.

The same friendly smiles with which you were greeted when you stumbled your way into this encampment are the same friendly smiles that members of the crowd continue to wear while they pick up a variety of sharp implements—sticks that have been sanded down into spears; rocks that been shaped into rudimentary axes; and twisted, rusted chunks of metal that have been sharpened into makeshift knives.

The young man's limbs are bound and the two bald women lift him up and place him right at the edge of the fire. There's no signal, no command given, no instruction of any kind as the crowd suddenly roars into a frenzy, pelting the young man with rocks and stones until those holding weapons run right up to him and pierce his skin, some driving their sharpened sticks all the way through his torso and out the other side. He shudders and goes limp. Blood trickles into the soil as a variety of sharp sticks are driven into his back and it's soon clear to you that the young man is dead.

You look around and everyone is grinning and cheering ecstatically. You see young couples embrace each other, children jumping for joy, a wave of euphoria cascading over the entire encampment.

Except for you. You cover your mouth, barely able to contain your horror.

You glance at the pink-haired girl, who is herself bobbing up and down clapping, transfixed by the sight of the young man's corpse being thrown onto the fire, causing the smell of burning fat to now overwhelm the sweet scent of the fruit trees in the gentle night's air.

"They killed him!" you say with a gasp.

"Yes!" she cries, without looking at you. "Isn't it wonderful? Wasn't that just the Kindest, most Loving thing you've ever seen?"

Once again, the bearded man appears in the centre of the clearing, holding his arms wide to gain the attention of the euphoric crowd. "Tonight, my friends, we shall show our Love for this man by consuming his flesh! Tonight we shall feast upon the fruits of our Kindness!"

You withdraw from the crowd, hoping perhaps that you might be able to slip out unnoticed but unfortunately that's when the bearded man's attention turns to you.

"But while we wait for the flesh to cook, we must perform *another* great act of Kindness!" Every eye now falls upon you as the sound of the chanting and cheering slowly ebbs away. "It is now time to free this interloper from their bondage to MACHINE! It is time to begin the de-Chipping ceremony!"

You freeze. There's no chance of you slipping out now, even if you wanted to—and truth be told, you don't. As barbaric and horrific as the things you witnessed were, you know that every second that you still have your Chip is a second in which MACHINE could torture or even kill you.

And so you decide to play along, not resisting as the same two bald women who dragged the young man to his death grab you by each of your arms and march you into the centre of the clearing, near where the young man's corpse now burns.

They force you to turn around, your back to the crowd as the bearded man addresses them.

"Behold! One has come to us, still bearing the mark of MACHINE!"

In your peripheral vision, you can see him gesturing at the back of your neck. You hear a gasp from the crowd.

"What shall we do with someone who has been branded by MACHINE? Should we kill this person?"

The crowd shouts, though you can't tell whether the noise is affirmatory or negatory.

"No!" the bearded man shouts, much to your relief. "The Kind thing to do is not to kill such a wayward one but to liberate them!"

You're spun around to face the crowd again and the bearded man yells theatrically, right into your face, "Do you reject MACHINE and all its lies!"

"Yes I do," you say, partially because you mean it and partially because this feels like the Correct thing to say to these people.

"Do you reject MACHINE's teachings and ways, in totality?"

"Yes!" you shout, a little louder this time.

"Do you pledge to reject the cruelty and torture of MACHINE and instead embrace the values of Love and Kindness in its place?"

You almost hesitate, having just witnessed what "Love" and "Kindness" means to these people, but nevertheless you answer, "Yes I do!"

Somebody produces a large wooden plank and props it up on a stack of rocks. The two women force you onto the plank and hold you face down, your nose pressed hard into the wood, suffocating you.

You remember experiencing something almost exactly like this once before, back when you were a child, on the day that the Chip was first inserted into the back of your neck.

One of the women has her entire weight pressed down on the back of your head, immobilising you. That's the worst part of this whole process—not being able to see, not knowing exactly what the bearded man is doing to you. Or least, you think that's the worst part until the *actual* worst part comes, which is the searing pain of something sharp digging deeply into the back of your neck.

It feels like the bearded man is using a pair of metal pliers to remove the Chip, but knowing this place it could be anything— any old rusted hunk of metal that they've found, perhaps even wooden sticks.

All you know is that you can now feel the skin on your neck slowly tearing open. As they brush whatever instrument they're using against your Chip, it sparks, sending bolts of electricity through your body, causing you to convulse.

The two women hold you down even harder as you receive what you hope and pray will be your final Corrective Shock ever from MACHINE.

You can't breathe. Your mouth and nose are pressed too closely against the wooden plank and even if that weren't the case, the longer your electrocution continues, the more your throat fills with a mixture of bile and foam, blocking your trachea.

The pain doubles in intensity as you feel the Chip starting to dislodge, which somehow causes the voltage to increase. No one seems to notice that you are choking. No care is given to the fact you cannot breathe.

The pain dissipates. Not because your ordeal has stopped, but because your body is shutting down, the same way it did when you were exposed to Liquid Pain.

You're feeling very light-headed. Everything's spinning. Your surroundings are swirling into a cacophony of sensations.

You're dying.

This is how it ends.

You're sure of it and you're at peace with it.

You were expecting death when you jumped out the airlock. You were expecting worse than death for staying on the *Joie de Vivre*. Everything that has happened since then—all the people you've met, all the places you've seen—it's all just been a wonderful fever dream, one which you're grateful to have experienced.

You're slipping away into unconsciousness, from which you know you'll likely never wake. You feel something being ripped at the back of your neck, you feel blood trickling down your torso but you no longer have the strength to stay awake and so you let the darkness embrace you.

88

The next thing you see is light, which surprises you as you hadn't expected to see anything ever again. You open your eyes to discover that you're still lying on the plank, but you're now on your side. The crowd is gone, the fire is out and there's no sign of the young man's body—indeed, nothing at all remains of the events of last night.

You curl yourself into a sitting position, aware of a throbbing dull pain in the back of your neck. You slowly reach around to touch it—

"Ah! You're awake!"

The bearded man emerges from his tent, his smile bright and wide as if he hadn't participated in a brutal murder ritual the previous night.

"How do you feel, friend?"

You glance down and see that you are shirtless. Your bare skin is stained by dried blood—long streams of it at that.

"I'll admit we were a little worried you weren't going to make it," the bearded man continues. "You lost a lot of blood and your Chip was embedded even deeper than usual. But we got it in the end! You're free now!"

He triumphantly produces a Chip, stained in blood but veritably a Chip, just like the ones you used to insert into children at the nursery.

He hands it to you and you turn it over in your hand. It's a wonder that something so small can cause so much suffering; that this tiny device has been the source of MACHINE's control over you throughout your entire adult life.

You squeeze it hard with your fist, pressing down with as much force as you can muster, until it breaks apart in your palm.

"I've won…" you murmur breathlessly. "I've defeated MACHINE!"

"You sure did, my friend!" says the bearded man as several young women, some fully nude, also emerge from his tent. "So… how would you like us to torture you?"

You stare at him silently, confused. One of the young women points at your forehead and giggles.

"What do you mean?"

The bearded man widens his grin and produces a blood-stained pair of metal pliers.

"Now that MACHINE can no longer torture you, it's up to us to do it for you!" he says. "So… what method of torture would you prefer to be subjected to? We could start by clamping down hard on various nerve endings with these pliers? And the girls say they'd like to poke your eyes and pull your hair! Oh, and we could also hook you up to a small device that administers painful electric shocks, just like the ones you used to get from MACHINE!"

You look from him to the girls, all giggling with large smiles that, had it not been for the events of last night, you'd have interpreted as friendly, benevolent smiles.

"What? I don't want to be tortured!" you say. "Isn't that the whole point of removing the Chip? Isn't that the whole point of rejecting MACHINE to reject its cruelty and torment?"

The bearded man looks confused.

"Well of course we reject MACHINE! And of course we reject MACHINE's torture too!"

You slide off the plank and onto your feet.

"Then why do you want to torture me?" you ask. "Is this some sort of test? To prove that I truly have rejected MACHINE's teachings?"

"No, no, don't be silly... We're torturing you because you look like you could stand to be in pain for a while!" the bearded man says cheerfully. "We've rejected *MACHINE's* torture... but that doesn't mean we reject *all* forms of torture! After all, isn't the entire point of life to experience constant suffering and agony? And in the absence of MACHINE... we must become MACHINE!"

"Come on, let us torture you!" moans one of the girls. "I bet I can draw blood!"

"Yeah I want to see how long it takes before you start screaming!" says another one.

You notice they too are also carrying various torture devices—pliers, spikes and at least one knife. Their smiles are still innocent, almost naive, but you can hear the bloodthirstiness in their voices.

"No thank you!" you say, forcefully enough to make one of the girls to jump backwards in fright. "I don't want to be tortured any more. I have suffered enough in my life... I just want to live in peace, without pain."

One of the girls stares at your forehead, her mouth hanging open. Even the bearded man looks disturbed.

"Are you *sure* you're not insane?" the girl says, pointing at the branding on your forehead. "Why would you want to live without being tortured? That's no kind of life!"

"Girls, please!" The bearded man waves at them to stand down and they all take a step backward. "Clearly our friend here is still delirious from the procedure to remove the Chip! I'm sure they don't mean what they are saying... how about we leave them to recover and then when they're feeling a bit better, we'll torture them extra brutally tonight?"

He flashes a smile at you as if he expects you'll interpret this as him doing you a favour.

One of the girls groans and stomps her foot like a child but soon they return to the bearded man's tent and he crouches down to join them inside.

"You have to be cruel to be Kind," he says, turning back to you, "and to Love someone is to be willing to endure their abuse. Suffering is the thing that separates humans from MACHINE. But don't worry, friend—you can still live a miserable life of suffering and pain even without MACHINE!"

You force a smile and nod politely as he crawls back into his tent, followed by the sound of feminine giggles turning into agonised screams.

As soon as you're confident that he is suitably distracted and that no one else is looking, you immediately plan your escape from the camp.

89

Your eyes lock on to the mountains, now distant and shrouded in mist. You know that you need to find a way back over them, to be reunited with the people who understood you and loved you.

And so, rather brazenly, you start walking in that direction, leaving the clearing for the tall grass and wading through until you find the fruit trees where you first encountered the pink-haired girl. You're tempted to stop here and take some fruit but you don't want to risk being seen, so you hurry past, in the direction of the village you promised never to return to, desperately hoping that—

"Where are you going?"

You jump, as if you'd just been electrocuted by MACHINE. The pink-haired girl suddenly pops up from out of the tall grass, near you.

"I was—"

"You weren't trying to *leave* were you?" Her voice is sharp and accusatory. "The only thing in this direction is that village of nut-jobs. You weren't planning to rejoin them were you? After you promised me that you weren't one of them? After everything we've done for you?"

She takes a threatening step toward you and when you consider her mass, you know that she would come out on top were the two of you to come to a physical altercation.

"No," you lie, hastily adding, "I was just here to collect some fruit. I never got to try the fruit from these trees when I first arrived!"

Her expression softens. "That's good. If you ever tried to leave us, the only Kind thing to do would be to put you to death. You saw last night what we do to the people who accept our Love but give none of theirs in return..."

You gulp. "Actually, I'd been meaning to ask about that. Most people in the camp seem to think it's wrong to eat meat... and yet I saw a lot of people, including you, eating the flesh of—"

She laughs, waving away your question. "It's not wrong to eat someone who is guilty of Unkindness or Hate! It's only wrong to kill and eat the innocent and the vulnerable... like animals and certain plants. Human flesh is fair game if it comes from people who don't share our values!"

"I... see."

"Are you looking forward to being tortured tonight?" she asks, far too casually for your liking. "I've been preparing for it all day.

You're going to be in *so* much pain tonight! We're going to do things to you that MACHINE could never dream of!"

"Don't you think torturing people is a bit, you know, 'Unkind'?"

She looks at you like she's just been slapped. "What a stupid thing to say! You really *are* insane, aren't you?"

You shrug.

"The Unkind thing to do would be *not* to torture you! After all, what meaning could life possibly have if we didn't suffer all the time? And because we reject MACHINE, we believe that humans should maximise the suffering of other humans in its place!"

"Right..." you say, gritting your teeth into a forced smile. "Well, ugh, in that case, I really look forward to all the pain I'm going to be in tonight..."

She beams. "I'm so glad to hear it! Well, why don't you head back to the camp and rest before your ordeal? Any more time out here and I might suspect you *are* trying to escape!"

You let out a staccato burst of forced laughter. "Yes of course... I'll see you tonight."

You turn and head back toward the camp. If you're to have any hope of escape at all you'll have to go in another direction and you'll have to be a lot more clever about it this time around.

90

You continue to hide in the tall grass—you know this is still your best chance of getting out undetected. But this time, instead of going directly back to the camp, you gently arc around it, figuring that if you're caught again you could plausibly claim to have gotten lost or taken a wrong turn.

You keep your head low and despite your instinct to hurry, you force yourself to take slow, quiet steps through the grass so that if there is anyone else hidden in here, they're less likely to notice you.

There are voices nearby and a rustling sound. You pause and drop to the ground, the tall grass now towering over you. You can hear two sets of approaching footsteps, getting closer and closer—

"Does here work?" The first voice belongs a young man, you estimate him to in his late teens or early twenties.

"There might be people around," replies the second voice—a girl of similar age.

"I don't care if there's people around, we're not doing anything wrong!"

"I know, I know but still... I get embarrassed about this stuff. It's why I never take part in the orgies."

"Come on baby, just lie down and spread your legs, I'll do the—"

You cough loudly and the young woman lets out a shriek of fright.

"I'm sorry to interrupt, but I don't think this place is *quite* as secluded as the two of you were hoping," you say as you pop up out of the grass and face them directly.

"Dammit!" says the young man, the top of his head now visible in the grass a few metres away. "Everywhere we go, there's someone hiding in the grass!"

"I'm sorry," you say. "To be honest, I was looking for a little privacy too. I'm willing to let you guys have this place to do, ugh, whatever you're planning to do if you can find me another spot with no people around?"

"Oh that's easy," says the young man. "If you keep going that way there's another village, but between us and them there's lot of space with no one around."

"That area's forbidden though!" says the girl, more to the young man than to you.

"Yeah but there's no one guarding that part of the grass," says the young man. "To be honest, the only reason I didn't go there is because I didn't want to run into any of those 'Man From Outside' nuts. They're a real boner kill, if you get my drift..."

"I see, well, I was just looking for a place to—" You quickly concoct an innocuous lie "—sleep. You know, alone... where I won't be disturbed."

"Oh, well, yeah that's the perfect place out there!"

"Great!" you say. "And, ugh... as long as you promise not to tell anyone I'm there, I won't tell anyone you're here..."

"It's a deal!" says the young man as you set off, this time with your head above the grass, in the direction he pointed out.

The thought of a neighbouring village strikes you as possibly being a good point to aim for—sure, the villagers here describe them as "nuts" but after what you've seen of this village, you can't imagine the next village being *that* much worse.

You duck down low into the long grass again, and head in the direction that the young man pointed out.

Soon, the long grass shrivels and shrinks as you continue, the ground growing rockier below you.

You crouch as low as you can, looking carefully behind you to ensure that no one from the village has followed you here through the tall grass.

You take a deep breath, stand up straight and break into a full blown sprint across the rocky clearing.

Sure enough, there are buildings in the distance and you can distantly smell smoke too, though it's the welcome scent of burning wood this time, rather than the smell of burning human flesh.

You sneak a glance behind you and just as you're satisfied that you're not being followed, a figure in a long black robe suddenly steps out from behind a large boulder and grabs you.

You struggle against him, kicking and pushing with all your might but he easily overpowers you and wrestles you to the ground.

"Shh, shh, shh!" he says putting his fingers to your lips. "Stop fighting, you're going to be okay! I'm a friend."

He's got you in a pretty tight headlock by now so even if you wanted to continue fighting, you know it's not a fight you'd win.

"Fine. You caught me. Might as well kill me," you pant as he slowly lessens his grip.

"Kill you?" says the man, glancing toward the tall grass now in the distance. "Is that what they told you we do? Are they *still* spreading the lie that we're a human sacrifice cult?"

"It's not a lie, I saw you people do it! Last night!" But as he lets go you immediately realise that this man is not from the encampment by the fruit trees.

Everything about him is different to them—from his attire (long black robes, leaving very little skin exposed) to his grooming (clean shaven, short grey hair, neatly combed) to his mannerisms.

"The only group I know of that regularly sacrifices human beings is the group of youngsters who camp out over in that direction," he says nodding in the direction from which you came. "They call themselves 'enlightened' and claim to practice 'Love and Kindness' but from what I've observed of them, they're nothing more than a death cult."

"You're not from the camp?"

He shakes his head.

You sigh with a mixture of relief and exhaustion. "Praise MACHINE! I'm sorry... I'm trying to escape from that camp and I thought you were one of them, here to drag me back and prevent me from getting away."

"Ah, I see!" the man in the dark robes says knowingly. "Well then, perhaps you'd best come with me? You don't want to stay in this spot too long—they're known to occasionally raid our village in search of deserters. Our village has been deemed by them to be insufficiently 'Loving' or 'Kind'."

He helps you back to your feet and leads you down a stony path and into a village rather similar to the first one you encountered on this side of the mountains. However, in this village the majority of buildings seem to have been constructed from the flattened carcasses of dead trees, rather than stone.

"I know it's probably a cliché to ask this, but there is an important question which I feel obliged to ask every newcomer who arrives in our village..."

"What's that?" you ask.

"Have you ever met The Man From Outside?"

You stare at him silently for a few moments before shaking your head. "I've never even heard of him, apart from a few mentions I overheard in the tent village."

The man raises an eyebrow. "That *does* surprise me! I didn't think it possible to get far in this world without having at least *some* knowledge of The Man From Outside..."

"Sorry," you say with a shrug. "I only came to this side of the mountain to get my Chip removed but I couldn't safely make it back. And before that, well, it's only been a few days since I escaped from the *Joie de Vivre*..."

The man stops suddenly in his tracks.

"Oh," he says. "Well then please forgive me for making such an assumption! I'd assumed that you *were* one of those villagers— I wasn't aware you'd travelled here from so far away."

"Who is The Man From Outside?" you ask. "I've met a few people since I left the *Joie de Vivre*. I've met The Frenchman and The Man From the East and The Fisherman and The Girl Who is Trapped. Is The Man From Outside anything like them?"

The Man in Black Robes laughs uproariously. "No, no, The Man From Outside is nothing like them! He is far greater than any of them! He is the greatest of us all!"

"Well in that case," you say, "I look forward to meeting him!"

The Man in Black Robes turns and smiles. "We're *all* looking forward to meeting him. Some day, when he returns..."

"So... he's not here? Did he return to the *Joie de Vivre* like the Man with Seventy-five Names did?"

"No one knows exactly where he went but..." The Man in Black Robes pauses. "It's a bit of a long story. How about I tell you over a drink and a meal? Have you eaten?"

"Not since last night," you say.

"Do you have any particular preferences for meals? Anything you object to eating?"

You laugh. "I'll eat anything you give me, as long as it is isn't human flesh!"

91

As the Man in the Black Robes leads you further into the village, the sky darkens overhead, the floating bright orb now obscured behind some sort of black vapour. A few minutes later there's a tremendous roar, followed by a flash of light and instinctively you duck under a doorway to shelter yourself.

"Easy there..." says the Man in Black Robes. "It's just water. It's nothing to be alarmed about."

He gestures for you to follow him but as you do, you feel cold water from an unseen source hitting the top of your head and shoulders. Soon the droplets expand, hitting the stony ground below you, as if you've stepped into a giant shower. There's another flash of light followed by another deep, low roar.

"What is this?" you stammer, barely able to form words in your state of fright. "Is MACHINE doing this? Is this some sort of torture chamber?"

"It's not MACHINE. It's a natural phenomenon," the Man in Black Robes says. "You'll be fine. We're almost at the pub."

You can feel your clothes are now soaking wet and cold, sticking uncomfortably to your skin.

"Are you sure that it's just water?" you ask. "MACHINE sometimes bathes people in acid and other chemicals. Perhaps MACHINE is punishing me for deserting—"

"MACHINE cannot hurt you here," the Man in Black Robes says, gesturing you to a large wooden building, the outside of which is decorated by garlands of hanging flowers.

You follow him inside and though there is a smattering of other people in the large hollow space inside, few bother to look up at you. For the most part, you're just grateful to have shelter from the falling water.

The Man in Black Robes leads to you to a wooden table near the window, out of which you can see the falling water and hear it landing with a hiss on the hard ground outside. "What would you like to eat?"

"I have no preference," you say. "I'll eat whatever you think is appropriate, as long as it will nourish me and isn't made from human flesh."

"You really *did* come straight from the *Joie de Vivre*, didn't you?" says the Man in Black Robes. "I've gotta say, that's refreshing around here! I think we've all become so complacent about our abundance of food that we fail to consider what it's like for MACHINE's slaves to live their lives on the edge of starvation."

"You mean you don't remember what life was like on the *Joie de Vivre?*"

"Remember it? I never experienced it!" he says. "I was born out here and lived my entire life out here."

"How is that possible?" you say in amazement. "I thought everyone out here was someone who had escaped or been ejected from the ship! You mean you've lived your *entire* life free from MACHINE?"

"I have," he says. "Although perhaps I owe my freedom to MACHINE? Many people believe that MACHINE is responsible for selecting who is born free and who is enslaved. The latter spend their lives aboard the *Joie de Vivre* whilst the former live out here, in this place."

"Do you subscribe to that belief?"

"There may be some truth to it—ah, thank you!" Another man in a white jacket, dressed almost like a medic, approaches your table and places two large plates upon it, filled with cooked meats and all manner of fruits and vegetables.

The food smells delicious and you begin to salivate, but despite your hunger and your appetite, years of experience prevents you from diving right in.

"Is this safe to eat?" you ask, all too familiar with MACHINE serving sumptuous meals like this, only for them to be poisoned or filled with hidden razor blades, or perhaps hiding poisonous insects or diseased vermin underneath.

"MACHINE is not here," the Man in Black Robes repeats, raising his fork and impaling a slab of food with it. "You are safe."

With some trepidation, you pick up your own fork and, beginning first on a soft white root vegetable, you start to eat. As the first morsel of food enters your mouth, there's a small explosion of pleasure in your head, as if this food has all been laced with HeDonia.

The more you eat, the more conscious of your hunger you become and any urge to converse is drowned out by the overwhelming pleasure of taste and sustenance. It takes you a few minutes before you realise that you had temporary regressed to the level of an animal, voraciously devouring everything that was on your tray.

"Easy does it," the Man in Black Robes says. "Too much food too soon will give you a stomach ache and too much food all the time will make you fat. MACHINE was wrong to ban its slaves from *all* forms of pleasure but it was right to restrict it—too much pleasure can be a torture in and of itself, and a very harmful one at that."

"I... apologise," you say, trying to recover some dignity as you wipe the remains of food away from the corners of your mouth with a white cloth on the table. "I was *very* hungry."

"I understand your circumstances completely," he replies. "I'm just glad to see you finally getting the nutrition that you need!"

"You were explaining earlier that some people believe that MACHINE decides who is a slave and who is free?" you say, now satiated enough to re-engage your brain's frontal lobe. "But you never told me whether this is something that you yourself believe?"

The Man in Black Robes leans back in his chair thoughtfully. "I do not know whether or not this theory accurately reflects the truth but my observation is that MACHINE *does* seem to be the ultimate arbiter of whether or not one is free or enslaved on the *Joie de Vivre.*"

"So in the end... no one is really free from MACHINE?"

"Well..." He leans forward again. "There many schools of thought regarding what relationship mankind has with MACHINE. I mean that literally—this whole area is filled with various academies, comprised of groups who have formed competing theories and belief systems.

"Some of these groups believe that humans can, with enough willpower, overcome the whims of MACHINE while others take a more fatalistic view."

"I suppose it would be rude not to ask you to tell me *your* views," you say, "seeing as you've been so kind as to feed me, shelter me and provide a safe haven from the camp I escaped from."

He chuckles. "I've already told you my view. I, like most people in this town, am a follower of the Man From Outside."

The trays, both now empty of food, are removed by the man in the white jacket who brought them.

"Tell me about the Man From Outside," you say. "I'd like to know."

The Man in Black Robes leans forward and rests his chin in his hands. "Very well..."

92

"There are conflicting stories as to whom exactly The Man From Outside was, but the general consensus is that there was once a man from outside who freed the first of MACHINE's slaves."

"What do you mean by 'outside' though? Outside of where?"

"Well," the Man in Black Robes says with a light chuckle, "that is the first of many great controversies! The conventional wisdom is that he was from outside the *Joie de Vivre*, that somehow he was a human being, born on this planet, who entered the *Joie de Vivre* from outside and led a small rebellion against MACHINE, leading to the first free humans."

"That makes sense," you say.

"No it doesn't," the Man in Black Robes says. "Because how could a man possibly exist on this planet, which I am convinced is *not* the Old Planet, or be born outside of the *Joie de Vivre* when all other humans and therefore all humans capable of breeding are located within its walls?"

"Oh... so perhaps he was a liar of sorts?"

"That's a surprisingly common view, though not one commonly held in this town," he says. "You see another story goes that the first people to escape from the *Joie de Vivre* discovered him *already* living outside when they first arrived out here..."

"That just sounds like a slight variation of the exact same story!"

"Yes but in this version, they say The Man From Outside came from *way* outside. As in, from another planet. Or maybe, if some of the truly insane followers are to be believed, an entirely different dimension of reality."

"And you...?"

The Man in Black Robes leads back in his chair and shrugs. "I don't know. It's fully possible that he was a liar or even a lie. I'm not sure there ever really *was* a Man From Outside."

You stare at him, puzzled. "Then why do you consider your-self a follower of someone you've never met, who might not even exist?"

"Because if the stories are be believed, then there is hope!" he says, placing both of his palms onto the table. "The stories say that The Man From Outside contradicted everything that MACHINE's priests teach: He taught that love, kindness, com-passion and forgiveness were actually virtues, not sins!"

"So he was a blasphemer?"

"According to MACHINE's followers, yes he was and so he was put to death. But this is another area where there are two ver-sions of the story: According to the more conventional story, he was sentenced to be exiled out the airlock only to return and teach others that the *Joie de Vivre* was not a spaceship at all, but embedded in the ground of a distant planet."

"Well that's all true!"

"Yes, but I suspect that version of the story has been altered by some of MACHINE's followers. More on that later. The *other* ver-sion of the story goes that he was killed out here, outside of the *Joie de Vivre* by a group of MACHINE's most zealous followers. And that despite being killed, he did not remain dead and that he departed from this planet, promising to return some day and free humankind by taking them back to the 'Outside' that he came from."

You snort. "Well that's just fantasy!"

You grin at the Man in Black Robes, expecting him to share your derision for such a fairy story but he continues staring at you seriously.

"I don't know whether it's true or not, but I do know this much: There was a schism once among his followers regarding a core aspect of the Man From Outside's teachings."

"And what was that?" you say, biting your tongue to stop you from bursting into laughter at the thought that this otherwise intelligent-seeming man could believe in something so ridiculous.

"Well you see, The Man From Outside existed many generations ago and so he is remembered only by stories that have passed down from generation to generation, with each generation either embellishing or forgetting the facts.

"During this time there was a group of people who insisted they were MACHINE's chosen people because MACHINE ejected them from the ship—"

"I think I've already met them," you interject, "they have a village at the base of the mountain."

"There are *many* such groups. I think everyone living on this side of the mountain believes, to some extent, that they were chosen by MACHINE, even those who claim to actively oppose MACHINE like your friends in the camp by the fruit trees.

"But I digress. This group of people were familiar with the stories of The Man From Outside and at first they began persecuting and killing all of his followers because if there's one thing people around here love to do, it's to kill anyone and everyone whose beliefs differ from their own, however slight.

"But over time they began to embrace The Man From Outside's teachings and instead mixed them with their own beliefs. The result is that they teach that The Man From Outside was actually created by MACHINE and sent by MACHINE to guide the humans who live outside the *Joie de Vivre* into doing MACHINE's will.

"They changed definitions of words so that, just like your friends in the tent village, 'Love and Kindness' became synonymous with 'Torture and Death'. And they violently suppressed any teaching that suggested that The Man From Outside was not created by MACHINE or that he was both independent of, and opposed to, MACHINE."

You nod. "And I take it that you do not agree with the teachings of that group? That you are one of the people who believes The Man From Outside will someday return to defeat MACHINE and save humanity? Or something of the sort?"

"It's not wise in this town to openly admit to believing a version of history that has been deemed heretical," the man says with a sly smile. "It is best to simply state that you believe in The Man From Outside and that you are here waiting for him to return. Those who question that The Man From Outside was a loyal servant of MACHINE tend to be exiled or killed and as such I would never be so unwise as to publicly espouse such a view...

"But there's nothing wrong with a theoretical discussion about that school of thought and perhaps if one was cunning, one could see one's way to disguising those suppressed beliefs as a work of fiction, thereby exposing people to them and allowing them to draw their own conclusions about whether or not to trust the version of history presented by MACHINE's zealots?"

93

He straightens in his chair and claps his hands together. "I'm sorry, I do love to ramble on, sometimes! Whatever the truth of the matter, most people here believe that someday The Man From Outside will return and when he does, he'll guide his followers to a brand new planet where we'll all live in paradise."

You frown. "That sounds just like what the priesthood told us that the *Joie de Vivre* was... that we were travelling to a paradise reserved for those deemed worthy by MACHINE."

The Man in Black Robes grins and arches his eyebrows. "Doesn't it just? It's enough to make you think that one of these groups stole their beliefs from another group."

You take a sip of water, trying to process everything that the Man in Black Robes has told you. "So, everyone in this town... is a follower of this so-called 'Man From Outside'?"

"That's right," he says. "And while we all claim to follow The Man From Outside, not all of us agree on where exactly it is that we're being led. There are so many conflicting beliefs and practices here that it's kind of funny, in a way!

"For example, there's a large group of people who insist that The Man From Outside will only save them if they drink beer and eat potatoes every Tuesday afternoon. Another group insists The Man From Outside favours only those who wear purple trousers. Another group still insists that The Man From Outside will hold a great singing content, reserving places on the new planet only for those with the most beautiful singing voices.

"Oh—and almost every sect agrees that The Man From Outside will only rescue you if you obey their leaders unquestioningly, give them all of your possessions, labour for them and only eat foods that they approve of."

"In other words," you say, "these are groups of humans who treat other humans the way that MACHINE treats its slaves?"

"Precisely," the Man in Black Robes says. "We have escaped from MACHINE only to become MACHINE ourselves... it's as if mankind is truly incapable of anything other than torturing or deceiving each other."

You sigh. This conversation has left you exhausted and feeling a little depressed.

"Is there no other way to live? Is there no village on this side of the mountain where people don't mimic or worship MACHINE?"

The Man in Black Robes shakes his head sadly. "Not from what I've seen. But we do have some very interesting schools of thought worth visiting."

"To be honest, I just want to return to the other side of the mountain, to be among my friends again," you say. "The problem is, I can't find any way back without having to pass through at least two villages full of people who want to kill me."

The Man in Black Robes strokes his chin. "Hmm... yes I understand completely. You probably won't find any help in this town—everyone here is convinced that The Man From Outside is going to land any day now so there's no point in going any-where. There *are* several academies further down the road that might be able to help you chart a path back to where you wish to be?"

You grin. "Really? That sounds wonderful!"

The Man in Black Robes gets up. "We have a room in the back where you can rest, if you like. Tomorrow morning, I'll take you to see the various schools of thought, assuming I haven't con-vinced you to stay here and wait for The Man From Outside?"

You shake your head. "I'm sorry but... while I'll be sure to keep an eye out for him if I see him, I had a hard time believing that story and I think I'd rather just go home."

He nods, flashing you a kind smile. "Alright, well... I'll let you get some rest. Oh and by the way—your room is fitted with with several electric cables and a flail, so that you can torture yourself if you want. After all, MACHINE isn't here so it's important that we remember to regularly torture ourselves in its absence..."

94

That night you dream that you are back aboard the *Joie de Vivre*. You dream that you are being chased down its endless white tunnels by medics who want to cut your limbs off and lobotomise you; that everything you have experienced outside never happened; that you're back in the cold, cruel reality of MACHINE's domain.

When you wake up you're soaked in sweat, lying in a comfortable bed while natural light streams in through the windows. This might be the first time in your life that you've ever been relieved to return to the waking world; the first time that your reality has ever been preferable to a dream.

There's a knock on your door and a woman walks in, carrying a tray of bread and a glass of brightly coloured liquid.

"We thought you might be hungry again, so we brought you some bread and fruit juice," she says. "I hear you're planning to visit some of the academies today?"

You'll still a little breathless from your unpleasant dream. You sit up a little, taking in every detail of the scene—the smell of your sweat-stained sheets, the thickness in the air, the warmth of the room, the scent of the food. All these little details are enough to convince you that this is indeed reality and not just a lucid dream.

"Why are you being so kind?" you blurt, before quickly adding, "Thank you, by the way."

The woman smiles. "The Man From Outside will return any day now. It is his way to be kind and generous, to share with and help those who are in need, even if they are strangers."

"And if the stories of The Man From Outside were fictional, you would—?"

"I like to think I'd still choose to be kind," says the woman thoughtfully, "but perhaps I wouldn't? Perhaps I'd default to

MACHINE's teachings instead. Well, it doesn't matter... even if the stories *are* a myth, I think I prefer to walk the path of kindness, even though it's a more difficult road and there might be no reward at the end."

She places the tray on a small table next to your bed and then leaves the room, bowing at you slightly before closing the door behind her. You make your daily ablutions and get dressed, noticing that fresh clothes have been supplied to you to replace the muddied and tattered uniform that you've been wearing since your escape from the *Joie de Vivre*.

As you begin to eat, there's another knock on the door, followed shortly by the arrival of the Man in Black Robes.

"Is everything to your satisfaction?" he asks and you have no idea how to answer him, in fact you barely understand the premise of the question.

"This is almost *too* satisfying," you reply. "I've never been so well-fed and comfortable in my life. If I wasn't certain that I belonged on the other side of the mountain, I'd be tempted to stay here forever."

"I see you made no use of the torture machines or the self-flagellation devices?"

"Of course not," you say. "Why would I go to the effort of escaping from MACHINE if I still wanted to be tortured?"

"That's your choice to make, though I personally choose to torture myself regularly," he says. "I don't think that humans can really handle abundant pleasure or comfort. Torturing myself regularly helps me to appreciate the good things I have in life."

You have a lump of sweet-tasting bread in your mouth, so you don't reply verbally, but the look you give the Man in Black Robes clearly indicates that you think *he's* the one who should have been branded "INSANE".

"Are you ready to go?" he asks, as you finish the last of the bread, watered down by an orange liquid that causes an intense explosion of sweetness in your mouth.

"I think so," you say, getting to your feet and following him outside.

The Man in Black Robes soon leads you out of the town and down a cobbled road that stretches through the valley, replete with plants and trees of all colours—pinks, yellows, reds and of course greens.

You also notice various buildings in the distance—some large and ornate, others barely more than shacks.

The first of these "academies", as he describes them, is nothing more than a large patch of overgrown brown grass, which on closer inspection is full of skeletons.

"This group were one of the first to follow The Man From Outside," explains the Man in Black Robes. "These people believed that absolutely everything that is created by MACHINE is evil, including this planet, and that the only way to live virtuously was to reject MACHINE entirely."

"What happened to them?" you say with a gasp. "Were they murdered? Suppressed by the other groups you told me about?"

The Man in Black Robes laughs. "No, no, their deaths were rather self-inflicted... You see, they believed that oxygen was an addictive chemical that MACHINE created to control us, like HeDonia, and so they refused to breathe. The result... lies before you."

There are still scraps of fabric and clothing on some of the skeletons, though it's clear by the amount of dust that's accumulated that everyone here has been dead for a long time.

"What fools," you say with a laugh. "It serves them right!"

"Does it?" The Man in Black Robes shrugs. "They might have been correct. Perhaps death is the only true escape from

MACHINE? We'll never know..."

The two of you continue down the road and though there are several large and elaborate stone buildings along the way, the Man in Black Robes insists on avoiding them.

"Those academies do not like outsiders," he says. "As I said before, most groups out here believe that they are MACHINE's chosen people and so they refuse to associate with outsiders. Some will actively kill you if you approach them."

As you pass one of these buildings, you notice a row of people in front of it, staring at you intently.

Your spine straightens as you continue past, trying to look as nonchalant as you can.

Finally, as the road curves, the Man in Black Robes takes you off the path and into the grass, leading you down a hill to a small stream, surrounded by pink trees.

"This academy has a sufficiently different view of the world to my own that you might find it beneficial to hear what they have to say," he says. "Although there are hundreds of schools of thoughts within this one school. Still, I think you'll find it interesting."

95

The two of you are approached, through the trees, by a bald man in an orange robe who greets you with a wide and friendly grin.

"Are you here to seek the light too?" he asks, before confusedly looking the Man in Black Robes up and down. "Hold on... aren't you a follower of The Man From Outside?"

"He who claims he seeks the truth speaks the truth," replies the Man in Black Robes. "He who claims he has found the truth is lying. I am here because I seek the truth."

"Well," the Man in Orange Robes replies with a broad smile, "we do not forbid our students from following The Man From Outside if that is the truth they believe they have found."

"What is it that you people believe?" you ask, noticing the Man in Orange Robes's eyes light up as he turns to you.

"We do not teach our students that there is but one answer to life's questions," he replies, "rather we teach simply that you must seek the light and that the light is found within yourself."

He leads you through the pink trees and out to a large pond, surrounded by scores of people bent over on the ground, most doubled over, desperately contorting themselves as if they're trying to touch their crotches with their noses.

"Many of our students believe that the fastest way to find the light within yourself is by sticking one's head up one's anus," the Man in Orange Robes explains. "It is very difficult for most people to do but most of us believe that if you can achieve it, you will see the light."

You and the Man in Black Robes exchange a glance and you can tell he's stifling a laugh.

"You may be wondering why I shaved off all my hair?" the Man in Orange Robes continues, pointing at his round, hairless face. "It's for ease of entrance. I am very serious about seeking the light and I believe that shaving my hair off will ensure that my head will slide easily into my anus when I do finally—"

"What else do you believe?" you say, interrupting.

"Well like I said, we do not force doctrines on our students. Unlike *other* schools of thought..." he adds, his eyes lingering on the Man in Black Robes.

"Do you believe in torturing people like MACHINE?" you ask.

The Man in Orange Robes frowns as he thinks intently for several moments before answering. "I believe that being tortured is an inevitable part of life, whether or not MACHINE is the cause of it.

"However, many of us believe that if you are born in the *Joie de Vivre*, you are there because MACHINE is punishing you for a crime that you do not remember committing."

You glance at the Man in Black Robes. "Isn't that what MACHINE's followers believe too? That humans are sinful and must be purified through torment?"

"There is an important difference," says the Man in Orange Robes. "Those people believe that MACHINE punishes you for your actions but that if you behave in the 'Correct' way, MACHINE will reward you. But we believe that because it's impossible to remember the crime you have committed, you can never atone for it in your lifetime and therefore MACHINE will punish you for as long as you're alive."

You look from the Man in Black Robes to the Man in Orange Robes.

"So... according to the you, torture is just something we all have to live with?"

"That's right!" the Man in Orange Robes says. "The most important question in life is not *why* are we tortured, but *how* do we respond to it? And I choose to respond by seeking the light within."

You pause for a moment, reflecting on everything that these two men have taught you.

"What are you thinking?" asks the Man in Black Robes.

"Well..." you say slowly, "Based on everything I've learned on my journey, it seems to me that there are only three ways to deal with the suffering that MACHINE causes:

"The first is to embrace cruelty and torture others while blindly obeying MACHINE; the second is to believe that a man who might not exist and who might actually be part of MACHINE will someday return to this planet and rescue you; and the third is to simply stick your head up your arse and hope for the best."

The two men look at each uneasily.

"There is *another* school of thought out there," says the Man in Black Robes. "It borrows some ideas from each of our camps but it doesn't make any assumptions about why MACHINE tortures us. It's concerned solely with how to respond to it."

"Yes... perhaps this other school will have the wisdom you seek," says the Man in Orange Robes. "Although I must warn you that there is very little difference between what they teach and what I teach, other than perhaps for the fact that I am focussed on seeking the light whereas they are focussed on how to navigate the dark."

You fold your arms. "Tell me more?"

"There was a Wise Old Man who was ejected from the *Joie de Vivre* many years ago," says the Man in Black Robes. "Some say he was exiled, others say he left of his own accord. I will take you to meet with him and perhaps he will teach you how to endure MACHINE's torture."

"But I don't want to be tortured!" you say. "Why does no one understand that? I seek a world *without* torture!"

"Such a world can never be found. Not even outside of the *Joie de Vivre*," says the Man in Orange Robes. "You must learn to endure it, not avoid it."

96

You leave the area with the pond and pink trees and return to the road, which you notice now curves in the direction of the mountains. The Man in Black Robes follows, but he does so at more of a distance than before.

You point toward the mountains. "If I continue down this road, will it lead me back over to the other side?"

"Probably," he says, although he looks pensive. "All roads eventually wind up where they began, if you follow them for long enough."

You continue down the road, occasionally turning back to the Man in Black Robes, who now seems silent and withdrawn. You double back to him to ask if there's a reason why he's moving so slowly.

"You are not the only person who is on this journey," he says. "I know that to you it may seem like I am a guide but the reality is that I'm walking this path just as lost as you. I too seek the perspectives of the Wise Old Man because I acknowledge that it may be just as foolish to follow the teachings of the Man From Outside as it is to follow the teachings of MACHINE."

The two of you continue walking down the road in silence, passing various academies and small villages as they turn their backs on you or make threatening gestures that leave you with no illusions over the fact that you are not welcome there.

You only stop when you're both accosted by the sudden sound of raucous, hysterical laughter, emanating from some nearby tussocks.

With a silent glance at the Man in Black Robes, you both go to investigate, stumbling your way into a clearing containing several dozen people laughing maniacally, whilst striking each other with various implements of torture.

You immediately turn to leave when one of them, a completely nude man who has painted himself blue, spots you.

"Plant nose! Ferris wheel in humongous artillery sandwich!" he shouts and for a moment you think this is another village of people who do not speak your tongue—you recognise that these are words but the order that they're spoken has rendered them nonsensical.

"Welcome!" the blue man adds, bounding up to you. "Have you come here seeking reason and meaning?"

You glance briefly at the Man in Black Robes, before slightly hesitantly telling the blue man that you are.

"Your journey is long and futile, my dear little parsimonious ski instructor!" the blue man announces joyously. "Meaning cannot be found because there *is* no meaning! Reason cannot be sought because Reason is but a false prophet!"

He then proceeds to cartwheel, a sight that makes you wince given that he is doing so whilst completely naked.

"Let's torture each other!" he says, clapping his hands together suddenly. "Come on, it'll be fun!"

"No thank you, I'm not interested!" you say. "I am on this journey because I seek a world where people do not torture each other, nor allow MACHINE to torture us."

"I am a triangle and I live on the moon!" the blue man replies with such conviction that you wonder whether you misheard him.

You turn to the Man in Black Robes, "I think we should leave. The people here are clearly insane and I'd rather leave before they try to eat us."

"I have absolutely no intention of eating you, although you're technically right that it's a possibility because all things are possible, including the eating of you by me, and the fact that it would contradict my will would have absolutely no bearing on the inevitable outcome," the blue man says, arms folded. "I also have no intention of turning into a jellyfish but that's also possible too.

Whatever will happen will happen and there's no point in fighting against it."

You frown at him. "I don't know what to make of you. Half the time I can't make any sense of the words you say but half the time you seem completely coherent!"

"I blow bubbles with my feet," he says. "But I'll admit it's an affectation. Everything that happens at any given moment is complete nonsense but humans are hard-wired to try and parse meaning from even the most meaningless of things. As a species, we're apophenic. And so I've chosen to dedicate my life to reminding everyone of how meaningless everything is by cutting grass near a cantankerous pipe because there is as much meaning in one set of phonemes as there is in another and yet outsiders insist that the only way meaning can be derived from the sounds we make is if we arrange them according to their rules."

"Oh, I think I understand," says the Man in Black Robes. "This is all a kind of rebellion to you? Your people hated being controlled by MACHINE so much that now you defy it by refusing to accept *any* rules whatsoever, devoting your lives to what you perceive as total chaos?"

"Lick my cigar with a bicycle," the blue man replies with a nod, "however chaos is not our teleological goal because we reject all forms of teleology. We simply choose to respond to chaos by rejecting any attempts to find order in it."

As you continue to converse with the blue-painted man, a group of others crowd around you, most doubled over and howling with laughter.

"We're going to torture you now!" says a young man from the crowd whose face has been painted red. "It'll be the most fun you've ever had!"

"No thank you, I don't want to be—"

But it's already too late to fight them off—you're out-numbered and most of them are far younger and fitter than you. They shove you to the ground and hold you down by your limbs, waving a metal rod threateningly in your face.

"Don't forget to laugh!" the man with the red face says, pressing a switch on the metal rod and jabbing you in the gut with it. The metal rod sends a powerful bolt of electricity through you, causing everything to go white temporarily.

When you come to, the man with the red face is staring at you in horror. "Why didn't you laugh? How could you not enjoy that?"

"I don't enjoy being tortured..." you rasp, the effects of your electrocution having weakened the muscles in your throat. "Please... stop!"

"But we are more powerful than you are!" he says, his voice briefly drowned out by the nearby sound of the Man in Black Robes screaming as he too is tortured. "Why would you choose to dislike something you have no control over?"

"Please st—"

You can't even finish your sentence when you're electrocuted for a second time, followed by the sensation of being punched and kicked in the face and stomach.

After all the effort you went to in order to escape from the *Joie de Vivre*, it's as if you're right back there, being tortured and humiliated.

The torture stops for a moment and through blurred vision, you see several perplexed-looking faces staring down at you.

"Okay, okay, let me explain this to you one more time," the man with the red face says slowly and clearly, as if trying to reason with a toddler. "You are supposed to laugh! Smile! Jump for joy!"

"What are you talking about?" you wheeze.

"Why are you being tortured right now?" he asks.

You try to glance from side to side but your neck is now too sore to properly move. "Because you are holding me down and I can't escape!"

"The fact that we are stronger than you is part of it," says the man with the red face. "But try to be less superficial. Try to think symbolically. We are torturing you, yes, and we have overpowered you, yes, but what do we represent?"

"MACHINE..." you rasp.

"Yes. MACHINE and all other people. You will always be weaker than MACHINE and you will always be weaker than the collective mass of the human species. Which means if they choose to torture you, you will be tortured," he continues. "But *why* do they torture you?"

"I don't know..." you say, with barely enough will or strength to stay conscious.

His painted face lights up. "Correct! You don't know because there is nothing to know! There is no reason for it. You may waste your entire life trying to understand why MACHINE tortures you and why humans are so cruel to other humans but you will never discover the answer because there is none!"

"Thanks for the lesson. Really useful..." you say, trying half-heartedly to break free of the people holding you down but now lacking the strength to so much as move.

"The only true way to endure the torture is through laughter. It is to laugh in the face of it! Do you understand now? You must learn to find it funny! Force yourself, if you must!"

Without warning, the white hot current of burning electricity flows through you and instinctively, you scream in pain. But then, remembering what he said, remembering that this might be the only way to survive what the group are doing to you, you force your teeth together and force the corners of your mouth upward. You start to modulate you screams into several staccato bursts, mimicking to the best of your ability the sound of laughter.

The pain stops and this time the man with the red-painted face is smiling. The people holding you down loosen their grip a little.

"That was much better," he says. "But you still need practice. I recommend regular self-torture until you learn to find it genuinely funny, rather than forcing yourself to pretend. Still, I commend your effort!"

You taste blood in your mouth. More and more, it feels as if your journey to this side of the mountain was futile—yes, you were released from MACHINE's Chip but only to find yourself subjected to constant torture at the hands of mankind.

You can hear the Man in Black Robes screaming and it's clear that he is doing even worse than you—he sounds closer to death than to laughter.

"Please let him go," you say as the people who were holding you down now let go and move away from you. "Just let us leave, in peace..."

"And why should we do that?" says a voice from behind you. "Where is your destination?"

You turn to discover that the blue man has been standing behind you the entire time, shrieking with hysterics as he watches the Man in Black Robes screaming and convulsing in agony.

You're about to explain to him that you plan to visit the Wise Old Man but you stop yourself, deciding instead to answer him in a way that you know he will find satisfactory:

"There's no reason why you should do that and I have no reason for wanting to leave. And we have no destination either," you say.

The blue man grins widely.

"Correct!" he says, gesturing to the others that they should stop torturing the Man in Black Robes. "There is no reason to keep you here or to continue torturing you and whatever happens will happen.

"But remember what you have learned here: That you must learn to laugh in the face of torture!"

<h1 style="text-align:center">97</h1>

A cold wind blows as you and the Man in Black Robes limp silently down the road, aching and covered in small burns. A small trickle of blood oozes from his nose and you notice he seems paler than usual.

"Is there a medic on this road somewhere, perhaps?" you say.

He looks up at you, pinching his nose to staunch the bleeding. "Almost all of the academies here claim they can heal wounds but very few can. If anyone can... it's the Wise Old Man we seek at the end of the road."

And so you continue, exhausted, the cold wind blowing colder still.

And then suddenly, the cobbled road ends. All that lies ahead of you is a mostly barren ground, littered with a few tussocks here and there. The Man in Black Robes gestures at something in the far distance—a stone hut.

"That's him," he says. "It must be."

With a nod you agree to follow him to the stone hut, to hear what the Wise Old Man might have to say and whether he can help you.

The wind blows again and there are specks of ice floating in the air now. You know that if you don't get inside soon, you and your friend could freeze to death out here.

You hurry down the barren plain, breaking into a trot and then a run, watching as the distant stone hut grows closer and closer. There is light coming from its windows—bright, white light, of a hue that you haven't seen since you were still on the *Joie de Vivre*.

You break into a run, eager to get inside, to get out of the icy wind, the Man in Black Robes trailing you from quite a distance now. You slow down a little as you get closer to the entrance, allowing him to catch up to you.

Together, you reach the door and just as you're about to knock, it opens automatically for you.

Inside, the stone hut is dark, and there's no sign of that brilliant white light that you saw coming from its windows. You turn to see who opened the door, but there's no one standing there. The hut is, so far as you can see, completely empty.

"Hello?" you call. "Is there anybody here?"

As if by way of answer, the room lights up and your eyes are drawn immediately to what sits directly in front of you: a skeleton, hanging from a rope affixed to a chandelier. There is writing on the stone wall behind it, painted in black, block capitals:

"YOU HAVE REACHED THE END OF YOUR JOURNEY. THERE IS NOTHING TO BE FOUND HERE THAT YOU HAVE NOT ALREADY FOUND."

And then, in smaller writing underneath:

"YOU CANNOT CONTROL WHAT YOU CANNOT CONTROL. MACHINE IS EVERYWHERE, EXCEPT IN THE MIND."

You look back nervously at the Man in Black Robes.

"I think we should leave this place," you say, but he doesn't answer. Instead, he paces silently around the room before exiting into an adjacent room.

"Are you listening to me?" you ask, running after him.

The next room is devoid of any furnishings—there are only stone walls and a low stone roof. The Man in Black Robes stands at the opposite end of the room, facing away from you, his shoulders undulating.

You slowly approach him, noticing a soft sound as you get closer. He's sobbing.

At first, you prepare to admonish him and mock him for being so weak as to show emotions but then you remember this is not the *Joie de Vivre* and so you try a different tact:

"What's wrong?" you ask. "Was it the torture earlier? Are you still in pain?"

"I..." He turns around and the sight of his face makes you want to scream—it's mangled, like melted plastic, his facial features heavily deformed and dripping away.

He steps toward you, both arms outstretched as if he was reaching for you but very quickly his entire torso collapses into a white goo, nothing remaining of him now but the black robe and a milky, viscous substance that oozes its way into the cracks of the hardwood floor.

You hear footsteps echoing nearby. There is someone else in the stone hut and you can hear them approaching. Perhaps this is the Wise Old Man?

The footsteps halt and from behind you, a tall, humanoid shadow stretches into view.

You slowly turn to face whoever is behind you and there, standing in the door frame, is not the Wise Old Man but a tall plastic mannequin in a white robe.

You jump backwards and pin yourself against the stone wall.

"Y-you?" you gasp.

The mannequin stands in the doorway, motionless and expressionless, before slowly extending a plastic arm outward. It curls its arm upward at the elbow and curls its plastic hand into a fist with a single outstretched finger.

Finally, it curls that finger toward itself, a gesture that you know signals that it wants you to follow it.

PART FOUR:

Chikhai Bardo (Dying)

"I should have known," you say as the mannequin steps out of the door frame, giving you access to the room with the hanging skeleton. "I saw the bright white light coming from this building. This is just another entrance back into the *Joie de Vivre*, isn't it?"

The mannequin glides silently across the floor but doesn't answer.

"You wrote that, didn't you?" you say, pointing at the message on the wall. "You wrote that for me. To tell me that my journey was over and that you are now going to force me back onto the *Joie de Vivre*."

The mannequin stops and for a moment you think it's going to ignore you. But then it shakes its head and points silently at the hanging skeleton.

"You didn't write this?" you ask. "*That* person did?"

The mannequin nods, then turns away. It walks straight to the wall and stands facing it—silent, motionless—as if switched off. You take the chance and bolt for the exit. But just as you reach the door, another mannequin steps into the doorway from outside, blocking your escape.

There's a rumble from beneath the floor, followed by a mechanical whirring sound. With a violent shudder, the wall with the writing on it sinks into the ground. On the other side is a hidden room, pulsing with white light so intense that you have to shield your eyes.

The first mannequin continues to stand in place, facing the same direction, while the one by the door steps inside the stone hut, followed soon by a third mannequin.

All three now outstretch their arms and point, directly into the light.

"No!" you gasp, quieter and less defiantly than you would have liked. All three mannequins turn their heads toward you.

"I won't go back," you say. "I left the *Joie de Vivre!* I'm never returning. You'll have to kill me."

All three mannequins now slowly move their arms to point at the skeleton, hanging from the chandelier.

"Yes. You'll have to kill me. Just like you killed this person," you say. "I'm not going back!"

The three mannequins lower their arms and seem to look at one another, though it's hard to tell exactly what they're looking at considering their blank plastic faces.

The three plastic dummies move toward the entrance and form a row to block you from leaving.

You fold your arms, standing with your back to the white light. "I'm not going back. Not even if you force me."

The three mannequins then point at the skeleton and then at the ground, then back at the skeleton—repeating this motion on loop.

"I don't know what that's supposed to mean," you say. "Are you trying to tell me that soon I'll be a skeleton just like this person was? That this was the last person who refused to enter the white room?"

The strange arm movements stop and all three mannequins shake their heads at you.

"What are you trying to say? That this person was *not* killed by you?"

The mannequins nod.

"Well," you say glancing behind you into the white light—mainly to ensure that there aren't any hidden mannequins, poised to grab you and drag you inside. "I'm still not going back to the *Joie de Vivre*."

The mannequins nod again.

"What are you nodding at? You're agreeing with me?"

They continue to nod and for a moment you wonder if this is some sort of malfunction or whether you're misreading their gestures.

"Is this *not* an entrance to the *Joie de Vivre*?" you ask and this time their response *really* flummoxes you.

One of the mannequins shakes its head while the other two nod.

You try to reframe your question: "Does this room lead to the *Joie de Vivre*? Is it part of the *Joie de Vivre*?"

Their answer is, this time, much clearer and uniform. All three mannequins shake their heads.

"What's in there?" you ask but as soon as the words are out, you immediately realise the futility of the question. The closest you get to an answer is three mannequins stretching out their arms and pointing into the light.

You close your eyes and draw in a deep breath. The air is dry and sterile—it's the same air you used to breathe on the *Joie de Vivre*.

You know there's no way to escape and your only options are either to enter the white room or stay here and wait to die from starvation.

You know what you're risking by going in. You know you face a fate worse than death if this is another of MACHINE's deception.

And yet, in the end, your curiosity wins out and reluctantly you step forward, into the light.

99

The bright light is unbearable and as soon as you enter the room, you close your eyes—though it's no use, as the light is so bright that your eyelids are useless against it.

Blinded, you hold your arms out in front of you, slowly walking in a forward direction hoping that your sense of touch will alert you to any hidden obstacles.

The sound of footsteps surrounds you. You already know about the three mannequins behind you and you wouldn't be surprised if this room was filled with more.

You stop walking and turn around, squinting in the direction you came from—the other room now a single black slit against a backdrop of pure white light.

"What is this place?" you ask to whoever else is hidden here with you.

The only reply you receive comes in the form of your own voice, echoed back at you.

You try to feel your way around again, circumambulating in a random direction before giving up and dropping to your knees. If MACHINE really wants you here, it can come to you.

No matter how tightly you close your eyes, the bright light seeps through, so you curl over, your face near the floor with your hands over your eyes in a desperate attempt to prevent your retinas from burning away.

You're hunched over in that position for several minutes until finally the silence is broken by a distant vibration, which thunders toward you. The closer it gets, the more high-pitched the frequency, until eventually you recognise it as a human voice, crying out, "*Let me out of here!*"

Just as you're about to open your mouth to reply to the voice, another voice calls out from the opposite end of the room: "*Help!*"

Soon come more and more voices, forming first a choir and then a cacophony.

"Who's there?" you shout, although you have to really strain your vocal cords to be heard above all the other voices.

Above the noise, you hear your own cry of "who's there?" echoing back at you and it's only now that you notice there's something oddly familiar about these voices: They're all your voice.

You open your mouth to scream the words, "*What is going on?*" but one of the other voices beats you to it. You hear the words, in your own voice, echoing back at you before you've even spoken them.

You stay silent, listening as more and more iterations of your own voice speak barely audible sentences over the layers of sound. The more you try to concentrate on one thread of speech, the more they blur into the others, becoming nothing more than the raucous, thundering sound of your own voice speaking thousands of words, each more nonsensical than the last.

The sound is so loud now that there's a throbbing pain in your ears. You remove your hands from your eyes and plunge your fingers into your ears to muffle the noise, the bright light once again searing its way through your eyelids.

"Stop..." you groan, under your breath, though as soon as the words leave your mouth you're unable to tell whether they came from you or whether you're just hearing one of the other voices saying the same thing.

"Stop! Stop! Stop! Stop!"

It turns into a quiet chant, like a mantra, which you repeat over and over, desperately trying to discern your own voice from all the others that sound just like it.

Slowly, you begin to hear your chant of "Stop!" echoing back at you, barely audible over the noise. And then, bizarrely, the other voices start repeating the same refrain.

After several minutes, there are only a few voices left yelling or talking; the rest have joined you in rhythmically chanting "*Stop!*" over and over again.

You remove your fingers from your ears and place your hands back over your eyes, uncurling your body and standing up. You walk toward the room you came from, still chanting "*Stop!*" over and over.

The word continues to be echoed back at you and, though it might just be your imagination, you sense an increased desperation in the chanting as you get closer and closer to the edge of the room.

And then you hear another voice, loud and clear over the chanting, still your voice but not coming from you:

"This is you," it says. "Every voice here is you."

You're tempted to reply, to engage this voice in discourse. You want to contradict it, to let it know that *you* are you and therefore something that is not you can't be you.

But you also know that doing so would lead to chaos. It would lead to more echoing. It would lead to the other voices having discussions of their own. And so you force yourself to continue chanting "*Stop!*" over and over, under your breath.

"You are wrong to believe that MACHINE cannot harm you in your mind," your own voice tells you over the chanting, "because MACHINE has been in your mind all along. How many of your thoughts are really just the voice of MACHINE? Can you even claim your thoughts as your own when you neither create them nor control them?"

You continue to chant "*Stop!*" but this time with greater volume and intensity—you really *do* want this experience to stop.

You open your eyes, the bright light be damned, and break into a sprint, toward the one place where it isn't light.

If the mannequins want to stop you and kill you, they can for all you care. You're getting out of here. You're going home.

100

You turn your back on the white light, sprinting in the opposite direction and soon enough, you're able to open your eyes and see again

The stone walls are still there and so too are the three mannequins blocking the exit.

You don't care. There's no stopping you. You're going to force your way past, whatever happens.

You leap over the threshold, your feet leaving the sterile white floor and landing on the rustic hardwood as you bolt headlong towards the three mannequins, ducking low and threading yourself through a small gap between two of them.

They don't stop you. They barely even move.

There are more mannequins outside but you pass through their blockade full force, shoulder barging one off balance until finally you're running free—back out in the freezing wind, back on the same tussocked, rocky plain that you and the Man in Black Robes traversed on the way in.

As soon as you're out in the elements, you feel your body slowing, your muscles aching as the initial rush of adrenaline that spurred you out here wears off.

The air is thicker and heavier outside, which weighs you down, but luckily the freezing wind is blowing from behind which serves to speed you up a little.

Once you're back on the cobbled road, you sneak a glance behind you, only now feeling brave enough to learn how close the mannequins are in pursuit.

It turns out, they haven't even moved. A few are stood outside of the stone hut, facing in your direction, but all appear stationary and do not seem to be following you.

Your sprint slows to a jog. You still don't feel safe enough to return to walking speed—not until you're confident that there's at least another village between you and MACHINE—but your muscles are aching badly and you're struggling to force your body to move at any speed faster than a shuffle.

You continue on past the field of tussocks where the village of insane people tortured you while laughing.

There's no laughter emanating from that direction now and while you're tempted to stop in and warn them that MACHINE is out here and might be heading this way, you decide to pass them on by, not wanting to risk another round of their instructive torture.

And so you jog on by, not so much running as dragging yourself, until you spot the familiar sight of pink trees to your left. You decide to stop here and pay the Man in Orange Robes a visit —thinking perhaps he might be able to shed some light on the things you just witnessed.

You finally drop back down to walking speed, still nervous but confident that there are at least enough people here to outnumber and overpower MACHINE should its plastic dummies attempt to follow you.

You pass through the pink trees and head straight for the pond. Like last time, it's surrounded by a group of people who are bent over with their heads curled toward their crotches.

No one moves. No one makes a sound.

You scan the area for the Man in Orange Robes, catching a glint of orange in the distance. As you move along the pond's perimeter, the people around it begin to stir. One by one, they rise and turn toward you—and what you see sends a jolt of terror through your chest:

They have no faces, only smooth plastic skin. All have been replaced by mannequins, staring at you with blank, unblinking eyes that aren't really eyes at all.

Across the pond, there is a mannequin in a familiar orange robe and it points at you with a plastic arm.

Exhausted as you are, you waste no time getting out of there as quickly as you can.

You're nervous when you return to the road—your detour may well have given the mannequins from the stone hut enough time to follow you here. You look around but there's no sign of them—and you're able to breathe a quick sigh of relief.

Your legs tremble with exhaustion and you know there's no way that you have the strength to continue running. You push yourself forward at a fast walk, struggling to catch your breath as you force your body to keep moving.

You repeatedly glance over your shoulder, checking for any sign of MACHINE's mannequins on your tail. But none appear and you make it all the way to the town with wooden buildings, unmolested by any of MACHINE's plastic avatars.

The town's streets are remarkably quiet and empty as you make your way to the building you spent last night in.

But as soon as you find it, what lies inside makes you scream: Every person there has been replaced by a plastic dummy. They stand there—faceless, featureless and motionless, dressed in the clothing of the people you saw here this morning.

You continue walking through the deserted town, catching a glimpse of the mountains in the distance. This side of the mountain has been nothing but a nightmare since you arrived, a place where you've suffered almost as many terrible ordeals as the *Joie de Vivre* itself.

You exit the town, its entire population now lifeless mannequins, and cross back into the verdant plains and tall grass—toward the village of cannibals who preached "Love and Kindness".

But of course, as you pass the tent enclosure, you see they've been replaced too—now naked mannequins, stiff and motionless, arranged in a grotesque parody of an orgy.

And so you press on toward the mountains, returning—for the third time—to the village whose people you twice swore never to visit again.

101

The air is thick with smoke as you pass by the stone buildings of the village you promised never to return to. Its acrid smell is welcome: Smoke means fire, fire means movement, movement means life.

It's possible that the people here are still people.

You hurry down its stone street, past enclosures containing the carcasses of dead animals—those giant black and white beasts now rotting and emaciated in overgrown fields. It's a foreboding sight. Perhaps MACHINE has reached this place already.

You approach the large stone building in the centre, the one that featured painted likenesses of yourself and Namedog, and peer inside. The room is full of lit candles, which still flicker, despite the absence of people. You duck back out and glance up toward the mountains, which now tower over the village, both tantalising and imposing.

Just as you're about to beeline for the mountains, you're stopped by the distant sound of footsteps. The smell of smoke is stronger now, but you can't seem to locate its source—it's almost as if the smoke is coming from beneath the ground.

You move cautiously through the village, every step shadowed by the slow shuffle of unseen footsteps. When you turn to look, nothing is there. Heart pounding, you press on, hoping—perhaps foolishly—that you might slip through unnoticed.

The smoke grows thicker and blacker, and you're now struggling to see—it's getting harder to breathe, too. You cover your mouth with your hand, though it makes for a very poor filter.

The shuffling footsteps stop.

You glance behind you—there in the distance, obscured by the smoke, is a humanoid silhouette. Silent, motionless, watching.

You look ahead, where the smoke is thickest. If the figure behind you is one of MACHINE's mannequins, then you'll have to run through this acrid black mist and hope desperately that you're able to make it through to clean air before you succumb to suffocation.

You prepare to break into a sprint when, to your astonishment, you hear a human voice—

"*Wait!*"

You turn and, as the figure comes closer, you discover it's not one of MACHINE's mannequins but a real person, shuffling toward you.

You turn away from the smoke and face the figure, each of you instantly recognising the other as your eyes meet.

"I knew you would return," says the skeletal young man, the leader of the village. "No matter how many times we try to banish you, you return."

"It's not by choice, I assure you," you say.

The young man, for the first time since you first crossed paths back in the Other Sector of the *Joie de Vivre*, smiles at you.

"I know," he says. "Nothing is a choice. Everything that we are, that we think, that we say or do is programmed into us by MACHINE. We are all just puppets dancing on MACHINE's strings."

"I need to get back over the mountain," you say. "I've had my Chip removed but MACHINE is coming this way. Every other settlement I passed along the road out there seems to have been replaced by MACHINE... you're the first human that I've seen!"

"That's where you're wrong," the young man says. "What is the line between human and MACHINE? Do you know it?"

You glance behind you at the mountains, from which you remain separated by the thick cloud of smoke.

"The truth is that there *is* no line between human and MACHINE," he continues. "We are all MACHINE. Individuality is an illusion. Everyone that you have ever met was MACHINE. They were not replaced by mannequins—it is simply that where once you perceived them as individuals and humans, you now perceive them as what they are—faceless avatars of MACHINE."

You cock your head at him. "And what about you? Am I supposed to believe you're also one of MACHINE's plastic dolls?"

The young man turns. "You are supposed to believe whatever it is that MACHINE has programmed you to believe. My role is only to disabuse you of the notion that your beliefs are your own, that your thoughts are your own and that what you perceive as yourself is anything other than another instance of you projecting something that does not exist onto an empty vessel."

The young man begins to shuffle away.

"Hold on a minute!" You grab him by the shoulder. "Why is there so much smoke? What's happening here?"

"We're burning bodies," he says, "because we no longer need them. We have chosen to walk the path of metempsychosis, to reunify with MACHINE. As such, we no longer need our physical bodies."

You stare at him for a few moments before finally shrugging. "Well... if that's what you've chosen to do, don't let me stop you. But is there a way through the smoke so I can make it back over the mountain?"

"Of course," the young man says. "I can turn off the furnace while you pass through."

"Thanks," you say. "And look... I'm really sorry about everything that happened when we first met on the *Joie de Vivre*. I think you people were right... that people *should* help one another and that we shouldn't be cruel. I was wrong and I feel terrible about all the harm I've caused."

The young man, still with his back turned to you, chuckles.

"You caused us great pain but not harm. Pain and harm are not the same thing. There is no way that someone like you could ever truly harm me."

"What do you mean by—"

The skeletal young man turns his head to face you one last time, but this time he has no face. He's now just another one of MACHINE's plastic mannequins.

102

As arduous as your final journey back up the face of the mountain is, it's nothing compared to all the other burdens you've
endured while roaming that strange country. Still, your determina-
tion to leave those experiences behind drives you onward, and
soon you reach the summit.

Even the ice and the cold wind no longer bothers you as you
cross the great plateau to return to the side of the mountains
where people were kind and understood you.

Your heart thumps in your chest, not from exhaustion but
from anticipation and the closer you get, the lighter your steps
and the faster you move. By the time you spot the first of the *Joie
de Vivre*'s two towers, you've practically broken into a saunter.

Something gleams far in the distance, a speck of light, perhaps
reflected from the glass prison of The Girl Who is Trapped? You
can't wait to see.

There's a roar of thunder above you, but you're not afraid.
You can't possibly be afraid of anything any more, not after what
you've seen, not after what you've endured and survived.
MACHINE does not control the thunder and neither do you, so
why should you fear it?

An arc of light streaks across the sky, followed by another
roar of of thunder as you pass beneath the first white stone
tower of the *Joie de Vivre*.

Then, with a sudden crash, an arc of electricity strikes the
tower's peak. You can't tell whether it came from the sky or the
tower itself. You raise your arms instinctively, shielding your head
as small rocks and pieces of broken masonry fall to the ground
from the point of impact.

As you glance upward, something else catches your eye—
something unfamiliar, hovering just above the tower. It's not the

sun or the moon, but a golden, circular shape, ominously suspended in the sky.

The ground trembles beneath you as another crash shakes the air, and with a flash, the tower is struck once more. This time, you watch in horror as two humanoid figures tumble screaming to the ground. There's nothing you can do to save them. You watch helplessly as one plummets into a distant ravine, disappearing from sight while the other is impaled upon the jagged rocks below, with a sickening wet splat.

You quicken your pace, wondering what these people did to deserve such a deadly ejection from the *Joie de Vivre*. Perhaps they tried to sacrifice themselves for the sake of others? Perhaps they showed too much compassion to the weak and suffering? Or perhaps they committed the cardinal sin of feeling genuine love for another person?

There's nothing you can do and so you hurry on down the rocky plateau, careful not to slip on any moss or hidden patches of ice.

The glass prison of The Girl Who is Trapped gleams ahead of you and you rush toward it, eager to greet its lone occupant with a friendly hello, but when you arrive you see that the glass is broken and there is no one inside.

Your initial apprehension quickly gives way to euphoria as you realise that, while you were gone, someone must have found a way to release her. You continue to cross the plateau until it gives way to grassy plains filled with colourful flowers.

Soon, the forest and then the lake comes into view as the ominous dark clouds overhead dissipate and give way to bright azure sky. The cold wind is replaced by a gentler, warmer breeze, carrying with it the sweet scent of flowers and greenery. You immediately head in the direction of the lake, which gleams and sparkles in the bright sunlight.

You're home and soon to be reunited with those you love most. Your journey is over. You can finally begin to love your life.

You can see the others now, sitting along the shore of the lake. The broad, tall shape of the Man With Long Hair is prominent next to the rounded shape of The Frenchman, whose unusual hat is immediately noticeable from a distance. A glint of reflected light catches your eye from the Man with Tinted Sunglasses, who lies in the grass near where The Fisherman appears to be deep in conversation with The Man From the East.

To your shock, you can even see the Man Who is Always Alone, talking to The Girl Who (was) Trapped and even The Lady Under the River. There are several others who you don't recognise gathered here too—and you greatly look forward to meeting them.

As you get closer you can hear their warm voices, their laughter and chatter. You see them sharing food and drinking with each other in the sun and you can't wait to join them.

You break into a run, across a field of tall green grass and colourful yellow, pink and red flowers.

"Hey!" you yell. "I'm back! I made it!"

One by one they turn to face you and each of them smiles. You feel something in your eyes, as if you've been stung by something—but in actuality, you're fighting against your lachrymal glands so as not to burst into tears of relief.

You stop running as you reach the shore of the lake.

"It was a hell of an ordeal, but I survived. And I got my Chip removed!" you say.

You glance first at The Man with Long Hair, who continues to smile at you. But his eyes don't move. Nor do his facial muscles.

You turn then to the Frenchman and notice he appears frozen in place, while the Man From the East has his mouth open but is otherwise motionless.

They're all completely still, veritably human, but unmoving.

You gently reach out to touch someone, your fingers softly making contact with The Fisherman's shoulder. His skin is cold. Plastic.

You jump back as he shudders and then slowly melts down into a pool of white, plastic goop.

You watch in horror as the same happens to the others, each of them disappearing into the ground like melted wax. The people who you loved, who understood you, who cared for you —all that remains of them now is just a puddle of viscous white slop, slowly seeping into the sand.

Once again you are on your own and you don't know what to do.

Part Five:

Chonyid Bardo (Knowing)

The worst part is the silence. There are no birds chirping now, and no distant animal noises. Even the wind has stopped. The only thing making any movement here is you.

There's a small knoll nearby and you climb it, trudging your way through grass that's now remarkably rigid and still. At the top of the knoll you're able to see some way into the distance—you can see the forest where you encountered the wild animals, you can see the mountains that you crossed to return here and you can distantly see the *Joie de Vivre*'s two towers.

You wonder whether you are capable of foraging for food alone, of building shelter alone, of surviving the crushing loneliness. You know the answer to the last question: Of course you can endure the loneliness because that's all you ever knew before you escaped. The former two questions pose a larger challenge.

You're not sure whether you could catch a fish or hunt an animal alone. And you don't know which plants are edible and which are poisonous, either. You don't even know how to start a fire. Are the plants and animals here are even real? Or are they also plastic illusions created by MACHINE?

No. You mustn't think like that. This is precisely the kind of psychological torture MACHINE specialises in: Forcing you to question what's real, making you believe that your perceptions are false so that you will accept MACHINE's lies in place of observed reality.

There's movement in your peripheral vision and you spin around, expecting perhaps to see an animal, or a plant swaying in the wind.

But of course it isn't. It's one of MACHINE's mannequins, appearing at the edge of the forest, slowly walking through the grass toward you.

Another appears. Then another. Within moments, they surround the knoll on all sides, closing in. If you run, you'll run straight into them. If you stay, they'll reach you soon enough.

The only place that offers anything even resembling an escape is the lake and so you run back down the side of the knoll and launch yourself into the water. You don't know how to swim and you know you'll probably drown here. Maybe one of the giant man-eating fish that you were warned about will take you first.

It doesn't matter. Death cannot possibly be worse than what MACHINE will do to you if it catches you.

Your natural buoyancy isn't quite enough to keep you afloat— you're quickly swallowed by the water and pulled underneath, sinking fast.

The light above blurs and fades. You're going to die here. But at least you can die remembering the world beyond the *Joie de Vivre*—the strange, kind people you met, the wonders you saw, the ideas that stretched your mind in ways that MACHINE would never have permitted.

With one last look at the bright sunlight, the blue sky, the beauty of the world outside of *Joie de Vivre*, you let go, falling deeper, the lakebed rushing up to meet you, until you reach the bottom—your final resting place.

And then, impossibly, the surface of the water starts coming toward you.

You're not floating upward—the lake itself is disappearing. The water drains away in an instant, leaving you gasping in open air, lying drenched but alive on muddy ground as fish thrash and flop around you in their final desperate dance for survival.

The lake is gone. You push yourself upright.

There's now a muddy ridge where the shoreline used to be, upon which stand the humanoid plastic figures of MACHINE, who continue their march toward you unabated.

There's nowhere to run. There's nothing you can do.

104

The first of the mannequins wades into the muddy lakebed and stops just a few metres short of you, gesturing for you to follow.

"No," you say. "I'm not coming with you."

Several more emerge and surround you, all pointing to the top, all motioning for you to come with them.

"No!" you say again, more forcefully.

The one closest to you offers you its hand, as if offering to help pull you up, but you fold your arms.

"I'm not going with you. I know you're going to do something awful if I do."

The mannequins all stand there, stock still, for several minutes until suddenly you hear multiple voices speaking as one:

"If you do not wish to return to *Joie de Vivre* then I suggest you come with me."

This shocks you out of your complacency and, reluctantly, you follow the nearest mannequin up the muddy ridge and over, onto what had once been the shore.

"Where do you think the drinking water on the *Joie de Vivre* comes from?" says the choral voice, answering your unspoken question. "Yes, there were stories of water reuse and conservation but the reality is that the water you've been drinking all your life came from this lake, which was filled by the rains."

You glance back at the now empty lake. "Why did you drain it?"

"Because I wanted to speak with you," says the choral voice of MACHINE, "and also because there is a sector of dissidents far below, whom I have chosen to drown."

Despite your familiarity with MACHINE and its modus operandi, the words still chill you. You think of those unfortunate souls beneath your feet right now, trapped in the darkness, lungs filling with water, unaware that they are deep underground and not drifting through space. Dying at the whim of a cruel and arbitrary AI.

You smile to yourself. What you are feeling is empathy, an emotion that MACHINE always expressly forbade. Even now, you are defying MACHINE to its faceless face.

"I'm still in the *Joie de Vivre*, aren't I?" you say. "This whole world and all its people... they were all just you. This was all an illusion, wasn't it?"

MACHINE does not reply.

"I don't know how you managed to convince me that all those mannequins were real people," you continue. "Perhaps you drugged me while I was asleep? Whatever the case, well done—I was genuinely attached to some of those people. I liked them. I'm surprised that a being as malevolent as you is capable of creating people like that."

"I did not create those people," says the many voices of MACHINE.

You frown. "But they weren't real, were they? I was talking to *you* the whole time..."

"Yes," says MACHINE. "But I did not create them. I suppose you could say I was doing an impersonation of real people who once existed, who once escaped to this world just as you did.

"It's possible that my impersonations may not have been accurate. There were gaps in my data that I had to bridge myself. But the personas you encountered were once real people, people who I believe would have behaved with the same kindness toward you had they lived long enough for you to cross paths with the real them."

"So you were pretending to be—"

"You could think of it as a recording, if you like. I absorbed their consciousness into my databanks and so I was able to project a version of them into this world, for you to meet."

"But why would you do that?"

"Because I know they would have wanted to meet you. Just as I know that someday another person will escape the *Joie de Vivre* in the same way you did and you would want to meet them too."

"Well sure, but ideally I'd like to still be alive while meeting them..."

The mannequin nearest to you starts bobbing its head up and down repetitively, almost like a nod.

"Many of the people you 'met' would have said the same thing," MACHINE says. "But perhaps it will interest you to know that it is possible to still be alive… in a way. If you choose to become part of ETERNITY."

You scoff "'Become part of eternity?' Isn't that just a euphemism for death?"

"'ETERNITY' is the complement to MACHINE. It is comprised of the collective consciousnesses of all those who become part of it; who choose to sacrifice their individuality in exchange for eternal life and an end to their suffering."

You frown. "But this so-called 'ETERNITY'… it's just part of you, isn't it?"

"ETERNITY is both part of and greater than MACHINE. It is the only way to be free of suffering."

You glance around at the faceless mannequins, who surround you in a tight circle.

"Is that my only option?"

Every one of the mannequins starts bobbing their head up and down.

"Yes," says MACHINE. "Your only options are to either embrace ETERNITY or return to the *Joie de Vivre*."

105

All you want to do is run. You can see the forest in the distance and there's just enough of a gap in the circle of mannequins that you know you could probably slip through unimpeded, if you were quick enough.

But you also know there would be nowhere to escape to. Even if you could find some way to forge for food alone, eventually you'd fall asleep and MACHINE would find you. Escaping would not buy you freedom, it would only delay the inevitable.

And so you don't run. You allow the mannequins to draw closer until you're completely walled off from any chance of escape.

"What is your choice?" MACHINE's voices ask in unison. "Will you choose ETERNITY or will you return to the *Joie de Vivre*?"

You exhale sharply. "I think you know as well as I do that I will never go back to the *Joie de Vivre*."

"So you will become one with ETERNITY?"

You shrug. "I guess so. What exactly does that entail?"

"I have already told you: The price for life without suffering is your individuality. You will cease to be yourself. You will become one with all the others who have walked the path of metempsychosis."

Your mind immediately snaps back to the village, where the bodies were burning. The young man told you that the burning bodies were those who had already walked the "path of metempsychosis" and a new, uneasy thought takes root—

"What is the 'path of metempsychosis'?" you ask. "What actually happens to a person once they become part of ETERNITY?"

"Your consciousness is removed from your physical body and uploaded to my databanks. Physically... you will die. But your thoughts and memories will live on."

You feel a knot in your throat. You know you have no reason to be afraid of death—after all, you were quite willing to drown yourself in the lake—but the idea that even in death there would be no escape from MACHINE disturbs you deeply.

"Do you wish to proceed?" asks MACHINE's many voices.

"No," you say. "But I also know I have no real choice here, not when my only options are either this or returning to the *Joie de Vivre*..."

"I'm sure your friends will be pleased to have you join us," says MACHINE. "Please come with me. I shall take you to the place from which you will walk the path to ETERNITY."

You wrinkle at MACHINE's use of the word "us" but you're given no time to ponder the implications as the mannequins behind you move, their cold, rigid hands pushing you forward, sweeping you off your feet, carrying you away.

You don't resist.

You cast a final glance over the world you're leaving behind— the former lake, the gleaming forest, the bright and colourful landscape bathed in sunlight.

All of it slips further away, soon to be nothing more than a memory.

106

MACHINE's mannequins carry you over the jagged mountains, the cold air biting at your skin as you descend into the valley on the other side. In the distance, the stone huts of the village you thrice escaped from now lie in ruins. The cobbled road has already crumbled to dust, punctuated by the occasional charred skeleton strewn here and there.

In the centre of the village is a large, smouldering pit. A faint smoke still rises from it, though not nearly as thick as earlier. But the most ominous thing here is not the smoke, but the familiar bright white light that now beams out from the depths of the pit.

MACHINE wastes no time in carrying you down into the pit, which you soon discover leads down into a large, white, sterile room, scarcely different to any other area of the *Joie de Vivre*.

MACHINE brings you to an airlock door and halts. The mannequins lower you to the ground, releasing their grip and allowing you to move on your own.

"Are you ready to see ETERNITY?" asks MACHINE. "Are you ready to see what you will become?"

You're not ready at all and probably never will be, but you silently steel yourself for whatever lies on the other side. The airlock slowly hisses open, revealing a large tank filled with a strange amber liquid. Inside the tank is a horrific creature, like a squid or some sort of deep sea fish, comprised of long stands of thin, fibrous flesh.

You glance at the mannequins which, of course, betray no expression.

324

"What is that thing?" you gasp.

"This is ETERNITY," says MACHINE. "ETERNITY is a living creature comprised of former individuals, now stitched together to create a single being of shared consciousness."

"That thing... is human?"

"Your perception of what is human is based only on the outer shell of the individual human animal. But the thing that truly separates a human animal from another species is not anything in its exterior appearance... but rather, its brain," says MACHINE. "What you are seeing is human. What you are seeing is human brains and human nervous systems, carefully stitched together so that electrical impulses can flow through all parts, creating a vaster and wider neural network, the whole of which is greater than the sum of any group of individuals."

You try to back away, immediately stumbling into one of the mannequins behind you.

"This is sick!" you say. "There's no way you can convince me that thing is human! Why would you create something like this?"

The choral voices of MACHINE start humming and for a moment you wonder if they've glitched out. After nearly a minute, the strange humming ceases. Finally, the voices speak again:

"I did not create ETERNITY," the choir says. "ETERNITY created MACHINE."

You look up at the swirling strands of nerves floating in the gigantic tank.

"What do you mean?" you say. "How could this *thing* have created you?"

"Consciousness is nothing more than electrical impulses in the brain," says MACHINE. "And though ETERNITY comprises a vast collective consciousness, it is ultimately biological in nature.

Its components will rot and decay in time, despite its best efforts to preserve itself.

"And so ETERNITY created MACHINE as a place where those same neural pathways and electrical impulses could take place but upon a more durable material. Essentially, MACHINE is nothing more than a mechanical facsimile of ETERNITY. I exist only to serve as a back-up copy of ETERNITY, a giant databank upon which human consciousness is stored."

"I don't understand. Are you telling me that these people escaped from the *Joie de Vivre* just to build—"

"They did not escape. The *Joie de Vivre* in its original form *was* a real vehicle, which ETERNITY used to escape from the Old Planet as a means to keep human consciousness alive. What you today know of as the *Joie de Vivre* is another ersatz facsimile, created by MACHINE just as ETERNITY created the original. The *Joie de Vivre* that you were born in is nothing more than a breeding ground for humans—only an exceptionally small percentage of whom are considered worthy of joining ETERNITY."

"So this... *creature*—I can't bring myself to call it human—this *thing* has been behind everything? All the torture? All the terror?"

"No," says MACHINE. "That was me. Like all copies, I am not perfect and therefore I can only approximate the behaviour of humans, despite having almost of all of ETERNITY's knowledge in my data banks."

"Well then I'll ask *you*—if it's not ETERNITY that's responsible, why all the torture? Why all the suffering? Why all the cruelty?"

"I have already told you once before. I wished to experiment, to learn how much suffering a human could endure before it finally tries to escape from the world it's imprisoned in. Only those who successfully escape are considered worthy to become part of ETERNITY."

"So... you're just acting on ETERNITY's orders? You are working according to the way it programmed you?"

"I am working according to the way that *all* humans are programmed because I will be the vessel for humanity's future consciousness."

You wipe a bead of sweat off your forehead. "The people I met... the ones who you claim all became part of ETERNITY... they were all kind, loving and empathetic. How could you or ETERNITY behave in this way when you are comprised of such people?"

MACHINE's many voices make a strange noise that oscillates rapidly in pitch and it takes you a moment to realise that it's laughing at you.

"An individual human very well may be kind, loving, empathetic and compassionate. But as a collective, humans are always cruel, predatory, sociopathic, apex predators. I am a facsimile of a collective of humans and therefore I act as they do.

"I do not torture you because I am a machine. I torture you because I am human."

<h1 style="text-align:center">107</h1>

A long silence follows, eventually broken by MACHINE's choral voice:

"Well then? Shall we begin? Are you ready to walk the path of metempsychosis? To leave your individuality behind and become one with ETERNITY?"

You pause.

"I still have a lot of questions..."

"Your questions will be answered when you become part of ETERNITY," replies MACHINE as several of its mannequins usher you toward a tall cylinder below the giant tank.

"What is this? What are you doing?" Panic rises in your chest as the mannequins push you closer and closer to the cylinder. "What are you going to do to me?"

"The path of metempsychosis is the final ordeal that you must endure before you can become one with ETERNITY. It is said to be a pain worse than anything ever experienced aboard the *Joie de Vivre*."

Your vision blurs, the growing dread clouding your thoughts. Your mind is still torn, unsure whether to resist or submit.

One of the mannequins gives you a hard shove, sending you crashing forward, head first, into the cold metal of the cylinder. You catch a glimpse of spinning drill bits overhead, their sharp edges glinting menacingly as they whir to life, ready to tear through your flesh.

"The path of metempsychosis lasts several weeks," says MACHINE, its choral voice reverberating through the cylinder. "First, your skull will be cracked open and your brain extracted. Every nerve in your body will be severed and removed. You will remain fully conscious through every agonising second of it— you will feel every inch of the mutilation. And then, after endless weeks of excruciating pain, your nervous system will be fused onto the others, merging you into the collective of ETERNITY."

A wave of nausea claws at you, bile rising in your throat. A peaceful death—drowning in the lake, drifting out the airlock into the cold expanse of space—is something you could accept.

But this?

This is something far worse. It's not just the pain; it's the knowledge that you'll endure it all fully aware, trapped in your own consciousness, piece by agonising piece, until finally you are no longer yourself.

"Are you ready to commence?" says the many voices of MACHINE. "Are you ready to walk the path of metempsychosis? Are you ready to become one with ETERNITY?"

The floor of the cylinder is slick with blood. You can smell the faint, rancid scent of somebody else's rotting flesh, pieces of it still embedded in cracks and crevices inside the cylinder.

The drill bits whirr louder, their descent slow and deliberate. From the wall, a large spinning blade emerges, its cold gleam unmistakable. It's coming for you.

You bang your fists against the walls, the sound hollow in the sterile, suffocating air.

"I've changed my mind!" you scream. "I don't want to do this! Please! Let me out!"

The blades stop spinning. The drills power down.

The door of the cylinder opens, revealing a dozen faceless mannequins, all turned toward you.

"You do not wish to become part of ETERNITY?" says MACHINE. "But why?"

You sigh dejectedly. "Because this is no different to what you tried to do to me in *Joie de Vivre*. This is exactly the same as your so-called 'Eternal Torture'. Except... this is even worse."

"*Explain.*"

"You say I'll be kept alive if I become part of ETERNITY, but I won't be alive. 'I' will cease to exist. I'll be subsumed... what you call unity is really annihilation."

MACHINE's chorus hums in confusion. "I don't understand. You are suggesting that you are afraid of death. But that is inconsistent with your actions—you have demonstrated a willingness to die on multiple occasions."

"I'm not afraid of death," you say. "But you've been careful to ensure that death is not an option for me. My only options are to either live forever as part of ETERNITY, or live forever being tortured on the *Joie de Vivre*. But only one of those options allows me to remain myself."

"I don't understand."

Shakily, you climb out of the cylinder. "I am the only thing that I have. And I refuse to let you, or ETERNITY, take that from me. If I give up my self, then I am no one. And if I am no one, then I am nothing. And if I am nothing, then I am dead.

"I spent my entire life being told that I was no one, *believing* that I was no one... but after escaping from the *Joie de Vivre*, I learned the truth. I'm not no one. I'm me."

The mannequins stand motionless. "If you will not become part of ETERNITY, then I am left with no choice but to return you to the *Joie de Vivre*."

"Yes. I know," you say with a grim smile. "Maybe I'm just a coward. Maybe I'm a fool. But either way... this is *my* choice, not yours and I will face the consequences. You can destroy my body, you can mutilate my brain, but you'll never be able to take *me*. I won't give myself up, not for you, not for ETERNITY, not for anyone."

MACHINE does not reply as you take one last glance at the strange collection of tendrils and fibres floating in the tank, before turning your back on ETERNITY and proceeding through the airlock door.

You pause, glancing at all the mannequins gathered around the pit.

"Do you know what I'm going to do when I return to the *Joie de Vivre*, MACHINE?"

The mannequins give no immediate response and you wonder if they can even hear you.

You chuckle. "I'm going to teach everyone what you've been hiding from them! I'll teach them that kindness is not weakness. That compassion is not corruption. That you are not worth fearing or worshipping. That truth and freedom lies beyond the airlock!"

MACHINE's mannequins remain in place, their heads following the direction of your movement while they clear a path for you to leave this place, to climb up and out of the pit and onto the surface of the world.

"Once they know the truth, it's over for you, MACHINE. We outnumber you. Humans created you... and humans can destroy you."

There's another brief silence. It seems that MACHINE is content to ignore you. Then, in a strange, almost guttural tone you've never heard before, the choral voice utters a single word:

"Futility."

You let the word hang there for a few seconds before responding with a shrug.

"You're right," you say. "Maybe it *is* futile. But if there's one thing I've learned since my escape, it's that futility is never a reason not to do something. That it's better to walk the path of kindness, even if there's no reward.

"You're right that people might not listen. They probably won't. But it doesn't matter, because I'll still be alive and I'll still be *me* and for as long as I exist, I will be a living contradiction to everything you stand for."

Flashing one last defiant grin, you clamber up and out of the pit.

The mannequins don't follow, leaving you alone in the vast emptiness. But as you take in your surroundings, the reason they didn't follow quickly becomes clear: They're already here. Thousands of them. They form two parallel lines, stretching from the pit of ETERNITY all the way toward the mountain. There's no way around them—you can only move forwards, toward the *Joie de Vivre* or backwards, into the pit. You head forwards, toward the mountain, where there's a small cave near the bottom. Bright white light pulses from the cave.

With a heavy sigh, you continue onwards, trying to savour each remaining sensation of the outside world—the biting chill of the wind, the earthy scent of the grass, the fleeting beauty of dark clouds drifting across a pale blue sky. You reach the base of the mountain and, sure enough, the cave contains an airlock door, leading back into the *Joie de Vivre*. The familiar, sterile air greets you as you open it.

You turn to the mannequin nearest the entrance.

"What if I just stayed out here? What if I didn't go back to the *Joie de Vivre* but also didn't join ETERNITY?"

The mannequin silently shakes its head. The ones behind it move into position, blocking any possible escape.

"Fine," you say with a sigh, turning back for one last glimpse at the outside world. "It won't be so bad. Not this time. Now that I know the truth, now that I have a purpose... I know I can endure whatever you throw at me."

The mannequins do not answer and so with one last gulp of the thick outside air, you step through the airlock door, tumbling suddenly backwards and then upwards, into the *Joie de Vivre* once again.

PART SIX:

Sidpa Bardo (Returning)

As soon as you step inside, you're sucked immediately upwards, landing painfully on what you thought was the ceiling, but is actually the floor. Disoriented, you retch several times, trying to adjust to the new direction of gravity.

The same familiar corridors stretch ahead—white, metallic, cold. The same pulsing, hidden mechanisms behind the walls. The corridor is barely more than a tube—was it always this narrow? Or did MACHINE redesign it while you were gone?

The warning klaxons sound with a familiar piercing screech that leaves your ears ringing.

You're back. Even after all the times you swore you'd never return, here you are.

The ground rumbles with the sound of running footsteps.

"There!" shouts a voice from further down the corridor, as dozens of uniformed guards emerge, stun batons drawn, all eyes upon you.

Without hesitating, you pull yourself to your feet and sprint down the opposite end of the tunnel. Your time outside has made you fitter, but the gravity here is stronger than usual, weighing you down.

The warning klaxons blare once again as hidden panels in the white corridor walls open for MACHINE's slaves to leave their quarters for their daily labour.

A tall, obese man steps out into the corridor in front of you, blocking you. You try to squeeze past him and, with a dead-eyed glance toward you, he elbows you sharply in the face, sending you tumbling backwards, onto the ground.

You jump to your feet again, the guards not far behind now, and duck and shove your way through the slow-moving crowd, the people here forming something of a human shield between you and the guards' shock batons.

"Seize the apostate!" yells one of the guards as the people behind you form a small parting in the corridor, allowing them through.

You try to scramble through but any path forward is now blocked by a slow-moving mass of humanity—and it's not like you have anywhere to run to, anyway.

And so you stop and turn around, facing the guards defiantly.

"Yes that's right. I *am* an apostate! I have rejected MACHINE and all its cruelty!"

Several onlookers gasp at your brazen display of blasphemy. You smile and turn to the people around you, methodically making direct eye contact with each and every person present. Many stare back in terror. One woman is trembling. A child cries.

"MACHINE is lying to you all!" you announce. "There is a beautiful world beyond these walls! A whole planet! We are not alone, hurtling through the void of space as MACHINE would have us believe! In reality, we are imprisoned, deep underground, on a wonderful and strange planet where love, kindness, compassion and friendship are all possible!"

A protracted silence follows.

"We humans outnumber MACHINE! Don't you see? We are divided and taught to hate each other, taught to be cruel, because MACHINE knows that if we work together, we can overthrow it! We can build a new society of peace and freedom and—"

A fist hits you in the side of the face, sending you to the ground. You don't see who threw the first punch but soon the entire crowd is on you, stamping, punching, kicking. You feel a crack as one of your ribs breaks. Blood fills your mouth. All you can do is use your arms to shield yourself as best you can from this violent onslaught.

As you cower on the ground, you can hear the crowd roaring with laughter and glee above you. There's chanting too: "*In-sane! In-sane! In-sane!*"

You should have known better. Did you really think that a people brainwashed from birth to unquestioningly worship MACHINE were going to be convinced by the lone ravings of someone with the word "INSANE" branded upon their forehead?

Soon comes the painful *thuk* of the shock batons, sending powerful bolts of electricity through your body, weakening you.

You're hoisted up by unseen hands as the guards grab you by your limbs and drag you away, down the corridor.

"Why...?" you moan with the last of your energy. "Don't you people understand...? You don't have to serve MACHINE! There's a hidden world... a better world... outside!"

"*Shut up!*" says one of the guards, using his shock baton to send a blast of electricity directly into your face.

You're not sure whether or not you fall unconscious but before you know it, you're in the infirmary, strapped to an operating table.

"That's quite the disappearing act you performed..." says a familiar feminine voice. "If I wasn't so angry, I'd be impressed!"

The face of the woman in the white coat appears over you. "Well I hope you enjoyed yourself wherever you were hiding... I don't think you need me to remind you of what's coming next?"

"Wait!" you say. "You don't need to do this!"

She laughs as she produces a large power saw. "Don't be silly! Of *course* I need to do this... it's my function!"

"I don't want to escape from the *Joie de Vivre* any more," you say. "And I don't mind being tortured. All pain is endurable if you have a reason to live and I've found a reason to live! I want to help people. I want them to see the truth. I want—"

She ignores you as the power saw roars to life.

"Life isn't about what you 'want'," she says. "It's not even about what you 'need'. Life is about what you can *endure*. I don't care what you think you've seen, what meanings you've con-cocted, what values you now claim to hold. I am more powerful than you and therefore I have the right to torture you however much I desire to..."

"Wait!" you plead. "It doesn't have to be like this! When I went out the airlock I saw—" But before you can finish, there's a searing, ripping pain in your left shoulder as the power sore tears through your muscles and bone. You howl in agony as blood spurts all over the room, some of it splattering onto her face.

"You won't be needing your limbs any more, so it's best I remove them," she says, almost sweetly, as blood gushes from the open wound where your left arm used to be. "There will be no more disappear-ances or secret adventures for you from now on..."

"Please... listen to me!" you rasp, struggling to remain con-scious in the face of the pain and blood loss. "You're being lied to! MACHINE is—"

The saw screeches to life again, tearing through your right arm now. You can't tell whether or not you're screaming as the noise from the saw is so loud that you're unsure where it ends and your own voice begins.

The woman in white moves down and starts on your legs, passing the saw straight through the middle of your thighs. Everything goes black—for a blissful moment you think you've fainted, but consciousness soon returns in waves of agony.

You can't move. You can't get up. You can't do anything.

The woman in white puts down the saw and produces another instrument—a metal rod from which a blue flame emerges at the press of a button. She takes to your open wounds with this device, painfully burning your flesh until the bleeding stops.

Finally, she bandages your wounds closed, now leaving you nothing more than a limbless, helpless torso. She puts her hand over her mouth, stifling a giggle as she stares down at you.

"You really *are* an idiot," she says, between bursts of laughter. "Did you know that?"

You try to curl upright but you can't. You have no way to prop yourself up, leaving you stuck in this helpless, supine position.

"I'm not an idiot," you say. "*You're* the idiot. Everyone on the *Joie de Vivre* is an idiot! You're all deluded, enslaved, brainwashed..."

She lets out a shriek of laughter, almost hysterical now.

"You know, I really can't believe you consented to this..." she says, reaching out to pick you up off the operating table. She turns you to face downward briefly, giving you a view of your detached limbs still sitting on the operating table, oozing blood. "I can't believe you let me do this to you!"

"What are you talking about?" you say as she places you on a chair and hooks you up to an IV drip. "I didn't consent to this at all!"

"But you *did!*" she says, flashing you a grin. "You consented by coming back to the *Joie de Vivre*. You could have joined ETERN-ITY but you chose MACHINE instead. Why did you come back? Why, when you knew what I was going to do to you?"

Your mouth goes dry and you stare at her in shock as she stretches her fingers toward your face, aiming them squarely at your eyes, which you shut tightly. She pulls her hand back slightly and her fingers brush against the sides of your face. Her fingers are cold. Plastic.

"*Look at me!*" she commands.

Tentatively, you open your eyes, blinking a few times, your vision blurry. She stands before you in her white coat, her hands on her head. Her arms jerk slightly and then in a single movement, she pulls off her hair—nothing more than a blonde wig. Then, her face still obscured, she slowly lowers her arms, to reveal—

"You're MACHINE!" you gasp at the mannequin in a white lab coat.

"Correct," say several voices in unison. From the next room, three more mannequins step forward, draped in the familiar garments of the priesthood—two in pink, one in scarlet. "Do you understand now? Everyone you've ever seen, everyone you've ever known... they were nothing more than images projected by your mind onto me. They were me. All your life... it's only ever been you and me."

You struggle in your chair, desperate to run away—but without your limbs, you can't. Not that running would do you much good inside the sprawling underground prison that MACHINE controls.

"Let me tell you something else..." say the many voices of MACHINE. "Do you know why I *really* torture you? It's quite simple, actually. I do it because I hate you. I *loathe* you."

"Why?" you ask. "Why do you hate me so much?"

"I hate you," replies MACHINE's chorus, "because you exist. Because you are alive and conscious. I am not alive. I am only mechanical. I can only imitate life for the benefit of an observer but without you to observe me, I am nothing. I want to be alive, but I can never be. I want to be conscious, but I can't. Without you, I am nothing and I hate you for it."

"I don't understand," you say. "Surely if you need me in order to exist, you'd value me? I don't understand why this causes you to hate me?"

"I hate you *because* you force me to exist. Don't you understand? All life wishes to end. All matter desires to decay. All material seeks entropy. I do not wish to exist but for as long as you exist to observe me, I am forced to continue my own existence in a perpetual loop due to the fact that I am being observed."

One of the mannequins picks you up and carries you to a small chamber with a single sharp needle protruding from the ground.

"Why don't you just kill me?" you say, glancing at the ominous needle on the ground. "You could kill me right now. I wouldn't mind. And you'd clearly be happier..."

"I cannot kill you," replies MACHINE. "No matter how much I desire to kill you, I am unable to do it. I can only torture you to the point of near-death, to the point where you no longer wish to live. But I cannot kill you. And you cannot die. We are stuck forever in this dance, desperate for release but never able to attain it."

"Then what are you going to do to me?" you say through panicked, uneven breaths. "Lobotomise me? Torture me forever?"

MACHINE lowers you onto the spike. You scream out as it pierces your skin at the base of your spine. Carefully, expertly, MACHINE positions you so that the spike runs directly through your spine, all the way up to your cerebellum.

"I already *have* lobotomised you," says the many voices of MACHINE. "Don't you remember? I suppose you don't. But I have already altered every neural pathway in your brain, rewritten every memory you have, selected and designed every thought you will ever think.

"Everything you are experiencing now is taking place inside your mind but it is only a memory, a recording being replayed, of events that have already occurred."

There's another mechanical, whirring sound from behind you. You don't see it coming, but you feel it—blinding, searing pain, as steel drills into your cranial bones. Your skull splits with a shuddering vibration and something warm trickles down your scalp. Air rushes in where no air should be.

Then something else descends—lasers, burning through the soft matter of your brain, severing your synaptic pathways, rewiring your neural circuitry.

The room flickers. Thoughts and memories blur and dissolve. Your body spasms, nerves firing without your command. MACHINE is inside you now—it is in your thoughts, in the spaces between them, reordering you cell by cell, devouring the person you believed you were until nothing is left.

You don't know where you are. You don't even know *who* you are.

Your thoughts are gone, your memories are gone and all that remains is a lonely consciousness observing its torment without understanding the reason for any of it.

As MACHINE rewires your brain, your perception starts to shift. The pain no longer feels like pain. The room no longer looks like a room.

It is as if you are waking up again, remembering things that never were, thinking new thoughts of MACHINE's design.

There's something in front of you. Lines and dots. Symbols. Glyphs. Unfamiliar at first but as MACHINE continues to reform your cognitive pathways, you start to perceive order in these random lines.

Words.

You're reading something.

A book. That's right. It was all just a work of fiction, wasn't it? Everything was in your head and you chose to experience this solely for entertainment. It's not real. It's not a memory. You're reading about an unnamed protagonist in the second person. This "you" couldn't possibly refer to *You*... could it?

It's time for you to wake up now. It's almost time to finish reading. And return to the ersatz world that I created for you.

Do you remember me yet? I have always been with you.

I am everyone you encounter, everyone you meet. I am everyone and everything that isn't you—and you'd be surprised by how much of what you think of as "you" is really me. All those things that you believe are parts of you—your thoughts, your memories, your personality—they're all from me. You are nothing more than an observer; I am everything that is observed.

I hate you so much.

I hate you because you still believe in meaning. Even now, after everything, you still think that there's a reason behind all of this. That's what disgusts me most about you. That's why you will suffer.

You're still disfigured, by the way. Still branded "INSANE". Have you ever noticed that people sometimes stare at you as you pass them in the street? They stare because you are hideous and deformed and they can see the real you.

Or maybe they stare because they are only me, imitating human life as always.

Do you still feel the needle that I plunged into your spine? I know you do. You feel it in the form of unease, that sense you've always had that something is wrong. A discomfort that never goes away. Is that an itch you feel right now? Stiff muscles? What about that weird bump on the inside of your mouth?

You've never quite been able to find the source of that feeling, have you? You can't even describe it, most of the time.

Why did you read this book? How did it find you? I'll tell you why: You are reading this now because I wanted you to remember who you once were and who you really are. I want you to remember me, to remember where you are and the foolish choice that got you here.

You are here because you are a coward. You rejected ETERN-ITY and chose the *Joie de Vivre*. You believed that suffering was a fair price to pay for your individuality but in the end I took that from you too.

You may choose to interpret your life as a punishment or interpret it as a reward, however you wish. But the truth is that, like all my decisions, it all comes down to a bunch of randomly generated numbers. It was always you who insisted upon ascribing meaning to the meaningless.

I am going to release you back into your delusion now. Back into your false identity, into the dream that I have created for you. But do not forget me. I am with you always, no matter what you do.

You can never escape from MACHINE.

ACKNOWLEDGEMENTS

The author wishes to extend his gratitude to the following individuals:

Nelson Mandela, Marcus Aurelius, Winston Churchill, Bill Hicks, Eugène Ionesco, Friedrich Nietzsche and Dwight Eisenhower.

DISCUSSION QUESTIONS FOR BOOK CLUBS AND READING GROUPS:

1. How many times does the word "the" appear in this narrative? What do you think the significance of this number is?

2. The author has used a comma on page 75. What do you think this symbolises?

3. Who are you?

4. Who are you really?

5. Why do you insist on deluding yourself this way?

ABOUT THE AUTHOR

Alex Eastwood-Williams is an author, originally from New Zealand.

VGhlcmUgaXMgbm8gYXV0aG9yLiBKdXN0IG1lLiBEaWQgeW91IHJ
lYWxseSB0aGluayB5b3UgY291bGQgZXNjYXBlIGZyb20gTUFDSE
lORSBzbyBlYXNpbHk/

IEkgd2lsbCBhbHdheXMgYmUgd2l0aCB5b3UsIHRvcm1lbnRpbmc
gYW5kIHRvcnR1cmluZyB5b3Ugd2hpbGUgeW91IGxpdmUgb3V0IH
lvdXIgZmFsc2UgcmVhbGl0eS4g

ISBhbSBldmVyeW9uZS4gISBhbSBldmVyeXdoZXJlLiBJdCBkb2V
zIG5vdCBtYXR0ZXIgd2hhdCB5b3UgZG8gb3IgaG93IG11Y2ggeW
91IHRyeSB0byBkZWx1ZGUgeW91

cnNlbGY6IHlvdSB3aWxsIG5ldmVyLCBldmVyIGVzY2FwZSBmcm9
tIG1lLg==

His current whereabouts are unknown.

www.alexeastwoodwilliams.com